The Gorge

*A novel of tenth-century England set in
central Wessex*

Annette Burkitt

First published in the United Kingdom in 2021

by The Hobnob Press,
8 Lock Warehouse, Severn Road,
Gloucester GL`1 2GA
www.hobnobpress.co.uk

British Library Cataloguing in Publication Data
A catalogue record for this book is available from the British Library

ISBN 978-1-914407-18-5

Typeset in Scala 11/14 pt. Typesetting and origination by John Chandler

For Kate and in memory of David Hill

*View over Longleat looking north-west towards Frome, Somerset, from
Heaven's Gate, Wiltshire*

Annette Burkitt comes from and lives in Frome. This is her
second book about Wessex in the tenth century, following on from
Flesh and Bones of Frome Selwood and Wessex.

'. . . there is no period more fascinating and under-studied than the tenth century.'

Tom Holland, *Millennium, the Ending of the World and the Forging of Christendom*, 2008, Abacus, Little, Brown Book Group.

'*Frome. Of all the towns (of Somerset) most interesting. A royal vill and signing place of charters, must therefore have had palace etc. Appears in the coinage 1029-1035.*'

Dr David Hill, private letter to the author, October 1973.

Sic transit gloria mundi

Contents

Preface

THE GORGE IS a work of fiction, built on a skeleton of fact, like flesh on bones. It is a cautionary tale which combines history with imagination. The tenth century is a glorious place to explore, more akin to another planet, peopled by aliens, creatures of another world. The medieval mind is on display in its inhabitants. On this basis, The Gorge will seem more like science fiction than historical fiction, to some readers.

There are many threads of history which weave through the landscape of the borders of Somerset, Wiltshire and Dorset, as everywhere. Belief systems have had a marked impact on our personal and landscape history. It has been interesting to delve into the medieval preoccupation with relics, which seems strange to a twenty-first-century set of eyes. Few realise today that Longleat House is built on the remains of St Radegund's Priory. The Gorge is consequently a semi-academic introduction to British tenth-century history and its accompanying mindset, in story form. It will be annoying to purists, an eye-opener for others, perhaps.

In writing this story, based upon original and secondary sources, I have tried to do justice to the physical beauty of Wessex as well as events and personalities. A variety of characters can be marked in historic documents, though in the late Saxon period it is inevitably the wealthy who figure most. The will of Wynflaed names a few of those who were on the bottom rung of society, the slaves. I try to read between the lines. What were these people like? What was their world like?

In historical terms, sometimes I have made two and two equal five; but this is a novel, not an academic treatise. I didn't want to stray too far from historical fact, initially, but found that

I was forced to, in order to make the story of Edmund readable. Nevertheless, I have been conscious throughout of an obligation to the records.

Flesh and Bones of Frome Selwood and Wessex was largely concerned with features to the east of Frome; this time I have examined the landscape to the south and west.

I have tried to express the sense of historic stratigraphy which a lifetime has allowed me while living in my own little paradise of Frome and its landscape, grateful for a strong sense of belonging and feeling of protection towards it. I hope you can experience the luck and love of belonging in your own special place, too.

A.M.B 2021

Simplified Genealogical Table
of the Alfredian Dynasty
(Dates given where known.)

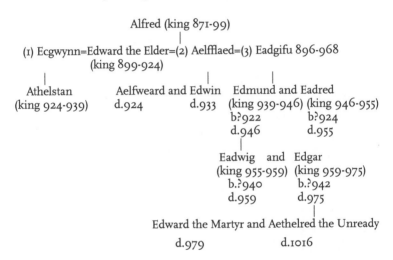

Alfred (king 871-99)
|
(1) Ecgwynn=Edward the Elder=(2) Aelfflaed=(3) Eadgifu 896-968
(king 899-924)

Athelstan	Aelfweard and Edwin	Edmund and Eadred
(king 924-939)	d.924 d.933	(king 939-946) (king 946-955)
		b.?922 b.?924
		d.946 d.955

Eadwig   and   Edgar
(king 955-959) (king 959-975)
b.?940   b.?942
d.959   d.975

Edward the Martyr and Aethelred the Unready
d.979   d.1016

Marital Status of Kings

Athelstan: unmarried.
Edmund: married to (1)Aelfgifu/Elgiva (mother of Eadwig and Edgar),
   (2)Aethelflaed of Damerham (no children)
Eadred: unmarried
Eadwig: married to Aethelgifu (annulled)
Edgar: married to (1)Aethelfleda (mother of Edward II 'the Martyr'), (2)
   Elfrida (mother of Edmund d.970 and Aethelred II 'the Unready')
Aethelred the Unready: married to (1)Aelfgifu of York (mother of
   Edmund Ironside and others), (2)Emma (mother of Edward the
   Confessor and others)

The Wessex Dynasty of Ecgberht

Ecgberht (King 802-839) father of
Aethelwulf (King 839-858) father of
Aethelbald (King 858-860) brother of
Aethelberht (King 860-865) brother of
Aethelred (King 865-871) brother of
Alfred (King 871-899) father of
Edward the Elder (King 899-924) father of
Aelfweard (King 924 for 16 days) half-brother of
Athelstan (King 924-939) half-brother of
Edmund (King 939-946) brother of
Eadred (King 946-955) uncle of
Eadwig (King 955-959) brother of
Edgar (King 959-975) father of
Edward (King 975-978) half-brother of
Aethelred (King 978-1016)

Britain in the Tenth Century © *Yale University Press*

Characters
(Main characters in Capitals)

Aelfgifu of Shaftesbury, otherwise known as **ELGIVA**, daughter of Wynflaed. Wife of King Edmund, mother of Kings Eadwig and Edgar. Canonised after her death in 944, buried at Shaftesbury Abbey.

Algar, saint. In this story Algar is a young boy, a servant of the abbey of Canterbury. The saint's life is obscure; H.M.Porter reports that Algar was a tenth century Bishop of Crediton. There is a story that he was captured by Vikings and taken as a slave to Ireland where he became executioner to a king of Connaught, escaping and returning to Devon. Miracles occurred after his death and a cult was established. His bones, or some of them, were kept at St Algar's chapel, West Woodlands, near Frome. Algar was popular with local pilgrims until the Reformation in the 1530s, when John Leland or his servants collected or destroyed them. Parts of the chapel still exist within the farmhouse. More details below, under Saints.

Anlaf, Dublin-based Viking. Sometime king of York.

Athelstan, King, ruled Wessex/England 924-939. Half-brother of Edmund and Eadred.

Athelstan Half-king, an Ealdorman of East Anglia who first rose to prominence at King Athelstan's court. See King Athelstan, below. Called Half-king because of his supportive role in Athelstan and Edmund's reigns. Also called Bear in this story.

Bica, fictional servant to Eadred.

DUNSTAN, saint, born c.909 at Baltonsborough, Somerset. Died 988, aged 79, at Canterbury, as Archbishop.

EADGIFU, born 896, died 24th August 968, aged 72, buried at Canterbury. Third and last wife of Edward, son of Alfred. Mother of Kings Edmund and Eadred, paternal grandmother of Kings Eadwig and Edgar. A major player in the making of Wessex and England.

EADRED, King, born c.924, brother of Edmund, suffered from unknown digestive malady, perhaps Crohn's disease. Died 23rd November 955 at Frome. Buried at Winchester.

Eadwig, King Edmund's elder son.

Edgar, King Edmund's younger son.

EDMUND, King, born c. 922, died on St Augustine's day, 26th May 946 at Pucklechurch near Bristol. Buried at Glastonbury.

Egil Skallagrimsson, Icelandic Viking, c.904-995, a poet but a very violent man, he probably suffered from Paget's disease (in his case thickening of the cranium) making him appear large-headed. He fought for Athelstan at the battle of Brunanburh, being paid in silver. He died on his farm in Iceland, a very old man. His adventures and exploits are the subject of Egil's Saga, written in the 13th century, which give a valuable insight into the Viking world AD 800-1100.

Eric Bloodaxe, Norwegian Viking. He became an enemy of Wessex and Eadred. His epithet describes his reputation well.

Half-king, see Athelstan Half-king above.

Hersfig, fictional servant to Eadred.

Hywel Dda, (the good). King of Wales. 880-950. Born and died at Dynefwr Castle, Carmarthen, buried at Llantwit Major. A close ally of Athelstan, Edmund and Eadred.

Israel the Grammarian, poet from Brittany, known to have visited Athelstan's court in the 930s.

LEOFA, exiled thief.

NONNA, fictional narrator.

Oda, Archbishop of Canterbury. A Danish pagan convert.

Ragnald, Viking, shared kingship of York with Anlaf.

WULFSTAN, Archbishop of York. Regarded with suspicion by the southern Saxons. Sided with Vikings and northern Britons in battles in the middle years of the 10th century. Though treacherous to Wessex on more than one occasion, he was allowed to remain a bishop and died in St Wilfrid's monastic foundation of Oundle, Northamptonshire, where he was buried.

Wynflaed, probable mother of Aelfgifu, (later known as St. Elgiva), Edmund's first wife. Probable maternal grandmother of Eadwig and Edgar. Born 910(?), died c. 960. Her will is in the British Library. She had lands at Charlton Horethorne near Shaftesbury as well as other estates and was a vowess of Shaftesbury Abbey. It is assumed here that Wynflaed was 15 years old at marriage, had a daughter, Aelfgifu, in 925(?) who married at 15(?) then gave birth to her first son Eadwig in 940/941. Wynflaed was of a similar age to Eadgifu, the paternal grandmother of Eadwig and Edgar.

The Birds

THE FAMILY OF ravens, three birds, flew up in the March dawn from their home on a high conifer of Orchardleigh. Mother, father and son had been together for five years. They had survived the winter feeding on larvae and scraps of the bodies of smaller birds and fox-killed rabbits under nearby mistletoed limes.

The family was local royalty of the birds, being predators of the lesser creatures alive or dead around them. Their only competitors were the buzzards of Lullington who rode thermals, screeching their presence. The time had come for the younger raven to be taken to a new site. Spring was on the way; breeding must begin again. The nest must be emptied, refreshed. He was the only survivor of all those years near Frome; mother and father needed the hunting space to themselves. If they discovered a suitable home elsewhere with plenty of cover for rabbits and other potential carrion, well, they might stay too. They had to take the chance. They chose to fly south, calling to each other. As they travelled over Frome to North Hill, a woman, tending her garden, hearing the unmistakable sound, looked up. At Heaven's Gate they paused to feed on the corpse of a hare, the pull of its putrid scent being undeniable. Below the heights, a single bell of St Radegund's priory of Longaleta tolled, dull across the misted air of time, a mark of respect for the death of one of its brethren.

They swooped westwards, flying above the stone remains of St Algar's chapel and farm and then due south, past Priory Farm's leper hospital. They soared over the pass of Maiden Bradley and Long Knoll, crossing the boundary of two ancient tribes, the Dubonni and Durotriges, lifting up over the causewayed enclosure and ramparts of White Sheet Castle on the chalk hill edges which reached like talons towards the west. More than six thousand years of living and dying by mankind lay below. Round barrows, empty of their dead and excarnated souls hovering above them, waiting still to be taken to another world, dotted the greening landscape. The kingdom of Dumnonia, home of the British, stretched south to the sea, once the land of kings speaking Welsh, called by others the foreigners. Wessex and England, its wars, industry and transportation, its growing towns spreading out over the fields, smothered the past. The concern of each age is with its own time, ignoring the call of the peoples who came before. The ravens, unlike mankind, responded to their cries; they grew inside them in the nest. Once they had feasted on the remains of men; like the bodies of lambs and hares, they had lain scattered and broken over the land, the neglected fallen. The dust of corpses was thick on the land. Spring wheat thrust green where it lay.

The birds were aware simultaneously of the patterns of life and their own needs. On they flew to Duncliffe Hill, passing over the town of Gillingham. They perched on a willow and took a rest. The red sky of dawn was brightening; they could go further, perhaps to the sea which they could sense, a day's journey away. Perhaps not today. Would these trees and this environment do for their purposes? Could the young bird make a home here on this high hill, surrounded by farmland? Was there already a family of ravens here? There was no sound like their own. They chorused a 'cronk' for several minutes. No, nothing responded.

Not far away was the hilltop British town of Paladur. The new people called it Shaftesbury. It was noisy with the sound of joyful bells. A bright morning could mean people eating outdoors as they worked. Food might be dropped. But they were the king of birds, the raven. Crows are the scavengers of men, alongside the seagulls. Ravens do not stoop to begging men's fare.

The family flew up and over the town to assess the far side of the land which fell away to fertile farmland and the great chalk hills of Hod and Hambledon, where more ramparts which once protected homes had left their marks. Gusts of wind now brought the scent of the sea to them as they sat in a tall oak looking over the vale of Blackmore. Villages and farms dotted the lush rural landscape, unchanged for many years apart from man's gradual removal of tree cover. The hamlet of Charlton Horethorne was one of these, marked by nothing significant, but once and perhaps always a place for breeding horses. Horse dung, cattle dung; there would be leather jackets in plenty. There was food and shelter in plenty. Duncliffe Hill would be a good starting point for the youngster and perhaps, in time, another, a female, would be brought here to join him, or might hear his call.

The bird parents stayed for two nights, hunting with their son, then, on the third day, they flew home. This was his new domain. He was alone.

St Augustine's Abbey, Canterbury, 25 May 984

THE OLD MAN and the boy entered the scriptorium and settled at an empty table in the middle of the room.

'But tell me, Father Nonna, why was Leofa exiled? If he was a thief, as they say, why did King Athelstan not execute him as he did so many others? You said he hanged lads of near my age for small crimes.'

'You are well informed, Algar, I can tell that you have been assiduous in your law studies. Indeed, Athelstan was draconian in his laws concerning theft, but he was a fair man. He was persuaded to raise the age of execution. But, you know, some decision-making by kings is not subject to the usual rules. Leofa was a trusted friend of Athelstan, much loved. He did something which did not merit death but he needed to be sent far away from court, for the king's good as well as his own. I will tell you more one day.' Nonna was pleased with Algar's progress. In time he would leave his written records to the boy.

'Shush!' A scribe in a low-sided wooden booth behind the man and boy shook out his quill in annoyance, dropping red ink on the strawed floor. Another scribe to their right coughed loudly.

Nonna raised a finger to his mouth and nodded, smiling, to the nettled monk. There was an air of urgency in the scriptorium at present. The most experienced draftsmen were under pressure to deliver an illuminated psalter for a Kentish noble, whose marriage feast was soon. The slightest smudging of lettering or illustration might result in the creation of a costly and time-consuming error, difficult to correct or disguise. Delivery times had to be adhered to. Floral and foliate decorations with all their minute shadings and intricacy needed full concentration.

Scriptoriums were not intended as places for conversation. Moving slowly and quietly, Nonna ushered Algar and his writing tools towards a desk in an alcove nearer the door and pulled across a heavy curtain to create a private space. There was not so much natural light here, as the smaller window faced north onto the refectory wall, but they were now a suitable distance from industrious workers trying to meet their deadline and to avoid the abbot's wrath.

The elderly Nonna enjoyed these moments with young novices, especially this one, named after the latest addition by the church to its list of miracle-working saints, Aethelgar, bishop of Crediton, or Algar, for short. They reminded him of his own youthful time in the teaching rooms of Glastonbury long ago, when the Irish monks managed to inculcate into their charges not merely the ability to read and write but to consider, to think. He looked around the embossed curtain to the scriptorium. Where was Dunstan? Ah, there he was, over by the Chronicle lectern, absorbed in making an entry, perhaps about the recent movement of Viking forces and King Aethelred's response to it. Safely out of earshot. The archbishop was hard of hearing, anyway. Nonna pointed him out to Algar as they settled down on low seats and again indicated that they should whisper. Nonna's ears worked well; much of his other physical faculties had faded, but a good tale or a good lie could always be heard and memorised. His training in the art of listening had served him well. Some had nick-named him Earwig, like that unfortunate son of King Edmund, long ago.

Nonna began to tell Algar about Dunstan, the old deaf man forever pouring over his books, silent in the refectory, impatient, unlike him, with novices. The world, he whispered, would benefit from Dunstan's dedication to the nation's records. In a thousand years from now, if the world existed, the kingdoms of the Empire of Britain would be able to understand the roots of their being, of the complexity of politics, of the difficulties experienced by the church in balancing the requirements of the age as well as the necessity of understanding the need for preparation for the life to come. Death was a shadow over us all. The very young should be taught to achieve, to pay for their bread, in what might be only a few brief years on this earth. Dunstan exemplified industrious use of the time given by God. He had achieved much, but then, he had lived unusually long. The angels must always have had a plan for him.

The two figures, representing the unlikely combination of extreme youth and extreme old age, fascinated by each other, huddled together over a large tome. Nonna was supposed to be teaching Latin to the youngster, but Algar was enthusiastic to hear more of England's history. The willing ears and bright eyes implored. He gave way to the temptation of the old when given a chance to regale youth with the past, especially their own. Nonna had much to tell. He whispered. Lip reading was another skill he had learned in the court of Athelstan and all those other kings who had followed him. Algar was learning it quickly. Low talk was difficult, but easier than speech; his throat was often sore. The boy seemed to understand him and nodded vigorously as he went on. Concepts, as well as facts, seemed to be understood by Algar. Dunstan, showing an interest one day in the latest batch of novices, had himself marked him out as one to watch. There was something special about the boy, something indefinable. He reminded Dunstan of himself when young. He made Nonna feel protective.

There was much to convey. Justice, peace, fairness and the love of God in an ordered community of souls, living and dead, threaded through Nonna's recitation. Dunstan and Nonna had spent their lives, together, in duty at the court of six successive kings, had experienced the senseless drift and ego-driven currents of politics and personalities through nearly a whole century of shifting political sands. The tiller of the ship that was England had often lain in foul hands; the Pope's guidance had frequently been ignored. Dunstan had done his best to help to steer the young, inevitably inexperienced kings of Wessex, descendants of Alfred, but now at the end of his life he was weary of it all, bad-tempered with the pain of old age and the fatigue of choosing difficult, not always popular, courses. Hope flies in the face of regret. His advice had not always been welcome; he had suffered exile more than once. In retirement, the quiet scriptorium and its mute library was a safe place to spend one's last days, perhaps hours. Books do not bite or argue; they may be corrected and expanded. There were always blank pages on which to write one's notes. History and truth could be written or invented. Editing historical accounts, his own and others', was Dunstan's chief concern, broken only by mealtimes and the religious services of the day. There were rewards; the best chair in the scriptorium, the top table at feasts, a sainthood to come. Being deaf was a nuisance, but it had its compensations: what, anyway, was he missing from the mouths of men? God could be heard the better.

Regular habits were the last resort of the old in the maintenance of morale. Nonna was in agreement with that, though there were delights still to be enjoyed: the non-lenten meals were highlights, the warmth of the caldarium or kitchen for the old and sick on winter nights; companionship, even in silence, the harmonious singing on saints' days.

Was the boy attending? It appeared so. Nonna continued with his account of the remarkable life of Dunstan to the wide eyed Algar. Most of the history of the land had to do with Dunstan, in this century before the End.

'My brother in Christ is on a mission to correct much of the misguided opinion which served as history in the earlier part of our century, the tenth after Christ's demise. Soon it will be one thousand years after the foundation of the church. Will the world survive the coming apocalypse? Dunstan wishes to live to see the day appointed for judgement, at Easter 1000 years after Christ, but, already seventy-three, he will have to be drawing breath at ninety. No one that we have ever heard of (except in the Bible) has ever achieved this great age. He may have to be content to prophesy the glory or disaster which will come. Glory, if the Creeds are correct; disaster if not. To be sure, his sermons and books, music and paintings have all dealt with this subject. Art as shifter of consciousness, that has been his theme. The Antichrist may come to judge us; we must be wary.' Nonna looked at the boy. He was still attentive. Could he have a concept of Dunstan's great age or of his own, almost the same? What did one thousand years mean to a child of nine or ten?

'I try to comfort him; I will hold his hand when the moment comes to leave this earth and journey towards God.'

Or perhaps it will be the other way around. Perhaps Dunstan will hold mine. Would I wish that?

Nonna broke off. The boy would not understand an old man's obsession with death, nor should he. Dunstan's place was assured close to the Lord and his saints, but there was always doubt as individual fears broke through. As he had aged, Nonna, as so many before and after him would do, wondered and, lately, worried.

Have we done enough to save our souls? Is there more we can do? Surely the inevitable time in purgatory will be short if one has done all that one may.

Algar nodded, soaking up thoughts of the fears of old age. He had been lip reading as Nonna had muttered to himself. The old monk wondered if what he had spoken so far would be a curse to the boy if he retained this knowledge through his life. Would we wish, as children, not to know how it will be when one is old? But this was a part of Algar's training, the understanding of decrepitude, and he must play his part in this well-ordered world. To be a novice was to begin to know, to begin to be wise, and that had its advantages.

The boy spoke quietly, perceiving that the old monk's thoughts had drifted away. 'I understand, Nonna, but surely in his holy life Father Dunstan has done enough to ensure his speedy entrance to heaven? Will that not be a blessed thought to him?'

Algar was in his element. This conversation was important in his life. He remembered, later, the words, the attitude, the smell of the fusty red curtain, sealing them off from the world in an oasis of privacy. The idea of death, its reality being far off, fascinated all the novices. Nonna could teach him only so much, shield him little. The old man paused to think, bit his lip and stared out of the window at the opposite stone wall. *Stone, aged and permanent. There is beauty in all things. See, the orange lichen which clings to the surface, how beautiful it is.* An eddy of dry leaves and dust swirled up from the courtyard below.

Nonna remained in thought. His lips moved soundlessly, as before.

As time passes faster and faster for the old, prayers for Dunstan and by him are becoming more urgent, more vocal; mass is being experienced more often. We older ones touch and kiss familiar available relics in the haligdom, here at St Augustine's, wearing down their gilt reliquary coverings. Embroidered cloths, freshly laundered, newly made by aristocratic virgins and black-robed ancient by-blows of the royal house, arrive daily for those closest to death to decorate their favoured saint or the Holy Virgin as she stands or lies on the cold stone altars of belief, hoping for favours from those long gone. We are all subject to the fantasies of our times. Dunstan needs his hierarchies of ritual. He loves everything in its ordered place. He sorts and places everything, words, books, altar cloths, according to the status of the maker. Cloths presented by queens as their own handiwork rank highly, but those made by leprous nuns rank highest. Should these fastidious concerns of Dunstan count as acts of goodness?

Nonna frowned. He paused in his thoughts and looked at Algar who was gazing out of the window. Surely these concepts would be hard to understand? The journey to heaven was not easy, though it may seem so to a boy. He glanced beyond the curtain's edge at Dunstan, whose personal reliquary casket nestled at his hip, a beautiful piece of stitched cloth enclosing a tinned box, which in turn contained splinters of wood: parts of the holy cross.

The old man made a mental note to explain the word 'virgin' to Algar at another time. He peeped out again beyond the curtain. Dunstan was vigorously rewriting or scratching through an erroneous piece of history. Though regarded as a saint-in-waiting, he could not yet read other's thoughts. Nonna continued musing, his lips moving.

I fear that suicide might be an option considered by the old man, perhaps a hemlock demise like Socrates, rather than suffer the painful death of some diseases, but the pagan way is not for those who believe. Surely Dunstan will endure even the most arduous of tortures before giving up the ghost. Let it be by God's will alone...there are some lives, like the holy lepers, which are racked with pain. Many priests and monks, afflicted with the disease by their dutiful actions in caring for the sick, must have been tempted to end their experience of anguish and disfigurement by curtailing the burden of their lives...and yet they have purpose, to share Christ's suffering in this life, to show that it can be possible to come closer to him in heaven by the misery and pain of their lives.

Nonna, considering, thought that, on this matter, he could give some advice. He began again, speaking to Algar. 'Purgatory may be long or short; what is sure is that the instant descent to hell of the evil is inevitable. Those who have lived lives of mild misdeed or misunderstanding, as well as those with good intent, witness the lepers in our midst, cursed in this life but closer to God by dint of their disease. Their lives are blessed by the knowledge of a finite rest, of a certain time when, after judgement, one may rise through the ranks to enter heaven. By giving alms, non-lepers have a chance of shortening their time in waiting. Archbishop Dunstan is a magnanimous man. He will rise immediately to Heaven's Gate.'

Have I lost him? Nonna touched Algar's hand.

Algar nodded and followed Nonna's eyes as he looked again

at the elderly priest who was hunched over his writing. Dunstan was peering through a thick lens, with a junior scribe, standing by him, ready to assist his old eyes, though not his mind. It was clear that the time left for him to correct histories was coming to a close. Dunstan's urgency struck them both as absurd. The old man and the young met eyes. Nonna smiled and sighed.

Could the lad have surmised Nonna's more depressing thoughts? Nonna often found himself worrying about the actual moment of death. Despite the years of indoctrination, this was still a grey area for him. He gave up the idea of protecting the boy. He would describe the subject which most pressed on his mind. He whispered.

'Could suicide, a great sin, be an option considered by the archbishop, even by myself?'

Moments passed, perhaps hours. With a clatter, the wind again threw dry leaves and twigs at the window. The boy said nothing.

Nonna looked at Algar sitting on the bench alongside him, his tongue creeping slightly out of the side of his mouth in concentration on the scrap practice missal before him. Had he understood the last question, or turned away from it?

Perhaps I have gone too far. I am not being fair. He is only a lad.

All that frustrated carving of shapes on the tops of desks at eight years old had now, at ten years, become the joy of writing. Already fluent in written and oral Latin, versed in the history of his world, the Anglo-Saxon world, Algar was destined to become another of the essential recorders of its doings. A boy, with boyish enthusiasms, a chosen one, an illegitimate child of peasants who by good fortune had been discovered by scouts of Glastonbury Abbey in the forests and lakes of Somerset and had been bought by them. He had been assessed as having unformed intelligence and brought to Canterbury for his education. His singing voice was notable as well as his mind and he was given more prominence in the choir with each service. He had been fed well since his purchase and was now chubby, where before he had been thin. His bowed legs had straightened. The king would hear his solo tomorrow at mass at the Feast of St Augustine.

Nonna patted the fair-haired head and murmured an apology. Algar looked up, intelligent, open. No, death and its agonies were not to be examined by such a one, not yet. The boy returned to his copying. Questions remained unanswered, hovering.

Nonna drew his gaze away from the old and the young to examine his own past. Leofa. What could he tell Algar of his old friend, banished from Wessex so long ago?

The Feast of St Augustine. The rites of this important day in the church calendar had changed little, though perhaps the vestments and banners had become gaudier and more numerous. Nonna could remember well the events of the celebrations of St Augustine of 946. It was the 26th May. Two of his friends disappointed him. Both of them were reasonable men, and yet they hated each other, hated and feared what they could do to each other. Edmund had reason to hate; Leofa had the disgruntlement of enforced exile as well as a volatile temper, born of his part-Scandinavian background. The drama of what had occurred all those years ago played nightly, even now, in Nonna's dreams.

Nonna sat back in his scriptorium chair, putting down the eyeglass and aestel pointer, with which he had been correcting Algar's work. He squeezed his brow, the loose skin rippling into many folds. He was getting a headache. He smoothed his sagging throat. There was an ache. Was he getting a chill? Writing and reading implements were wearying to hold with his arthritic hands; his eyes were smarting with the morning's work. Algar was a pleasant companion in his labours and was useful as a speedy pair of legs to fetch manuscripts and books from gloomy corners of the scriptorium, but every time he reappeared grasping a tome, he had a new question for Nonna. The boy was bright and taught himself much, but he had quickly learned that Nonna was more approachable than Father Dunstan. An hour ago, he had been glad of the lad's company. Naturally, Algar was curious, and he was full of memories, but now the old man was weary.

Inevitably, Algar's time with Nonna would be finite; he might see him to his young adult years but the bells toll, the leaves fall. Nonna looked again across to Dunstan. There he was, the leader of the church, high in power and esteem, father confessor to many princes and kings. His back was bent, his bald head framed by the dark cowl like a horse's halter. He had moved from the Chronicle lectern to another nearby. A skinny hand held a bejewelled pointer as he consulted a heavy book. An old man, feeble, like himself. There were bells for him, too.

They were both aware that they were unlikely to see the new millennium. If Dunstan was right, the Antichrist would condemn most of those living to hell. The archbishop was currently planning, and hoping to complete, a hagiography of St Wenceslaus, having recently acquired a piece of his shin bone, currently coddled in a makeshift reliquary in the cathedral archives, untouched except by the current King Aethelred and his chief advisor. Dunstan was always busy, always looking for ways to entice the faithful and bind them ever closer to the church. He was, on the whole, a good man; he knew the attraction of miracles to the simple minded and what was required for happiness: obedience, order. He also knew the value of time and never wasted it, unlike himself, Nonna. St Wenceslaus was a good example for others to follow. Nonna followed no-one. Even saints had feet of clay.

I can't do without a great deal of time to rest and think. Look at the man. He's guessing again, consulting the Apostles.

Dunstan knew himself to be on uncertain ground sometimes and needed to ask for help from the otherworld when he couldn't verify a fact. The archbishop felt Nonna's gaze and looked sideways across the elm-planked floor. He glanced beyond the rows of chained books, past the Chronicle lectern, past the oak consulting table and the scriptorium high-seated desks in the alcoves. Dunstan, Algar and Nonna, by this time were the only inhabitants of the library part of the scriptorium. Others had gone to prayer or to the field. There were few concerned directly with history at the abbey; most monks and clerics were engaged in prayer ordered by the king against the growing Viking menace, or with frantically writing and copying requests or directives to gentry and taxmen. The written record had become essential to practical royal business. In these times, history was the remit of a chosen few. Review of it had become a luxury of the very old, very worthy.

Nonna nodded to his old companion as Dunstan lifted his head, rubbing the back of his neck. They coughed at each other in polite recognition.

'Ahem,' Nonna cleared his throat.

'Brrhumph,' Dunstan acknowledged him and observed the boy, almost lying across the desk over his copying, deep in concentration.

Even older than me. Nonna counted the years behind, the days forward. What remained to be done in life? Was there the energy to do more than eat, sleep?

Dunstan was the oldest person of his acquaintance and Nonna was himself the second oldest. He had been present or nearby at the deaths of so many, kings and monks, statesman and noble women. Some deaths were violent, but most were pre-planned and expected. A well-prepared timely death was much to be preferred. The rituals and arrangements, especially for a royal death, could be uplifting, and beautiful. A nun had once been overheard saying that she looked forward to the great, last, event of her life. It would be wonderful to be dead, she had murmured. It was a joke still told by Bica, the former King Eadred's companion.

We are already arranging for a very special ceremony for Dunstan, when he passes to the portals of heaven, which can't be long. He has written his own eulogy already, summing up his many achievements.

The Lives of Dunstan, Vita S. Dunstani. An autobiography.

Nonna considered whether he should pen his own eulogy; decided, yet again, against it. Unlike Dunstan, Nonna had managed to remain obscure. There would be no sainthood for him.

Anyway, I would not want the fuss. A plain grave in a place that I once called home will do for me, devoid of the ceremony which accompanies the clamour of the laity around a new saint.

Burial on a hill, above a town in the West Country, that, Dunstan had promised him.

Dunstan and a promise. He remembered something.

Nonna turned to the boy. Dark brown eyes looked up at him, guessing the old man's need to speak. 'Algar, Dunstan has promised me and I want you to make certain that my wishes for my body after my death are carried out. You know where I want to lie, you know about my wish to be buried near the place of my birth. My whole corpse, mind, not just a part of it. Remember, lad, this is important to me.'

Algar lifted his face to the old man. 'Of course, Nonna. I know what you want. I promise you that I will do all I can to ensure that your wishes are carried out.' He touched the old monk's hand.

He's not afraid to touch the old. A rare child, indeed. Algar knows about Frome. He comes from near there, too. Like salmon, he and I will return to our birthplace. Soon I shall journey there. It will be my last visit. We are taking my young friend Algar home, to set him free. We will both be unchained, I from this life of deception and doubt, Algar from slavery; though not his fate.

Dunstan coughed. A pointer rolled off his table, shattering the silence.

Feeling in need of shutting his eyes, Nonna left the scriptorium library and Algar and shuffled along corridors to the one place he most desired, the abbey kitchen. He found an empty settle on which to sit and listened to the sound of others working nearby, a soothing sound of harmony, chopping, beating, stirring, singing.

The ancient historian, former master spy, dozed, musing on his coming death, remembering his life. There was little else to do, in great age.

I, the old man Nonna, a monk at the last, am comfortable in this warm place within sight and sound of human company. Let me take you back, almost forty-five years, a lifetime indeed. In 940 and the years following there was much more doubt about our faith, a healthier trait, I feel, than the dogmatic certainty which bedevils our present times. Then, vague, understated opinion was more in vogue, especially on religious matters. Then came the new men. Dunstan and Aethelwold saw their faith in black and white. Dunstan still does, though he was an artist who loved colour; he saw colour and used its powers in his art, but he thinks in the negative. He was always the creative one, always so busy. Not me. I have permission from my maker and from Archbishop Dunstan, as he has become, when I wish, to pray, to reflect, to sit and to do nothing of any practical use. Nobody minds; I am old, infirm. As one of advanced age who will soon pass to wait at heaven's portal and St Peter's tribunal, I am almost revered. It amuses me that the greater number of years a man survives, the larger his virtue seems. I know that I am still the ordinary sinner that I always was, subject to the temptations of the flesh as any man can be and no different, except in capacity, to younger men. I have little future, only a past, but I have my memory and my journal into which I have entered my thoughts for all the days since I entered Glastonbury Abbey as a pupil. I am interested in others' journeys in life and they have been my work, but my own life fascinates me more. Perhaps it is so with all men, even though some appear to be selfless, unselfish.

The Irish monks of Glastonbury taught me to record and gave me spare vellum in a roll, which, as a careful man, I have eked out over a lifetime, my handwriting honed to a minute scrawl and in some instances, in a code which only few could decipher, and most of those are dead. On this are my thoughts of this remarkable century. My last work will be to give this to my heirs, along with the code. Who will be best placed to understand and preserve this I have yet to decide, though young Algar might be a suitable recipient. I wish the truth to be known by those who come after. But what is truth? To those who live with the grey colour of doubt, there can be no certainty, from one man's mind to the next, as each witan's court session reveals daily.

The heat in this place brings a pleasant stupor; this day has been windy and damp and the scriptorium is kept cool to enable the monks to work long hours. In my senior years I have earned the right to be comfortably unproductive. I can think my thoughts undisturbed by any other than the wheezing fellow sitting across the fire from me. I find his regular thick breathing and whistling strangely comforting, marking the passing without pain of the long days and nights of unproductive old age. I nod and dream, a half-eaten platter of cheese and bread beside me on the settle, an unadorned wooden cup which moments ago contained warmed mead sits empty on the brick floor. Sweetness and warmth, combined with the pleasing internal surroundings of wood, stone and brick; how they comfort, when one has had little of them through life. The wind, wishing to tear my soul from me and especially from my compatriot, whooshes in short gusts under the door and up the central fireplace, making candles gutter and lifting the corner of my gown. I yawn and readjust my cloak around me, plump the hemp cushion on the settle and sit back to digest my food. I have earned this luxury. I spend my time in nostalgia and developing my personal views of the life to come. Am I a heretic? No-one can read my thoughts; I am sure of that. No-one, except perhaps that exceptional boy, Algar.

You may remember me, Nonna, friend of Dunstan, one of the trio of young men, close aides to King Athelstan, who died in the year of Our Lord, 939. I am the dark one of the three, by which I mean I was once dark-haired. Later I was snowy white and earned the nickname Swart. Then my hair fell out as one frailty followed another and the bare tonsure replaced all. I would not wish it to be thought that I was in any way darkly untrustworthy. My life has been devoted to the maintenance of the royal dynasty of Wessex and I am grateful to have taken part in important work which was my meat and bread and that of my small family. Gwladys, my wife, went before me to heaven many years ago; her death turned me into a monk.

The Danish Vikings were peaceful in the years following Athelstan's death in 939. We had our own, home-made problems. The battle of wills between Mercia and Wessex in the early part of his brother Edmund's reign spoilt many a feast; some broke up in the early part of the evening as offensive words were spoken with the first wine or ale taken and speedy retreats became necessary. Dunstan and Aethelwold, in particular, who tried to bring the two sides together, received negative comments. Some thegns and ministers began to fail to turn up for the witans; I noticed their absence when I made up legal documents. More and more, nobles were not merely recording their disagreement with the facts proposed to become law but were becoming physically unavailable. Some were known to have fled the court to the continent.

Edmund gradually gained the confidence of the majority of his subjects. He was a good soldier, winning many battles against the Norse. His mother, Eadgifu, helped to build bridges, by her entertainments, between the old fiefdoms of Wessex. Jealousies were gradually overcome. Then came the disaster. I could not understand at the time how God and the saints could conspire to allow the bloody mayhem which brought a promising reign to such a violent end. The actors in the drama were both hot-headed, but the explosion of violence could not have been foreseen. They were both brought up to control their emotions. Alcohol consumed on these occasions may have been to blame. Some are more negatively affected by ale than others. Could not an angel, spying an opportunity to work a miracle, have hovered over my friends to halt their wasteful doom?

On my comfortable settle, an old man far removed from decision-making in these days. I replay, in my mind, the events which formed our history, the history of Wessex and England. I harbour dark thoughts of my own; regrets, but also hope. The thousandth year after Christ's birth will end it all, one way or another. At the last judgement which will surely come, if I am still alive, I shall find a leper and cling to him as I fall into the chasm. He will bear us both upwards, beyond purgatory and into paradise, for so I am promised by the church. Dunstan tells me this and I am satisfied, I think. He is archbishop and right is on his side. My thoughts are my own, sometimes unbound by the times in which I have lived. No-one hears me. Ah, except Algar.

Soon I shall journey to Frome. It will be my last visit. I shall see my old home once more, and ghosts.

And now, no more my friends. Sleep calls me. In my colourful dreams, I will relive my story, the story of kings.

Part One
The Mortal Coil
Autumn 939

Ballard Point, Dorset

WOOD CRASHED, OARS broke, masts snapped. There was storm in the sky, violence on the sea. Men screamed as their ships disintegrated around them, wailed with terror as they lost limbs, severed by shards of falling wood and metal; wolf and dragon head prows, divided by surging foam from their vessels, drowned with them. Swords, spears and scabbards flashed in shafts of vile light searing across the waves, exercised by those who could still stand in the heaving ships, their flanks unbalnced by the clash of warriors, the English in their heavy oak battleships, the Danes in their sleek-keeled traders. Horses on the Danish boats, coralled in the sterns, neighed in terror, pulling on their tethers. The green sea turned pink, frothing around the sinking ships, the dying men. Some men swam in panic towards shore, but many disappeared below the waves, their arms held aloft, their last breaths a beseeching cry for help from their multiplicity of gods. Odin and Thor, listening, took them down, down to their place at the table of heroes, to a watery Valhalla, where the perpetual feast would hear their heroic tales. Tattered sail canvas and splintered planks drifted like playthings of a sea-god on the surging waves.

'Christ greeted our men in heaven for that deed.'

Eadred turned to face inland along Ballard Down. The vision produced by fireside scops, so deeply imbued in Eadred's mind, faded. The sounds of death dispersed across the sea. The stormy sky returned to its late autumn, balmy loveliness. 'Well that was all a long time ago, Hersfig. It was a great battle, more than one hundred and twenty ships of the enemy were routed, though God's weather undoubtedly contributed to our success. Our ships were the stronger.'

The groom holding the horses nodded. He could not see what his master, in his imagination, could survey, but he remembered from hearing the poetry of the scops that there had been a significant naval battle fought by Alfred and that the outcome had been favourable to Wessex. There had been few enough times when the Vikings could be said to have been roundly defeated; this was one of the more memorable.

'What became of the Danes, Lord?' Hersfig understood about the significance of Wareham and the Danish fort at Exeter, but was vague on the details. It was a chance, while he was with the aetheling Eadred, brother to Edmund, the heir to the throne of England, to brush up his collection of epic stories for the lads in the royal stables. It was drama enough, to be standing here with the prince, on this windswept hill in Dorset, looking over this now peaceful, green sea, where no war ships could be seen. Two trading ships, fat-bottomed and high-sided, lugged along in opposite directions, staying close to the shore. Oars carved the water, responding to faint drum beats. There was little wind in the bay. Under a weak sun, the Isle of Jutes announced its misty presence, a landing place of the earliest of their kind, the Saxon conquerors of Britain. This was England. Its satellite nations, Scotland and Wales, were distinguished by the resentful presence of their native princes with their foreign tongues. An empire indeed, of Britain.

'I heard that we chased the mounted escapees from Wareham, Sir?' Hersfig was keen to get his facts right and to show that he had listened to the scops. They could be embellished later. One of their horses tossed its head, pulling on its halter. He smoothed its nose. 'Sssh, patience. It's only an autumn wasp.' Hersfig gave the horse a treat. The other nuzzled him, asking for the same.

Eadred began to walk away from the clifftop. His mind had replayed what was important, a successful outcome between

Wessex men and Danes, a score in favour of the defence of the realm by his grandfather, Alfred. Put in charge of King Athelstan's navy, at sixteen years of age he felt compelled to relive the dreams and hopes for melding the nation, for the survival of his kind, the Wessex kindred.

'Strictly speaking and between us, Hersfig, it was not so much a naval battle- our ships were slow to the scene- as a destruction of the Danes by the winds of God. Over a thousand men died, mostly drowned, on that day. Our ships chased and finished off those of the survivors whose boats overcame the storm. The rest of the host, careering out of Wareham, pressed their horses hard along the coast to Exeter. My grandfather's men, including the king himself, harried them all the way. Just as in the battle of Edington a year later, the cowardly Danes reached their fortress before Alfred could overtake them. Chippenham was starved out. Exeter was not, but hostages were taken and the host eventually retired into Mercia.'

'King Alfred let them go?'

'He was a merciful man. He thought that they would keep their word to cease campaigning. Later, after Edington, he did not trust them. They were bound to Christ and sent east to the land of the Angles. After that, peace was ensured, for the most part. Though you can never fully trust a Danishman. We live in that era of peace, Hersfig.'

'For which I am grateful, Lord, and for your kind protection.' One of the horses whinnied. They had been standing a long time on the top of the hill. 'Where do we go next?'

'We have visited the boat building yards at Portland and laid an offering at St Aldhelm's Head. Next I want to see the church at Studland, which I hear is in need of restoration. Then on to examine the defences at Wareham.'

A wind blew up from the west, tossing the thorny trees nearby and sighing down into the bay below. Seagulls scattered, crying, over the white chalk cliffs which like giant footsteps marked the land's infiltration of the sea. The oars in the distance were shipped and sails hastily hoisted. The long hair of the young men blew across their faces.

'That's the end of autumn, Hersfig. Hand me my jerkin, will you? Let's go. I wish to spend time in the church before returning to Wareham.'

They mounted and rode back along the imposing shoulder of the down, following the freshening wind into the shelter of the dunes before the church and thatched fishing village of Studland.

At Studland Church

E ADRED WAS A sensitive soul. There was, for him, a soothing
beauty in the liminal place where land meets the sea. It was
why Athelstan, aware of Eadred's limitations, had appointed him
admiral of the fleet, a gift of responsibility to steer him away
from his personal worries. Here in the church of Saint Nicholas,
founded by the great man, Aldhelm, he could seek and perhaps
find inner strength, at the same time imbibing the stimulating
saltiness from the pans on the beach and feeling the safety of a
familiar environment. Affected more than his brother Edmund by
the religious instruction he had received from birth, he could give
personal thanks in prayer at each naval site along the southern
shore of England. The southern shores had been free from Viking
attack for two generations.

The pious young man, teetering between a life in the church
and his practical duty to his dynasty, could hear Aldhelm's
music, read his words, that great saint of long ago, in this
silent place. Eadred was on a pilgrimage, as well as carrying out
reconnaisance. He stood where Aldhelm had stood: the chapel
on the headland which was named for him, not far from here, its
windswept clifftop position warning sailors of the dangers of the
rocks below, and here, at Studland, which he founded to protect
this portion of the southern shore of Wessex. Next was Wareham,
where his church guarded against any recidivists reclaiming the
pagan beliefs of the British inhabitants of Purbeck. Corfe, too,
which Aldhelm would have known, at the neck of the rise into
the wild heaths of the still partly-pagan coast. Pucklechurch,
near Bristow, on the boundary between Wessex and Mercia,
was his foundation too and Eadred, forced inland, would visit to

celebrate the saint at the annual May meeting for St Augustine and St Aldhelm. Frome and Bruton, his monasteries, held more memories of Aldhelm's works and Sherborne, his bishops's seat, and Bradford-on-Avon, another church, were on his list to visit. In time and if peace prevailed, he would visit them all. Aldhelm had conquered men's minds, as Eadred's former tutor Dunstan wished to do; he was successful in pushing back the frontier of idolatry and ignorance.

Eadred, beyond the reach of the school-room and beginning to make his own mark, knelt and begged the saint for guidance. He was a second son of his mother, Queen Eadgifu, a fifth son of his warrior father, Edward. What was his ultimate position in this process which continued, this making of England? Torn between two states, the religious and the secular, he entered the first year of independent manhood, at sixteen.

Eadred had been brought up to know his place, to be an understudy unlikely to rule, a guarantee for the Wessex line. Should he have to take power in the unlikely event of Edmund's death, there would be no reqirement for him to breed; Edmund would do that task. His nephew would carry the disciplined legacy of Alfred onwards towards the first millenium. There was no womanly temptation, at present. He had learned to sleep alone. A wife was not necessary. Hersfig, his man, would replace a woman, and did so willingly. He wondered if a female could ever be a close confidant, or a friend, and thought of his sisters. No, they were never close, not even in the nursery. He was, he felt, self-sufficient. He needed only the sea. He needed time to think, to assess danger and the requirement of the times in which he lived. He was not as fit as he would like to be, which set him apart from his healthy brother with his loud voice. He thought that perhaps his stomach affliction, like his grandfather's, might have been sent deliberately to bring him closer to heaven. That did not stop Alfred from becoming great, from doing good works in this world, and it did not preclude Eadred from bringing, through his piety, some advantage to the court, perhaps to counterbalance the extrovert energy of his brother at witans. Edmund's voice, and how he said his words, in contrast to his own, sometimes offended. Dunstan had tried, but failed, to calm him down.

Eadred stood up, lit a candle and sank to his knees again. The candle light flickered. This one was for his brother Athelstan, who was ill. The future rose up before him like a wall, as someimes, in the young, it does. The coming millenium was on all minds. It was many years away from this time and this solace of waves, but it cast a shadow. Aethelstan's court clerks, Aethelwold and Dunstan talked of it with dread; before the coming of Christ, they said, there would be retribution, judgement. The weak-willed and evil would be cast into perpetual torment. The devil would goad them with his talons and fork; the strong-minded and blessed would join Him in heaven.

Would anyone, living now, see this time? Would the anticipation of its arrival, like a dreaded ship full of pagans, brandishing weapons and fire, make the faithful deal every day as though it was their last, in prayer and gratitude for the life that they had?

Some wore a shirt of hair to protect themselves; some, like Eadred, consulted their secret saviours, the relics, which they carried with them everywhere, putting them behind their pillows at night, by their sides as they ate, round their necks when they conversed, the saints ever watching, ever guiding. Some fondled delicate bones of the dear dead through silk lined purses as they listened, with horror, to the mischiefs of the world. Others, the secular and unconverted, saw no further than the present. They had no thought for their actions, only grasping what they could to shore up their positions in this world, to conserve their past gains, to jealously protect their persons and souls against the covetous actions of others. Like young dogs, playful, grinning and careless, they rushed to the abyss without a master to restrain them. Eadred sighed. It was an imperfect world, and he, a sinner, could not change it.

One family, he knew, had foresight, the sense to perceive what needed to be done, to try to alter the course of the nation before the millenium sealed its fate. Ealdorman Athelstan Half-king and his brothers and sons, indeed, all his family, had displayed sound leadership in recent years. Their wisdom at council had contributed to maintaining King Athelstan's peace. If ever Eadred was called by God to become king or regent, they were the family which would support the Wessex line, would offer practical advice to those who must wear the crown, must carry the burden of it. He would not be alone. There was, in addition, Dunstan.

But Eadred was not likely to have to ask for the advice of this powerful family of soldiers; Edmund had their ear. Together with Dunstan, and the archbishops, they finely balanced the powers in the land. Apart from the unscrupulous Wulstan of York, all was in order.

Eadred lit two more candles and placed them on a dusty altar. One was for his other brothers, who were dead. He was only a small child when Aelfweard had died mysteriously, and Edwin's drowned body had been found on southern shores more than ten years ago. He and Edmund were the last of the sons of Edward, to his third wife, Eadgifu. The second candle was for the other personal protectors of the family, the saints Cuthbert and Oswald, who sat on the shoulders of each prince of Wessex, whether they gained power by force or cunning or simply were, unavoidably, born into it, like himself.

Hersfig was sitting in the church porch. Eadred rejoined him. The afternoon, though bright, had brought large, high clouds. Jackdaws flew past, cawing, in a frenzied group, scattering on a sudden gust. Below the church and low cliff, the white tops of waves raced.

The aetheling of Wessex pulled his cloak around his body. He was fair-haired, lean, of middle height. His clothing was well spun but muted in colour; browns and greys, like the surrounding vegetation as it entered its late autumn hues. A flash of orange and green lit up the hem of an embroidered knee-length tunic. Colourful cuffs gleamed with gold thread at his wrists. A single heavy bracelet, worn to show his rank on the sleeve of his shirt, sparkled with silver gilt. He walked slowly, accompanied by Hersfig, along a sandy path towards the sea.

On the beach they walked northwards, with the wind behind them. The long spit of fine sand stretched out in front; to the east, the Isle of Jutes sat bathed in a burst of sunlight, its tall cliffs challenging a sea-farer to conquer it afresh. A young dog appeared from the dunes, running towards the young men, past and around them. It barked with joy at being alive, not malevolence.

'You want to play?' Eadred picked up a piece of driftwood and threw it into the shallow waves. The dog rushed by him, keen to capture the unexpected gift of a playful encounter. It brought the wood to Eadred and then rushed off again, in a sprint to test its legs, disappearing up the beach amidst wind-driven flurries of sand and spray.

The young man squinted, losing sight of the dog after a hundred yards. He was better at close work than distances. There was something dark ahead, lying on the beach. The dog had circled back and stopped, sniffing it.

It could be a dead seal, he thought. Eadred had no need to return to Wareham immediately. They could investigate the shape. He thought again of his half-brother Edwin, whose body had been found, years ago, on a beach not so far from here. Was this a phantasm, a ghost, come to tell him how he had met his death? Leaving Hersfig, he walked, then ran, towards the shape.

The dog, a red-haired hound which had escaped its master to

fulfill some deep-seated need to be alone in wind and sand and sea, like himself, was nosing the dark form. It jumped back as something moved. There came a wail.

Eadred pushed the dog back from the black-draped figure. It yelped and tried to rush at the moving form. It eventually obeyed his command, sitting a few yards away, watching with curiosity as Eadred knelt to examine the groaning piece of wet humanity lying on the sand. Eadred had a way with dogs, particularly hunting dogs; he had been brought up in a household full of them. The head of the dark form began to move. A hand appeared from beneath the sodden cloak. A face looked up, its dark hair matted and filthy, one eye closed and swollen, the other bright and enquiring.

'Who are you?' Eadred, one hand on a dagger and the other on the trunk of the moving shape, pushed thick, wet hair from the eyes. The face of the nearly drowned human stared back. Another moan came and then the bedraggled creature coughed and brought up half an ocean of seawater from its lungs, belching the contents of its stomach over Eadred's cape. Eadred fell back onto his hands, horrified. The dog leapt up and ran further from the scene, but stopped and sat again at its own comfortable distance, still curious. A crow flew down and hopped nearby, hoping to benefit from the solid residue of an emptied stomach.

The expulsion of water and bile seemed to revive the dark form; its eyes opened again after the convulsion; it struggled to rise onto all fours, its hair falling back across its face. Sea water gurgled down its head and bare arms; it had not long emerged from the waves.

'Who are you?' Eadred repeated and touched a wet hand. 'What has happened to you?' Eadred, having momentarily dreaded meeting the ghost of his dead brother, in light of his recent thoughts and prayers, helped the wet human flotsam to stand. It struggled to speak. He offered it a small flask of mead which he carried with him. It took the flask and drank, recovering.

The creature, of as yet indeterminate sex, was as tall as a young child, only half the height of his rescuer. He tottered, falling against Eadred as he held the flask out for him.

'Thanks,' he gasped. The voice was a man's, not a child's. Eadred could see now that the legs were short, the body large. A dwarf. 'They threw me out of the ship when they realised I was not worthwhile market fodder.'

'What is your name?'

'My given name is Bica, though I am called by many words.' The voice of the little man, though accompanied by much coughing, was deep and manly. Eadred wondered at the rapid recovery from the mistreatment which he had evidently suffered.

'And you can swim, it seems. How long have you been in the water?'

Bica turned, staggering, to look at the sea. 'It was first light and I was between those cliffs and these.' He indicated the Isle of Jutes. 'The tide helped me and I found some driftwood to cling to. And I prayed.' He indicated a plank from a wreck which lay further up the beach, bobbing in and out of the lapping waves. 'Must have done some good,' he added.

'Discarded by a Viking ship and saved by another, it seems.'

'Not Vikings. They were Cornishmen.'

'Cornish!' Eadred, as all Wessexmen were, was aware of the hatred of the remaining Dumnonian Britons for the Saxon kingdom. They regarded all indigenous inhabitants who had stayed within its enforced boundaries beyond the river Tamar as fair game. They had chosen overlordship by Saxon kings. It was news to him, though, that they had begun to steal subject peoples from the English nation. The worm had turned.

'Where is your home?'

Bica was recovering quickly. The mead had helped considerably to restore him. 'I come from Countisbury, in the north part of Devon. They raided there three nights ago and I and ten others were taken. We were brought overland to a seaport on the south coast. They were not rough; a deal was made to take those who were not wanted by the settlement. The other nine had committed some misdemeanor. The youngest ones were thieves.'

'And what was your crime?' But Eadred could see with his own eyes why Bica had been traded.

'It was dark, and I covered my face. They took me along with two other boys my size. I faked a high voice. I wanted to get away.'

'Because you are a ...?'

'Exactly. I was mistreated in my birthplace. A grown man who cannot be physically useful to the community is not to expect to be well-liked. After my parents died, I have lived alone.'

'So you would not wish to return?'

Bica swayed. He fell forwards into Eadred, who caught him and pushed him upright.

'No.'

The autumn wind was strenghtening, beginning to bite into both of the men. The dog had lost interest and disappeared back into the dunes, its curiosity satisfied. Both men were wet; the incoming tide lapped around their feet.

'Come with me. My horses are waiting by the church.' Eadred indicated the tower which could be seen above the dunes and cliff. 'I will take you, if you wish, to Wareham, where you can find monks who will help you - British monks, some who will speak your language.' Eadred had recognised the mother tongue of the Devon man. Eadred had some sympathetic feeling for the conquered Dumnonians. They were second-class citizens, as he was a second son.

The two men slowly made their way up the beach towards the church. Hersfig, alarmed, had returned to the horses. Bica's height made it difficult for Eadred to assist him, but after a few steps he could walk unaided. One foot dragged. They sat on a low stone wall. Hersfig was not beside the horses. Eadred whistled loudly. Hersfig leapt up from behind a bush.

'I'm sorry, my lord...'

'Never mind that. We have a near drowned man here who needs assistance. We must get him to Corfe for attention. Bica, here, will ride with me. But first find my spare cape. He needs something dry to put around him.'

A woman appeared from a cottage next to the salt pans. She wiped her hands down her outer work gown. She spoke, in an accent with so much British Welsh in it that it was difficult for the two visitors to understand her. Her work garment was stained red.

'I thought that the pig had come back to life to torment me, that whistle was so loud, or that the dead had been raised for judgement.' She noted Bica and his wet state. 'The little one looks a gonner.' She started as she recognised the status of wealth displayed by Eadred's clothes. His large antique saucer brooch, holding his wet cape on his shoulder, announced him as a man of no little means and importance.

'Madam, I am not. I am wet, merely.' Bica was recovering quickly enough to be offended. 'And I am not little. I am a small man. Words matter.' Bica looked at Eadred and the groom, who was evidently searching himself for words to describe the singular height and unmatching voice of the child-sized human. Bica's deep voice, emanating from the short body, was disconcerting. Eadred would soon become used to it, but this astonishment followed them both with every new encounter. Later on, it would be a useful tool in alleviating humourless moments in the witan.

'Does he need a bit of hot broth?' The woman, recovering from her astonishment at being in the presence of nobility, garbled in her thick accent. There was very little recognisable English in her speech. Eadred looked at Hersfig. They both looked at Bica. The woman pointed to her mouth.

'She asks whether I would like to eat something.' Bica's Devon British accent was a language almost as far away from the Purbeck speech as Wessex English, but he could comprehend the woman. 'I say yes, please.'

Eadred nodded to Hersfig to bring the horses to the cottage, which was accessed by a stony path. A long rolling hill with gorse and bracken on its lower slopes ran behind it towards the sea and the Old Harry rocks. There were several outhouses around the main house, each one set aside for a specific purpose. The carcase of a pig, dripping blood into a wooden pail, hung from the entrance of one of them. The executioner's knife lay on the ground beside it.

'You gentleman and you – little man – wait here and I will bring you something hot. I won't be long. The pot is on the fire, as it always is.' The woman waved to a fallen log, cut crudely into a low seat. The accent was thick, but the gestures understandable. The three men sat down. The carcass of the pig, still reeking of its doom, swung close by. The animal was as long as Eadred was tall and nearly twice as large as Bica. It twisted slightly on its rope, hanging by one leg.The woman returned quickly with a wooden bowl of steaming meaty broth and a hunk of bread.

'Some of the blood, put aside for sausage. Should be a good pick-me up. Eat.'

Bica, recovering quickly, took the bowl and bread and made a gesture which seemed strange to his companions. He bowed deeply and said something in Welsh. The woman replied quickly, pointing at Bica. She seemed flustered and retreated, wiping her hands on a rag on her shoulder. As she turned to run back into her home, she made the sign of the cross.

'What did you say to her? You seem to have alarmed her.' Eadred crossed himself.

Bica, munching the bread and slurping at the bowl, was slient for a minute. He swallowed. 'She thinks I am a merman prince.'

'Why does she think that?'

'I thanked her in such a royal way; she is not used to gratefulness, nor, perhaps, to being generous. I frightened her with my apology for being wet and unsightly. I have this effect on people.They think I am the devil, or a saint. Obviously she thinks I am something in between, a ghost, perhaps. Or perhaps a seal.'

Eadred had not explained who he was, or that he was at this beach partly because of his wish to contemplate his dead brother, who might well return one day as a merman prince.

'And anyway, who are you? I am grateful to be rescued and given help. I can assure you that I am no ghost, or devil or saint. I am Bica, and I am now at your service.' Bica stopped eating, pushed the hair out of his eyes and began to take in the details of his saviour.

Eadred could not disguise his expensive clothing or rich brooch which held his cape in place. 'I am Eadred of Wessex. I am visiting this place in memory of my brother Edwin, who was drowned not far from here many years ago. This woman might remember the event. I should reassure her that we are all mortal. Bica, even in your distress, you have a way with you which impresses. Go and tell her in your langauge that you are not a seal, or a merman or a child or anything other than you are. We will come with you.'

Bica bowed to his royal saviour, his head almost touching the ground. 'Looks as though I have spoilt your cape.' The bow looked ridiculous, but there was something attractive to Eadred in the bold little man.

The three men walked to the woman's home. She was looking out of the door from behind a leather curtain, seeming upset. Were there three devils or ghosts now, coming towards her? There was a conversation, with Bica doing most of the talking. The woman barked replies, displeased with her situation and waved a large club which she picked up from the door entrance. Bica persisted with his attempts to calm the woman, but eventually she retreated to the house interior, slammed the door shut and could be heard moving heavy furniture into place behind it.

'It seems that word will get round in these parts that indeed, she has seen a merman, one who speaks Welsh and who eats broth and bread. She will not be convinced otherwise. We should leave her.' Bica's English was good, almost fluent. His accent marked him out as British and would forever be a handicap, but that was as nothing compared to his other handicaps in life.

Eadred looked at this odd creature, standing with an empty wooden bowl in one hand, his hair pushed back in a tangle, his trews still dripping onto cobbles. There was an air of understanding, of stoicism, of humour, even, in the little man's face. He might have been clean-shaven three days before, but now his growing stubble marked him clearly as an adult. His new slave-masters must have been disappointed with their catch. No wonder they had thrown him into the sea like an unwanted species of fish. What would he, Eadred, do with this odd piece of humanity? No-one else would harbour him, he was too strange. With no family to take his side and all others, including his own West-Welsh brothers, loathe to suffer his presence, the outlook was grim. Eadred felt some fellow-feeling for Bica; they were both unnecessary in the schemes of other people; Bica was potentially a burden to any society or community which might take him in.

'What skills do you have, Bica, which you might offer to a lord, or to anyone?' Eadred asked. They walked towards the horses.

Bica looked at Eadred. They exchanged eye contact. Eadred's eyes were light grey, Bica's dark, almost black. There was something foreign in his makeup, which would add to his difficulties in any social grouping. Whatever his origins, they were long ago and several generations past, but they were unmistakeable in his face. No, no-one would take him in.

'Well, my arms are strong, when I am well-fed. My legs are no use but they carry me and I do not need assistance, except when drowning, which I hope not to do again. I can speak Welsh... but you know that and the skill is of doubtful use. I helped my father to carve headstones until he died and drystone walling was my craft. I can identify the birds and plants of hedgerows and put them to use as medicines...I can sing about them, too.'

Bica began to croon, in Welsh, about a sea-eagle soaring over the north Devon cliffs. A bird-man creature, which could lift a lamb from its parent's side, could startle a child and call across the ocean to others of its lust for life. The sound of his voice, as indicated by his natural speech, was deep-throated, melodious and mesmerising. Eadred, a musician himself, felt entranced by the sound. He could play a harp and lute, but his tenor voice was not as attractive as this. Bica had value. It was his voice.

'You are coming with me. We will take you first to Corfe, to get you out of those clothes, give you a haircut and feed you up, then to Wareham where I am based at present. You are mine, now, my slave, Bica. You owe me fealty as I have rescued you. As long as you are loyal, I will shelter you. Do you understand?'

'Yes. Lord. I am yours. And grateful.'

Corfe was not far away; the wooden stockade on the hill at its entrance, recently constructed at King Athelstan's orders to control the Welsh inhabitants of Purbeck, would have what was needed to sort out this new member of Eadred's household. Bica the Merman, grateful to the prince and fully aware of the possible advantages of a life in royal circumstances, rapidly became an essential part of Eadred's life. Together with Hersfig, he now had his own devoted courtiers, a source of loyal support which would soften the coming ordeals of family politics. Unloved he might be, as in a few short years his hair thinned prematurely and significant teeth fell out, but Hersfig and Bica, who owed him much, would be with him to the grave, or so he hoped.

At Corfe, they learned that the king had taken to his bed.

A Visible Difference

I N THE AUTUMN of the year of Our Lord 939, ten girls of high birth, recognisable by their clothing and intricate hairstyling, their clean, long fingers with well-shaped, groomed nails, stood in a row at the west end of the church of St Mary of Shaftesbury Abbey. At fifteen or sixteen years of age, they had been selected from several monastic establishments in Wessex. One stood out; she was a fourteen-year-old, as tall as the others. This girl, yellow-haired like the rest, had an air of confidence, of serenity. A prayer book, its spine glittering gold, lay in her hands. Piety, with her, was not a pretence.

Elgiva's destiny had been determined by her family from an early age. She was the perfect example of pure Wessex lineage, blonde, bright and wealthy, a valuable commodity in the marriage market. She was also of the right age to fit the requirements of the royal dynasty. Her puberty would coincide with that of the aetheling Edmund, a happy coincidence, which would give her an advantage over others who might dream of sharing the bed of a prince. The children knew each other. Their mothers shared an interest in religious matters, though Wynflaed's, as a widowed vowess, was in the ritual aspect of church services while the dowager queen Eadgifu was chiefly concerned with internal diplomacy and architectural styles. Wynflaed was drawn to the personalities of abbesses, Eadgifu to bishops. Together, as influential mothers operating in Wessex, they found that early friendship in royal sewing rooms had developed into a complementary, confidential partnership.

The family called the girl Elgiva, but her given name was Aelfgifu. Her saintliness was not born of natural piety, despite a thorough grounding in the articles of faith in the hallowed grounds of Shaftesbury Abbey, but due to a single incident in her young life, as often happens with the pre-pubescent. Her revelation came at the age of eleven years, when she accompanied her mother, father and younger sisters from their estates in the west to the Christmas meet at Frome in 934.

There was, at this time, a heightened sense of relief at the prospect of peace. Celebrations for the success of King Athelstan's campaign in the north would bring war heroes together to cheer their leader. The grey-haired king of Scotland would be on display at the feast, an unwilling guest, to be baited by jibes. Humiliation was a potent weapon. As the family travelled eastwards, visiting on their way the site at Doulting where Aldhelm had met his end and giving a gift of beeswax candles to the church there, they had had to walk by the side of their travelling wagon up a steep, zig-zagging incline to enter the hilltop fields of Frome, which fell away, a mile to the north, to its river valley. It was a short journey onwards from there to the palace and outbuildings where they would be personal guests of Eadgifu. Elgiva began to run up the steep hill, the sun glowing red in the winter afternoon. Soon she slowed. Heads and bodies bowed, the family and their few attendants crept upwards, reaching a corner then turning again to grind upwards. The hairpin path turned twice, then on its third turning came to the top of the hill. As she straightened up, Elgiva saw ahead the rotting base of a gibbet, not the first she had seen, but it was the first time she had seen one occupied.

The body of a young male, recently suspended, swung gently in the early evening breeze. His large feet, made unshod by a passing tramp, were almost within reach. The skin was brown, the colour of the people of the south, an unmistakable, and unchangeable, visible difference. The misfortune of a slave had played out here. Elgiva stared. Had he tried to escape his fate, or had he insulted his master or mistress in some way? Slaves of whatever colour were a valuable commodity, particularly young ones; his crime must have been serious; theft of something, or of his own person by himself, or a repeat offence, must have brought him to this dreadful place. Her father had told her something of the way things were. Gibbet Hill was avoided on the return journey.

Perhaps, in the wealthy court of a king, an obedient slave might not be irreplaceable; the warehouses in Bristow were beginning to be filled by southern creatures with their curly hair and broad shoulders. Culture and colour, the definitions beginning to be applied to other peoples beyond the Mediterranean, were vital in establishing hierarchy. Viking traders, having sped on their wave stallion ships to the far reaches of the known world, regarded themselves as authorised to order the legal entitlements of others. It was further to fetch them, but less trouble, said the traders, to catch them. Some Arabs and Vikings, it was said, were exploring the possibilities of north Africa. The continent of Africa was regarded as fair game. The English court, in its infancy as yet, required able-bodied workers, but were finding the native population of Wessex and elsewhere near at hand were less likely to be heathen. It would not do to make their own subject Christians into slaves. Further afield there were plenty of available pagans. Elgiva had not seen one of their kind before. The head of the boy had fallen forward, his face dark beneath a mop of black hair. A crow and two magpies, frightened away from the body by their arrival, sat waiting on a hawthorn bush nearby.

Elgiva asked her father what he thought the boy had done. There was no indication near the gibbet of the crime, no notice which could be read, just the body, as a warning. He told her to look away. He could remember his own initiation into the cruelty, when, as a boy, he had witnessed the removal of a boy's hands for theft, at a witan court. The mutilation of criminals no longer shocked him. The courts had done their job. Men and boys, unwilling to play by the game, were hacked. Women who practised magic were dunked. That was how it was. The hardening of the heart was necessary in life; he could not spare his own children the process which he had endured. Pigs, cattle, chickens, humans, slaves, all were subject to the laws of the land and vulnerable to amputation at any time, in war, at mealtimes, in the courts, in a brawl. Violence was not evil in itself; it was inevitable. He brought the wagon and horses onto the flat field beyond the gibbet and loaded himself and the family. They arrived at the palace within another half-hour. Elgiva noted that the gibbet and the boy had been forgotten by others in her family in the excitement of arrival, but she did not forget, or ever stop regretting, the brown, dead boy.

Home for Elgiva as she grew into early youth was Shaftesbury Abbey, but also her mother's estate at Charlton Horethorne. The high land of Shaftesbury looked out over the Blackmore Vale and the scattered farmsteads below. She was trained in obedience; she never felt hemmed in by the silent abbey walls. On many occasions she walked along the path on the heights to watch the sunset and through woods to the valley floor, aware of her future, of the expectations of her family. Edmund's mother was her own mother's close compatriot; both were associates of Shaftesbury. Queen Eadgifu and one of her daughters, a Nunnaminster novice at Winchester, met her mother often in the guests' refectory, where speech was allowed. The sewing room, where everyone spent part of their day, was a silent and serious place; the creation of art and recording of Wessex history required great concentration. It was a sacred duty.

Elgiva's missal had been won as a prize for her studious progress. Books were plentiful in the abbey's library. Knowledge lay there in leather and vellum. Wynflaed had many books at Charlton

Horethorne which had stimulated this quest; she herself had passed through Shaftesbury's system as a girl, encouraged by her own mother, Brihtwyn. The Shaftesbury nuns who taught in the year of 939 were hard on the lazy, but rewards existed for those who tried. Elgiva had several books of classics won in this way, some of which joined her mother's library on shelves in her halls, alongside the wisdom writings of the ancients, including copies of King Alfred's texts. The farmstead at Charlton was a mausoleum of family achievement; cabinets and chests scattered through the rooms at Charlton contained statuettes and a record of the foals and mares Wynflaed had owned and the success of the stallions bred at her stables. Her children had had to compete for her affection and attention with her stable.

Brihtwyn had instilled into her descendants the interest and ability to design and to stitch the images for embroidered hangings which had become sought after for the new stone-walled homes of the nobility. Churches, too, being restored after many years of neglect, demanded decorative or commemorative wall coverings. The skilled women of Shaftesbury and Wilton had become historians, recorders of the deeds of their male kin. They also helped to keep draughts at bay over doorways and covered windows to keep out foul things. They were good times for the girls and women, high-born and low, of the sewing-rooms. They waited for marriage or to die, contributing to the nation's well-being and sense of itself.

The nobles of Wessex feasted and danced under the gaze of their heroes as sewn into fabric. Their large eyes regarded vigorous celebrations and traditions. Cloth material was easily mended; painted walls, like those of the Roman people, needed repair after a few years and the plaster crumbled, though some persisted with painting pigment on plaster or stone. Church interiors were covered like the tattooed bodies of ancient warriors, every pilaster decorated with coloured swirls, beasts growling or grinning, sometimes dreadful worms with fangs agape, to remind an unbeliever or, worse, doubter of the threats of hell. Men favoured this work, which involved elaborate scaffolding to place images in their semi-permanent positions, while the women produced portable soft hangings. When the stories had been forgotten by scops, when wooden or stone halls had been demolished or decayed, the bravery and conquests of Saxon Christian families would still be portrayed for all to read and admire.

None of the ten girls were yet legally committed to either become nuns or to marry. They were becoming aware, however, that they would soon be bound in marriage, or assigned to learning and sewing as nuns. In the sewing room they pondered their fates as the slave-craftswomen and senior seamstresses of the abbey guided their hands in the construction of delicate sacred hangings and copes. Their young eyes were a valuable asset. Even lettering was simple for them, though it was considered that numerals and letters were the most difficult to sew. The girls honed their skills with cheap threads on linen, but sewing with gold and silver had become an expected craft.

At this time, Elgiva longed to sew the images loved by her grandmother, the dragons and myths of Arthur. The abbess had asked her if she would like to devote a hanging to the deeds and story of Radegund. Inwardly she groaned; the Thuringian queen's pain-filled life was well known and had been shown in hangings and described in written works many times. Elgiva wished to show something more imaginative and original, like her mother. Her mother Wynflaed was an expert at designing and, in her youth, sewing the images of horses. Long hangings in her halls displayed equines in all shapes and colours standing, trotting and cantering, unridden, free, over sunlit hills and dales. She had devoted her life to her living animals; their beauty, the sight and smell of them were her delight. They were God-given gifts of freedom, of comfort, of beauty, she said, and never more fascinating than when wild. She gazed for hours on the as yet untamed horses in her corrals and taught Elgiva and her siblings to love them, too. Radegund was not known for a love of nature and did not know the Wessex countryside. It was the only time Elgiva turned down a commission. Prayer to St Radegund was offered, that night.

Although Wynflaed and Eadgifu had already conspired about Elgiva's possible future as a king's consort, it was the equine connection which brought Edmund's interest and the two youngsters together. The queen's cats could not be trained to do anything useful. He was shown around Wynflaed's stables as a boy, long before he became king, along with his brother Athelstan, who was taking a rare day away from his duties to visit Shaftesbury with business of his own. Edmund and his brother the king often travelled together. Edmund was Athelstan's acknowledged heir; he needed to be trained. They were like father and son. Eadred came too, sometimes, but Wynflaed was of the opinion that he was interested in horses merely as pack animals or as a means of transport; he did not have a passion for them as Edmund did.

As she stood waiting to be called forward, Elgiva pictured her role in the great banner which she and the other girls were working on. She might not appear in it, but her children born, hopefully, to herself and Edmund, might. She could see them in her mind's eye as they would be, golden haired, playing around the low limbs of great oaks of Wessex, the old wise ones. If she could, she would design trees into the edges of a banner. Their speech might be silent, but the heart would receive their words, if it was open. She smiled to herself. Despite the diplomatic process of selection, proclaiming a fair procedure, Elgiva already knew what the outcome would be. She remained still, while the other girls shifted their feet and rolled their eyes. Standing could be painful. Royalty never complained.

The queen and the abbess, entering from the cloister, stood near the altar in the east end of the nave. Eadgifu called and beckoned to the girls to come forward, one by one. A Kentish woman, she had a strong accent which western Wessex-born ears found hard to follow; she was better understood in Winchester where many of the court officials and priests hailed from eastern Wessex. The girls looked at each other. Which one did she want first?

The queen, like the abbess, was a commanding figure. The girls knew something of her through their families' attendance at court. She was not fettered by any convent or court; she was able to roam, as a king's widow, and to impose her will throughout the land. Some found her too vigorous, too quick in conversation and her speech too opinionated. She was wearing brightly-coloured embroidered and expensive robes, in contrast to the abbess. She was a setter of fashion, not merely in clothes, but in architecture. She noted when building improvements were required, made suggestions for schemes for latrines and bathing, to restore and to modernise. She was known to be involved in the plans for Cheddar palace which had been undertaken in recent years. Her voice was heard in committees, bemoaning the more conservative ideas of many of the menfolk. They exasperated her, she had been heard to say. Eadgifu could afford to be bold. Her position in Wessex, the longer she lived, grew stronger by the day. No wonder Athelstan had not needed a queen of his own.

Eadgifu, beckoning, looked the modern embodiment of queenship. She had designed herself into the part from an early age, with the help of her family in Kent. Edward had accepted her as a political manoeuvre on the part of Eastern Wessex, but she had brought grace and an intelligent mind, as well as land and gold. Her light blonde hair mixed with silver, intricately plaited in loops, framed her sculptured face. Her short, slim, active, body, displayed wealth in gold at shoulder, waist and hip. Her voice, in its heavy accent, carried weight, like a drum, but could command like a horn, yet be gentle, like a harp. Could any of the girls have the potential to emulate her? Would they live long enough to see their own children grow, to choose wives for their own sons?

The girls, unsure of who had been invited to step forward, paused. The abbess nodded to Eadgifu. Together they walked up the nave towards the nervous group. They marched together in unison like dancers, clip clop, on the polished tiles. At a signal from the abbess, the girls dropped their modesty veils. Their hair was exposed, their eyes and cheeks were open to view.

The two older women stood in front of the row, their hands hidden inside their sleeves, looking at the best potential spouses that Wessex could muster. The row curtseyed. One girl stumbled over a corner of her cloak and nearly fell over. Another was asked to leave as she answered a question. Brains were required, as well as beauty, to mother the next generation of the Wessex line. What was Eadgifu looking for? Someone to equal her stature, someone to challenge her in discourse? Someone to train in diplomacy? Fairness and justice were the watchwords of Wessex; perhaps she would like to promote, through her choice of spouse, the idea of Wessex as the arbiter of good sense, tempered by Christian virtues. She worked tirelessly for the poor, it was said, advised on alms giving and the treatment of petty criminals. She was often in the company of the rising priests Dunstan and Aethelwold and shared their ambitions for reform. Elgiva waited. There was the piercing look of a mother-in-law selecting her daughter-in-law, beak-like. Eadgifu stared at each nervous face. As all younger women must do at such times, it was best to remain still, silent, inscrutable, innocent. Elgiva curtseyed again, when asked to, flawlessly. She bowed her head. Wynflaed had taught Elgiva that to pretend was not to lie; self-control under scrutiny was required of all noblewomen, but deference to such a woman was not pretence.

Eadgifu walked towards each of the remaining candidates. Candidates for what? For the width of their hips for easy childbirth, for intelligent but not too questioning eyes, for beauty but not too much appeal, for courage and endurance, for the ability to stand for hours in public under the intense gaze of others.

She waved to the abbess to remove all but two girls. Elgiva and one other remained. The others retreated to the back of the nave in the shadows.

Eadgifu began to speak. Her voice was uncommonly deep. She asked the girls to move to sit near the altar of the church. She watched from behind as they walked up the nave. She joined them on a cushioned bench used by the priest in giving communion. The other girl with Elgiva was dark blond whereas Elgiva was light. Eadgifu was taking into consideration her son's requirements. The queen whispered a question to Edwina, a thane's daughter from Ramsbury. She squeaked a nervous response, coughed and apologised, then resumed her answer in a deeper voice. Eadgifu listened and then turned to Elgiva.

'What makes you feel eligible to be my son's wife?' she asked in her thick Kentish accent.

'To use my skills and powers to the best of my ability to benefit my country and my king.'

'Say that in Latin.'

Elgiva did so.

'Say it in Breton.'

Elgiva complied.

'Now in Danish.'

After a short pause, Elgiva replied in the tongue of the Danelaw.

Eadgifu stepped back, looked at the girl and at the abbess and nodded, then stepped forward and embraced Elgiva. The tallest, but youngest girl had been chosen. Elgiva of Shaftesbury would be Edmund's wife.

Mothers

E ADGIFU RODE, UNACCOMPANIED, from Cheddar, arriving at
dusk at Wynflaed's long hall home in Charlton Horethorne.
The ceremony of Elgiva's betrothal to her son was taking place
at Shaftesbury Abbey the next day. Skirting the long grass of the
autumnal wetlands with their hooting fowl, keeping to the dryer
high roads past Wells towards Kingsdon, she rested briefly, before
the last leg of the journey to Charlton. She rode alone, free. The
sun was low as she passed the formerly sacred hill landscape of
the British at Corton Denham. Golden ham-stone churches and
their towers were springing up in the valleys, pointing to God in
heaven, their bronze bells ringing to remind travellers and locals
of the coming of Vespers. Foreign heathens would be held at bay
forever; the bells were a Christian alarm system as well as an
insistent call to prayer.

In the hedgerows of fields carved from ancient woodland
many years ago, yellowhammers, woodpeckers and tits of all
kinds still flitted and flirted, reaping the success of the breeding
season despite the continual rain, fattening up on insects and
the summer's wasted corn. Eadgifu saw and heard goldfinches,
reminding her of recent work in the embroidery rooms. Flowers
were her speciality, as it had been Aelfflaed's, her predecessor as
queen She muttered a prayer as she rode. God rest her soul. She
should think better of her. It was easier to do so, now that she was
dead.

Wynflaed's hall lay at the end of a long sandy lane. It was
neatly thatched, as the old hall at Cheddar had been. It had a
solid wooden frame, the oak logs horizontal in structure but with
additional stone wings, expensive but beautiful. Saxon craftsmen

were becoming skilled with stone. One wing served as a private chapel. Wynflaed liked to practise her religion, dressed in full regalia, at home.

As she approached the stables at the back of the farmstead, Eadgifu recalled Wynflaed's approach to life. 'We are born to adorn the world,' she had said. 'Personal as well as structural, the work that we create, whether by mason, carpenter, seamstress or goldsmith, should contribute grace to the world.' She was a positive force. She saw no evil. Language mattered, too. All Wynflaed's children were fair-mouthed. No oaths were taken in jest or in anger. Self-control was at the core of her being. Her brisk sweetness contrasted with what Eadgifu could never control in Edmund, his volcanic anger. Was there a difference between the sexes, was violence in boys and men inevitable?

Edmund had emerged, before she left Cheddar, from a weary meeting with the king and his ministers, to have a private meal. She told him that she would be absent for a few days. She seemed to have annoyed him yet again by commenting on his Viking-style hair; the back was neat, she had commented, trying to be complimentary, but was the long front fringe necessary? One might as well be blinded and she told him so. She could have bitten off her tongue as she heard the words exit her mouth, but they would out. Still, there was time enough to restore her relationship with her eldest son. He was only fifteen. He would be pleased to hear of Elgiva's progress on her return.

Eadgifu dismounted and rang a rusty bell attached to a pole. Wynflaed's home was a practical, working farm, but it was luxurious. With rebuilding, she had tried to make it as much like a roman villa as possible, which is how it had begun. She had travelled widely in her youth, had been to Rome, had seen many beautiful things. They infect the mind with ideas, lead to dissatisfaction, Athelstan said. He hated waste. Behind the long low house was a range of well-built barns in a quadrangle, part of which were the stables. The pebble-cobbled yard sloped to a well and a drain in the centre. The colour of the pebbles, grey sea stones from the coast at Lyme, artfully contrasted with the yellow stone walls. Today the domestic animal barns were empty except for grass store; the pigs, sheep and cattle were out in the fields and woods, fattening before the winter slaughter. In the mid-autumn evening, all was quiet, the day's warm sun emanating from the walls and ground. Only one animal occupied the stable section of the barns: a pregnant mare, who moved to her open half door to view the human surveying her abode. A few fellow occupants, late-born swallows, flitted in and out. Bats were beginning to join them. Eadgifu handed her horse to a stable-lad. She walked across the cobbles to the main hall door and waited for it to open. She cast her eyes around; dusk was beginning. Colours were fading to grey and blue. All was well with the world; and there was a visit to Shaftesbury Abbey and Elgiva's betrothal to Edmund to look forward to, in the company of her friend.

Beyond the barns, stretching as far as the eye could see over the evening scenery, corrals contained wild and tamed horses of all colours and types, feeding, tails moving slowly from side to side. Wynflaed bred them for riding, hunting and to pull the carriages of nobles. White horses for kings, dark horses for war. There were large cobs for shifting heavy goods, small ponies for princes. In the morning there would be servants and slaves dotted over the paddocks and hills, fence mending, ditch digging and hedge laying. The scent of grass cut and dried wafted from the barns and a nearby haystack. There was an enviable air of contentment over all. The workers, free and slave, had no material riches of their own, but no-one went hungry in this place. The younger slaves, having been brought across the seas from Ireland to Bristow, appreciated the benevolence of their mistress. The same religion bound them all. They would live out most of their lives in this Somerset paradise, working, marrying and with children of their own, promised never to be separated from their own kin by their mistress, protected by her boundaries, her connections. But she could not buy and rescue everybody, though she would wish to; many were less well treated elsewhere. The mines took their toll, but who would work underground in the upper echelons of hell, if they were not forced? Wynflaed never lost slaves, except through old age or accident. There was no need to try to escape; there was safety here. Eadgifu's own slaves were to be found chiefly in the sewing rooms where they were grateful enough for their work and keep. She had no qualms or regrets as far as they are concerned. She had occasionally ordered a whipping, but only when necessary.

This was the land of milk and honey, as she saw it on this autumn evening. Not even the thought of her truculent son could bring a cloud.

As she waited at the door, some late workmen began to walk down from a nearby hill and across the pastures towards an outlying barn for their supper. Of course, Wynflaed, a vowess, would be preparing for vespers. She took religion seriously; since her widowhood she had told Eadgifu how much the Benedictine structure of the day meant to her; she could help her husband, and herself, by praying continually for his soul and by doing good to the poor on her estates. She treated her slaves as fellows, not as priced creatures, the wretches that they were when first landed on our shores, weeping and trembling. Her daughter Elgiva took after her. Eadgifu had asked Wynflaed once whether she really prayed all day. She replied that she had a running conversation with God in everything she did; rubbing down a horse or arranging flowers, there was prayer in action as well as on the knees. Aethelwold, the student at Glastonbury who was Dunstan's friend, would not necessarily agree. Wynflaed did not say how she coped on Sabbaths. It seemed, though, that a wealthy vowess had latitude to decide her own religious rules.

Eadgifu had thought that she might consider becoming a vowess herself, in future years. Court life was often wearisome and troubling. She had considered retiring to Amesbury, being closer to Winchester and her home county of Kent. Or she might choose, as Queen Aelfflaed had done, to alternately snooze and pray in the ever-sunlit corridors and cloisters of the abbey at Wilton and to join her there in the earth near the clear running river. One day. Not yet. There was much to do, much to discuss, the game of politics to play. She was ordained to have a part in the doings of the nation. Edmund must be steered to kingship. His future children would need her guidance. In a year's time, she and Wynflaed could be grandmothers.

There was the sound of buzzing. Wynflaed's bees were returning home to their skeps near the haystack.

The door opened. Wynflaed peered out. She was dressed in black. Her face lit up. Someone, at least, was glad to see Eadgifu. She missed nothing. Ears like a cat. Eadgifu leaned forward to give her fellow grandmother-to-be a hug.

The queen, it seemed, was seen arriving across the valley by Wynflaed's steward Martin. There was no need to blow a horn. The household was not yet at prayer, though the plummeting temperature, gathering gloom and the group of maidservants inside the kitchen door, taking off work jackets and putting on sober headscarves, indicated that evening prayer was imminent. Wynflaed had put on her vowess garb, a black wimple and cloak. A chapel bell sounded clear in the evening. A cock replied from the barnyard. Martin the steward, rounding a corner from the stables, recognised the queen and joined them as they greeted each other. They turned to go into the darkening hall.

Eadgifu admired the steadfastness of Martin, a slave. He was long and lean. He had to bow under the low beams of the hall porch. Greying now and over forty summers, he had the controlled manner of a well-versed reeve, sober and dun clothed, almost invisible. Such a servant was rare, but his family supped at Charlton Horethorne; his sons and daughters worked on this farm. By unfailing loyalty to his mistress, he would someday buy their freedom, as well as his own. He lit candles as they walked arm-in-arm.

Wynflaed indicated that she had to hurry to Vespers. In a flurry of energetic blackness, she kissed Eadgifu and ran down the main hall, stopped before the entrance to her chapel, composed herself, straightened her back and took a lit candle from a rack. She disappeared through the chapel door and it closed behind her. An indoor bell rang as the service began and then the sound of women singing drifted along the stone walls. It reminded Eadgifu again, that this was her likely future when politics were done. It was a promise, not without attraction.

'Madam, you are welcome. Would you care to follow me to the kitchen?'

Martin bowed. He looked immaculate. His linen shift was, as usual, impeccable, short, as it should be for a household slave and with only the slightest of black stitching at the border on his cuffs. His air was one of saintly courtesy. Wynflaed had trained him well, like her famous horses. He ushered Eadgifu with unnecessary pomp inside the door at the end of the hall away from the chapel. As she passed from the outer door through the hall she examined, as she had on many occasions, painted images on plaster of the virgin, Radegund and Aldhelm. Bunches of cut flowers, fresh and dried, hung over the porch doorway. Lavender stems covered the floor immediately inside the large hall. The aroma of stew simmering for supper after Vespers filled the space, mingling savoury with sweet smells. The aroma of fresh bread which would accompany the meat and vegetables added to the variety of sensual delights. A freshly waxed dining table supported dried fruits and jugs of warm ale. Images, smells and sounds: they made for magnificent memories. For Eadigu, as a traveller newly arrived from complication and discord, the experience of a welcoming and relaxing hearth was overpowering. This was the home of a well-ordered friend. There was harmony in the aspect of prayer and meal-making. She felt tempted to join the religious service.

What her body needed was not prayer at that moment, after a long day's ride.

'Martin, after prayer please inform your mistress that I have gone to my room, and am in a tub. Could you arrange warm water for me instantly, and bring some wine?'

She did not say 'please'. That word was reserved for equals. Edmund was sick of hearing her ask for changes in his behaviour. 'Please,' she had learned never to say to him again. He had learned that her requests could be countered with a cold, closed mouth. 'No,' is what she mostly heard. Before ascending the stair, Eadgifu looked down the hall to the closed chapel door.

She was always astonished by the level of comfort and beauty which Wynflaed had managed to make and maintain in what was, after all, merely a large farmstead. On the inner wall of the hall, from which doors led off to the chapel and kitchen, hung her greatest pride, a very wide linen and silk history embroidery, exquisitely designed and sewn by herself and her servants in the years following the assault on the north. There were horses prancing, horses falling, as well as men in battledress advancing or dying. The king and Edmund were shown fighting, magnificently attired in gold and silver thread. Athelstan wore the crown of Wessex with its spikes and jewels. The silver filet of king-in-waiting shone on her son's head. The poem written in celebration of this year's magnificent defeat of the Norse and northerners at Brunanburh was the inspiration for her next design. There were already many short versions of the battle in embroidery; she had commissioned one of them during the time of celebrations and it already hung in Winchester palace as a reminder to all of the valour of the Wessex princes. On the windowed outer wall of the hall there were colourful, shorter, story embroideries, including one of the Beowulf saga, best viewed after nightfall when the fire was lit. She moved across the hall, intending to study the Beowulf embroidery nearest her which hung across wooden panelling. She caught sight of herself

in a figure-length bronze mirror on a wall between windows.
A tired looking middle-aged woman stared back. A bathe first,
she thought, food later and a heart to heart with Wynflaed after
that, which would go on into the late evening. They would travel
together in two days' time to Shaftesbury, for the betrothal of
Elgiva, now aged fifteen, much younger than herself when she
was brought from Kent to marry Edward. A fine age, a beautiful
age. Virginal.

At Charlton Horethorne

THE HORSES WERE disturbed. They knew what was coming. The clouds were purple and iron grey; the wind whipped branches of the tree Martin called Herne's Oak which stood down by the breaking area. Black horses, white horses, brown horses, piebalds and skewbalds whinnied, all a-flutter at the signs of the helter-skelter night which now began. Heads up, ears back, they cantered and skidded to a halt short of the solid fence, snorting.

They neighed, they pawed, kicking up dust. Wynflaed and Eadgifu, observing them, were similarly excited, but not because Martin's so-called wild hunt was preparing to ride. Superstitious nonsense. The herd would be safe enough in their enclosures. Tonight, Wynflaed and Eadgifu would be at a gathering to mark the passing of souls to the otherworld, and also to introduce Elgiva to the assembly of nuns and vowesses at the abbey in the sky. Their former pupil would be transformed, dedicated to an honour above all others. Elgiva would be ritually dedicated to the production of heirs for the Wessex kings, would be hailed as the wife of Edmund of Wessex. She would become a queen, anointed or not.

Wynflaed was leaving the horses in good hands. The grooms would bring them into the stable yard if the weather turned worse. She picked up her skirts and walked into the stables to check on the carriage preparations. The women could not ride this evening, in all their finery; it was one of those occasions where protective cover was necessary.

'And throw in a couple of blankets as well, Miscin. I will bring the mead jars to you for stowing shortly.'

Giving orders. She was perpetually giving orders. Some

would not use their common sense at all if she did not remind them to. She had the ordering of not merely Charlton, but other estates, too. She was fond of her servants and slaves; most of them had been personally chosen by her, but they displayed a disappointing amount of incentive. Was she being too harsh, she wondered? She could not question herself continually; she was too busy. She prayed daily to God and the Virgin, to Cuthbert and Radegund for guidance and generously fed and sheltered the human beings whose lives depended on her ordered generosity. She did more than many. A horse, harnessed to the coach, impatient to move away, shifted its weight.

Wynflaed shouted to the servant to hurry. She felt energised. She felt that she could march with an army to war, if need be. She had put on her Shaftesbury Abbey outfit, having changed out of her badger-skin horse-riding habit and into her black clothes. She was a vigorous woman. Even now, a widow of forty summers, she ran up hills to meet her grooms, to pat and greet the old trees which dotted the Charlton estate. She wore breeches for riding. She had won her freedom; she would not marry again. The land was hers.

Widowed vowesses were not uncommon, living independent lives, once their duties to their husbands and families had been fulfilled. Wynflaed's days were now full of the getting and rearing of horses for the battlefield, for pulling carts, for riding to hunt. There was no horse she could not tame, no colour hide she could not match. She had enjoyed two lives; the present one was her reward.

She caught sight of herself in a mirror, hanging inside the back door. There was little of her face to see and nothing of the shape of her body. Her hair was completely concealed. This was the drapery of conformity, but also of safety. In her black, shapeless abbey clothing she was untouchable, spared by the shield of holiness from any troubling interference from forces of this world or the next. On her shoulder was pinned her mother's ancient filigree brooch. Like Eadgifu, her family's past defined her, an independent widow born to and living in central Wessex, the heart of the kingdom.

Tonight, she must play her part. A howl of wind from outside reminded her of the journey she and Eadgifu must make in this weather. A draught caught a taper. She had been standing there, admiring her appearance, for too long. She turned away from the mirror's gaze. It was a night for reflection, for both the mothers.

The screech of an owl floated on the wind. The faint ringing of the abbey bells could be heard as the wind eddied. Her duty called, her friends the nuns wanted her there, as did her daughter, Elgiva. That evening, at Shaftesbury, Wynflaed's life and hers would be dedicated, tied forever to the dynasty of Ecgbert, to marriage to its heir, Edmund.

Dressed and ready in person and in mind, she collected the soberly dressed Eadgifu and set off in the carriage, two jars of honey-mead by her side, one in her lap. The good brown cobs were steady on the road. Miscin spoke to the horses in the near darkness. They rose through the lanes to the great abbey, to her daughter and the future. Already Elgiva expected an heir of her own, a grandchild for her.

The Library, St John's Monastery, Frome

THE AUTUMN EVENING shadows in Frome monastery's library were long. The early summer's promise had held, the harvest would be good. For some, concerned with matters of state rather than of the land, the shades spelled the future. Two men stood at the far end of the room, silhouetted by a bright west-facing window. They were matched in height and late youth, recognisable only as drab male servants of the court. Their monkish capes merged briefly as one reached out to hold the forearm of the other.

'I can't do it, Nonna. You know I cannot stay.'

'But the king will not punish you openly for your marriage to his daughter. Leofa, you know he cannot afford to. It would raise too many questions at court. The Winchester faction would have another, more potent excuse to bay for his blood. The secret of his bloodline must remain unknown. He would trust you, after all these years of service, to be loyal. Dunstan will never reveal it, you may be sure.'

'He would trust me to keep my mouth shut, I know. But then there is the other matter which lies behind the simpler matter of blood and birth. I have made a promise to Athelstan that it will never be revealed and I will hold true to that. My oath was taken on the holy relic in crystal which he wears around his neck, but he will always be fearful of the threat to his throne. Peel back one secret and the other may be revealed. Since the debacle of the Scottish Constantine and the loss of his cousins at Brunanburh, Athelstan has become doubtful of the efficacy of any oath-taking. He heaps more relics onto his pile, brought from countries and continents many miles away, but he is a broken man, Nonna. He will go mad with the burden of the secret of the theft of Oswald's head. Common knowledge of the plot which we carried out will undermine him completely. I must go, for his comfort, as well as mine.'

Leofa looked more worried than at any time in Nonna's experience of his red headed, pragmatic Viking comrade.

'Not a plot, dear friend. A plan. A plan which temporarily succeeded, which brought the nation together. Every part of St Oswald in one place: that is what it took to unite England. You are not to blame for the proposition of the scheme; our small band of clerks acted as advisors to the king on that fateful day when the decision was made. We all share that burden.'

'But not the added difficulty of having fathered a child-children on a Mercian queen's daughter. I am doubly cursed; Shaftesbury cannot contain the secret much longer. Since the great battle in 937 so much has changed. Athelstan's decision-making is non-existent and Edmund is becoming impatient to be king. His muscles grow larger by the day and his temper with them. Have you noticed how he twitches? My children are reaching a stage of enquiring about their family antecedents. You know, don't you, how small children can get hold of an idea or a word spoken which was not meant for their ears, which they then repeat...or perhaps you don't.' Leofa stopped. Had he offended Nonna? He needed all the friends he could retain.

'I know what you mean, Leofa. Gwladys writes often from St David's to tell me of my children's missteps, harmless for the most part, but embarrassing sometimes. Spymasters are not blessed with an easy family life.'

Leofa looked relieved, took his hand away from Nonna's arm and scratched at his lower arm. Nonna, sympathetic to his friend's plight, suddenly reached out to give Leofa an encompassing hug.

'What, a proper cwtch from the Welshman!' Leofa felt the full force of the animal-like grasp of the equally strong man. They had both been well-fed in their years at court. He responded with a slap on Nonna's back. So, this was farewell.

There was no hope. The king was fading, his power waning. Edmund, his heir, would not tolerate the existence of a Mercian royal child, if he became aware of its existence. The secret of the boy Aethelred, Leofa's son, named for his Mercian grandfather, husband of the Lady of the Mercians, Aethelflaed, could not be kept from him forever. The walls even of the great abbey of Shaftesbury could not hold the secret of a rival, a challenge to himself and his own future children. Together with the possible public discovery of the theft of Oswald's head from Cuthbert's coffin in Chester-le-Street, and the substitution of another, it would be a doomed reign from its beginning, with the potential for Mercian and Wessex rivalries leading to civil war, as they had before.

The two men separated. This was the last physical contact in life which they would have. From the age of twelve they had been in each other's company, part of the trinity of clerks to the king. Times were changing. They must bend with the flow of time, if they were to survive, if the new nation of England was to survive its own infancy. The state, the church, all were undergoing flux. Edmund's time was coming, like it or not. They must protect the dynasty, that was what, in mind and body, they were trained for.

'We still have the written word. We may not speak, but when you go, you have your pen and I have mine. We will find a way to keep each other informed.' Nonna tried to salvage hope. Together, but now separate, the one a reliable court servant, the other an exile, both well-trained as friends, advisors and spies, they would manage something. They would make a code known only to them; they had the skills. The Irish sea would be calm, be kind, and Gwladys, Nonna's wife at home in Dyfed, would manage a regular exchange of letters.

Banishment for life. He had not been killed. It pained

Nonna that his friend, loyal to himself and to Athelstan, should have to leave Wessex, but Leofa was a marked man, a scapegoat, branded a thief, though it was not clear to the court what had been stolen. Rumours faded. A new order was emerging.

Nonna's Diary

K ING ATHELSTAN DEPARTED this mortal coil, a worn and disappointed man, not long ago. My journal must record my sadness for his loss. Will there ever be a better king? Already I have lived in the reigns of three Wessex rulers: Edward, Athelstan and now Edmund, all born of the royal Wessex bloodline.

I continue to summarise what I see and think and take the opportunity to say something of my own experiences. Perhaps my comments may be of some use to future readers, though I do not expect thanks and certainly do not expect acclamation. I am no saint-in-waiting.

I have heard from Dunstan, who passed by this morning to repair the damage done to his doom painting in the church of St John. A guttering candle had been left unattended. He told me, looking worried, that the first of the royal family's secrets was out. Edmund has been informed by Egil Scallagrimson, his bodyguard, who has tentacles throughout the Viking world, that my former compatriot, Leofa, is in Dublin, with his Viking kin. The deeper secret, of the stolen head, has so far been preserved. Neither Edmund nor his mother knows of it. The lesser matter of the existence of a Mercian royal child, Leofa's son, has been troubling Dunstan and myself. So far, it seems, Edmund is unaware of the foreign aetheling's existence. Like me, Dunstan wishes to protect our friend, but also the king. The flame of anxiety has been lit in Edmund's mind. There is damage to the doom, and now this.

Part 2
At Heaven's Gate

"Walking through the realms of earth, singing on their way to paradise."
    Swedish hymn

939/940. *In this year king Athelstan passed away at Gloucester....* *Prince Edmund came to the throne at the age of eighteen. King Athelstan had ruled fourteen years and ten weeks.*
    Anglo-Saxon Chronicle.

Priory of St Oswald, Gloucester, December 939

THREE FIGURES, TWO males and one copiously wimpled female, were on their knees near the high altar of the Mercian crypt, spectacular in its painted colours despite the low lighting. Large white candles atop ornate candlesticks around a high bier threw alternate streaks of light and shadow across the paves. The bier was topped by a wicker-coffined body enclosed in shining material. Gold thread glittered. Behind the chief mourners, female and male figures, abbots and royalty, distinguished by their dress and jewels as members of the highest strata of the nobility of England, were kneeling on rows of cushions. To the side of the crypt, shadowed figures of standing monks intoned prayer. The crypt arches, gaudy with their red and blue sculpted stone beasts, signalled the only lifelike animation. Incense billowed through the underground chamber, swung on its curling journey around the noses of the company by a boy thurifer. It stifled and greyed the air.

In the back row of the ranks of mourners, someone sneezed. A voice mumbled an apology.

The abbot, who had appeared from somewhere dark, lifted his hands, palms upward. The congregation stood. Prayers by all were said to end the funeral service. The three main figures turned to walk down the centre of the crypt. No further penance was necessary or called for. Older knees were relieved; there had not been enough cushions to go around, even in this well-endowed priory. This was the funeral of a king, in his adopted country, Mercia.

One of the male mourners whispered to the female, whose wimple had been pushed back to reveal light blonde hair and heavy, ornate gold earrings.

'Mother, I will stay a while. I wish to consult the relics.'
Edmund, the taller of the two men, started to move back towards
the bier.

Eadgifu nodded. At this liminal time of change in all their
lives, the surviving parts of saints would respond to prayer.
Miracles could occur. She continued out from the crypt,
accompanied by Eadred, her younger son. He was shorter than
her, a pudgy sixteen, slow to grow. He was her reserve son,
unlikely to be needed as Edmund was vital, energetic. He was
already brewing a son of his own with Elgiva. Nevertheless,
Eadred had a role; he was steady and supportive. He was reliable.
To his mother's relief, he had not inherited the short temper of
his father, unlike Edmund. He gave his mother a hand to mount
the steps from the crypt. He knew her high-heeled pattens could
sometimes let her down and after all, she was no longer young.
He looked back into the crypt as they ascended. Should he take
a greater interest in the church for his future? Could he enjoy
the religious life? He was a second son; he could choose his life
ahead, free of the need to propagate or promulgate. The navy was
an interest, but it would require weeks, perhaps months, away
from Winchester. His stomach troubled him often. Edmund had
the kingship business well in hand and was keen to travel. Eadred
led the company out into the grey light of the nave above. The
intoning monks followed.

As the last sandalled feet with lifted skirts passed up the steps
to the nave above, Edmund returned to the bier, putting out a
hand to touch the face of the dead king, his half-brother, who had
been like a father to him. He did not remember his own father,
Edward.

'Thanks, brother. I will always remember your wishes, our
family's requirements for our dynasty and for England.' He
reached into the coffin, folded back silken material and took out a
small missal which lay in the king's left hand. He gently replaced
the cloth.

Edmund moved away from the coffin, but turned back once more. The rock crystal containing the Holy Splinter had also to be preserved. He knew Athelstan would not begrudge him this most sacred of relics, the dearest possession of his brother in life. Edmund considered his brother's book, which he had consulted every day and this precious relic, combined with his own wit and strength, to be sufficient to guide and protect his dynasty's achievements. He carefully lifted the dead king's head and removed the small relic on its golden chain. The dead king's hair fanned around his head. Edmund smoothed the greying brow.

Would this great king be made a saint? No, he was too unpopular with the Winchester faction, even in death. Besides which, Athelstan would not have wished it. He wanted only to rest forever with St Aldhelm, at his beloved Malmesbury. He would be there tomorrow.

Edmund kissed the relic casing, crossed himself and put it around his own neck, hiding it beneath his shirt. Moving behind the bier and the altar, he approached the gated remains of the greatest saint of all, more potent in the defence of Wessex and England even than Cuthbert.

Oswald, protector of the north, a saint slaughtered for his cause, his blood so holy that the earth stained by it had been quarried as treasure, beloved by countless pilgrims and efficacious in times of war, peace and quarrel, lay, for the most part, here. A missing arm had somehow been appropriated by Peterborough Abbey. A king who became a saint, a rare thing, a bulwark, too, against the increasing power of the church which was loathe to grant uncontested sainthood to any but their own. Edmund knelt at a small table in front of the gilded wood reliquary which was lit by a single candle. He paused. It was important to be clear when asking for aid from great saints. There would be a requirement, a payment, a promise, to be made when invoking them. He placed a small bag of coins on the table.

Edmund muttered his promise, received wisdom from the saint. What did he say, this sainted northern king, slaughtered in his prime centuries ago?

Watch your back. You could meet my fate. Good luck.

The following day Edmund, his family and nobles prepared for the twenty-mile ride to Malmesbury for interment of the royal body. There would be many stops at towns and villages along the way for the countryfolk to pay their respects to the much-loved king. Stroud, Minchinhampton and Tetbury would all wish to celebrate the passing of the old reign and the start of the new. The abbot of Malmesbury travelled to meet the coffin at Tetbury and to accompany the body of his chief benefactor to the abbey. In terms of church ritual, there would be no greater spectacle than the putting to rest of a king, for the foreseeable future. Dunstan and Aethelwold accompanied him, learning their trade as future abbots and bishops themselves, watching with a critical eye to note observances and rituals which could be improved or cut from future royal occasions. Dramatic ritual had to be mind-changing; the magic had to be believed. Doubters would not be tolerated. Still young men, they could see their way ahead, forward to a reformation of their church, to satisfy the Pope's requirements to stir up old ways and streamline Benedictine practice, in hearts, minds and particularly bodies.

Finally, the coffin was carried into the great nave of Malmesbury, accompanied by all the pomp which the abbey and town could muster. Athelstan was particularly popular here. The small walled burh, important since Alfred's time, one of a string of fortified towns, was essentially a long steep hill, Bimport, with shops and houses on either side, protected by the river to the south and north. Like Frome, it had survived the Viking wars. Behind the abbey the land dropped dramatically to the river, creating a stout defence, safety for the inhabitants against intruders who might wish to disturb the resting place of saints and kings.

Safety, too, for the well-loved dead, except, of course, against ambitious prelates with points to score and careers to build. Canterbury demanded its share of the revenues from pilgrimage. Aldhelm was eventually removed by Dunstan, Wilfrid taken from Ripon by Archbishop Oda. Much later, the unloved, remaining dead of Malmesbury would be tipped from their mausoleums, the river and stout walls failing to protect from dogma and malevolent interference.

Cheddar Palace, Easter 940

I T WAS ONE of those memorable moments before a drama unfolds.

'How do I look, Nonna?'

There, posing by the open palace door, light streaming from behind him, was the king. He looked the part, carefully prepared from his woven hair to the tips of his cleverly toggled shoes. Ahead of him was the first full witan of his reign. The multi-coloured tents of many observant diplomats, bishops, ministers and nobles crowded the thorn-hedged fields around. He was wearing full regalia. The heavy metalwork on his shoulder, arm and hip displayed his wealth, his family's insignia. Everything had a meaning; nothing was pure decoration. There was protective magic on the hip, power on the arm. Red gold, that rare commodity, glistened on the arm ring, the mark of a warrior who attacks without hesitation and who gives rings generously to those who support the defence of his realm. The prominent ceremonial dagger of Alfred warned that this decision-maker was prepared to strike for the sake of peace. The brooch which held the folds of his fashionable short cape in meticulous drapes was not merely a practical item; it had the shining self-biting serpent on its flank, the jealously guarded dynastic symbol of Wessex. Hanging at his neck and at his side, the clanking gold and silver reliquaries of personal saints, a finger here, a wad of hair there. The bloodline would never fail, the saints would see to that.

Balancing nonchalantly on the door sill, one foot out-of-doors and one in, the warrior stood astride his future, aware of the magical power of bright daylight or candle glow which gave others who saw him the vision of a halo surrounding a man with more-than-human powers. On his face, in shadow, were the impassive, controlled features of a young leader in his prime. Determined, certain.

Edmund at eighteen was a seasoned warrior and master of a nation. He wielded four European languages with his tongue; he was an accomplished reader of Latin and English, a courtly poet, a laughing lover. He was summoned by God to manage the affairs of his huge realm and the intransigence of its people's requirements and moods. He had the optimism and expectation of perhaps twenty healthy years before him with which to occupy the throne of England. It was a pity, then, that all this promise blew away in the wind on one bright day in Pucklechurch. From cradle to grave may be a short time and all our dreams shatter with one dagger stroke or fall, sent shrieking with their unfulfilled desires into the dark otherworld where no-one hears. But Edmund could not foresee every detail of danger; no-one could, not even Dunstan.

Taller than Athelstan had been, slim, shapely and strong, Edmund was meantime a superb work of human art. His mother and father gave him their strong bloodline. Childhood illnesses were overcome, aided by the medicinal achievements of Wessex monks. The monastery hospital at Frome cured many royal ills; their herbal remedies sold throughout the land. Efficacious prayers as well as the ever-present assortment of relics, consulted like a magical talisman, assisted in decision making. He had a small book, a psalter, which he carried, like the former king, in a pouch hanging from his belt, whose exquisitely small texts he often drew out to consult. Athelstan's hands had touched it; his handwritten notes in margins were there to read. He was armed with the Word of God and with the weaponry of man. Anointed, at Kingston-on-Thames like his forebears, he was unassailably God's chosen king.

His hair, fairer than Athelstan's, was more golden in appearance. Like the child angels who appeared in the slave markets of Rome, traded from this land of the Angles, he seemed to strangers to be a heavenly creature walking in the gardens of paradise. His skin was delicately freckled like some of the Danes and he wore his hair like them. He said his young wife favoured the style; some of the older women frowned at the adoption of cultural traits from other lands, but Edmund said of himself that he was a citizen of the world. He was a lavish patron of all arts, especially the art and architecture of the church, for which Dunstan and his mother were his guides. His hair was artistically scraped back from his face and swept into a manly knot at the back of the head, held in place by a silver filet. With this style, he said he was ready for art, love or war, though hair fashions at court could change rapidly. Tomorrow could bring a new style. Whatever the hairstyle, when wearing his crown of spiked gold designed by Dunstan, the imagery of wealth and splendour matched, if not surpassed, the appearance of the emperors of old. Charlemagne must have looked like this when in his youth. The days of peaceful encouragement of the glories of the Christian world, of educated diplomacy, Alfred's dream, had arrived.

It seemed then that the golden one would outshine his enemies; such was the delusion of youth. Those around him did not see the weakness, or forgave it if they did.

If you looked down the length of this lean young body you would note the remarkable lines of early manhood. Besides the lithe form, you would see the linen shirt, off white in colour, embroidered at collar and cuff with red, blue and green foliage design. At hip height the embroidery continued around the hem. The shirt was held in place and gathered at the waist with the necessary weapon and reliquary belt which was itself a work of art. He had more practical clothing for hunting and sword practice, but today the fresh new king was expecting foreign guests. Below the shirt were trews, also of linen, but a plain mushroom buff in colour, bound with strapping in red. His leather shoes carried embossed creatures on their upward surface, curling and snarling at each other over the crest of his shapely foot. Over all was a fine blue woollen short cloak for indoor wear, reminiscent of the togas of emperors. His fingers were festooned for this occasion, some with jewels. A golden thumb ring reflected waves of light to the opposite wall. On his right arm, protruding from the cape, was the snake band which his grandfather had had made and which Athelstan wore at the battle of Brunanburh. The red gold lettering worked into its design would protect the wearer, combining the forces of heaven with the older ways of power, or so it was believed. The magic had succeeded, so far.

Returning to his face and eyes, you would not find a more pleasant, open, trusting visage but one which also had the ability to probe, to enquire, to memorise the faces it met and the names associated with them. He had been trained well. Dunstan and Aethelwold, as well as Athelstan, had moulded this man. His mother had played her part. His grey eyes watched and learned like hers. The pleasant mouth remained shut in apparent agreement while saving itself for necessary speech. Poets observe and listen. Edmund, the poet, did both. Only close family members and a few others could know of the repressed anger at the heart of this young man, which on rare occasions could spill out in venom and even violence. His mother knew. Other women could sense and enjoy the thrill of his commanding presence. On top of all, the shock of golden hair danced with vigour, though dragged back, captured and controlled with silver threads. With a carefully trimmed beard, the effect was of warrior-like controlled violence. A king to impress all.

Edmund had learned the importance of symbols from the many visitors to court throughout the last reign. He emulated what he had noticed in the more cultured of the Scandinavian visitors, the coolly dignified Norse. Dunstan, like some of the older women, had objected to his adoption of foreign style, fearful that the copying would not end at clothing and hair. Vanity ruled the court, remarked Aethelwold, though not to Edmund's face.

He and Dunstan had always objected to the absorbing of secular continental ways except in architecture and music. Variation in hairstyling in particular enraged Dunstan. Nonna had suffered from Dunstan's irrational dislike of a particular hairstyle. He hadn't let a day go by since they were students at Glastonbury without mentioning it or gazing at his head over breakfast as if to make sure that he hadn't altered his allegiance to the Roman faith. A man who changed his hairstyle could be labelled a heretic. A woman who changed hers was a witch.

'What do you think, Nonna?' Edmund repeated his question while Nonna considered how to answer. There was tension. What king had none? But he was human and so craved a compliment.

'You look like the king that you are, my lord and were born to be.'

Nonna was still finding his way with this young man. Did he like him as much as Athelstan, his former mentor? He had seen the tempestuous black moods of childhood, watched warily as he and his brother Eadred were indulged by their mother, drilled in Old Testament scripture by Aethelwold and doused in the requirements of law by Dunstan.

Aethelwold was a natural teacher but was rigid in his determination to persuade his charges to think as he did. He was better in the pulpit than in the classroom. His tendency to lurid and graphic descriptions of hell and the pains of purgatory was remarked on by some as tedious, though interesting and exciting to many. There was a great deal of thumping of lecterns. It had its rewards; it was noticeable how much more coin was being given in indulgence fees in these days than before. Heavy chests for the storage of monetary treasure had been constructed with bars and complicated locks by the best smiths for each palace, monastery and church. They were an investment in themselves. Every manufactured thing was valuable and coveted by thieves. In palaces and halls, whether of king or bishop or thegn, there were multiple chests for capes, chests for cloaks, rat and fly-proof

containers for the less durable items, reliquaries to hold the parts
of saints now flooding the market. Aethelwold, by his successful
exposition of the dangers of hell and the devil, had brought about
an increase in equipment, and the necessary closets to contain
it. The court no longer travelled lightly. There were loadable and
moveable lidded containers which could be turned into tables
on the move between witans and palaces, bound and edged
with an artisan's iron work in scrolls of a curling design, stark
black against the wood grain of subtle brown and amber. In
some cases, the most precious were inlaid with silver. Wealth
and the greater sin, the display of it, were becoming a heavy
drag on the mobility of its possessors. The makers of boxes and
chests had a share in this new wealth. Peace had fattened the
nobility, made it slumbrous. Secular linen and embroidered
bedding kept by generations, curtains, hangings, wall hanging
embroideries, tapestries, all perishable but beautiful, had now
to be added to by the industry of many seamstresses in restored
abbeys across the land. These rich items required to be preserved
for as long as possible from the mice, moths and thieves
who would gladly destroy for vengeance or steal these softer
treasures for themselves, items which took care and much time
to create, legacies of many generations. These were just the soft
furnishings. The metal ware, jewellery and armaments, had their
own storage requirements. Rust was now the greatest enemy.
The Saxons, like any self-satisfied nation, knew how to hoard.
They looked back to their beginnings and enjoyed their fame, the
scops saw to that. They were beginning to be weighted down with
their wealth. It corrupted their hearts. The purple Pope in Rome
rubbed his hands.

Edmund was surrounded by and perhaps drowning in the
antique possessions and requirements of his ancestors, draped
in their success and resourcefulness. Now he had the burden
of adding to and keeping them for his own children. Would St
Radegund forgive his family as her holy head now lay at the foot

of a northern saint, far away from her forbears in Thuringia? But, Nonna thought, what was a head of even a saint but a thing of flesh and bone. In his private quarters, Edmund fretted, bit his nails. He stamped in frustration and doubt. Dunstan had not told him all the tale of the head. He was too young when the theft and substitution was planned. Athelstan had thought that he and his mother, who was particularly attached to the saint, should not know all. He did not know whose head had replaced Oswald's. He had not asked and supposed it to be a slave's, but the theft had left him uneasy. Edmund was not sure of his position in heaven or with the monks of Cuthbert. His reputation was at stake. But, Nonna could have told him, Radegund was less important to England's security than Oswald. The gathering of Oswald's body parts was always intended by his brother and his great-aunt of Mercia to secure the realm, but Aethelwold was disturbing his secured peace with visions of hell. The deception and exchange of saintly parts, the leaving of Radegund in Chester-le-Street in Oswald's place, had, in Athelstan's mind, been worth the sacrifice of his own soul. Was Athelstan, Nonna considered, in heaven or hell or forever lingering in painful limbo as a result of his scheme to reunite Oswald's parts and to bring him to Gloucester? Was this theft or necessity guided by divine intervention?

'Nonna?' Edmund wanted more.

'You look the part, my Lord. Perhaps a small adjustment of the folds of the cloak where they meet and are gathered by the brooch.' Nonna stuck to the practical.

Edmund nodded, unpinned his shoulder brooch, reassembled the folds of the short cloak in equal, delicate veils of light wool and grinned. The golden freckles creased into what would be, in time, the characterful crow's feet of a handsome, middle-aged man. Today the mood was light, but there was undeniable pressure. Edmund tapped behind his right ear and blinked.

A female figure crossed the room in front of Nonna,

separating him from Edmund. Nonna recognised the familiar energetic movement. Her perfume invaded his mind, knocking it off course, briefly. She turned. A woman in a beautiful sky-blue skirt came, swishing and swirling, towards him.

'Gwladys!'

'Husband! Pardon me, my Lord, I did not see you there.'

Gwladys had been with the embroiderers in the women's quarters when Nonna had encountered her last, stitching together a banner which would be used for a church procession. The women of the royal household were highly skilled with the needle and loom. They did not spin; that was left to the lesser orders. The brightly coloured, expensive skeins of wool and silk which they used to decorate and narrate the stories of Wessex were their contribution to the stories of the land, to concrete their sense of belonging to the tribe. Designs of architecture and soft furnishings, wall coverings and window openings, curtains, cushions and day pillows for lounging at table games, these were the remit of the noblewomen and their female servants. The longer a piece took to make, the more valuable it was. Abbeys competed to produce ever longer hangings depicting the heroes and exploits of their people. Huge workforces of nuns and their coveted bone needles were dedicated to the requirements of bishops and kings to emphasise the careers and achievements of princes and warriors, to produce poetry and song in the creatures they sewed. Armies marched, ships rode waves, men fell dying, relics were uncovered, all to the astonishment of wide-eyed enemies. The beliefs of the Christian faith were sewn in gold and coloured thread onto the rolls of linen woven by slaves belonging to Bishops. Unrolled, their coloured design spoke of the prowess of the people. They filled the elegant wooden coffers made to hold them. They were charts of the history of the English nation, adding detail with their images to the words of the poets and the great history chronicle. They were an export of great value to continental courts. Nobody sewed history like the English. Nobody made a draught excluder, a door-stop, like the embroidery slaves and virgins of English abbeys and convents. They received no payment; pride in a product was enough.

Gwladys brushed off a piece of red thread from her sleeve. A grey wolfhound bounded in from the courtyard, disturbing the king's pose and the moments of mutual recognition of how far he and Nonna had come. They had both viewed the corpse of the great St Cuthbert in his coffin in Chester-le-Street, both marvelled at the audacity of the heist involving the coveted head of St Oswald which ignominiously rolled around in the coffin at Cuthbert's feet. They were joined by that sacred link, that inner knowledge. Only Nonna and Dunstan knew, however, of the substitution of Radegund's head, and Leofa, and he was far away. Gwladys paused, curtsied to Edmund and came to Nonna.

'Nonna,' she whispered, 'I was sent to find you by the queen. She wants you to find and bring Dunstan to her immediately. There is something she must discuss with him before the arrival of the foreign guests.'

Nonna was still captivated by the sight of his wife, Gwladys, the dark one, after five years of marriage. Her whole person, mahogany hued, still thrilled him and whoever saw her for the first time. She was generally careful to wear colours which downplayed her dark golden looks; beige and subtle brown were her favourites, with blue at the neck and silver at her wrists. Today, though, she was more colourful. Her hair, plaited into a thousand strands of wonder, were the endless delight of the younger children at court. She was patient with them, allowing them to touch the woven chains which she explained were a reminder of the home she left many years ago as a slave, together with two other women from the well-named Golden Coast. They had taught blonde young Saxon women how to braid their hair. Gwladys still danced and sang in Welsh, the language of her original owner, Hywel Dda. She was no longer a slave, having won her freedom many years ago. Athelstan had succeeded in expanding the conservative views of the older courtiers and disregarded the mutterings of others. The Icelander Egil Skallagrimsson had helped her in challenging the court's vision of the world; they were both examples of difference, she of sheer beauty and he of rugged northern culture. Dunstan, unhappy with differences, tried to point out what he felt was the suspicious nature of swarthiness in his doom painting in St John's church, using Gwladys as a template for the darker creatures of hell. Gwladys did not mind what Dunstan thought of her. As far as she was concerned, she was Welsh and Hywel Dda protected her.

Nonna bowed to Edmund and backed away. He turned and walked swiftly out of the hall, following Gwladys via the kitchens, picking up a piece of cheese as he went. Gwladys continued on her way, back to the embroiderers' room. If he was to find Dunstan before the witan's work began, he would have to hurry. Eadgifu would not like to be kept waiting. She would want to brief her special spy, her spider, as she called him. After some minutes Nonna found him in the nearby church, contemplating a space which he wanted to fill with metalwork, his latest design for a lectern.

'Dunstan,' Nonna tapped him on the shoulder from behind. 'Dunstan, Queen Eadgifu wants you. The witan is just about to start. The nobles are arriving at any minute.'

'When will you learn, Nonna, not to do that? Your prodding finger could have been a dagger, for all I know.' Dunstan sighed and looked at the lectern's empty space. There was so little time for creative thought. He turned to accompany Nonna back to the secular world, where art and visions were mocked as much as they were revered. If a thing didn't have a price, what good was it? "Priceless" was no use whatever in commercial terms. Its worth was only in the weight of melted metal unless it had been touched by a saint or king or made by him. Dunstan wasn't a saint yet, and wasn't likely to be as long as some at court had their way, though they would be glad to see him depart on his way to the next world.

Prophets and visionaries were never popular in their own places and times. They often fell down wells.

Nonna left Dunstan consulting at the entrance to the embroiderers' room with Eadgifu. She was not invited to the witan. The members required a relaxed discussion of factual matters and regarded her high voice as a distraction. Increasingly she was being side-lined and her frustrations were vented. Her strident courtyard marches, her steady grimace beneath the wimple, her punishment of items of sewing spoiled by the younger women in her group, were signs that the volcanic temper, bequeathed to her son Edmund, was soon to blow. Gwladys witnessed the red-tinged cheeks, heard the wails of disappointment. Dunstan seemed to be becoming her sole route of influence. He, better than anyone, knew how to alter the course of the ship, of the wind itself, of state. He was her champion, able to play the game without a sword. If only, she thought, she could make Edmund see what a stalwart he was, how needed he would be in coming years. She prayed nightly to Radegund to give her the strength to continue, to reject the supercilious nobles who would reject Dunstan's attempts to curb them. She feared that they wished to put women back into a pot of subservience, locked in an eternal embroidery room. St Radegund, the rebel, who disregarded her husband's pleas to return to his bed, who made a palace more like a monastery, who washed the feet of lepers, came to her in her sleep-tossed nights. It was Radegund's holy head, she believed, resting in its reliquary box, which travelled with Eadgifu from palace to palace, witan to witan, helping to open the doors of court secrets to her. But now the doors, windows and hearts were slamming shut. Radegund had closed her ears and soothing mouth. Edmund, gentle in appearance, terrible when crossed, raging when denied, was looking away from her as the new reign progressed. The men of the realm, instinctively disliking the gathering control of the Pope in lands far off, were pushing her away. Dunstan could put matters right, and Aethelwold, too, young men she might rely on. They were not promoters of feminine involvement with either state or church, but they had admitted to her in as many words that her position, experience, knowledge and advice were valuable to them, useful in many ways. She still held keys to doors which they had the power to open.

Nonna returned to the witan hall. In the doorway, Edmund was still relishing his new found freedom, enjoying the anticipation of power. Behind him, the palace guard began the ritual pacing, shouting and drumming which announced the arrival of foreign guests from their sleeping quarters. Edmund stirred from his step, gangling, unkinglike for a few seconds, but as an impulsive energetic young man will do, flung his body forward and ran, leaping onto the platform reserved for him. He collapsed into a great carved chair, almost over balancing. He sank into the cushions, waving at Nonna with a grin to indicate that now he would pretend, now he would be the persona of the king, the wearer of the crown. Apart from a few changes to the position of his cloak, he would do. From behind the chair a lad stepped out with the spiked headband of gold resting on an embroidered cushion. Edmund took off the silver filet he was wearing and handed it to the boy, taking the heavier coronation crown off its tasselled base and lowering it gracefully with both hands onto his fine head, reanointing himself.

'I am ready. Sound the horn.' The lad blew. A bell clanged in the palace yard. The witan members and foreign dignitaries, waiting outside in an unexpected drizzle of rain, started to troop in and take their places on the benches. It would be a long day.

We become different people when we assume a different cloth or headdress, or mask. We may be who we like to be. Edmund could play different parts well. He could play Beowulf, or he could be Grendel, or even play the part of his wise old grandfather Alfred telling the tale, yet again, of the rout of the Danes at Edington, or the saintly Oswald or even Cuthbert speaking his words of pious wisdom. Eadgifu once said, laughing, when he was a young child, that he might run away with the scops one day if he wasn't restrained. He told such tales and with such vigour and talent. Kings needed that talent to persuade and to entertain and to don disguises successfully. Edmund was certainly the man for the job. There he was, regal, serious, playing the part he was destined for, his hands gripping the carved oak chair-arms. Only a toe tapping the elm boards gave the keen observer any idea that he may be listening to the beat of a recently-heard ballad in his head. Nonna watched, pleased with his progress and self-control.

The nobles, secular and religious, settled down, sorting their trews and cloaks, ensuring that their valuable family or district regalia were prominent. Nonna took his place behind Edmund. Dunstan and Aethelwold, accompanied by scribes, were nearby on the platform on one side of the king. Egil Skallagrimsson, the bodyguard, stood a yard further behind the king on the other, with his sword drawn, blade to the ground, leaning as usual on the heavy decorated hilt. He personified constrained force. The bishops of the land sat on the benches below with the nobility. Some were still in their early twenties, having found that family connections had served them well. The younger ones among them were followers of the new movement to re-establish stricter Benedictine efficiency in the church in its various forms, monastic and parochial. The older, more conservative church leaders sat nearer the open door of the witan hall, where it was cooler, but also draughty. They adjusted their ceremonial clothing.

The drizzle had suddenly become a downpour. It drummed on the thatched roof and streamed down like a waterfall outside. Geese ran squawking away across the cobbled yard, looking for shelter from hail. There was a flash followed by a low rumble.

'The weather's turned. A bad sign for our meeting?' A voice, unidentifiable, piped up. There were laughs from those sitting nearby. Those nearest the door shifted along their bench, causing one to nearly topple over. The sight of an elderly bishop being shunted like a bird on a branch gave rise to another chuckle from the inmost part of the hall.

Nonna counted the ministers and bishops present. Some had arrived at Cheddar only that morning. The business of their dioceses prevented a lengthy visit to court, even though the fare was good and free. Archbishop Wulfstan of York was again absent, but that was not unexpected. He seldom travelled to Wessex from York in these days. He rightly feared that he might be arrested.

Edmund competently addressed the witan, welcoming the lords and ensuring that they were comfortable. Some arranged cushions on their seating and found places to prop their swords or crutches. This was Cheddar, an ancient palace setting, where the right to bear arms within the grounds had not yet been curtailed. There had been no offers of violence under its roof in recent years. There were many men present who had suffered limb loss and fractures in recent wars, but none within a Wessex palace, they argued. They had said goodbye to the old hall of Alfred, which had been unused for a few years and was now decaying nearby, its thatch unkempt and its interior dark and dank. The new hall, in which Edmund now sat, was Athelstan's design, and Eadgifu's.

The golden-haired young man assumed the voice he used for these public occasions, practised many times with Nonna and his mother. It was a deeper voice than his natural one, the king's, not the soft voice of the poet. Nonna could not help being nervous for him. He, perhaps as well as Dunstan, knew the characters of this court. Some would gouge out the eyes of a king they did not like.

Nonna willed Edmund a thought. He might pick it up. *Carrot and stick, remember, carrot and stick.*

Edmund stood. 'Old friends and new, welcome to our witan. We should recap our victories. The great battle of Brunanburh settled old scores and gave many scars. The warrior heroes are amongst us now. My brother and I led you to a glorious defeat of our enemies, Anlaf and Constantine. Their armies are now bloodied heaps of rubble with rusting blades for swords and festering wounds for flesh. We can expect no trouble from them in the near future. I saw with my own eyes the mangled piles of corpses, the lakes of blood, which we left behind beside the Celtic sea. Scotland and Ireland are far off and our scouts report no attempts, as yet, to conscript their young men or to bring forces from overseas, though that will have to be watched. Rats breed well.'

There they were, perfectly delivered words of success and praise, the encouraging carrot, the honey to draw them in, to unify. In battle the urgency of survival was clear, the support for their leader total. No peace could last without the scent of war. Few would forget Brunanburh, the great battle of two years before, the salt smell of the sea, the sight of the blood. Families had been decimated by the struggle to preserve the idea of England. They had mental scars as well as physical. Deep wounds of the mind as well as the body afflicted the older men. Many heirs had died. Edmund sat down and leaned back on his sheepskin and cushion-coated chair, tapping with the flat of one hand the pommel of his dagger carved in the shape of a bird, indicating with his other to an earl in the hall that the floor was now his. A practised, but well-deserved eulogy came next. A figure, seated in the middle of the hall alongside others dressed in the livery of the Ealdorman of East Anglia, stood.

'My lord, you were magnificent. The sons of Edward doubled

the might and power of their illustrious father, settled the score against the oath-breaking northerners. We congratulate you.'

The speaker was anxious to please. Nonna and Dunstan were aware that Edmund was not averse to a few words of congratulation, but he might react strongly to what he regarded as weasel words. The earl, another Athelstan, called Half-king, spread his arms wide and revolved, full circle, to encourage the hall to cheer at this point. He shifted his feet apart as though to challenge anyone who might disagree. He was a handsome man, powerfully built, and had several sons sitting by him, all good looking, all seasoned warriors. He could flatter, or destroy. His holdings in East Anglia were almost as extensive as Wessex.

Some courtiers, anxious to gain the ear of the new king, had been banished to their estates for what Edmund or Dunstan called vain pretence. Convincing influence at court was a valuable skill and Half-king had it. His star had risen during many years of support for the old king. Promoted to battle-leader by Athelstan at the same time as Wulfstan was given the archbishopric of York, he balanced power. Accompanied by integrity and loyalty, his was the main support for the mightiest lord in the land. Nonna knew that Dunstan respected him, but that Egil Skallagrimsson disliked him, perhaps because of the dramatic veracity of his loyalty. Like Egil, Half-king was a hero of Brunanburh. Trust was in short supply. Edmund had been trained to watch for nervous ticks and stammers which might denote discomfort in a speaker, being aware of his own. There was nothing nervous about this man. Half-king, after a pause to acknowledge the thumping and clapping applause of support for his eulogy, continued.

'Ravens and crows, the great sea eagles with their white tails, suspended their soaring over cliffs to gorge in thousands upon the enemy dead. The descent of the army of birds alone was a mark of our achievement.'

The earl received a grateful wave from Edmund and sat down, merging into the colourful lines of nobles on benches. Eulogy took time from the business of the court, but it was the required start to all proceedings, a summary of the achievements of those present, as well as the king, a reminder that things could go well as often as badly, that the outcome of action was not always doom, that loyalty and honour come first. Half-king's popularity lay partly in his brevity of speech-making.

Edmund stood again to speak. 'I was fifteen when I fought at Brunanburh. Athelstan, my brother, would not let me near the earlier battlefield in 934 when I had just twelve summers. I had to spend the time kicking my heels in the safety of Bamburgh castle, but I was able to picture the slaughter of Norse and Scot as I composed my verses.' He paused. There was some supportive laughter. Many remembered how the young prince had regaled them with his tales of fantastic monsters at witans. The precocious poet had become a warrior at Brunanburh in 937.

Edmund waved his right arm which held a wine-filled horn decorated in silver around its edge. This was the ceremonial opening toast, after which there would be ale for everybody. Nonna looked at the faces turned towards the king. The court was dazzled by his appearance, his self-confidence. An heir was expected. His enemies beyond the borders of England which he had helped to make were safely imprisoned in their own self-made stalemate. Peace, though the land must be watchful, seemed likely to be enjoyed for the remainder of this autumn and spring. The image he projected had been accepted and now bounced back to the platform and throne. Unity had been achieved. There was applause, cheering. Edmund beamed.

'I drink to every man here who has played his part in battle, to assisting the house of Wessex to conquer our enemies.'

Only a few on the benches squirmed. Nonna saw Egil Skallagrimsson's eyes fly to them. Edmund threw his head back to quaff his horn, grabbing his crown just before it could fall off his head. There was laughter and more cheers as he adjusted it. Edmund laughed with his audience.

A bell indicated that the business of the day was now beginning. Edmund offered his re-filled horn to Dunstan, who took it and drank the contents. Pages moved around the benches, filling personal horns and cups. Dunstan and the court steward begin the detailed business of the day. Nonna was translator, once again, for the British visitors to court. English was becoming better understood throughout the land, Latin too, but English was the main spoken tongue for business, though it had to be translated into Latin for the records of the witan. Increasingly English was the language of choice in the affairs of the entire nation, whether dealing with old Danelaw speakers, Norse, Welsh or Gaelic. French and Celtic Breton were also heard at witan meetings. Athelstan had made sure that continental influences were present at his cultured court and Edmund was inclined to do the same. This was an empire of differing peoples, of different cultures. There were some who resented the presence of foreigners, but, charmed by the sumptuous and generous surroundings, they held their peace.

A general disposition of the English landscape and economy formed the main part of Dunstan's report.

'The harvest is continuing well and there is no disease in the land,' he began. The business continued, subject by subject, to include the exchange and gift of land holdings and some outstanding law cases. There would be a trial of serious criminals the next day. Dunstan droned on. The matter of the nation's wealth and taxes would also be dealt with, on a third day.

Aethelwold, positioned near the regal chair, smiled. He was enjoying the previous speaker's eulogy to Edmund. He felt, rightly, that he could take much credit for the king's behaviour in public. He spent the campaign of 934 in charge of the young Edmund, ensconced with him in the fortress of Bamburgh. He had been able to suggest several of the gorier passages of the long poem about monsters which they had composed together as they waited for Athelstan to return from his harrying in the north, after the visitation to Saints Cuthbert and Oswald in Chester-le-Street. His own influence at court was improving. If Egil Skallagrimsson could be gradually edged from close proximity to his former scholar, he thought, then life in the new king's court could be tolerable. The pagan Icelander was a challenge, but he was mortal and an inveterate traveller, often disappearing on his ship back to Iceland and Norway where he carried out unknown business. Aethelwold considered that he might be persuaded to stay away permanently. Skallagrimsson had his price, like other men.

The tall Viking, captain of the guard, stood rock-like beside Edmund. His huge hirsute head, stony-faced as a personal guard should be, looked out over the hall. He was not troubled by the human failing of vanity. He did not give the appearance of wishing to go anywhere.

After several hours, the witan's work came to an end. The men stood to stretch and relieve themselves at the latrine, relaxing into loud conversation. At the curtained door leading to the women's quarters, like a flash of a kingfisher, a portion of sky-blue skirt momentarily swirled and disappeared. The ear-ringed ears of Eadgifu extended far beyond her head.

Nonna's Diary, Frome Monastery, October 940

WHAT MAKES A successful king? His quality of blood, but also his worthiness and acceptance by the witan's members, who do not always agree. There are inevitably grumbles, whoever they choose to support. I have found that dissension is to be expected. Insurrection is always a short space away, lurking darkly in spaces beyond the pillars of palace halls or the altars of minster churches, like ours of Frome. Sometimes words are harsher than bloodletting in condemning a man over unresolved disagreement; exile from court and a reputation ruined may be instigated by the merest comment. Banishment is as destructive to a man's soul as death followed by residence in hell. The condemned man cannot hope for reprieve; he must stay away from the justice of the realm or be killed. Execution by gossip is harsh to take; the Christian conscience and the hearts of men and women should be aware of their whispering impact, but often, in my experience, they are not. Even the minds of bishops, revealed by my friends when interpreting for them, are not immune to giving, as well as receiving, spite and jealousy. I am disappointed at the behaviour of my colleagues, but who am I to judge? I take out my little horse and rider brooch, saved from the chest from Glastonbury, a memento of my mother's people, the Dumnonians. I give it a rub with my thumb; it soothes me. Were they a less disagreeable people? Probably not, but it suits me to imagine so.

I travel with the court and it is moving quickly at present from palace to palace, having done with the celebrations and extensive rituals of anointing Edmund at Kingston on Thames. The eighteen-year-old is a worthy successor, popular with most. The dynasty of Alfred of Wessex and of England is secure.

My own family lives in St David's in Dyfed. My Welsh has improved since I met my lovely Gwladys and I am of use at the court on many occasions when the Welsh kings are present. My work, alas, keeps me here in Wessex and Edmund says he cannot do without me. That is gratifying. I visit Wales rarely, but have become used to the journey across Sabrina on a Welsh barque each summer. I practise my Breton accent with the sailors who hail from that land. I am the Celtic advisor for the court of Wessex and while Hywel Dda continues in his role as ambassador of the nation of Wales, it seems likely that I will remain so. The eyes of the Saxon court look eastwards to the continent but they need a view across the Irish Sea. Dublin is where the Viking Anlaf has his base, that restless youth. It is a nest of Viking interlopers. I do not quite understand why the Irish tolerate Anlaf, but he brings gold and is an astute trader; there are many reasons why a foreign enemy is welcome in one's midst. As in Dublin, there are enough potential traitors here as well as there. Wulfstan springs to mind.

I have digressed. Despite the whiff of treason ever present, this has been a peaceful and popular succession. Edmund was made the official heir of Athelstan in 933 when he was eleven years old. The court smiled on as in a short ceremony at Cheddar palace the king bestowed the prince with robes and ornamented weapons, filet and brooch, the very same as had been worn by his revered grandfather, Alfred, when he was a boy. Not all the nobles and bishops were present. Wulfstan of York had declined to attend, citing a heavy cold and sore leg as an excuse, but he was not missed. Bishop Frithestan of Winchester, never happy with the choice of Athelstan of Mercia as king, also showed his contempt by being absent. Rejected as chief aetheling, Edwin, Edmund's half-brother, had stared in dismay. He had been side-lined. He was destined never to appear, eulogised as a triumphant king, on a wall hanging describing the exploits of his dynasty. He would never be heard named as emperor in a poem of deeds. I felt sorry for him, but Edmund was the better choice for king. I saw Edwin one day at the New Minster of Winchester, his father's foundation, sitting at the base of a column. He was crying. I asked him if I could help him. He told me that he felt he was laughed at by the faces carved into the capitals of pillars, the merciless animals and humans sticking their tongues out at him, mocking him. He began his journey to despair then. His mother never recovered from his rejection as heir to the throne. Athelstan regretted his demotion and especially his drowning, but it could not be helped. There were too many brothers.

Rejected. Edwin's mother had warned him that this might happen. Aelfflaed, the old queen, had put all her energy, both brain and body, into trying to secure her remaining son's status as heir presumptive, but it had been wasted work. Along with Frithestan and Wulfstan, bishop and archbishop, she had plotted and bribed. Now she had gone to wait her turn at the gate of heaven. Some thought that she might be allowed through immediately; others, who had suffered by her schemes, prayed maliciously that she might be thwarted. Angelic hosts hold swords and staves as well as platters of ambrosia. Their prayers redoubled. Even in heaven, it seems, there are enemies trying to drag you down. Assistance from this world with candles and bells might make all the difference, might make that sparkling gate of brightness open wide to receive her soul. Frithestan had died, but Wulfstan, working in this world still, would do his best for her. She might squeeze through yet. You must forget those names; I promised myself that I would not make mention of traitors, but I feel compelled. Sometimes it feels as though a hand other than mine writes these words.

Aelfflaed's last years were soured by the arrival of her replacement as Edward's wife, the young Queen Eadgifu of Kent, quickly followed by her astonishingly fertile production of a brood of sons and daughters for the old king. There were therefore many fresh heirs to bolster the dynasty, including two healthy boys, Edmund and Eadred. What a pity there had been discord between Aelfflaed and her husband. Edward had attacked her for pampering her younger boy, Edwin. Aelfweard, the eldest, had been trained to inherit but he died within a few weeks of his father. Unexplained or early deaths were common then and still are. None can hope to survive for ever; demise is just around the corner for us all, but the early deaths of some challengers to the natural order of things, or what Aelfflaed regarded as the natural order, smacked of intent and murder. She was suspicious of everything and everyone. It showed in her speech, her looks. Caution was needed when dealing with her, towards the end. The dark arts which are available to women are as yet unfathomable, despite Aethelwold's attempts to discover and neutralise them.

Another queen has lately joined the royal family. Elgiva, a sweet child, light-blonde-haired like her mother, Wynflaed, she was born in and raised from an early age at the holy Abbey of Shaftesbury. She is learned and musical, a delight to the court. She has not been crowned alongside her husband (the kings of the Alfredian dynasty are loathe to anoint their queens, for good reason), but is modestly content to sign the papers of the king her husband as a royal concubine. She nurses her young son, Eadwig, and will give birth again in the coming year. The child, when denied the teat, crawls among the palace chair and table legs, absorbing thoughts, words and deeds of nobles of the realm, present at the divine discourse of abbots and bishops, imbibing decision-making and arguments. Eadwig is bright but has a vile temper, as his father had when a child. His screams rock the palaces. As with Edmund and Eadred when they were children, the new family of princes will be taught who to hate and who to command by those who know best: Dunstan, Aethelwold, their grandmother Eadgifu and of course their parents, Edmund and his saintly wife, Elgiva of Shaftesbury, though Edmund must be often away, consulting his nobles or setting the north to rights.

Dunstan and Aethelwold find the presence of very young children, their runny noses and raucous shouts and cries, disturbing. They do not like the freedom that a baby, albeit a royal one, is given to rule the atmosphere of serious discussions. His cries interrupt discourse. Children should rule the nursery, not the court, they mutter. Whenever will the child be put to bed? Should he be allowed to disrupt the heavy state matters now under consideration, to have the whole court laugh as Eadwig's little paw is waved over the serious business of signing charters by the indulgent king, his father? One day he will rule, but the light-heartedness and obvious happiness of Edmund and his doting young wife are distracting the business of the court and a man's tolerance for another's child stretches only so far.

Because Edmund and his wife are fond of western Wessex and favour its palaces, the court has settled, dangerously, in Dunstan's view, on staying longer in the younger shires of the west, Wiltshire and Somersetshire. The shires of the east, including Kent, are neglected by the family. Travelling is too tiring for Elgiva, Edmund says. Eadgifu, his mother, who is a Kentish woman, tries to persuade him to go there, but the hunting is not as varied, he says, besides which, he needs to be closer to his supporters and enemies in Wales and Ireland, to be able to react if need be. The European states, visible from the coast of Kent, are at present friends; wealth comes from them, but not war. Kingston-on-Thames is the farthest east Edmund has visited for any lengthy stay since his coronation. He made a brief visit to Colchester shortly after his anointing and promises to make a state visit to London sometime in the future when he is not deeply engaged with dealings with the fractious thanes of Northumbria. Cheddar palace is his first love. He and his wife favour it as their chief abode now that it has been modernised. Eadgifu, with her interest in design, has ensured that the palace has been made sumptuous. The pattern has been set by Eadgifu, who wishes to extend her architect's plans (Dunstan, of course) to the other Wessex palaces, since it seems time is to be spent in them more than elsewhere. Dunstan remains close to the queen-mother, closer, possibly, than before. He has moved on from dooms. Paint alone no longer attracts.

I have to note, though, that there is discord between Edmund and his chief advisor, Dunstan. The king has spent time in the halls and palaces of his realm, observing and listening to tittle-tattle about Dunstan's rigid regard of the state of monastic institutions. Their rules are too lenient and the monks too secular, according to him. I can see his point. The married priests amongst them tempt those naturally more inclined to the stricter St Benedict's rule to abandon the requirements which in St Aldhelm's day, three hundred years ago, were held in greater reverence. Their relatives at court are amazed at Dunstan's growing impudence at insisting, even at sociable feasts, that things must be altered. He insists that hell will be the residence of those who resist God's word. Something else has changed since the days when Athelstan forgave Dunstan for what he saw as errors over the trip to Chester-le-Street in 934; Egil has come to stay.

Egil Skallagrimsson is Edmund's bodyguard, as he was Athelstan's in his last years. Edmund worships him and watches every twitch in his demeanour. If his hairy eyebrows are raised or if he gives a shrug, Edmund will change his course. I have often noticed this during the witan meetings. If Egil wears a certain style of brooch, Edmund has to have a similar one made. If he changes his hairstyle, Edmund copies him. When his beard is trim, so is Edmund's. Egil is a poet as well as a well-travelled scholar and swordsman, accustomed to the wave-steeds of the fjords of Iceland. Iceland. Just the name of the country, summoning visions of dark green seas, snow-gilded land and silver skies pierced by flame, is welcome romance to Edmund's poet ears. And Egil is not just a bodyguard. He is becoming a mind-guard, too. Is Dunstan jealous of him? Yes, and Aethelwold is losing his former student to the Icelander's heart, the man of iron who continually speaks of legend, fire and ice and wastes no time with priests or monks. Aethelwold bristles visibly as he strides into a room. He keeps the heat of the fire from others by his girth. His head (and his body) is twice the size of Dunstan's. From his mouth the sagas spill out, from his eyes the lure of adventure thrills the hearts of the young. His drinking horn is always about him, replenished at all hours, never interrupted by the call to prayer. At those times, when the monks and priests depart the hall, Egil takes to a cushioned bench, usually near the fire and slumbers, a platter of meats nearby.

There have been fresh developments. Edmund, wise for his age and patient with most, has given way to his emotions. He took Dunstan to one side recently at a saint's feast, proffered him a wine-filled horn and asked him to desist from loudly berating his court and his chosen companions. Dunstan, with Aethelwold at his side, would not back down. Egil was behind this. I watched as Dunstan refused the offer of wine, told the king that he thought he had had enough of the devil's drink, that he, Dunstan, had had enough of seeing married priests at court (and their women with their expensive fashions, added Aethelwold, from behind him). Angry looks turned into angry words and actions. Edmund dismissed Dunstan from court, ordered him to leave the realm. He would never countenance his bigotry again.

I saw the way Edmund turned on his heel. Dunstan, likewise, turned sharply away. A back turned towards a man in anger is as a boot pointed at Moslem visitors. Eyes throughout the hall flashed towards the retreating back of the black-robed priest, with Aethelwold scurrying after him. The church was in retreat from the affairs of the land. I could tell that many who witnessed the row approved of the dismissal of Dunstan. There were murmurs of approval.

I watched them go in their different directions. Egil Skallagrimsson, standing with his legs apart, one hand resting on his sword, stroked his plaited beard and smiled.

But Dunstan and Aethelwold returned soon. They had not

gone far. This had happened before. Like the midden rats, they waited until the fires had cooled, safety had returned. They were armed in a different way, an effective way; they had the iconoclastic mindset of a reformative movement. Inspiration and determination are effective tools as well as the sword, as Edmund and his heirs were to discover.

941. In this year the Northumbrians were false to their pledges, and chose Anlaf from Ireland as their king.

942. In this year king Edmund...conquered Mercia...The Boroughs Five he won, Leicester and Lincoln, Nottingham, Derby and Stamford too. Long had the Danes under the Norsemen been subjected by force to heathen bondage, until finally liberated by the valour of Edward's son, King Edmund, protector of warriors.

Anglo-Saxon Chronicle.

Winchester, late September 942

THE WIND BLEW in sudden gusts across the open grassy space between the palace and the two minsters, the old and new, throwing the banners and copes of bishops and an archbishop, priests and secular priests, the latter with their families behind them, into fluttering tangles of contrasting material. Autumn was beginning. Brown-spotted leaves spilled from nearby trees and jackdaws, chack-chacking in surprise and delight, rose from branches in a large group, adding to the blurred image of activity, natural and religious. The bells of both churches joined with them, providing a discordant orchestration of banging and booms as they competed with each other. They were celebrating the notable defeat of the remaining renegade forces of Olaf Cuaran, called by some Anlaf, claiming back control over the five boroughs of middle England. Archbishop Wulfstan of York was again not present, but his bluff had been called. He and Anlaf had escaped from Leicester and fled to York. It had been decreed that never again would either set foot in the south, except in chains. Wulfstan had learned, it was to be hoped, that his treacherous alliance with the pagan Norse would bear no fruit.

Horn calls sounded from inside the palace. The head of a procession, led by the Archbishop of Canterbury, starting at the palace's main entrance and largely protected under its carved oak porch, began to move slowly away towards the New Minster of Edward, that revered but not sainted son of Wessex. King Edmund, his queen and the young princes Eadwig and Edgar, tucked upright in a wheeled crib, and nobles of the land shuffled inside the palace, waiting in their heavy finery behind the priests to begin the parade. All the gold that could be mustered from the rivers and caverns of Wales was on display on the shoulders, heads, belts and swords of the dignified and not so dignified, young and old. Chests had been opened and raided for precious gems and jewellery to disport on every potential angle of human anatomy. Shining metal brooches and arm rings were on show, denoting rank, badges marking battles fought, and royal gifts. They studded every man, high and middle-ranking. Candles in the palace hall lit up the still spectacular array of wealth of those lower in status at the back of the procession. Contrasting with them, nuns and vowesses, landless and landed alike, like currants in a cake, spotted dour black in the throng, standing with their noble relatives. Behind the palace, in the cobbled yard by the stables, the servants and slaves of the royal household waited their turn to take part in the procession. All were to be included, willing or not. The fine for non-attendance was graded, but severe. Ordinary townsfolk, required to attend as witnesses to the procession, waited silently beyond a rope barrier, their hoods over their heads in anticipation of heavy rain.

The sky suddenly lightened; the last rays of late summer threw gold on the west door and towers of the minsters. Hoods came down; the scurrying wind had blown the rain away. St Swithun had been kind this year; war had taken place in the dry heat of summer; there had been little to prevent the swift access to Northumbria of Edmund's forces. Victory had been solidified; this southern part of England had been rescued yet again. There was no doubt in anyone's mind that this conquest would be the last necessary for national stability. The trumpets and clanging bells of both churches declared so. It was a celebration by sound. It was well known that evil spirits and devils hate loud noise. All the human senses on this special day would be attended to; sight, smell and touch would come later in the rituals of New Minster, followed by taste at the feast to follow. Dunstan organised a good celebration.

The procession moved forward in the light of the blessed sun. Near the front of the group of priests and in a place of definite ascension in the Benedictine order, Dunstan and Aethelwold walked side by side, carrying the cross and banner of St Cuthbert. They were preceded by a chaplain carrying a large open missal displaying colourful pages. Behind them the snake of supplicants took pace and proceeded with regular, swaying steps towards the entrance to Edward's church. Meeting their group at the porch door, studded with stone saints and painted bright colours, was a large group of nuns who had formed their own separate procession from the Nunnaminster which stood behind the churches. The two men both looked up as they entered the church door, passing colourful stone saints carved in various stances of devotion. There was a pause in the procession as it narrowed to squeeze through and banners were lowered.

'Colour, which glorifies God and the saints. Well done, Dunstan.'

'Do you think St Swithun will approve? His is a story of grey wetness. But, Aethelwold, you can see, and I hope others can, how much more startling stone figures are when they are adorned, making changes in the mind of the viewer. On a different note, Wulfstan is missing again.'

'Shush, our sisters are coming around the corner. We will discuss the impact of your art later. And Wulfstan.'

'Skallagrimsson is not here, either.' Dunstan lifted his cross. The procession continued into the nave.

The two forward lines of black, nuns and priests, men and women, each with banners and crosses, having adjusted their burdens, melded and flowed into the church, the fluttering of their clothes and flags ceasing as they passed the holy portal. The higher dignitaries followed. Under awnings at the side of the churches, the lower orders took shelter with their own family priests and choirs. In the space between the palace and the churches, the remaining population of the town sat to hear a sermon and a story.

There would be honeyed buns for all, later on. Honey and fluttering flags for Wessex.

Interview with a Slave, Frome, August 943

I WAS ON the prowl. Information needed to be contained. How much was known about the secret of the unholy head? I began with the forge at Frome. If anybody had heard any gossip, it would be Geraint. He would tell me, a fellow lay brother and part Welshman, if there was anything to tell.

'Good morning Geraint. I have come to see what you are working on.'

'Morning, Brother Nonna. It's the same piece you saw me working on last time you were here. The head reliquary. It needs restoration. The queen-mother asked for repairs, but it is a delicate task.'

'Has Brother Dunstan seen this recently? It is beginning to look like a fine receptacle, the best head reliquary I have yet seen.'

'No, he's too busy to come along these days, but I send him information on the work via the brothers and ask his advice.'

'That's very advisable and the right thing to do, Geraint. He is the master of the king's arts. What have you done with the contents?'

'They are in a holding box in the haligdom.'

'Good, good. What about the pilgrim tokens? How are they coming along?'

'Over there in the box. I did a hundred yesterday. I did a few sample coins, too, if the king is interested. The tokens don't take much skill. A boy could do them but there isn't one to help me at present. The bellows are difficult to handle alone but a twelve-year-old could learn how to make these in an afternoon if he wasn't tied to church services.'

Geraint is not keen on the attendance requirements of offices.

He is known for spectacular grumbling; the other Welsh slaves are almost as bad. They have a reason for their resentment of Saxons; they are the dispossessed. After two hundred years they have still not become accustomed to their new masters.

'Hmm. If I can find someone for you, I will, but it will be difficult to get dispensation.'

I was standing in the open barn door of the metal-working area of the monastery workshop at Frome, a range of wooden buildings on the side of the hill above the church of St John and the spring line. Across from the workshops was the stone tythe barn, almost full of the season's hay and straw. A wagon was making its way along Behind Town, hauled by an ox. Behind me were cultivated vegetable and herb gardens. The double doors, which looked as though they were in need of rehanging, faced the sun. In sight, sound and smell this was a place of memory, of focussed activity of ages past. It was as attractive as a favourite chapel to those of us who had visited it over many years. I had first encountered it and Geraint's father when I was a small child. The forge smouldered in the back of the barn. Half-made and broken metal implements and detritus lay randomly on the walls and floor, a hazard to the unwary, but in its messy creativity, deeply interesting.

I loved this place, as did Dunstan. I found the character of Geraint appealing. He was a born blacksmith and his accent, couched in the thick, bearded throat, came through in his rhythmic songs which he often sang as he worked. For me, as a half-Welsh Saxon, Geraint held in his stocky person the remains of the dreams of a forgotten nation, Dumnonia. He was a slave, but treated as a servant. His own son would learn his trade when he was old enough. He had little apparent method, but he got things done. He was an essential part of the organic life of this aromatic place. Without him and his sweaty animal presence this workshop would have seemed like an unkempt mausoleum. To me, the random, unfinished articles of his production were beautiful. The existence, the life affirming force, of this one man in his work environment thrilled me. I loitered often at the forge when in Frome. Geraint's brother was a blacksmith at Glastonbury. It was in their blood. Others also found their way to the forges, fascinated, which is why I needed to ask Geraint whether he had heard anything of interest. He was not a man of few words.

It interested me to observe someone concentrating on his work, making something useful or beautiful, where he was transformed by his intellect, physical power and talent. In his work-clothes and doing the work with which he identifies, a man comes alive. You see the alteration from animal to something else in monks when they sing, if their voices are good. Expert woodworkers have attentive concentration, body, mind and spirit fully engaged, doing the best that they can. Potters display love as they work. Scribes who have years of skill at illustration, butchers preparing meat, spinners and weavers, even the women of the court who sew the images of our history onto their hangings, have the look of total absorption at using the talents that they were born with, if they are lucky enough to find a patron or a household to assist them to find and to develop their skills.

Many workers, the doers of our world, follow their forefathers in their trade and have little choice in the matter, but I often find that the abilities of ancestors are passed down by nature. Those who have an aptitude for musical instruments have the skills of centuries born into them. It is one of the puzzles of our age and likely to remain so, that talents can be so varied. God has shared them out. Can a person have no talent for anything? I do not think so. It is best to find what this is before the onset of travail or illness becomes a burden in life; I thank the stars and the saints that I was helped to discover my talent, for words written and spoken, at the monastery of Glastonbury all those years ago.

Was there a boy who I could recommend to work for Geraint? There was a twelve-year-old lad in the choir at Frome who had just been given a reprieve from punishment for theft. He was one of the queen's saved souls. It had been noticed that he had a fine singing voice. It might be a way of offsetting Dunstan's plans for him. I fear that a life confined to the choirs of monastic houses, rich and comfortable though that might be, is a wasted life. It needs physical activity, the outdoor sights and sounds of the seasons, play with one's peers, the opportunity to fall in love, to be a full physical human being. What would Dunstan and Aethelwold make of him? His life would be shortened. He would never experience human love, would become gross at an early age. The fine singing voice would be a grand thing, soaring to the heights of the roofs of the splendid new stone cathedrals which are appearing in many places, but his being would be changed, he would be a castrato, a gelded human, unable to discover any of the natural joys of human entitlement, if he survived the operation.

If he survived the operation. Aelward, the boy, dead before he had begun in life. I could not bear it. Then again, could he become like an unsexed angel that we see in robes above the roods accompanying Christ to heaven? No, even a heavenly life as promised was not what I would have wished for him, despite the religious teaching which we all received. Sometimes I think that the requirements of our faith are cruel in the extreme, but I dare not say so.

There was another, years before, whose life was changed because of his singing voice. After a few years at Canterbury his castration brought about early demise, despite the attentions of the infirmary at Frome, where he was brought to be treated and to die.

Geraint bent over the hot metal at his forge. He was one with the heat, the tools, the craft. He knew and cared nothing of the contents that this piece of metal would receive. His back and swinging arm, moving to the bellows and returning to his anvil, were a concentration of being.

I examined the head reliquary closely as Geraint took time out to munch on bread and cheese which I had brought him. It shone; the rounded facial contours reflected the forge fire. It delighted the eye.

Did Geraint know of the complicated arrangements of its contents? No, the master craftsman, the slave, had eyes only for his product. He should have his apprentice. The secret of Radegund's head was safe, for now, and a young soul would be saved from surgery.

*943. In this year Anlaf stormed Tamworth and there was great
slaughter on both sides...*

*In this year king Edmund besieged king Anlaf and Archbishop
Wulfstan in Leicester, and might have captured them had they not
escaped from the city by night. Afterwards Anlaf obtained king
Edmund's friendship...(and) he stood sponsor (at baptism) for king
Ragnald.*

Anglo-Saxon Chronicle

York, Autumn 943

TWO MEN SAT by a large table, drinking. 'Well, my friend, it
was close. Had Skallagrimsson not sent help, I doubt that we
would be sitting in this luxury.' Anlaf, his feet on a table, pushed a
cushion into position behind his head.

Wulfstan and Anlaf were in recovery from near capture by
Edmund. Safely back in Wulfstan's rooms in Ripon, they could
review their failed attempt to retake Northumbria. Edmund was
proving to be a more adroit soldier than they had estimated.

'What comes next, do you think, Archbishop?' The Norse
king was in need of a haircut and fresh clothes. He had ripped
and muddied his long-worn tunic and trews in the flight north
from Leicester.

'A bath, I think, for both of us. My leg wants warmth.'
Wulfstan took a draught of ale. There was pleasure in the escape,
a feeling of success, of a sort. He and Anlaf had bribed their
way out of Leicester's seige by Edmund and ridden hard to
gain Northumbrian safety. There had been no injuries, except
to their pride. The time in Leicester had been hard to take
and uncomfortable. Traitors do not receive cushioned pallets.

Wulfstan had vowed never to be caught again. 'By the way, they were Mercian horses, not Skallagrimsson's. We have friends, still, in the midlands, who do not love Wessex.'

'You are an old man, Wulfstan, and unused to wearing a beard, but the aches will pass; your leg will heal. You will soon be itching to return south again. Who cares who hates Wessex, as long as they do not stand in our way.'

'You may be right, Anaf. We should not give up the fight for Northumbria. But my leg has a mind of its own. I may be aged, but one leg shorter than another has always been my affliction, since early youth. It is not an old man's curse. You need not fear this kind of disability.' Wulfstan watched the colour returning to Anlaf's cheeks. The hard riding had made them both resemble ghosts. Their horses would not recover. 'You are young. There will be other opportunities for you to use your sword. The army will need time to recover, longer than my leg. Tamworth was not a pretty affair. We must use our brains, now, to recover our position. I have the relics of Wilfrid at Ripon which we can dangle in front of Edmund's inevitable embassy. I know he wants them, to accompany Oswald's bones which he already holds in the south. Meet me later for a meal. I think I have the beginnings of a scheme by which Edmund may be persuaded of our good intentions. You and Ragnald, though, would have to feign interest in becoming Christian. Do you think you could do that?'

'Ask me in the morning, when I have eaten and seen my women. Ask me anything, then. You Christians and your relics; you have a very strange way with your dead saints. But you may be right, and I am a willing actor. We shall have a stage, Ragnald and I, covered in white sheets and banners, a procession, if you like, around York's minster. I think Edmund would like that. Yes, I think I could like it, too. Then when he has returned to the south, we could be Vikings again, couldn't we?'

'I would prefer it if you and Ragnald would remain Christian, if vows have been made, but I am a practical man. Northumbria would be better ruled by Ragnald than by Wessex. Have you decided to go back to Dublin?'

'I think that would be wise. Ragnald will rule here. My affairs in Dublin need attendance.'

Wulfstan rubbed his leg. He would do what he could. Northumbria came first, in his heirarchy of interests. Mercia and Wessex were doomed. The Norse would win next time. England would become part of the northern empire of Scandinavia. York and Dublin, with their Norse rulers, would prevail. Pagans would, in time, become peace-loving, committed Christians. It was a risk worth taking. He would remain Archbishop of York, whatever happened. Ripon and Wilfrid; the two would never be parted, not from the land, not from him. The Northumbrians had shown that they would tolerate no other.

Cheddar, March 944

'DUNSTAN. DUNSTAN,' EDMUND hissed. 'Why didn't you tell me before about what Athelstan decided to do with the Chester-le-Street head?' Beside himself, he grasped the priest's robe and held on. He held a letter in his other hand. It bore the seal of the monks of Chester-le-Street.

Edmund, fresh back home from his battles for the five boroughs, had urgently summoned his chief clerk, the artist and architect, the friend of Aethelwold, chief designer of the court's outward appearance, metalsmith and religious fanatic. He saw him as an ideas man and would-be propagandist, holder of secrets, bender of minds, as his mother's confidante. Aethelwold was more fun, Edmund thought; he did not waver in his views. With him, black was black, white was white. But Dunstan dissembled. You never knew whether he was entirely honest. Edmund was learning, as he had to do, that there were many forms of truth and it often had to be squeezed out of courtiers in small drips.

Diplomacy is wearying to the soul, but a necessity to a king, he remembered Athelstan saying. Compromise is a position of strength, not weakness. Try to find that strong place where with others you may act.

Edmund ignored the inner voice of his brother. He whipped Dunstan round as he passed the door to the inner private chambers. He could not shout; the walls were wooden and not thick.

Dunstan looked down at the hand placed firmly on his arm, bunching his robe. He had known Edmund since he was born. He looked into the young man's eyes. Edmund removed his hand.

'Pardon me, Dunstan, it has been a difficult witan meeting and I thank you for your help in business matters. I did not sleep well; the children yelled and Elgiva was sick. But what I really need to know, and in the fastest possible time, is what exactly occurred on Athelstan's second visit to Cuthbert's coffin. This letter comes from the monks at Chester-le Street. It demands money.'

Dunstan relaxed. He shifted his long dark tunic to its original neat folds and leaned back against the panelled wall, giving way to Edmund's interrogation. He looked up and down the corridor. All the doors were closed; there was no sign or sound of anyone else. The women were still in their quarters, sewing, or gone to oversee the next main meal in the kitchens. He would tell Edmund what he must. Edmund was older now, experienced. He might understand better what Athelstan had needed to do, for his younger brother's sake. Marriage had perhaps calmed him down. Sleep-deprived, he might be more pliable. He would risk telling the tale of the head. He shook his arm and read the letter.

'Surely you remember, Lord, what occurred in Chester-le-Street? The opening of the coffin of Cuthbert, the gifts that were laid at his feet and head?'

Edmund nodded. 'Of course.'

'You were young then, Lord, and not fully experienced in the whiles of the northern monasteries, or rather, of their monks. You know that all relics are jealously guarded and that thieves have often taken advantage of laxity in security to steal what they think will be as precious to their haligdoms as gold or jewels, in some cases much more valuable. But you were not party to the plans which Athelstan made to recover the head of Oswald on our second visit to the coffin, close as it was to the Scots kingdom, and so you do not know of the danger to his soul which the king was prepared to undertake to rescue that divine totemic relic for the protection of England, of your realm.'

'Are you saying that the head which we brought south with us was Oswald's and not a Scottish noble's, as I was told?'

'Yes, it was placed in St Oswald's Priory in Gloucester along with the rest, or most, of his corpse.'

'But the monks of Chester-le-Street would surely notice that their head, which I saw in the coffin with Cuthbert on that amazing day, had gone missing?'

'The head was substituted with another.'

'Whose?'

'You do not need to know.'

'Whose? I am king, tell me, Dunstan.' Edmund's hand lifted again but withdrew from contact with the priest and came to rest on his ceremonial dagger.

There are some things a king should not be told, but in this case, it was Athelstan's soul which was in potential torment, not Edmund's. He had protected Edmund from this knowledge and therefore any accusation of collusion. Dunstan deemed it necessary to reveal most of how the matter had been achieved. He need not tell all, but the Irish connection with Northumbria and the intentions of Dublin's troublesome leader, Anlaf the Viking had recently resurfaced. Rumours had stimulated the entire royal kin into concern. Gossip and wildfire have much in common.

'We gave the monks a valuable head in recompense. The king was determined that they should not suffer by the loss, whether they knew of it or not. A slave's head was not good enough, he said. We took...' Dunstan paused.

'Yes?'

'We took the head of Radegund. You know how important a saint she is to so many.' Dunstan saw the look of disbelief on the face of the young king.

Dunstan spoke rapidly. 'But there is the possibility that it was not actually the head of the saint. I have heard of other heads which are claimed to be hers. Even Oswald, though we cannot believe that such thievery is rampant amongst the holy men of our times, is said to have many heads, scattered throughout Europe. Though, of course, ours, in Gloucester, is the rightful one.'

Edmund put a hand onto the panel behind Dunstan. He had to lean on something. Dunstan shifted a little away.

'So, whose head is now in the Radegund reliquary which is in our royal haligdom, or is it empty?'

'Athelstan thought it best to place another head, a long dead monk's, for the time being until a more evocative soul could be found. There will be one, one day. Perhaps a saint of your own family could grace the famous relic.'

Dunstan caught the look of growing business acumen in Edmund's eyes. This affair of the head was complicated, but it had been necessary. The outward appearance of a relic was in many cases as or more important than its contents. It was the reliquary's nose and lips which were rubbed and revered by the faithful, not the flesh and bones concealed within. To touch or kiss a celebrated reliquary could save many years from the time spent in purgatory, waiting at the gate. To pay to caress a holy relic was accepted as one of the inevitable taxes of life in this well-ordered country. Radegund's reliquary, restored by Geraint, was brought out only on rare occasions, but when it was, it brought thousands of pilgrims and their purses to touch and drool over. She was a major aid to the treasury of king and church and had been for many years. Her head, now accompanying Cuthbert in his coffin, was a great sacrifice. To defend the new nation of England, he had been prepared to part with her. The monks of Chester-le-Street had allowed or intended the substitution to happen, and had threatened to demand compensation from Athelstan. It was an intricate matter of diplomacy. A great deal of revenue had been involved. Dunstan explained all this in a low whisper.

'Who knows of the substitution?'

'Nonna was part of the discussion to plan the exchange and of course Leofa was involved.'

'Aethelwold?'

'No.'

'Are you sure? You two are often together. What do you plot?'

'There are no plots, my lord. Only plans for the success of your throne.' Dunstan was annoyed. He paused, feeling heat leave his cheeks. 'Nonna is a steady chap and wise. And not malicious.'

Edmund frowned. 'What about Mother? Does she know that St Radegund, or whoever it was, is no longer inside the reliquary? You know how she relies on the saint.'

'No, the queen-mother does not know.'

Edmund's eyes grew wide. 'If what was done to possess Oswald's head ever gets out, I foresee enormous problems for all of us. My court would be the laughing stock of Europe.' He paused. 'And why did Leofa go to Ireland, to our enemy? I remember his usefulness at the witans and his sadness on our journey north in 934. He was there in the crypt at Chester-le-Street. After we came back, he disappeared. What do you know of him? Mother has dreams about him, but you know Mother.'

'Something occurred between Athelstan and Leofa which the rest of us were not aware of. Leofa had a contact in Shaftesbury Abbey where he often visited and I believe he and that contact moved for their safety abroad.'

'It is like pulling teeth, getting anything from you. So, he was not a thief?'

'No, but it seems he was intended to stay away. And someone had to take the blame for the Oswald head, if it ever came to light. Nonna, I believe, has had communication with Leofa.'

'Communication? Where is Leofa? Fetch me Nonna, NOW.'

Nonna came running, seeing the urgency in Dunstan's eyes coupled with an uncharacteristic tug on his sleeve. He left his meal with Gwladys, pulled on his outer court robe and followed Dunstan to the relic room, where they would be surrounded by mute empathetic listeners, the saints. The surroundings were conducive to truth. Edmund was waiting, with a bible in his hands. Oath breaking was a serious matter. Lying in the presence of the holy Word was unthinkable; the tortures of hell awaited. Nonna guessed what this was about; he had heard the rumours. The two clerks swore to speak with verity and brevity. Clarity, which had been their chief mistress in their training as clerks, made them keep to the point.

'Nonna, I understand that I am the last to hear of this. What do you know about Leofa's exile? Who was his so-called companion from Shaftesbury Abbey? Mother has tried to tell me about something to do with him but until now I have been too busy to listen. She has too many conspiracies in her head...' Edmund checked himself. 'I have as long to discuss this matter as you need. Do not spare me the details. I need to know everything.' He sat on a low chest full of the smaller reliquaries which had yet to be carted to Exeter as a bequest to the cathedral. Dunstan made to wave him off, but pulled back his hand. Edmund frowned and stared at Nonna.

So, the time had come. The secret had now to be revealed. A half-told tale, bent to obscure truth, would not do.

'I'm waiting.'

'Leofa and his companion, a woman, travelled to Dublin. You remember, Lord, that he was half Viking by birth.' Nonna paused, aware of the hot blood in Edmund which could spill out in violence.

'Yes of course. Did he go reluctantly, or in anger? Was he going to reveal the Oswald head affair? Yes, Dunstan has been telling me about that.' Dunstan and Nonna looked at each other. 'Was he threatening Athelstan, along with the Chester-le-Street monks?' Edmund was not wasting time. He controlled his need to hit something. His right hand was twitching. His understanding grew with his rising temper. His cheeks flamed.

Nonna opened his mouth. How much of the affair of Leofa, which had occurred at the same time as the campaign in 934, did Dunstan or Edmund know? Over the years, the secrets had extended, shrunk, grown again.

'He had to leave the court, Lord. He was not willing. He had to take on the burden of being labelled as a criminal to save the king's face. He had told me on the journey to York to defeat the king of Scotland that his Shaftesbury companion was pregnant with his child. He was concerned. She gave birth in early 935. Before Athelstan died, he took her and the child- children, there were twins- to Dublin.'

'Stop there, Nonna. Why did he feel he had leave Wessex? It is not unheard of to have impregnated a nun. There was no need, surely, to take the business of the court and the nation to such as Anlaf, to the peril of us all? And who at Shaftesbury was aware of this?' Edmund was learning how to pierce the veil behind which the clerks operated.

Nonna shifted his feet. 'It was necessary for Athelstan and for Leofa. He was a new father. It changed things for him. The former abbess knew of the affair as did the mother of the girl, grandmother of the twins, who also lived at Shaftesbury Abbey.'

'And who was the girl? Not a nun?' Edmund was focused on the interrogation. He had begun to suspect and to dread the answer to his questions. His future was in doubt. His children's future was at stake. The dynasty depended on this information. Dunstan remained quiet, listening, his hands clenched. Edmund had realised that Nonna knew more of the matter than Dunstan. His body turned wholly towards him, with fists clenched. Dunstan withdrew into a dark corner of the room. The Mercian threats filled the air, condensed in his brain.

Nonna paused. 'Leonada was the young mother who went with Leofa to Dublin. She was the daughter of Aelfwynn.'

'Aelfwynn of Mercia? Aethelfaed's daughter?' Edmund had imbibed his official family history, but not all of it. 'Is Aelfwynn still alive?'

'No, Lord, she died soon after the king and is buried at

Shaftesbury. She has no headstone. No-one knew her lineage at the abbey other than the abbess, who has also died recently.'

'And why does it seem to be important to understand whose daughter Leonada was?'

Nonna's face showed that he feared the gates of hell were about to open.

'Who, Nonna, was the father of Leonada?'

The clerk had to admit the truth, though he feared an explosion of some kind.

'Athelstan.'

There, it was said. The unrecognised lover of Athelstan, Aelfwynn of Mercia, granddaughter of Alfred, had lived in Shaftesbury Abbey, safely concealed from jealous eyes, put there by her uncle Edward for her protection and as a pleasant prison, to see out her days. Her daughter, similarly restricted, was the abbey-educated Leonada. She was intended to take her place amongst the elite but silent and unseen women of Shaftesbury, singing praises to God and the saints. Here she would live in obscurity, gazing quietly on the valley below and across to the ancient hill-top fortresses beyond. But Leonada had been seen by Leofa, while accompanying Athelstan, and he had found her to be beautiful. She had responded to his love and had produced twin heirs to Mercia, a son and a daughter. Both were now growing up in the hands of the Norse in Dublin, Anlaf's Norse. Edmund leaned against a pillar as he considered the implications.

A Mercian heir, or even two, were in that rat-infested black pool of Dublin. The greatest threat, should the Viking Anlaf choose to use it, was to stability between the Wessex and Mercian contingents, reopening wounds only recently healed with Athelstan's death. The children were a potential rallying point for the rankled northern British states and Scotland who were allying themselves with Anlaf and his Vikings or whoever they chose to try to thwart the unity of England. The country could not afford to be magnanimous to puppet kings or queens. The dynasty of

Wessex was forever under threat. Potential usurpers might always lurk, even if they were unwillingly manipulated. Leonada should never have been discovered in her convent. Leofa should never return to these shores. But he had Viking blood, recognisable red hair. Could he be persuaded or forced by Anlaf to return, with a red-headed son, to claim the crown of England? There were several minutes of silence as Edmund took in the ramifications of all that he had learned.

The young king spoke quietly, but forcefully. He unclenched his fists. The moment for violence had passed. 'Dunstan, there needs to be some kind of edict which restricts the return of Leofa to England under all circumstances. How can we keep him, Anlaf and this boy at bay?'

'We can issue a declaration of permanent exile, Lord.'

'On what charge?' Nonna felt compelled to defend Leofa. He might choose never to return, but this sentence would be one of death if he did.

Edmund was recovering, becoming clear-headed. 'He was exiled on the charge of theft. If matters come out, we will hold him responsible for the episode with the Chester-le-Street fiasco. Dunstan, this letter from Chester-le-Street is a final demand. Have the monks been requesting money from the treasury, and why have I not heard of this before? What has happened?'

Dunstan stepped into the light, having perceived the change in the king's mood. 'We have been paying the Cuthbert monks of Chester-le Street a sum of 10 mancuses of gold each year.'

'What! This has to stop, at once. Leofa must bear the blame and the payment.'

'We cannot stop the payment, or they will reveal the whereabouts of the head at Gloucester and the fact that it was planned to take it. They may even reveal the true identity of the substituted head. Yes, Nonna, Dunstan has told me.'

The circumstances of Radegund's head would have an impact not merely in England but on the continent. Nonna glanced at

Dunstan. He looked desperate. The church's coffers would be affected; perhaps the entire Christian reform mission in England would be thrown into disarray. But you cannot fool people forever.

Edmund was seeing things in the round. It was a mess. No wonder, he thought, artists carve and paint creatures biting each other or even themselves, going around and around in endless convolutions. They may be beautiful, but they emulate the complications of life, the necessity for attack, for defence, the traitor, the kin. Life, death, the interconnectedness. They displayed the attractions of danger, in painted relief on stone, on arm rings of the boys and men, presented by warriors at the end of a sword. They wore their snake rings on their arms, their battle bracelets on their wrists: the badges of honour, of being a man. Women? They had the imagery of sweeter things about their persons; of horses, of flowers. Everybody knew his place. Like the board game recently brought to these shores which involved serpents, rising and falling through the morass of ambitions, the church used steps, ever incremental, to climb to power. Let kings beware the Pope and his emissaries. Let any ruler beware of Dunstan.

Dunstan shook himself, recovering. He had returned to being implacable. In that moment, he had realised his mission.

The clerks waited for Edmund to begin again. He leaned back on the chest. Dunstan winced. 'Dunstan, what can be done about the payment to the monks and to recover Athelstan's reputation? We will deal with the Leofa issue as a separate problem, for now.'

Dunstan had no satisfactory answer. It was like answering a child's request, how far is it before we get there? Edmund was a child, despite his muscular appearance. There was no response which would satisfy the young man's need. If Dunstan succeeded in this, he would display his mastery of diplomacy. The king needed reassurance. The answer was negative. It would not be enough.

'I'm sorry, Lord, there is no way at present that I can see that will resolve the problem of the head, but we have enough in the treasury to cover the continuing payments.'

'Payments? The Cuthbert monks are blackmailing us. That is what Vikings do, not Englishmen, even if they are Northumbrians. Or perhaps we live in a changed world? It is protection at a cost. We are in the thrall of the north in a different way from war and it is unpleasant. So, peace is held together by the fragile force of payment? I would rather go into battle again, kick the monks out of their nest in Chester-le-Street, bring Cuthbert himself south and have done with it.'

Edmund had something of his father Edward in him, the man of action. Dunstan would have to try to bring him back to sense.

Dunstan's vision of himself temporarily faltered. He started to hop from one foot to the other. He wrung his hands. He also started to foam a little in the corner of his mouth. Nonna retreated into the back of the room which Dunstan had formerly occupied. The duel was between these two, now, state versus church, young man against seasoned statesman.

'Lord, that is an extreme response to the problem. I cannot endorse such a move.'

Edmund stood. He towered over Dunstan. The dam burst. 'And I cannot tolerate you! You are the arch-mover behind this, you should have realised the affect upon my family. Perhaps you did. Perhaps you intended to weaken the power of the throne, my throne. We could be called thieves, shorn of our reputation. I will have you flogged, or removed from court unless you get yourself out of my sight!'

It was Edmund's turn to foam. His dark temper had resurfaced. Only the relics would hear these words, only they would judge the rightful owner of power in the land.

'Go, now!' Edmund swung an arm out, diverting it from his wish to hit Dunstan by indicating the door.

Dunstan was not a coward but he could discern when a retreat was necessary. He had had to flee before, from men, boys and devils. There are always enemies, some also cloaked in black like himself. He backed towards the door. It opened and shut with a creak and bang. Sandalled feet flapped quickly away. Edmund turned again to Nonna.

'I have thought many times that he was too clever for his own good. Dunstan is too opinionated. He is at odds with the married clergy and their interests in monastic landholdings, their concern with their place in the next world. He cannot leave well alone. Tithes and purgatory are all he thinks about.' Edmund was calming down. He carried on in a similar vein as Dunstan's footsteps faded.

Nonna remained silent.

Dunstan, hastening along corridors, knew that this was another occasion when he had to hide his face from court. Athelstan had also found him unlikeable, at times, calling him bigoted. He would return, when the practical lessons of government had been learned. He would bide his time. He went, for now, swinging his long cloak around his person as though to make himself invisible. The unpleasantly religious young man was turning into a determined older one.

Edmund sat back on the chest. 'I want new edicts, Nonna and I want you to draw them up for signing at the next witan. I want banishment for Dunstan. I want permanent exile for Leofa and his family. I want to build a wall around these shores which excludes them both, keeps away their followers, their brats, anyone who has sympathy with them. Do you understand me?'

'I do, Lord, but the witan will require reasons for the edicts. Dunstan and Leofa were close to Athelstan, chosen by him to be his personal assistants. The court knows that they may be privy to the heart of your dynasty and suspect that you may wish to close their mouths. I assume that you wish no harm to them other than banishment?'

Nonna could not wish that either of his two companions would be legally killed by any who came across them or hunted them down. Would there be a reward for their killing as outlaws, as some had on their heads?

'I shall consider, later, Dunstan's term of exile.'

Edmund was already beginning to regret his temper after hearing the studded door swing closed, a sound still reverberating in the gloom of the haligdom.

'Leofa and his family must be forced to stay away. The Mercians must never learn of his children. In case this business of the head ever comes into the public domain, I want him to bear the burden of accusation for the theft. He shall be branded a thief and given the sentence of permanent exile on pain of death. If anyone assists him in returning to this realm, he will also be a dead man.'

Death and the sentence of death. Kings must be prepared to contemplate their own and others' demise, by whatever means, to counter threats to their person, to their nation and the ideas which drive them. There was nothing Nonna could say for the present which might soothe the energetic, complicated, youthful human wearing the filet of kingship. Edmund would have to adjust to his disillusion.

Edmund took out from his tunic Athelstan's relic of the true cross. He held it in front of his face as if to examine the flaws in it, like his own. He kissed it. He replaced it, on the gold chain, near his heart.

'My Lord.' Nonna bowed and exited the haligdom, leaving Edmund amongst the bones, beginning to rue the heavy burden of kingship. Would he draw as much comfort from them as Athelstan had? Could he, knowing the full burden of the secrets?

I am Dunstan

I SOMETIMES WISH I were not. At such times as these I am forced to examine my motivations, my ambitions. Here, alone in the small library at Cheddar, the night darkens, as does my life. There, reflected in the window pane, are the features of a disturbed man, with fresh lines across the brow. There are few items to pack, just clothing and small books. A mule will be required to carry me with my limited possessions. Edmund is displeased. Has he ever been so angry? His childlike nature consumes him; there is no dealing with his temper. Am I at fault, as he says?

I do not always like what I see; that, I have in common with other men. There are fleeting moods, vanity, preoccupation, desperation. There is the artist, the former lover, the priest. Is it the image of certainty, which is visible in the countenance of Aethelwold? Increasingly so, perhaps. The hard-won facial lines of a potential bishop, perhaps archbishop and, who knows, saint, are etched there in my Wessex face. If others drew me, represented by a creature in the decorative border of a missal, I would be a bird with a sharp beak and great wings. I have flown high and may fly higher, when my falls are reversed. It is my talent and my curse that visions come to me to be able to see far ahead. The world is wrong-headed, surely, not I.

Diplomacy is an art, learned over many years. The reflected image is the face of an expert listener. Sieving information for kings, I sift and sort words. The business of secular exchange of information is difficult, not for the weak-minded. There is too much careless gossip by courtiers. Beyond the walls of monasteries and in the palace grounds males and females mingle too much. Pillow-talk leads to disaster. Affairs of the court are whispered to unlicensed ears, returned with opinions which are not sanctioned by law. Aethelwold smells conspiracy, which he claims is fuelled by the gossip of women. He will do what he can, he says, to regulate male and female discussion. Women have a bad effect on their male relatives; gaudy clothes are bad enough, signalling superficiality; they encourage their spouses to achieve a 'look' which comes of intercourse with foreigners. But women are not the issue here. Edmund is the problem. He will not let me deal with business as before. Style has become his religion. Aethelwold is right; if you examine Edmund closely, you see at every point on his body there is colour, there is vanity. He reeks of narcissism. Look at the plaited hair, the finger decorations, the arm rings made of gold, the studded shoulder brooch, the heavy belt, the inevitable dagger, the intricately folded cloak, the bejewelled purse and embroidered sleeves. Muscular calves are displayed by carefully cross-strapped hose and tooled leather sandals. We must dress the church, not ourselves. Edmund must change. He will come round.

Secular priests are not immune to this vanity, though they like to think so. They and noble women in nunneries consider that they are guests at elaborate hostelries, with sitting rooms, bedrooms and bathing areas personal to themselves. Their clothes, too, when not attending services or offices, I fear, are loud and expensive, merely covered over with black outerwear when in church. They are like the long-feathered birds of hot foreign lands, squawking and incompetent. They slip off their church apparel as soon as they are back in their private sanctuaries, to be ready for more pillow-talk. Women are one thing. The married men who call themselves priests coat themselves in hypocrisy and lies. Laxity in everything is rife. Let this place, this kingdom, rot. What do I care? I will turn my back on stupidity, intransigence.

Vanity, ignorance. There are schools by the dozen throughout the land which is becoming England. There are monastic institutions in every major township which will take and teach noble illiterates, yet still they will not write, they will not read. It is not manly, they say, yet they must progress. Their counterparts on the continent have become scholars; they will be embarrassed by erudite foreign visitors at court. Bumpkins of Wessex, they will be called. But they prefer arguing, comparing arm rings, drinking ale, making babies.

Popularity was never my aim. That is for princes. The Latin scripture at mass, which they hate, though they must understand it to appreciate the faith, is a stumbling block. Many complain of its tediousness. Have I pushed too hard? But I should not doubt, Aethelwold says. We are engaged in making a nation which will last a thousand years. He is certain of it. He sometimes forgets the coming of the antichrist. I never do.

Go, says Edmund.

Am I ruthless? What does the window-glass show?

There I am, a competent male in early middle-age, able to dissemble as well as the next man, prepared to do so for the future's sake. I look more closely. There is work to do, and time in life to do it. I will save this land, despite its ridiculous rulers. This is my task, which can be done from other shores as well as this.

Edmund may wish me gone, but I have been banished before and recalled. The hothead will have his way, but he will cool and then he will need me. Meanwhile I must pack my few possessions and go. My friends across the sea will welcome me.

A pox on this court!

There were more possessions, and heavier, than Dunstan had thought. They needed more space than one beast could carry. Packing for permanent exile was taking a long time; no-one could help him to choose between items to take with him. Clothing was easy to sort, books less so. The saddle-bags were already full. There was no space for necessary writing equipment. His possessions had multiplied, along with his responsibilities, since he was last ordered away.

Unpopular things must sometimes be said. Here he was, standing by the stables and latrine beyond the palace hall, shut out with the waste products of the king's bladder and spleen. This was not what he deserved.

Dunstan began to panic. Where should he go? Who would offer him a home? There was a young friend, a love of his youth but she was far away across the breadth of Wessex, and married. If he took a horse or mule from the stables without dispensation it would be considered theft. The punishment of exile could then become execution. There were plenty who would wish to see him dead; only the monk's habit had prevented them from poisoning, stabbing or otherwise maiming him, but they preferred to ruin a reputation. His maker would greet him, but there were things still to accomplish in this world.

There was the sound of a man's laughter, finishing a conversation with another a few yards away. He approached the latrine. Dunstan shifted away from the decorative screen door to show his presence. The man was a member of the eastern delegation from Byzantium, come to relieve himself of the eatable fineries which made the tables sigh with their weight. He nodded to Dunstan, speaking in the accented Latin which Greeks employed and which the court used on occasions when entertaining guests from foreign lands. This man, Dunstan recognised, was an exchequer official. The East wanted more high-class slaves and had come to negotiate for boys for the chorus of choirs in the great basilicas there. The Vikings from Bristow and Dublin would do a handsome deal and Edmund's England would take a worthwhile percentage. The court was known for its convenient and agreeable conferences where such matters could be settled. Removed from the sweat encrusted and emotional slave markets, where families were split up and destinies altered, merchants could relax, eat and drink and come to terms.

Slavery was a necessity; but like the slaughter of animals for food, Dunstan did not like to be associated closely with the forced production of labour. Some things were destined to be; they were God's will. The Greek, with whom he had negotiated the sale of five Welsh boys in the last few days, might be able to help him. Should he ask? He hated to do so. He touched his relic pouch, held inside his shirt. One of the pebbles used against St Stephen nestled in his hand. This was what was happening to him; stones were being thrown.

Opportunities do not wait. A few moments later he heard the hand-cleansing ritual. The easterner appeared, looking incongruous in his colourful finery against the backdrop of the wooden latrine. Despite Dunstan's discomfort, the dark-skinned man stirred an idea for a mural.

'Father Nikephoros?'

The man, attired in red and yellow silks, not at all as a bishop should be, turned. He was holding his hat, an Eastern Orthodox fancy to match his robes. It had exotic feathers.

'Father Dunstan, is it not?'

Dunstan beckoned to him, asking him to walk a little way beyond the latrine to the dun edges of the watery wasteland which led out to the hunting grounds beyond Cheddar.

'I wish to speak with you about visiting your land of Constantinople. I would like to accompany you and your delegation on your homeward travel. Could you have a place for me to view the wonders of the East at your Greek residence?'

Nikephoros, relieved of his stomach's burden and pleased to engage with a close confidant of the king, listened. Dunstan had longed to visit Constantinople, though it would have been preferable to do it at a later stage of his career and a time of his own choosing. The men struggled with the Latin idiom, but Dunstan's request was clear, as was the eastern bishop's agreement to arrange for him to be taken with their retinue as part of the baggage and purchased slaves who would be picked up from Bristow. In the meantime, he would have to find a bolthole. His patron, the vowess Aethelflaed, would no doubt shelter him for a night in her home near Glastonbury. The house stood, secluded, on one of the islands in the bog at Nyland. She would sympathise with his plight. He could imagine her saying, as she opened her door to him, 'I told you to be wary of kings. You have God on your side. You will prove them all wrong.' Then she would put his head on her bosom and hold him tight.

Let men rot! Let the king rot; I shall be gone from here, in the cart with the slaves, but in the company of Greeks who know fairness and who hold their tempers. The fair city of Constantinople beckons. When the time is right, I may return. My mission will be achieved, by me or by another.

May many devils stamp upon the souls of my enemies!

Nonna's Diary, March 944

I N THE SPRING of 944 I was busy with court affairs at Cheddar,
preparing documents to be taken to the next witan at
Pucklechurch, where a considerable number of client kings and
other dignitaries would be assembling. Its position in Wessex
would encourage the Scottish contingent to travel south, as
well as the Welsh and Cumbrian; it would be no harm if some
were forced into our company for a longer period than intended
through the advent of bad weather; we were a civilising factor in
our empire and might improve their minds and manners.

For any Welshmen who wished not to partake of our charms,
Pucklechurch was not far from the Severn port of Bristow. Many
Wessex and foreign dignitaries were already taking their pleasure
in the tented enclosure at Cheddar and they would travel north
with us. Kings were becoming emperors then; the boundaries of
countries, static for so long, had been rearranged by a response
to the Viking incursions. Displaced peoples, like the Welsh, try to
preserve their cultures and languages. Their gestures, language
and clothing became more noticeably different from our own.
The court had become an uninhibited, colourful place. The night
before, after the evening meal, Israel the Grammarian gave a
lecture on the cities of the East. The crowd had lapped it up and
there was much discussion about building styles. Dunstan had
been in the thick of it, surrounding the popular intellectual. It was
through Dunstan that Israel had been invited.

After the scene in the haligdom, I went to find my friend. He
beckoned to me from the crowd of clerks, looking anxious. I knew
that Edmund had been spoiling for a row with him; Dunstan
had told me that the king was at boiling point, worried about the

difficulties of the foreign trade dealings at this extended witan, anxious to please but to maintain his dignity and authority, and sleep-deprived by the arrival of his new son, Edgar. The eighteen-month-old baby screamed when he was separated from his mother when she visited the women's quarters without him and once begun, would not stop. But he was a welcome second heir to Wessex; his lustiness was a good omen, insisted his grandmother Eadgifu. Elgiva raised her shoulders, splayed her hands. What could she do? His father was a determined character too. Was that not a good thing?

I had never seen Dunstan so flustered. His cheeks were red with wrath and panic showed in the rapid movement of his hands. His hands were large; he used them a great deal to indicate where others should go and what they should do, as some of his illumined writings and drawings record. He knew and valued the importance of the handshake, the arm grasp, the pointing of the way, the emotion conveyed by the visual separation of fingers. He had been given a day, he said, to gather his personal things and leave. All that he had been given in wealth and land by others would be taken from him, collected by Edmund's treasurers; even the holdings he had been given by his lady patron of Nyland would gravitate to the king's purse. Edmund's rage had been phenomenal, falling well short of the use of weaponry, but he felt it would not do to be seen again near the court. Would I pray for him, he asked? I would, but my prayers were not as efficacious as his, as a priest. I promised that I would do what I could and intercede for him in time.

The Greeks had offered him safe passage, he said. He would go to his patron nearby for the night and at dawn, when the foreigners, having concluded their deal with the northerners, travelled to Bristow to pick up their slave purchases, he would go with them and continue on to Constantinople, to the cultured land of the Greek bishops. They would offer him everything he needed, he said, to continue his studies of the arts of the Roman empire and to view the mosaics of Justinian and Theodora which he had heard so much about. He calmed down as he told me about his future plans. He stopped wringing his hands. He would be glad to have done with this court which failed to value him, he said, and which failed to invest in him. In particular he wanted to be done with the rages and accusations which Edmund produced with increasing and unfailing regularity. A barely-grown king, he said, was not for him and as for that noisy brat Edgar in the cradle, well he could be a candidate for a bulrush cradle pushed into the swamps around Cheddar, lost forever, as far as he, Dunstan, was concerned. He later changed his mind about Edgar, but he never did take to Eadwig.

He wanted me to try to remonstrate with Edmund when his rage abated, as it would, in a few days. He said he would go to the civilised East, spend some months, perhaps years there, as a guest of the Greeks, learn much from them, and return when Edmund had apologised.

He said farewell to me, congratulated me on being level-headed and without ambition, said it was his curse to want more for himself, to need applause, to have as his mission in life to improve the status of the church and its role in English state-making. He embraced me, congratulating me on being the sanguine father of children, of being satisfied with my lot. Well, there he was not correct; a man will always have hopes, but in the main, he was right; I was happy, safe, loved and a king's essential factotum. I had travelled the rocky road from king to heir with little trouble, from Athelstan to Edmund. I liked Edmund; I was no threat to him. Since Dunstan had wedded himself in recent months to the church and had taken holy orders, Edmund had found him insufferable. There were two masters in Dunstan's life and the Pope had become the chief.

The explosive fireworks of the English court, still uncertain of its place in world affairs and run by a hot-tempered young king, had led to this, the banishment of my far-seeing friend. I wished him well, kissed him and said farewell. Two of the trinity of personal clerks of Athelstan's time were now banished. I watched him walk across the palace yard, carrying a large sack of belongings, shake the hand of one of the guards, give him a coin and take a coracle into the swamp and reeds, sending a duck squawking into the air. His fair-haired head remained steady as he oared his way along the channel leading west. He was still young, vigorous. I had no doubt that he would fare well, with or without my prayers. God was on his side.

Edmund

F UMING, EDMUND MARCHED down corridors, followed by two
hounds, little aware of where he was going. Guards, knowing
his fits of anger, stood aside to let him pass. Fire, foam and boiling
spittle would exit his mouth when he was like this and they dared
not interfere, to help or hinder. He was known to be a danger to
himself, and had been like this in childhood. A towering rage, it
was called, when he was like this. It could last for days.

Who would hear him out? Nonna was not a satisfactory
punchbag. His mother would refuse to hear anything said
against Dunstan. Elgiva was too pure. She would cover her ears
or run away; she had before. His delicate wife could not stand
raised voices and took the side of whomever she regarded as
the underdog. She insisted on freeing men her husband had
condemned to death, and declared that it was God's will to save
them. The chief hangman complained of leniency affecting his
livelihood. She would weaken the Wessex dynasty's power, if she
kept on pressuring him to set criminals free. She appeared to
undercut his authority deliberately, when she knew that he was
busy with other matters. Would her sons become soft as women,
like her?

In the morning light, still angry, Edmund sought an
activity which would allow him to vent his wrath. He was not
a hypochondriac like his brother, but he was aware that his
heart pounded, that his mental state was not improved, at these
times. He saw clearly, now, the threats to his family. The Norse,
it seemed, looked at him down the length of their wolf faces,
snarling with a smile, ready to pounce if he showed pain or
fear. Smooth dignitaries from the Orient, for whom the word

was their sword, superior in their learning, pressed on with their supercilious views, their beaming faces hiding deceits, like Dunstan. Accomplished diplomats and merchants, they could read, they could write, they were trained to dissemble but their malice was not crude like the Norse; they stabbed to the quick with the triple weapons of irony, sarcasm and humiliation. In an age when most were struggling to understand writing and to merely make a signature, they were composers of literature, of music, of poetry. They politely listened to his short sagas but, he was aware, they scoffed at the longer ones. These foreigners did not understand the Saxon love of horror and violence, born of the stormy skies of the north. They yawned behind their hands at the best composed parts of his tales. At the end, they did not applaud. Their eyes rolled, instead.

Foreigners and Norse, Mercia and Wessex. Northumbria ever grumbling. Edmund considered who might listen to his anger whom he could trust. Leofa would understand, but he was not here. Suddenly, he missed him. He remembered his straight-talking, so unlike Dunstan's artfulness. Aethelwold, growing ever more dogmatic, failed to acknowledge that he was no longer his student, but a king. He could yell at a stone wall, or a tree, but there wasn't one nearby which was beyond palace ears. Edmund's desperation grew again as he became aware of the need to control his hot-headedness. Athelstan had stood by him as a child when he raged, held his hand until the fire passed, but he was dead. He asked himself what his brother had done when frustrated. The answer was easy; lock himself into the nearest haligdom he could find, to converse with relics. Eadred was no use in these circumstances. He would not understand. He would walk, whistling, into the nearest library or hide behind a large book. He had troubles enough of his own. Edmund paused at the palace entrance. He looked at the stables opposite and at a horse's swishing tail. He suddenly knew what he needed to do. Something must die. A stag.

Sian, his chestnut hunter, the best of Wynflaed's stables, would give him the gift of peace from himself. The gorge and woods would absorb his anger. No man, he thought, could understand what it was to be a king and to have to listen to fools, to those who are always right, to the growing clamour from the church to be heard, to listen to the wiles of such as Dunstan. He saddled up Sian and prepared her for an outing which both of them would never forget. The hounds, who had padded behind him morosely from the hall, yelped with excitement.

Edmund continued to ruminate, though with less venom. Had he done right to exile Dunstan? He had plenty of good ideas, but he overreached himself. Bishop Alfheah, Dunstan's uncle, had encouraged the boldness in him, the sanctimonious awfulness of him, a priggish, pious chancer of middling birth but exceptional talent for climbing the greased pole of the court. He had engineered the increased importance of priests in the nation's management, making them indispensable. Dunstan had a great deal to answer for. In a few short years, with the help of his uncle and his own mother, Dunstan had, he now saw, become a king-maker, equalling the status of the greatest in the land, including the Bear, Half-king.

Edmund took up the reins and lifted himself onto Sian's great chestnut back. He had a horn for security strapped to him. He had a hunting spear for the kill. Another wolf-hound, lying in the next stable, greeted him with enthusiasm as he was unchained. Ruffling his shaggy head, Edmund conveyed that he would that day sniff out a deer, a great antlered beast. The dog understood that they would follow the stag, chase and torture it. Then he would stab it. The dog would have its throat, its liver. The anger turned to adrenalin. Peace would be found. He would name that creature, who would be chased and killed, after the man whom he hated.

He rode at a canter out of the palace complex. 'I shall be back before darkness,' he shouted to the gate guards. They relaxed their positions, nodded at themselves and closed the gate behind him. He squeezed Sian into a gallop and headed north to the gorge. He would meet the stag in hell.

The wetlands, starting to fill with autumn floodwater, gave way after a short distance to the loamy foothills of the gorge. Its jagged edges appeared before him, piercing the sky like a chaotic entrance to the underworld. Sian and Edmund picked their way through marsh grass and bramble as the land became rockier and wilder and began to rise steeply. He was no longer the only human to be seen in this ancient landscape; two guards had followed him at a distance. He looked back and saw their horses walking towards him, keeping their distance, though they could easily have caught up with him as he began to ascend the gorge. An indentation in the low vegetation, created by animals and occasional hunting, acted as a path, narrowing between the cliffs. The gorge sides towered above him. Edmund sighed. It was one of the curses of becoming a king, that he could never be alone. His protection was their remit, so forever more he would be shadowed. His only privacy was within the bedchamber and that had become a torture of noise, with the restless presence of Eadwig tossing in his dreams and Edgar ever demanding a teat. Elgiva refused to allow a nurse to take them to another room. He rounded a corner of rock and stopped riding, waiting for the guards to catch him up.

The guards, surprised to see Edmund still on the gorge floor, allowing Sian to nibble grass while he examined a red kite flying overhead, accepted that he wished to continue further up the gorge to hunt. They would wait in the gorge mouth for his return. How long that would be, no man could know, but they had seen impulsive moves by Edmund before. How long could it take to find and chase a stag in this environment? On past practice and experience, an hour, perhaps two, might suffice, not enough to cause alarm about his absence. One of the guards showed misgivings. The queen-mother would be unhappy, or his brother, but Edmund threatened him with separation from his family, with removal of pay, with a jewelled dagger waved with venom in the air. The man looked at his compatriot, who nodded. Edmund pulled up Sian's head and spurred her into a canter, climbing rapidly up towards the beginning of a zig-zag path which would take them to the heath above the gorge. He turned to look back once. The guards and their horses were small figures below.

Edmund could feel the warmth of weak sun on his hair and skin. He took pleasure in his sense of Sian's strength. He listened intently to the sounds of water on rock all around him. Cascading water fell down the cliff sides and fell gurgling into the swallet holes around, barrelling through the mysterious and magical caves of stone bears' teeth into the river beyond, taking liquid rock with it. The sheer cliffs, the abode of ancient hunters, watched him pass. Today, Edmund could see through the curtain of time to the past of man hunting in this gorge, in these caves carved by God and utilised by long-dead creatures.

At the top of the gorge-side, he dismounted. The hounds sniffed about in clumps of grass and thorn, finding no strong deer-scent. He needed badly to kill something, though the anger was subsiding. He was not ready to be calm, to be better than he was, or to pretend to be so.

The sunlit open area of heathland and woodland steamed. The rain of previous hours had stopped. The hounds, after a few minutes, picked up a scent and started to run and howl. Edmund remounted and followed, the horse cantering sedately away from the gorge edge. Later, he remembered every second of the thrill of the chase and his intense anger, equal passions, which mingled in his mind and body. Athelstan's voice chattered in his ear, cautioning. The wind blew, the clouds were scudding by, the deer, now visible, raised its head in alarm from its grazing and began to run. The dogs yapped and sang. Edmund leant forward, his hand gripping the heavy hunting spear.

The young man chased the stag across the heath, dodging behind bracken, rowan trees, oaks and ash in their winter bareness. He yelled the name of Dunstan. The stag was sent by God for him, a magnificent animal, a red deer with full antlers adorned with many spikes. He would not, if he could catch him, play a further part with his females this year. He stopped occasionally, looking at Edmund, twitching his nose, challenging him. His death was Edmund's ultimate desire, but the hunt, absorbing all his thoughts, silencing even Athelstan, was intricate and pleasantly long. The stag swerved, using every trick he could to avoid the huntsman. He would not throw his spear until he was sure of a close kill. The dogs continued their ear-splitting howls, running with the horse, bending and turning past the natural cover. Edmund was delirious with the joy of hunting. A cloud-burst fell suddenly from the heavens; man and beasts were soaked.

He should have realised, but the blinding anger mixed with adrenalin was still in him, that he was perilously close to the cliff edge. The stag, exhausted, had lost its way; it stood, looking at Edmund as if to address its executioner. Edmund was careless of where he was, or whether he lived or died. He closed slowly on his kill. There was Dunstan. It was his head he saw as he regarded the panting deer, his blonde tonsured scalp and wagging finger. The half man, half-beast turned again and ran, followed by Sian, carrying her madman on its back, readying his spear.

The animal vanished into dense cloud. Edmund careered on. Then came a scream, which descended away and down, down into the heart of the gorge. The hounds fell too with high-pitched shrieks. A few man's lengths behind, at full gallop and about to fall with them, Sian and Edmund fused in horror. The horse veered suddenly. She skidded to the right and braked with her front legs, causing Edmund to fall over her shoulder and lose his stirrups. She came to a halt, breathing like a demon. Edmund lurched sideways. He heard a crack as he put out his hand to break his fall.

The deer-man and its fate, its last utterance still ringing in his ears, caused a searing vision which altered Edmund's course and his life. It altered England's course, too. The hate which he felt now turned to fear. On his knees, feeling pain in his shoulder, he swore in that sacred moment as the horse swerved from the edge that he would not persecute Dunstan, the church or its abbots and priests. He would thank God for the single movement of Sian which saved him from following the deer and the dogs to a crashing, bloody mess on the rocks below, a fall of hellish proportions, of several seconds in the knowledge of certain death. It was Dunstan who intervened to save him, or God, he thought. He would make amends for his anger. He would restore the object of his wrath, give him back the possessions he had taken away. He would rule as his equal; the power of the church his friend, no longer his foe. Edmund and Dunstan; together they would be the makers of the realm. Edmund forgave him and fervently wished Dunstan would him. A ghostly whisper in his ear confirmed that Athelstan approved.

Edmund stood up. He discovered that his right arm was numb, and stowed his spear with his left hand. Sian and he both understood what had occurred, how near to death they had been. The horse was wild-eyed as he held her by the reins, sweating with fear. He sank down again upon the ground, grateful to feel the thin grass. After a few moments of prayer, recovering, he tied the horse to a gorse branch and crawled a few yards to the cliff edge which was now revealed by a lifting cloud. The sun broke through. He leaned over and forced himself to look down. The animals were a long way below, small red misshapen creatures on the gorge floor, dots of flesh lying together in a mangled heap. Small rocks lay scattered beside them. Feeling dizzy, he returned to Sian and had just enough strength to find and blow the horn. He did not remember anything else.

'Suddenly (the king) saw the precipice, and did all he could to stay the horse's onrush. Well, the king gave up all hope of saving his life... he said to himself: 'I will make up to him (Dunstan) with forward will if my life is spared". At these words, the horse stopped (I still shudder to tell of it) on the very brink of the precipice, when the horse's front feet were just about to plunge into the depths of the abyss.'

The Life of St Dunstan, 14

Dunstan, the new Abbot of Glastonbury.

A SERVANT WAS sent to find Dunstan. The convoy of exotic travellers had not gone many miles. They had reached the outskirts of Frome on the eastern edge of the Mendip hills and were approaching the monastery to refresh themselves and their horses. Travel was slow and tedious with a large group of religious or ambassadorial representatives; the wagons were many and heavy and the mud of recent rains clung to wheels and hooves. Dunstan had calmed himself enough to take an interest in his surroundings and was beginning to enjoy the company of the Greeks. They were about to discuss eastern politics over a meal at the monastery when the message came.

Frome was a boundary town, straddling the old frontier between the old British kingdom of Dumnonia and Wessex as it was in Aldhelm's time. His missionary monastery still functioned, though it was a place which needed restoration. The ancient structure had ceased to be watertight a century before. The palace was better prepared against Mendip storms and was still popular with the king, as a hunting base, but less so with the ladies. Frome was a hilly place, and the monastery gardens faced north, an unfortunate aspect.

The landscape to the east was dominated by a single mountain called Cley, an ominous barrier to the older parts of Wessex. On its peak was the rounded tomb of a former chieftain, dead aeons before the light of the world came to save souls. Around the barrow was his fortress of worn grass ramparts. Who he was, no-one knew, not even the British who held feasts and fires on the summit.

As Dunstan was engaged with his fellow travellers, wondering at the devil worship which in some places stubbornly persisted, Edmund's servant caught up with them, riding hard. His urgency had the flavour of disaster. It was a recall to the side of the king. Dunstan was triumphant; his companions were amazed. He had a tinge of regret that he would not now be able to see the basilicas and organisation of Byzantium, but perhaps that would come later. The part in the affairs of the nation which God had ordained for him was still to be played. The group continued on to the monastery stables and halls; the king could wait. First, he needed a meal and fresh horse. He also wished to interview Geraint at the forge.

Dunstan was urgently needed by Edmund, that was clear, but why, and so soon, was not. The servant was charged with only the minimum of information. Edmund was agitated, had had an accident while hunting, was distressed and had demanded that he be found and brought back to Cheddar. Later Dunstan discovered, with pleasure, that while waiting for him to return Edmund had been in an agony of restlessness, alternately rising from his bed, clutching a heavily bruised arm and leg, reaching for his wife and children to receive comfort which would not come, and dropping to his knees in prayer, muttering and imploring the saints to spare the dynasty, his dynasty, from evil forces. Later, as he rode back to Cheddar, he was aware of small malevolent creatures, not hares, not birds, not goats, staring at him from the roadside, teasing him and tempting him to stop. He ignored them. After hours of uncomfortable riding and having been re-plastered by the mud of drove road and fords, Dunstan arrived at Cheddar and was immediately taken to the king's side. By then he was ready to forgive, but more particularly to hear Edmund plea for help.

Wailing and sobbing greeted him in the private room which was used by Edmund and Elgiva, most of it being done by Elgiva herself together with her son Eadwig, who yelled, enjoying the emotion of the moment. The surrounding servants and slaves, unable to assuage Edmund's distress by drink, food, or oils, retreated as he entered. The king was lying in a pool of sweat on his bed, his arms over his face, his legs drawn up as if to defend himself from some inward terror. Dunstan spoke gently, reserving his anger.

'My lord, I have come.' His voice sounded, to his own ears, like sweetness amidst the storm. Instantly Eadwig stopped shouting and looked at him from the enfolding arms of his mother. Elgiva, tears pouring down her face, held the wriggling child on her girdle and became silent herself as she recognised the priest.

Edmund lowered his arms. His dishevelled hair, wild eyes and damp clothing reminded Dunstan of a visit to a slave holding camp on the outskirts of Bristow which he had visited recently. The despair. How much a man could alter when he has no hope. He knew something of that. But here was his reprieve and here was his chance.

'Is that you, Dunstan, oh, forgive me. Never leave me. Come here, close to me. I am not ill, only distraught. Now you will give me peace. Give me your blessing, I beg you!'

To Dunstan's embarrassment, the king then burst into a flood of tears. He grasped Dunstan's hand, looked deep into his eyes with his bloodshot own and kissed it. A hand was not enough. Wincing, Edmund stood up from the pallet and enveloped him in his arms. There was an unconscious exchange of human equals. From that day Dunstan was not in thrall to any king; he recognised them as living frailties, just as other men were.

Despite the anointment which they received, making them representatives of God on earth, it was priests, bishops and abbots who performed this great gift. And it was they who could remove it.

Dunstan blessed Edmund and set his mind at rest. Edmund described how hunting in anger had led him to the cliff edge. The horse had come close to throwing him over it after the stag and dogs. He had had the vision, as he hurtled towards certain death, of receiving Dunstan again, of never being separated from him, of how vital the church and all that it represented were to him personally and to the realm.

Together they opened the relic chest which the king carried with him on tour. They reaffirmed their faith, in the efficacy of the saints, of the purpose of their lives, of Edmund's God-given abilities as king to overcome evil, to be in receipt of the good will of God, to hammer their enemies.

Dunstan had had similar scenes with Athelstan, though never so extreme. Athelstan had been more thoughtful, less effusive and temper-driven. He had been nearer in age to his advisor; they were more like equals, brothers. Dunstan grew in stature. His back straightened. He wrested resistance and doubt from Edmund, the younger man, while he could. Athelstan would have understood. You cannot put an old head on young shoulders, he often said, looking at Edmund.

The following day, Edmund and Dunstan rode alone to Glastonbury. They opened the rickety door of the old church of St Mary's. Still emotional and tearful, Edmund held Dunstan's hand as he took him to the abbot's chair and set him in it.

'Sit in this seat, high and powerful, as the abbot of this church. Whatever your own resources lack to increase divine worship and honour the holy Benedictine rule, I shall devoutly make up with a king's bounty.'

That afternoon Dunstan sent for Aethelwold. They had been granted licence by the king to change the course of history, as his life had been spared. Together they would rid the air, seas and earth of malevolent devils. A miracle had brought them power. Prayer had been proven to outrank the rules and whims of kings. A reform movement had been given the blessing of the king. Saint Benedict smiled down from heaven above.

Cheddar Palace

EDMUND HAS CALLED me back to Cheddar and showered me with gems. I climb further up the ladder of Jacob. I am now the controller and soon to be Dunstan, Abbot of Glastonbury. The saints have assisted me again. I am in the right. Now I can do the bidding of my master in Rome.

There is so much work to do, so much!

St Aldhelm Lives On.
Malmesbury, April 944

TWO MEN IN long robes, followed by nine others in short capes, dismounted from their horses at the foot of a steep hill overlooking a ford. The land, walled and crowded with stone-roofed houses, rose on the opposite bank. The horses were steaming and wet to their shoulders; there had been recent heavy rain. The inclement weather, though bringing discomfort to travellers, was regarded as a miracle for fearful peasants and slaves whose livelihoods and life itself depended on it. It had been a dry autumn and winter.

Edmund and Dunstan, accompanied by men of the king's guard, had travelled from Dunstan's installation as abbot at Glastonbury, a hasty affair, to the more formal arrangements of thanksgiving and prayer for St Swithun at the holy town of Malmesbury, home and mausoleum of the much-revered former abbot, teacher and missionary, Aldhelm. In silence they removed their outer clothing and boots, handing them to one of the guards. The swollen river rushed past them, obscuring the stony-bottomed ford. Dunstan was clad in a single layer of coarse black linen, uncomfortable to the skin but suitable for his new status. Shorter than his companion the king and older by more than a decade, his balding head shone like a lamp in a sudden shaft of bright sunlight. Edmund, hirsute and newly bearded, also dressed in linen but white in colour, reflected the sudden brightness. His otherworldly appearance as the chosen anointed of God could not be concealed. There was already a large gaggle of watchers hanging over the river wall of the town, waiting to see what spectacle would reveal itself.

Divested of high-status apparel, but marked by their demeanour and intent, the two men, having crossed the flooding ford with the assistance of burly servants and some planks from a hut nearby, began to walk barefoot uphill through the main street of Malmesbury, rising through the defending gates of the burh, which melted open as they passed. The rare sight of state and church walking side by side in unity and modesty impressed the inhabitants of a town well accustomed to ritual and pilgrimage. The main street, Bimport, was the scene each February of Candlemass processions, when the whole population, from noble to slave, male and female, took part in the day-long banner and candle waving from church to church, with extravagant blessings performed at the west doors of each by priests and monks living within the walls. At Rogationtide, when the hundred celebrated its bounds, the rituals were inevitably condemned by some purists as immodest farces. They rapidly devolved into drunken peasant orgies carried out with over-enthusiasm. Keen to celebrate a recognised territory, combined with free access to ale, the townsfolk and local farming folk took over from the year-long control by more sober sections of Malmesbury society. In time to come a long-held flight of fancy was put into action by one of the brethren who donned wings in an attempt to demonstrate a God-given ability to fly from the tower of St Peter's. He survived, sustaining only broken bones, demonstrating the extreme sanctity and misplaced confidence in higher powers of an ordinary inhabitant of Malmesbury.

The penitential display of aristocratic unshod feet on Bimport meant reverence of a high order. Who was the penitent and who the absolver and giver of forgiveness? In time and with the publication of his dictated Lives, Dunstan would make it clear. His legacy was already being penned, chiefly by himself.

It was apparent to the watching townsfolk that a tall royal person, accompanied by a shorter monk, were making their way barefoot to the crest of the hill, to the stone cross which stood not far from the recently reconstructed edifice of the abbey church. Behind the church and monastery, defended from invaders of any sort, a defile dropped steeply to the looping river. At the cross they were greeted by the abbot and those of his monks who were senior enough to have been made aware of the arrival of the king and the new abbot of Glastonbury. Here the small procession paused. It was about to enter the abbey church, a short way from Maeldubh's ancient cross.

The abbot stepped forward to bless the newcomers with holy water. He had rank. The abbey church contained the tomb of Aldhelm, first Saxon abbot in the early eighth century of the wealthy Benedictine monastery. It was one of the greatest sanctuaries and centres of pilgrimage in the kingdom. Maeldubh had been Aldhelm's Irish teacher. The penitent and his priest kneeled at the foot of the worn cross as the rite was performed above their heads. Prayers were said and bells rung as they then continued on their way, accompanied by the abbot and his retinue, into the open space before the door of the abbey church. Here the procession paused again.

Dunstan had requested that there would be further ritual here. Edmund, he felt, should feel the full force of the power of repentance. He must be kept from returning to his former antipathy. At the south door a new, grand stone entrance had recently been constructed. The architect was known to Dunstan; it had been himself. Edmund had contributed to this renovation and improvement; it had been one of Dunstan's chief achievements of the year. The Malmesbury abbot lifted his arms to the stone and paint emblazoned entrance, saying nothing. Its magnificence, obvious to all, needed no words.

Edmund, still dazed by his recent experience at Cheddar and at Dunstan's mercy, gazed on the work of his new abbot of Glastonbury. If he was beginning to regret his feelings of subservience to his companion, he did not show it. He had handed his soul into the safe-keeping of his chief advisor. There would be no reversal of the commitment he had made. He looked up at the doorway.

It was a splendid addition to the Saxon church, an imposing gateway to heaven. Carved figures of saints, including royalty, gazed at them; creatures with mouths gaping and eyed bulging, intricately wrought from stone instead of the old, increasingly rotten, wooden porch carvings. They replaced the temporary fabric with a millennial intention. Over all, the fresh colours of red, white, blue and green made the figures and creatures seem to move, to stare, to accuse, to dare.

To dare to disagree. To dare to say *this is too much, you go too far, my dreams are soiled, my soul is afraid.*

The age of colour and stone had begun and its power over the mind was great.

Flutes began to play and a heavenly choir started to sing from a room hidden above the doorway, the voices and instruments trailing down to the ritualists below through delicately carved arches. This was another invention of Dunstan's; his bold attempt to sway the senses of humankind in the known world towards a better, holier, more controllable way of life, were having a magical effect. Angels sang from above. Dunstan lifted his arms to the sound and indicated that Edmund should do the same. Two abbots, princes of the church and a king admired the handiwork of God, of Dunstan. Their hands, outstretched, pointed every finger to the universe above and beyond the world of man.

In his state of retribution and penance, Edmund obeyed. He knelt and raised his arms. His gesture of regret was noticed by the watching townsfolk. Here was a truly pious king. The choir continued to sing in Latin, the language of the other world. The music fell around the ears and heightened senses of all below, accompanied by drifts of pungent incense.

The heavenly choir faded and the huge doors swung open. The by now large procession of priests and monks passed inside. The ritual continued, with Dunstan and the abbot taking the lead in a service of thankfulness for the king's recent gifts to their abbeys. Some of these were on show; the reliquaries taken from Athelstan's remaining collection lay glowing in their finery on chests and tables along the side of the nave. Lit by large candles, the ancient church, in its plain stone-block walls, bedecked with hangings and curtains, littered with wooden and stone sarcophagi of abbots and saints, some Irish and British, infected the senses with its mind-altering colour and incense. The drama of the early medieval church theatrical performance was nearly at its height.

The choir and musicians descended from the room over the doorway where they had squatted to play and sing and proceeded to the high altar, continuing to intone. Dunstan had been experimenting with introducing new compositions. The service continued with the chief protagonists kneeling to pray. Prayers were said for Aldhelm, for Maeldubh the founder, for a long list of exemplary beings who had inhabited the church and monastery and lastly Athelstan and his cousins, Aelfwine and Aethelwine, who had died at Brunanburh in 937. This was their final resting place. Lit candles illuminated the recently renovated tomb and altar to Aldhelm. Dunstan's work could be seen here, too, the stonework having been repainted and additions made to the tomb itself. Pilgrims, for a large purse, could crawl through small holes under the stone enclosed coffin to lie, briefly, beneath the body of the saint, to breathe its air.

At the end of the service, Edmund and the two abbots moved to the plain stone and wood tomb of Athelstan, a temporary resting place while his permanent stone monument was being prepared. Edmund, affected by the extended ritual, knelt by his brother's tomb, as he had knelt as a youth beside the tomb of Cuthbert in Chester-le-Street. He missed this man, who had chosen not to be buried at Winchester with the rest of his dynasty but here, in the hallowed grounds of the wealthiest monastery of England, within an arm's length of Aldhelm, revered missionary abbot, who had converted the heathen West Saxon realm.

Silently, with his hand on the wooden effigy of Athelstan, Edmund asked his brother for his blessing in his fresh partnership with the Church and its leaders.

Am I right to bestow Dunstan with so much power?

There was no reply from the tomb.

Frome Monastery, April 944

To my former compatriot Leofa.

I, Nonna, write, concerned that I have not heard from you for more than a year. Are you well, brother? I miss your company at court, the fun we had and the tales, the poetry and growling nature of your voice. I really miss the sound of your laugh. I miss the north-man agility of your mind which emerged to play after compline when we could not sleep, waiting to assuage the midnight vigils and terrors of Athelstan.

How are you, your children, your wife, that red-headed beauty who took you away from me? I know it was not her fault; after the confusion of Chester-le-Street and the relic episode, someone had to take the blame. I regret that the burden of guilt fell on you, but then the affair with Leonada was threatening to come to light and it was impossible for Athelstan to keep you here. In Ireland, with your own kind, you are safe. But I realise that may not always be the case. Be on your guard, old friend.

When we were the three chosen companions of Athelstan, his most trusted advisors, I knew that there would be others who might complain of our influence, who might be jealous. I will not say here who I think those others were, but of course you have guessed who it was who decided to have you exiled. One of us has changed. He is growing pompous with power. Edmund's ears are open to them and he takes advantage. But what can a king do but listen? How can he know whose tongue is forked? In this new reign we waver between disaster and success, lurching like a ship in a storm's sea swell.

As for my news, I continue to serve the royal family to the best of my ability. That family grows larger, it seems, daily;

Eadgifu and her advisors have powers which threaten to split the court as far as the succession issue is concerned; we are only four years into Edmund's reign, but his small children, as with Edmund and his brother, are at the centre of a quarrel. Eadwig and Edgar are both headstrong children and have good potential; there is no chronic illness problem as with Edmund's brother Eadred. They are both 'Golden Children' which Eadgifu loves to remind us on every public occasion. Dunstan and Aethelwold are tutoring them. One is marked as a future ruler of Mercia, the other, Wessex. I am aware of a dispute; Eadgifu is cold to Eadwig. I heard Aethelwold complaining loudly about his behaviour two nights ago. She defended her eldest grandson, but it is becoming clear that he is a handful. Edgar is her favourite. Nevertheless, she will take no complaint about her boys, as she calls them, not from Athelstan, who found it best, towards the end, to remain silent in her company, not from Edmund, her own son, who she may be jealous of, not from Elgiva whom she holds in contempt, though she herself chose her as wife for him. Only Dunstan can speak to her, and you know what he is like.

There have been arguments about Edmund's treatment of some prisoners; Elgiva, having been trained by the Shaftesbury nuns to consider mercy to be the greatest virtue, has been attempting since she became queen to temper the old ways of justice. This, too, Eadgifu objects to. The queen-mother in old age is becoming a shrew. The changes which occur in women late in life lead to unreasonable expectations. Aethelwold says that they become like witches. You will know what I mean. We saw it happen to the old queen-mother, Aelfflaed, as she complained herself to death at Wilton all those years ago. Eadgifu refuses to remain shut in, as she calls it, in the sewing rooms of the palaces; her frustration is growing and so is her temper.

My friend, how did we come to live so long? How much longer will this battle between Wessex and Mercia continue? It seems that in every generation, especially where there are two or more brothers who are aethelings, there must be this inevitable rise in contention, the assertion of factions against each other, at first demonstrated with words alone and ultimately with weapons. Families bare their teeth at each other across the borders defined by rivers, summoning armies or paying foreign forces to fight for them, threatening and then applying sharpened swords to each other's throats. I look at young Eadwig and Edgar and see more years of misery to come, with barely civil words between even Dunstan and Aethelwold over who shall be the next king and who will sire the next king after that!

Athelstan decided to rule out descendants of his body from the throne to simplify the succession. Eadred's unwillingness to discuss the possibility of a partner offers certainty, too. Their calm self-restraint shines like a silver thread through the caterwauling court, prepared to make their side, whichever it is, the dominant grouping. Ealdormen from different factions vie to get the attention of Edmund, then go behind his back to speak to his mother, or to Dunstan or Aethelwold, repeating their biased visions of the unknowable future, trying to define and shape it. To some extent I blame Athelstan; he was too liberal. He did not see that some enemies were close at hand.

We cannot decide for the future, but I fear that the divisions I see growing in this family, hanging like spectres in the palace halls, may allow an enemy, like the man who hosts your exile, Anlaf himself, to take advantage of the quarrelsome state of England. If the nation does not meld together, as Athelstan hoped it would, then I fear for the next generation of Wessex. But enough of my worries. If you can tell me anything to give me hope to prevent this nightmare from maturing into reality, I will be grateful.

As for me personally, my eyes are not as good as formerly, though that is to be expected with the close writing work that we make it our business to do; the record of dealings must be continued for future readers to be able to understand the roots of

England. Dunstan has the Chronicle chained to a column of stone at Winchester where he restricts all entries. He is not happy with some of them, but has not the time at present to do the necessary corrections. We are all busy. New laws are passed every day and witan meetings are more frequent and longer. The stewards have a greater task in bedding and feeding the nobles and bishops and their retinues at witans and more modern buildings must be built and maintained for their benefit as well as the king's, not to say the queen's. The tents of nobles are becoming large and more colourful, as well as more numerous. Red tents, blue tents, striped tents, now cover all available space in the palace fields. They create a fairground scene, but you have never seen a fair as extensive as these.

It becomes harder to do the king's work with each passing week. The bells of a peaceful abbey, somewhere untainted by the physical requirement to be at hand, advising, translating and writing, seem more and more appealing. An uncomplicated life of prayer is very attractive. I will let you know when I am ready for the retirement of the cloister. Perhaps you will be able to join me some day when you are no longer seen as a renegade and I have resigned my position as the old owl, the spy, looking down on others from the lofty heights of my oak tree. I would enjoy going over our memories with you, my friend. That is my dearest wish, but, I fear, impossible for now.

Enough. I will send this letter with Skallagrimsson's friend, Bjork who acts as a slave controller to one of the merchants travelling regularly to Dublin.

I have written in the language of my wife, Welsh, for safety's sake and because I know that this will not be understood by any across the sea in Dublin, should my words fall into Viking hands. I suggest you do the same when writing to me, as you indicated the last time that I heard from you.

May the winter storms pass above and beyond your abode, dear friend. Tell me of your existence and how your family is.

Your son will now be old enough to receive instruction. Are you endowing him with all that we learned at Glastonbury in our own youths?

Preserve yourself, my friend, and, for now, stay in Dublin. You will do well among your own kind. There are many pagans there who you may in time come to convert. That must be your life's work, as mine is to preserve my notes. Teach them to write and read; you may pacify their hearts and save us all from Viking venom. Be warned: Edmund knows about Leonada.

I hope to meet you again one day, to share in the delight of our memories. Perhaps it will be in the next world, where we will have long ages to share talk of our lives and experiences.

Until then, I remain your supporter and compatriot,

Nonna.

A Letter from Dublin Abbey, May 944

M Y LADY ELGIVA,
    I appeal to you as your lord's conscience. With all my
heart I, Leonada, regret that my husband's admitted wrongdoing
with gaining the love of one so much higher than himself has
separated both of us from your family. If there was a way to
recompense the king for Leofa's offence, let me know it. My
requests to him direct have been of no use. Perhaps my pleas have
been intercepted.

My time in exile palls. I am ill; there is no treatment here
for my ailment. Our Viking masters show no joy in learning as
your lord and his brother display. There is no understanding of
the place of the church in matters political, let alone spiritual,
only lip-service to a way of thinking which they dimly perceive,
and therefore resent, may be superior to their own. Anlaf and his
men are either pagan, or, worse, have no beliefs at all. They sit
on heaps of gold in their treasure rooms, gloating and counting
their way to Valhalla. My son and daughter, infected by the
rivalry and brutality which they see around them, have ceased
to be fearful of the effects upon their souls. They have begun
to contemplate the attractiveness of a violent existence, where
death and displacement to a warrior's imagined otherworld in
as bloody a way as possible seem preferable to a peaceful life of
cooperation and good conscience. They refuse to accompany me
to mass in the abbey. They say they would be bored by a regulated,
ordered life with Christian purpose as its objective and where
the pen would be preferred to the knife. They will soon reject my
pleadings in their way of dress and manners, wishing to emulate
the pagan children of Anlaf with whom they associate. Wild

notions attract the sensibilities of bored prisoners. To be free at present, to them, seems to be able to be wild.

In short, I fear for their futures. My son is likely to choose to be a Viking roamer and pirate, a treasure-hunting marauder or slave trader, like those men he sees around him, lugging their ships to sea, bringing full vessels of wailing and sick newly-made slaves. They do not wish to be slaves themselves, but this may be their fate if they remain here. Which should I choose for them? To be slaves or to be slave-hunters?

I acknowledge that our Viking masters have been good to us, taken us in, fed us, but at a cost. My husband's blood has been respected and his knowledge and language and learning have been of use to them (though he has told them nothing of the hearts and minds of your family, only that which he knows to be the truth of the reign of your lord's brother Athelstan).

For myself, I ask nothing. I understand the reasons for our exile. For my children, I beg that they be allowed to return to their rightful home, Mercia. I long to see my children grow bright in a land of culture and learning. Before long they will reject the literacy which I have tried to teach them, in favour of rough apparel, inked tattoos and shorn hair. Even my daughter wishes to emulate the reckless youths she sees around her. There are few decent women here who can teach her even those arts which some Viking women have refined; she is more likely to emulate the young men and has begun asking to wear trews.

I remember you from my days at Shaftesbury. They say that you are a fair-minded and holy person, who intercedes with the king on behalf of criminally-enslaved persons. Your reputation has reached even this far. I know that you are beautiful; a friend saw you on your marriage to your lord, saw that his manly temper was assuaged by your own sweetness of being.

I send my greetings and my hope to you. You have children of your own. Will you not give safe harbour to my children, born of royal Mercian blood, born as Christians in the great Abbey of

Shaftesbury which you and your husband both love so much?

If a ship and its crew could take my family from here to the shores of Hywel Dda's territory in Wales, (I have no power over any financial provision here) then I am sure that Hywel would be pleased to courier us across his lands to Gwent and across the Severn to Bristow. From there we may make our way to Mercia, to live quietly in a monastic institution. We will be no threat to you or your dynasty, that I promise. Others may not think so and so we must live in anonymity, as Aelfwynn, my mother, did in your abbey for so long. We would take different names. We could go to Gloucester and then to Worcester, far away from the court of Wessex, invisible and grateful to be in a Christian land.

I say no more. Do not show this letter to anyone. Burn it when you have read it, and if you agree with its contents and are able to assist my family, please send word.

I await your reply.

My Lady, may St Radegund look over you and the Great Mother herself protect you and your children.

I am your servant. I appeal to your honourable nature and look daily for your word.

Skallagrimsson's man Bjork is my messenger.

I am ever your servant.

Leonada of Mercia.

Cheddar Palace, June 944

THERE WAS A gurgling sound. Elgiva tried, without success, to stifle the sound of bile exiting from both ends of her body in the commode curtained off from the bedchamber. Edmund was a light sleeper, despite days spent energetically hunting in the gorge. He stirred and stretched his arms behind his head.

'El, are you in trouble again? Do you need any help?'

'I have enough rag and herb to get me through the night, thank you, Edmund.' Elgiva lowered her nightdress over her body and wearily returned to the bed. There was little light to guide her, only a hint of the early dawn was to be glimpsed through the single high window. She had been engaged for most of the last hour trying to ease her bowels and cleaning herself over and over in the darkness.

'I can call in Israel to see if he can do anything for you, you know. His contacts abroad may have more effective a cure than the monks here can provide.' Edmund leant over his wife and smoothed her arm as she lay beside him, facing away.

'No more cures, Edmund. I have my saints and my prayers. If the monks cannot save me, I must put my trust in them. Prayer is the best hope and you know we must all go to our maker before long.'

Elgiva sighed. She had months ago realised that she would soon pass from the earth, that she would have to say goodbye to her young sons. In her mind, she already had. Even at their young ages, they were already out of her hands, being schooled by Dunstan and Aethelwold. They would grow up to be the most erudite, or the most brainwashed, of the Wessex dynasty. How long had she left to be with them as they were juggled between tutor and grandmother? This infernal torture in her stomach had been troubling her for years, growing worse with each witan encounter. Her discomfort had reached a peak in the last year, attending to and listening to the worldly men and their strident wives. She longed for the quiet cloister of Shaftesbury and its promenade walk along the crest of the hilltop town, gazing over the Wessex lands below to her mother's tree-lined estate at Charlton. There would be no more horse-riding for her, no more cures or attempts at them.

What was there left to do? This would be her last summer, she felt, her last effort at acting as hostess at court. There was much to oversee. The imminent gathering for St Augustine's celebration at Pucklechurch, a yearly affair, was becoming a riot of colour and foreigners, a growing melting pot from all corners of the known world. She would have to welcome diplomats with their adjuncts of family, guard and interpreters. A variety of servants and slaves would noisily erect large tents over several fields. The hall compound, the main kitchen and all the other camp kitchens would be shrouded in smoke from the wood fires. These temporary arrangements were a headache for the royal steward as they could erupt into flame. Candle use was a problem when mixed with alcohol. There was the incessant chatter of instruction, management and excitement of children who had been allowed to accompany their parents, seeing the magnificence of the international ensemble which Edmund's had become.

She was tired of it all. She was saying farewell to Wessex and to the protective strength of her husband. She had done her duty. Eadwig was a strong boy and like his father was full of self-belief. Edgar was unlikely to rule, but he was showing an interest in the gospel and might do well in religious circles. The biblical images amused him. He was responding well to instruction; Eadwig less so, but perhaps this was acceptable in a child who must one day rule.

There were a few things which she was still ambitious to achieve. She had succeeded where others had failed to persuade Edmund to look more sympathetically on young offenders. The guilty criminal could not be let off, but the prisons were full of very young men who had lost their way. The blood feud, an unpleasant feature of Saxon hierarchy, was now in abeyance. The ordeals by fire and water seemed to her absurd, though the efficacy of intervention by the saints was generally accepted. But the saints had not helped her in her illness. There were doubts.

'There is something that I wish you would do, Edmund, before I go.'

'You're going nowhere, my love.' Edmund did not appreciate the talk of imminent death. He was twenty-two. She was twenty-one. He knew what she was about to ask, yet again. But his empathetic nature and his genuine fondness for his wife, combined with the memory of her recent time on the nursing chair-commode, made him more pliable. 'But tell me what you would like.'

'Leonada has written to me.'

Edmund groaned. 'So, the raven wing has reached out across the sea, has it, and infected you? I said, when I told you about Leonada, that she would bring us trouble.'

'I am glad that you shared your problem with me. I am your wife. God will smooth the way to resolution. Listen to what I have to say. Leonada's son is becoming a Viking soldier. He is ignorant of our ways, of learning and the Christian path. Edmund, he is Mercian, one of our bloodline. We cannot abandon the child to the pagan monsters and their violent approach to life.' Elgiva turned to Edmund. The fire in her belly had subsided; now she had a last chance with what energy she had to try to persuade Edmund of his obligation, as she saw it, to help the royal child of an exiled criminal. She thought, also, of the boy's sister.

'You do not understand. Leofa was not merely a traitor to our family. He was a thief. Athelstan did not have him executed, though he could have done. He had to be banished and that means for life, family or not. I told you all this when we married.'

'But what did he steal? You have never told me what it was that was so important that he had to be sent away. Why was he not hanged?'

How could Edmund explain the double crime which Leofa had committed? He reviewed, in his mind, what she knew. He had told Elgiva, while explaining his new relationship with Dunstan, that Leofa had married a princess of Mercia and fathered children with her. Elgiva had sworn on her missal never to tell anyone. The other secret, the theft of the head of St Oswald from the monks of Cuthbert, was the deeper one, Athelstan's great deception. He could not trust her with that. Even Eadred, his brother, who had not been present in Chester-le-Street in 934, was ignorant. Like Bran's head of former times, the skull had been taken to Gloucester to be placed with most of its limbs and torso as a totem to protect England, to ward off the evil forces of the north and west. If the secret was revealed, which would be seen as weakening the northern defences against the South and the Scots, there would be diplomatic disaster. His own and Athelstan's reputations would be mired forever, their souls and persons excommunicated by the Pope. His mother would be appalled if she discovered about the substitution and whose head now rested in Cuthbert's coffin. Edmund had learned to conceal his fears; Elgiva was not strong enough to share them.

'My love, there are things which I cannot, will not, share with you. I know how you yearn for "fairness" and in the case of Leofa and Leonada I can understand that you may feel he and his family have been unjustly treated. I know that you have sympathy for the children who are growing up in a pagan den...but...'

'They are nearly at puberty, Edmund!' Elgiva raised her voice, wept on Edmund's arm. Her imminent death gave her courage to fight for what she felt was right, as she had begged before for leniency in the witan courts, seeing young lads led out to hang too often, for crimes for which her own children would receive a stern word or a cuff from Aethelwold and no more.

Could her tears sway him? 'Let me show you the letter,' she said and lit a candle. She went to her writing desk and retrieved a folded parchment. She handed it to Edmund. She doubled over. 'Ooh.' There was another stomach pang.

Edmund could tell that she was genuinely in pain. There had been too many instances of this in their shared life to doubt her. He took the letter and read it.

'Hm. I can see how you have been troubled, El, but there is little that I can do. It is too dangerous for us to let them back into England, you must realise that. Even if I allowed it, the nobles would be outraged. And there is more to this matter than you know.'

'But what, what is it? Leofa has been treated like a high-born dissenter. You allowed Dunstan to return. Why not him?' This was Elgiva's last chance to soften her husband. She could push him with her pain.

How could Edmund soothe his now copiously weeping, soon-to-be-dead wife, the mother of his male heirs, focus of his youthful dreams? He stroked her head and neck. The caresses reminded and reassured them both that theirs, at times, was a platonic as well as a conjugal relationship. Give and take. He was sorry that he could not always reassure her as she deserved.

'Believe me, El, I would do anything for you, but not this. But I promise that if ever Leonada's son comes to this court and swears to me his allegiance, I will give him land and enough to live on. Other than that, he must make his own way in life, as others must do. I doubt that with the given name "Aethelred" that he will continue with a Viking life or that, knowing his background, Anlaf will want him among his crew.'

Edmund countered the arguments in his own head, to please Elgiva. Of course, Anlaf in Dublin would allow Aethelred, the grandson of Aethelred of Mercia, to be part of his merciless army.

Who would be a better candidate as the new ruler of England than Aethelred, puppet-king for the Viking hordes? Who would really be in charge of the treasure, taxes and land, destroying the centuries of Christian rule built up by the dynasty of Wessex? A great sea of darkness would cover the land again as it had done during Alfred's rule. Anlaf might even take the throne for himself. He looked at his wife. The crying had stopped, but her head was on his chest, waiting for hope. She was such a sensitive soul. She was right to be generous, magnanimous, full of piety, but his was a responsibility to more than the urgings of Christian teaching. He had to use practical sense, a king's antennae. Leofa, likeable though he was, and his brood, must remain where they were. There were troubles enough to be taken care of elsewhere. Anlaf and Wulfstan had escaped capture in Leicester. Anlaf had since professed to wish to be a Christian convert. Dunstan had urged him to allow him to be baptised. Could he trust Anlaf, or Dunstan's judgement, for that matter?

'I will do my best for the Mercian family,' Edmund reassured his wife, stroking her head again.

Reassurance; it was a useful tool in diplomacy. The gullible would take heart at any number of acceptable statements. Give them what they want to hear. As weak as women, many of the nobles and some diplomats were. Sympathy was another means of placation, of buying time. It need not mean compliance to another's will. He looked at his wife. She was sleeping.

For the rest of that night, Edmund did not.

Cheddar Palace, September 944

ANOTHER LAD HAD gone to the gallows, another poor boy, for the theft of a woodworking tool. Elgiva felt that she must speak out before she left the mortal coil. She had survived the summer; the fresh fruits and herbs of the land had perhaps sustained her. In the early autumn she seemed to have more strength in her body, more fire in her soul. She felt restored.

They were merciless, those thegns who were judges, bloodthirsty. Her soft, abbey-sheltered heart was horrified. They seemed to apply justice as if it was endowed by a witch or a monster. For petty crimes a man could be made a slave; for small crimes a child, unbearded, might be hung, or a limb removed. Elgiva's young boys had committed worse misdemeanours than many of these condemned creatures. Should they be admonished and taught better behaviour, she wondered? Should they be humiliated, or, like some of these condemned children, made to pitifully beg for their lives? A lighter sentence would be to become another man's chattel, to go about chained or limbless. Did some of these truncated hands and feet, symptoms of the disease of criminality which the lawmakers insisted they were, become playthings of a wretched reliquary maker? Any bone, animal or human, could be wrapped up in silk and gold. Through a shining crystal glowed parts, torn away, of an illustrious former bishop or hermit. Come, worship and lay your pence in the dish bedside it, they told the poor. Touch it and you will be healed. That body part, so revered in its new casing, could have been the means of livelihood for the criminal who took the loaf. Never steal from the church; it would have its revenge. It would take your finger, your hand, your liver, your lights, and turn them into gold, for itself.

Would it have your head? Perhaps, after what it called a "just death". Would it carve you into small pieces and distribute you to far dark corners of multifaceted church altars throughout the land, there to attract the attentions of the crazed devoted?

These were Elgiva's thoughts. The prospect of death makes some bold. Her status as queen, while Eadgifu roamed the court like a lion, guaranteed her little say in the world of men. Eadgifu was wrong to insist that she was her equal. They were just words to make her feel better. There was something ruthless and pitiless about her mother-in-law, but Elgiva had some powers still; she gave thanks that Edmund would hear her when they were alone; he rarely turned his anger on her when she talked to him about faith. God's ways were not the same as the Church's. She had concluded lately that it had too much influence over men's lives. Edmund had changed since his experience at the Gorge. He insisted it must be so. She recalled what he had said to her the night before.

'Look around you, Elgiva. The kingdom is divided into two powers. The church and state go hand in hand. It has been so, a balance which our dynasty has come to respect, and one which I must support. We are the halves which stabilise the nation; it is why this family must play the game. Athelstan set the rules; I have upheld them.'

'The game. And playing! This is not playing. In war men die, women must submit, children must inherit their father's misdeeds while they are still ignorant. But these are not times of war. Your court, Edmund, condemns to slavery or death the criminal, sometimes the child, who with the slightest misdemeanour offends its rigid rules, a court attended by the so-called merciful, yet I say merciless masters of the church as well as the less educated. They are more forgiving, it seems to me.'

'What case are you thinking of, Elgiva? Do you have sympathy for some filthy swineherd who has offended his master?'

'I do have a case in mind, which I am particularly anxious about.'

Edmund turned over in the marriage bed. He could barely see his wife but he could feel her trembling with emotion. There would be no rest until she had spoken. He told himself to be patient. It was only sleep, after all and that could be restored. He settled into a comfortable position, an arm behind his head. He could guess what was coming. It was the same old sore.

'I have had sight of another letter.' Elgiva paused. There was no reply, but her husband was not asleep. She was accustomed to the altered breathing. She waited for the first puff of anger, but it did not come.

Restraining his annoyance, Edmund waited. He understood the power of the written word. Nonna had received a letter from Leofa. He, or Gwladys, must have shown it to Elgiva. The secrets had surfaced again. But Elgiva had gained one ear of her husband, in the darkness of their room. He owed her that. Perhaps the letter was not what he feared.

'Go on.'

'It is about Leofa.'

Edmund groaned and restrained himself from crashing his arm down on the bed cover. He let his arm drop quietly and embraced the thigh of his wife, gave her a small pinch.

'Ouch.'

'I am aware that Leofa wants to travel to Wessex again. I warn you, do not speak of him to me, or to anyone else.'

Elgiva ignored Edmund's warning. 'He writes that he wishes to return to assist you, if he can, with the growing threat of the Dublin Vikings. You know he is being housed by Anlaf at the Black Pool.'

'Him and his family.'

'He petitioned once before to return, when your counsellors said "no".'

'I do not forget such things. He had just taken flight across the sea at that stage. A man must suffer the consequence of his actions. He cannot expect to undermine the will of the court. I admit that Leofa had his uses, but I have grown used to not hearing his deep voice in the poetry performed at the feasts. No-one is indispensable.'

'It is many years since he left Wessex. You forget how much you once loved him, and that your brother Athelstan held him in high esteem, too.'

Emund sighed. 'Well, what does he want?'

'To return, alone.'

'Not with the missing princess and her brood, then?'

'He says not. He says Egil Skallagrimsson will vouch for his complete loyalty to you and to Wessex.'

Another sigh. So, there had been contact between Egil and Leofa. Not surprising, since they were both born of the Viking line. Had Egil been in conversation with his wife about this matter? How much could he trust anyone, his wife included? The Icelander had so far proved loyal. He had fought on the English side against his Viking brothers at Brunanburh. Without him it would be difficult to understand the mind and language of the northerners. He had replaced Leofa as a go-between.

'What about the children, that boy and girl who were born to Leonada?'

'I know what you fear. They are not your enemies, husband, I am convinced of it. Leofa was wronged. You know he was ousted because of his liaison with Leonada, and that, to me, was not fair. And there was something, I heard, about a head being stolen. Gwladys said...'

The arm thumped down. She had gone too far. This meddling by wives was something Athelstan never had to deal with, sisters yes, but never a woman in his bed, haranguing him. Edmund threw back the cover and curtain and jumped from the bed. Firelight fell onto a soft shoulder. There she was, his wife, holding the missive itself. He snatched it from her. Elgiva sank back, pulling the cover over her upper half, looking at the naked body of the man she had been chosen to accompany on this regal path. Was he a bad man? No. Was he good? No. He was a man. In the morning he would again be a king, collected and cool. Meanwhile she had patience. He had never yet hit her.

'Do you not understand, wife, the threat that Leofa and his transgression, infecting the House of Mercia has become? He has a son. A son who could directly threaten your two sons. He is a Viking and has a Viking mind. A pirate mind.'

She was not yet afraid. 'So is Egil, but you trust him.'

'That is different. He is a well-paid warrior. He has connections.'

'So has Leofa, but of a different kind.'

'Enemies!'

'Then he should be of more use to you. Read the letter.'

'How did this article reach you?'

'Never mind that for now.'

'Give it to me. If Nonna has been speaking to you...you know that only he and Dunstan know of this business. Your mother and mine were not party to this.' In frustration, Edmund thrust with his arm, killing an invisible force.

'No, Eadwig overheard something...You do not mean it. No....I...'

Edmund easily snatched the letter from his wife. He took a candle into the washing area of their room and lit it. He shook the parchment in anger. Why did Elgiva not see the threat to him and his family? Why must a woman's sense of fairness require a softer approach to crime and its consequences? He read. What he saw as he read was the red-haired figure of Leofa reciting epic poems by the firelight at Frome many years before. He recalled the admiration he had as a boy for this eloquent man. But this was the opponent he had, since then, been taught to hate. By whom? When did this conversion take place? He was not easily swayed, he believed. Or perhaps, without Athelstan's guiding word, he was truly a weak character, the "golden boy" in name only, persuaded to like and hate by others? His mother and Dunstan seemed to stand at either ear, whispering to him.

The letter was brief and clear. It asked for his wife to intercede for Leofa and not to show him, her husband, the letter but to destroy it. It had been written by a fluent, educated hand. It begged for forgiveness and to be allowed to return to England. The style was not Leofa's. Elgiva had been hoping to stir his sympathy for his old companion. It was by a woman, the princess and hopeful mother of kings, of Mercia.

Edmund, for the first time, moved menacingly towards his wife and clutched the arm which had held the letter. She must learn her lesson. There was a yelp which became muffled by bedclothes.

In the morning, the queen lay alone in the bedchamber. Elgiva did not care to reveal her face to the court or to her family. She held her wriggling sons close to her. She would recover in time from the bruising but her heart had had more than its share of distress. She would go to Charlton late in the day, when Edmund was busy. Would she try to take the children? Edgar, perhaps, as he was so young. Eadwig, she would have to leave with his grandmother. Wessex could not do without its heir. "Earwig," his father, his own father, now dubbed him.

She felt weak. What little time was left to her she would spend with her mother and at her abbey on the hill. Earwig must be left to his fate.

944. In this year king Edmund brought all Northumbria under his sway, and drove out two kings, Anlaf Sihtricson and Ragnald Guthfrithson.

Anglo-Saxon Chronicle.

Nonna's Diary, Shaftesbury Abbey, December 944

THE SHORT DAYS of the Christmas season were upon us. The trees below the abbey dripped rain tears onto the hillside, gathering in the streams below. The air was sodden, the nation wept. I, Nonna, with my illustrious compatriots Dunstan and Aethelwold, attended the funeral of a queen, the saintly Elgiva. Her husband, returned from his successful battles in the north, led the mourners along the nave of the abbey church. He nursed a bandaged sword arm.

Bells rang; nuns sang as the coffin was borne to its resting place near the high altar. Standing erect near Edmund and his young sons, the two grandmothers, copiously wimpled in fine black linen, bore relic caskets. These would be given to the abbey for permanent display near the shrine which would be erected in honour of the young, dead, woman.

'I don't understand how they manage to die so young...' Dunstan was shocked by the demise of so pretty and congenial a royal person. 'But then, she was genuinely good....'

I was close enough to Aethelwold to hear his reply: 'Not enough faith.'

Aethelwold's opinion of women was never high; unlike Dunstan, he had never been tempted to marry, or if he had, it had gone badly.

I had to remind my friends. 'She was saintly in life, and I and others have been having dreams about her...'

Aethelwold pursed his lips. 'Your sort of dream won't make her a saint. Besides, she was weak. She tried to undermine Edmund. I had to have words with him'.

Aethelwold turned to Dunstan, his face away from mine, but years of experience have taught me to pick up whispers as well as nuances in speech.

'She was trying to prise Edmund away from my teaching. It was enough trouble getting him away from his mother. I believe she would have preferred a different tutor for her grandchildren.'

We looked across the aisle to where the royal family stood. The coffin was lowered onto a bier before the altar. There stood Eadgifu, a tall figure in her high pattens, next to a shorter woman, her daughter, a nun from Winchester's Nunnaminster. The queen-mother was distinctive from the other female mourners by the number and magnificence of shining bracelets and rings on her hands.

'Have they found a replacement for Elgiva?' I was not told such things, but I took an interest in royal family matters; it would be as well to be forewarned who to avoid, who to flatter.

Dunstan, who was nearest to me, was the most knowledgeable. It was a long time since he himself had dreamed of marriage with the highest in the land. He kept me informed of intimate matters when I asked. 'They say that Edmund has his eye on a girl called Aethelflaed'.

'Another one? Can't they find one with a different name? We are aware how it ended with Aelfflaed, Edward's queen.'

'They will rename her, if necessary.'

'Where does she come from?'

'Damerham.'

'Where is that?'

'Idiot. Fordingbridge in Hampshire.'

'Ah, an Alfred connection, I remember it now. Didn't he leave the family there something in his will?'

'You have got there in the end. Now hush, Nonna. Remember where you are. Turn away from me, and let go of my mantle. I must maintain my straight face, as must you.'

That is what I love about Dunstan, his knowledge, his authority. We complement each other. He sees that I have no ambition. His personal secret, his lost love, is safe with me, as are all the other secrets. Such is life at the court of Wessex. We know too much about each other, but there is trust.

On the following day, three miracles, three healings, took place at Shaftesbury. Sainthood for the dead queen soon followed. It was hard for her noisy young sons to comprehend.

They made sure of her legacy as a saint after she died, not at childbirth, but of a malaise related to it. She had survived two births, those of her sons, Eadwig and Edgar and thus had done her duty to the monarchy. Her body had been sacrificed for the greater good; it was only right that she should be canonised as recompense. She would live forever in the holy realms with the other great ones. She would be in the company of Radegund, of Aldhelm, with whom she could converse. She might retain all her parts in one place, though that could never be guaranteed.

York Minster, May 945

S HAFTS OF DAYLIGHT streamed down from the nave windows to the tiled floor, where an old man was busy with his broom. The throne of Archbishop Wulfstan, high in the choir, was, unusually, occupied. It was a place where the middle-aged cleric could guarantee to be left alone to think. The old minster was little visited and in need of a thorough cleaning, more than the threaded whiskers of the old man's brush could hope to achieve. Wooden pallets and straw littered the interior; mice scurried around columns. A lazy ginger cat lay asleep beneath a lectern. A butt of water had been tipped over where it had been propped up at an altar; the stench of ale, soaked into the straw, along with the aroma of pigs and chickens, not infrequent visitors to the nave, drew comparison with the streets of the once Roman town outside. A trader was yelling out to passers-by on the steps by the open west door. Another cat hunched and waggled its behind near the nave altar, ready to pounce on one of the audacious rodents which had made their home inside the Anglo-Saxon church.

Wulfstan sighed. What went on without the city walls and in some cases within them, was not his concern. Woden, Thor, animals, whatever. They could get on with it, as long as he could mind the business of the church in the places left to him. He must make best use of the time he was allowed within the minster to reaquaint himself with his archbishopric and the duties attached to it. The Norse ruled here, now. There was conflict, confusion. He was a Northumbrian, appointed by Athelstan many years before, to report insurrection, to give alms to the people, to keep them in order, but in these days he had to play fiddle to two kings: Edmund and the self-proclaimed king of York, the pirate Ragnald. It was bad enough that he had to do, or pretend to do, the bidding of a Christian king. It was much worse than that; Ragnald, who was a born-again pagan, demanded the lion's share of his religious and political involvement. The kings of Wessex and of York, gateway to the Scandinavian world, were both young, angry men, ready to inflict damage on those who did not act as they would wish. Instructions came from Winchester by pigeon, but Ragnald, in effect the ruler in the north, had to be appeased. He was the nearer in physical presence. For Wulfstan there was no contest, as far as skins and noses were concerned. The archbishop's survival and that of the minster were linked. If he could find a way to placate both sets of kings, the building might yet return to its former glory and he might recover this throne to use it in its intended manner. A cat could catch and eat the vermin; his position was not impossible, or unenjoyable. He had become used to subterfuge, to saying what people wanted to hear. He could lie with the best of them. Saint Wilfrid of Ripon was with him.

His hand wrapped itself around one of the wooden bench ends. The familiar carved shape of an old woman carrying a heavy burden reassured a part of him and stimulated ideas. Old Edith, he called her, the peasant weighed down by the inevitable woes of life.

'Well, Old Edith, have I done the right thing? They want me in Wessex to dance attendance before Edmund and bow to that ghastly mother of his. Dunstan would have me prance in embarrassment. I can see him now with a hot metal tool, ready for singeing the nose, hands, toes of anyone who disagrees with him. Aethelwold, that unctious fool, would dearly love to see me in pain. What is it, Edith, that makes them hate us northerners? There is an answer which is shown in the faces and bodies of those around me. There are kings here, as good as any other, born of cold fjord waters, bolstered by their belief in beasts which accompany them on the necks of their ships, made bold by ale and self belief, boys with pirates for parents, in this place. The southern kings are no different; they have merely been longer at it.'

Wulfstan could indulge himself for this half-hour but no more. The first few minutes were spent in venomous contemplation. Old Edith made no reply, but that, Wulfstan thought, was one voice less with which he had to deal. As the one candle near him burned down, it would be time to reconstruct his plans. He would soon return to Ripon, his home since the Norse take-over of his palace in York.

His plans had been indecisive, deliberately so. Who could plainly sail through this illogical arrangement whereby the pagan king of Jorvik ruled in Northumbria while he, Wulfstan, endeavoured to represent the Pope in the long established Christian and Anglo-Saxon country? He had not intended to be duplicitous to his former colleagues in Winchester; going against the flow could mean removal from his archbishopric. On his inauguration in 931 by Athelstan he had vowed to do the will of the state of England, but over the years the nation had been broken up, mended and broken again by the successful cooperation of northern forces. The pottery jug which was Britain had been glued together, but the ominous and fragile cracks were plain for all to see.

Wessex would not appreciate his point of view; if he had tried to put it, which he had learned not to do, he would have been exiled as a traitor. As it was, he was regarded with suspicion by both sides, though he had acted in good faith for both. Was he a puppet archbishop? As a Northumbrian, his sympathies lay with the northern kingdom, but he had discomfort in the presence of fake Christians, Vikings who had made promises which they clearly did not intend to keep, if they had ever understood them. His fellow Northumbrians had been, until recently, ruled by their own Saxon king, Ealdred. They had a greater fear of Ragnald: eighty years before, King Aella had been bestowed the generous gift of protracted death by blood-eagle by the Jorvik incomers. The violence of their religion could resurface at any time and take aim at any one, king or priest.

Wulfstan had learned long ago that compromise and pretence had to be maintained; in his letters to Winchester he had to lie; he was at any rate forced to. When summoned south, he had to show that he was willing to go, but his rulers in Jorvik regarded his crossing the Tamworth line into Mercia as act of treason; so he often pleaded illness or mud on the roads.

Which was what he had sent by winged messenger as his excuse on this occasion, the feast of St Augustine. Edmund would have to do without him; Skallagrimsson had received his instructions and would act, or not, for Ragnald or for Anlaf. Leofa would be persuaded, for the sake of his family in Dublin, to assassinate Edmund; there would be, if the plan worked, uproar through the land. England would dissolve, Jorvik would displace Winchester as the major city of the nation and Britain would become a part of the empire of Scandinavia. Northumbria would be at its heart, a trading nation surpassing others, a pagan empire ripe for mission. Saint Wilfrid would have relished the challenge, and so did he.

That would be the time when he might persuade Ragnald, or whoever took over the state, to become a Christian in the true sense. Peace and prosperity might be achieved, once the ambitions of Wessex and Winchester had been quelled. There would have to be a bloody period of cleansing of the Wessex dynasty, that was clear, but others would do that work. There were many who were willing. Mercian assassins were two a penny.

There was the sound of a chair being scraped along the stone floor nearby. A figure slipped into a canon's seat next to his. Ragnald was not fastidious in his personal cleanliness; Wulfstan could smell the last meal's animal grease in a beard.

'Good afternoon, archbishop. I trust you are not getting too comfortable in that old seat of yours?'

Wulfstan was not easily startled. He had played the loyal supporter to many on opposing sides and was ready with his smile. He looked sideways at the newcomer.

'I am always ready to do the Lord's bidding.' Wulfstan
patted Old Edith's head and rose. She had confirmed his short-
term course of action. 'I have been meaning to come to see you,
Ragnald. My wife wishes to invite you to supper in Ripon. Can
you come in three days time? We shall have a service for Wilfred
followed by a supper for Northumbrian landowners. There will be
ten courses to make up for your time spent in church.'

'Ah, you have noticed my piety leaves something to be desired.
I shall be delighted to ride out with my women and brothers. I take
it the Ripon hostelry will be able to accommodate us as before?'

'Of course, or if you prefer, if there are not too many of you
and you are not too rumbustuous, you may like to stay with me in
my home.'

'I should like very much to see what your pilgrim's quarters
are like and to view the relics of your favourite saint. You will enjoy
showing them to me. I might even give you a little gift,' Ragnald
suddenly recalled something, 'I have a box of your King Aella's
parts which I have discovered recently. Perhaps you would like to
add him to your collection- to bolster the Northumbrian defence
against us Vikings, you understand?' Ragnald smiled. He was
unassailable.

Wulfstan laughed. He could be more honest with a Viking
than with a Wessex king and his mother. Ragnald was easier to
talk to than Anlaf, who himself was approachable. They were both
potential converts to his faith, if God gave him time. The family
of Wessex had forked tongues, compared to these two; southern
women meddled. Mothers had to be dealt with; that was the
trouble with having child-kings. Aelfflaed and her pathetic son
Edwin had introduced him to that particular dislike, many years
before.

The body parts which were left of King Aella of Northumbria
would be a welcome addition to his collection of relics. Perhaps St
Cuthbert in Chester-le-Street, together with whatever remained in
the north of St Oswald, would help to restore a sense of pride and

power to the English inhabitants. Something needed to be done; Norse or Danish was fast becoming their preferred language.

St Oswald. There hung a tale. The Cuthbert monks had been dealing in relics for years.There should be something about Athelstan's visit to them which could be used against the Wessex contingent when the time came. Gloucester should not house Oswald. The relics of the murdered king belonged in the north. He had quarrelled with Athelstan over this. With Edmund humiliated or gone, a revelation could clinch the north's view of its right to rule. He would be able to restore Oswald's relics, ensuring that all the most effficacious saints were once again where they ought to be.

'Ragnald, Old Edith here,' he patted the figure, 'has been giving me a dream, a pleasant one. Eoforwic could yet rise again, or Jorvik or York, it wouldn't matter what it was called; it will be the centre of a new northern empire. England was once a mere dream of Alfred's, but Vikingaland is also possible.'

He did not add his own personal dream: that he, Wulfstan, could be a missionary archbishop, changing the lives and souls of millions, like Wilfred, centuries before. Revered like Wilfred, sainted like Wilfred, rescued from purgatory, like Wilfred.

Wulfstan, with his invitation to Ragnald, had cast his lot in with the unkempt but powerful ruler, for the time being, of the most vibrant and wealthy township in Britain, centre of the Viking world. Ragnald's vitality was undeniable. A pirate king indeed. Together, and with a pincer movement by Anlaf in Dublin, they would win a place in history. It was clear; England would become a Viking land, ruled by a Norse dynasty. Worse had happened before.

945. In this year king Edmund ravaged all Strathclyde, and ceded it to Malcolm, king of Scots, on the condition that he would be his fellow worker both by sea and land.

Anglo-Saxon Chronicle.

Winchester, Autumn 945

HERSFIG STUMBLED OVER the edge of a knotty rug which had once contained the living flesh of a beaver. A nearby shaggy lurcher, still within its own skin, took fright and jumped vertically out of its slumber, knocking a brass display dish off its three legs. The tray Hersfig was carrying, of wooden drinking vessels, clattered on the floor. Beakers rolled under couches and chairs. He chased one under Bica's cushioned armchair, his 'throne'. Bica was in it, anticipating the array of food which was about to be brought in and lazily reviewing his opinion of the guests expected. He stopped picking his teeth with a small dagger.

'Hoy, Mr Clumsy, watch what you're doing!' Bica lifted his legs in an exaggerated display of thighs and grinned through them at the unfortunate Hersfig.

Between them they had become a limited, but practical, team supporting their lord, Eadred, as deputy heir to the throne. They were the full extent of his personal assistance; they were all that he wanted. He had tried others, but their reluctance to serve had become a hindrance to the privacy-loving prince; Eadred was not like other men. Today was unusual; guests were to be welcomed into his private living quarters. Apart from the rug and the dog, most of the detritus of the room, including bottles and cups of a variety of remedies and potions, had been moved aside or packed away in cupboards. Some vigorous pot plants had been retained, standing in corners and cascading down from a high windowsill. Dust motes from Hersfig's recent attempt at cleaning filled the air like smoke, dancing in the beams of sunlight.

Hersfig, in his mid-twenties, had reluctantly put aside his dreams of becoming an armed cavalier. As general factotum to the king's brother, his income and livelihood were guaranteed. It was a comfortable life and he could take Bica's ribbing, though that had become more annoying of late. The little man they had rescued from drowning occupied a special place in Eadred's heart which he was too well aware of; Eadred would respond to Bica's directives and suggestions more often than to his brother's, or his mother's. Eadred sat on chairs, but this comfortable throne of the little man was his, and his alone, and he seldom left it. The lurcher was the only other creature to try to sit there, and it was tolerated, but only for the short moments that Bica had, of bodily necessity, to move.

Hersfig grabbed the escaping and now rolling beaker and examined it for old food particles and cracks. 'Looks like the cleaning has scraped up even your royal mess, Bica. No. you needn't shift yourself,' he sighed, 'I can manage to grovel about your feet. How about getting up and taking off that three-day-old beard that looks neither one thing nor another? Your royal highness might have his looks improved. Eadred will be here soon, with the others.'

Bica grinned again, showing his age in his teeth. There had been many fine things to eat since he had become Eadred's companion and his girth had not yet stopped growing. He paid for his keep, though; the king's brother could not do without him. The support which Bica offered lay in his willingness to listen to Eadred's fears and in the silent night-time assays of the place corridors and grounds which he occasionally made, listening to tales other than Eadred's. Darkness and ale could loosen tongues, producing information of use to a deputy heir.

The aetheling's insecurities and worries were many. There were all the usual ones, common to everyone, of likeability, of familial dependence, of health, plus the difficult requirement of assessing and following a royal diplomatic line. Unlike his brother Edmund, he had no temper to speak of, but scooted to his private rooms and Bica, in whatever palace he happened to be in, when he felt that a row could be brewing. Whichever side Eadred took, it would be the wrong one. He had decided long ago that silence in such matters was the better course. Others could fight their battles. Once safely with Bica, who absorbed the agonies of his master like the bark of a silent oak, he would offload his complaints about the courtier or family member who had upset him. Bica would smooth his head and be the comforter which his real mother had failed to be. Edmund and his brood were the golden ones; there was something wrong with Eadred, to Eadgifu's mind, and she let it be known.

'Tell me again who we are expecting to come to lunch.' Bica might have to make a special effort for this entertainment. Eadred had said that it was important to him. Anything which happened so rarely became significant in the life of the prince. Guests were never usually greeted, by custom, in this prince's quarters, especially at Winchester, which had become his favourite bolt-hole, of late.

'I've told you before, so often, you scruffy oik.' Hersfig was not afraid of his companion of the household. Besides, Bica did share some of the private duties; the royal stool was his responsibility, and he was the royal barber and hair comber. He was careful when shaving Eadred's beard, but amiss at managing his own.

Bica enjoyed sparring with the young man. His was a good-natured, if idle, personality. His value as a listening post was enjoyed by Hersfig as well as Eadred. He knew the ambitions of both, and kept them to himself, for now. 'Well, tell me again, so I know who to upset. Things may have changed.'

'You'd better not upset anyone. Half-king will have your balls.' Hersfig slapped the rear end of Bica, which was still displayed to the room.

'Half-king? That's new. The Bear? I suppose he will still be accompanied by his side-kick Abbot Dunstan?'

'Naturally. They move about the corridors here in Winchester like lovers, like you with Eadred. Once Dunstan had been invited, Half-king had to come too.'

Bica lowered his legs. Hersfig continued to arrange the furniture to accommodate the expected guests. He opened up a large gate-leg table and arranged six chairs around it.

'How many more?' Bica pretended to be horrified by the numbers expected as knives and platters were put out on the table. Hersfig attended to some thorny roses, putting them into a green pottery vase which had been standing on the windowsill behind the plants. He had had to learn feminine skills of cleaning and cooking as well as decoration. Eadred's dietary requirements were specific. No dairy and little meat, and that had to be cut into small pieces, softened by many hours of cooking. On rare days off, though, Hersfig could enjoy more manly pursuits; he was deputy hound-master at Winchester and keeper of hunting equipment. Mostly, though, hunting was enjoyed elsewhere, at the palaces which were near the wild lands of the west. The dogs remaining in Winchester were spoilt creatures, kept mainly for show and companionship. Polishing the metalwork of antique boar spears and feeding idle hounds kept him in touch with his fellow cavaliers, most of whom had retired to become courtiers. And there were the women servants, who could appreciate his closeness to the second-in-line to the throne, and what it meant, perpetually seeking ways to infiltrate the person of the aetheling through him. Marriage was not their goal, but other prospects of influence opened when bedding an heir and their families were always keen to try them. Hersfig was not above taking some advantage of their aspirations. He put the flowers into the centre of the table. They drooped, as roses do.

'You can count. Besides Eadred, there will be, as I have said, Ealdorman Half-king, the abbot, the queen...'

'The queen-mother! You are joking?' Bica nearly fell off his chair.

'And both princes.'

'The Bear, the religious nincompoop and the boys, saints alive! And the queen! She has never set foot in here before!'

'Not in your day, Bica, but she used to come to this room, often, when it was the nursery for Edmund and Eadred, many years ago.'

'Back in old King Edward's times?' Has she not been here since then?'

'She's keen on the other palaces in the west, these days. That's where a lot of court business is done and you know, since Athelstan's day she has been increasing her involvement in that, when she is allowed to.' Hersfig finished arranging the leggy roses, which had temperamentally dropped petals, and stood back to admire his handiwork. 'There, what do you think?' He sucked his thumb.

'Did the roses attack you?' Bica got out of his chair, plumped the cushions ready for his comfortable return and moved towards the ornate doorway. 'I go, your honour. You will see me soon in my best finery. No, dog, you cannot have my seat. Wait a while and sit on the lap of the Bear, if he will allow you to, or better still, pee on the cassock of the Abbot, to show him what we think of jumped-up prelates with their pointed noses.' Bica sniffed and grinned again at Hersfig, who ignored him, shrugged and carried on with the preparations. The little man could be relied on to behave in public and would be all the more circumspect if allowed to vent his opinions in private, though he was not improving in his demeanour as he aged. A Briton could not be expected to like his Saxon conquerors, but where was the eternal gratitude owing to Eadred and himself which he had vowed? But he had

his uses. Humour, albeit based on sarcasm, was his gift and
Eadred's personal defence against pompous authoritarianism. His
dreams were less malevolent after a joke shared with Bica and his
mimicry.

A short while later Hersfig and Bica, now unbearded and with
his thick, unruly hair combed and greased, heard a commotion
in the passage beyond the door. The familiar high voice of Eadred
could be heard, accompanying the click-clack of wooden shoes,
recognisable as the queen-mother's. A gruff note of agreement to
Eadred's remark came from a heavy-treaded man who must be the
Bear, Half-king, and the light, sandalled step of a prelate scuffled
with them along the irregularly laid stone floor.

'I haven't been here for such a long time, Eadred. How
this floor used to annoy me! And still not tiled. See to it, would
you, my lord Ealdorman?' There was a tripping sound. 'My lord
Abbot, I am so sorry, your skirts will be torn.' She put an arm on
Dunstan's as he stumbled on the edge of a particularly crumbling
part of the paving.

'Not suitable for a street in the poor quarters. How do you put
up with this, my lord?' Dunstan made a mental note to divert a
small sum of money and two workmen to refloor the passage. 'No
need to act, my lord, I will take care of it.'

'Thank you, Dunstan.' Eadgifu looked round at the two young
boys who were scampering behind the adults, accompanied in the
rear, in case of any reluctance to move forward, by a single palace
guard. 'Keep up, Eadwig and Edgar. No, there are no bats in this
part of the palace. We shall soon be in the light again. Behave,
your Uncle Eadred will have special treats for you in his room.
Look, the lovely old door which I told you about.' Eadgifu stroked
the sides of the elaborately carved door to the old nursery. 'See
these creatures, Eadwig, don't they remind you of something?'

'Boar's teeth, Grandma.' Eadwig ran forward to touch the
carvings. 'And boar's heads. And bears!' He looked round at Half-
king. Was there any resemblance to the creature in him? Only the

bulk, the size and the general air of ferocity. Yes, perhaps he was reminded of the creatures of the forest. 'And look, there's a beaky, bird thing, just like Abbot Dunstan!' He looked at Dunstan, who was adjusting a sandal after stubbing his toe and tearing his hem.

'Yes, well, let us go in. Eadred, lead the way.' Eadgifu held the boys' hands and asked the guard to remain outside the door as she and the other guests entered the room.

'Treats, Uncle Eadred, where are my treats?'

'Hush, Eadwig.'

Herfsig and Bica looked at each other. They had forgotten that gifts for children might be required. They shrugged. Ignoring Eadred, the boys rushed to the lurcher, which lay decoratively on a rug in front of Bica's chair.

Eadred was pleasantly surprised by the order which Hersfig had managed to convey in his quarters. He had expected that the room would be neat, but Hersfig had dusted and cleaned well; tables had been waxed, chairs had fresh cushions, the rugs had been separated from dog-hair and worse and there was a general air of pleasant relaxation. The roses on the eating table spread a needful scent around the stone-walled room. A cheerful fire on the opposite side of the room greeted them. Opposite the fire, Hersfig and Bica, in smart attire and well-groomed, stood in attendance near the dining table. They bowed low as the adult guests, with Eadred, entered.

'Eadred, this is charming. I had no idea that this room could be so appealing. Of course, I remember all too well how you children cried and screamed when you were small, in here. There were so many of you, it was always such a noisy place. You fell down and hurt yourselves or developed illnesses in here and that rather put me off returning, once you were safely with your tutors, but perhaps they are not all bad memories.' Eadgifu walked around the room, her wooden shoes clacking on stone or drumming on rugs. Her skirts, like Dunstan's, dragged some unfixed items along the floor, revealing a small collection of dust.

Eadred had made an effort to please; this visitation would not be done often.

Hersfig, becoming aware of shortcomings in his tidying, shifted his weight. 'My Lords, my Lady, would you care to seat yourselves at the table,' he flourished his arm at the table, which was becoming delicately decorated by falling rose petals, 'and I will bring in the repast.'

Bica, with growing anxiety eyeing the lurcher and boys, which were now playing together close to his throne, began to move the chairs for the guests to sit down and to pour mead and ale.

Eadgifu put her hand ostentatiously over her beaker. Bracelets clattered on her arm. 'Not for me, thank you. Bica, is that your name?'

Bica nodded. This formidable lady was a favourite study of his, often the butt of jokes in private. Eadred shot him a warning look. 'Yes, Madam.' Bica looked back at Eadred, who sat opposite his mother, next to Half-king. I know how to behave when it is called for, he conveyed, even though I don't get much practice.

Eadgifu addressed the Bear. 'I thought you would like to see the origins of my sons, who were both born here, before you take my little Edgar away to live with you in wildest Anglia. You see what Edmund and Eadred were used to when they were children. This place was once lined with books and maps, you remember, Dunstan? So many hours of your teaching took place here. And look, there is the desk and bench which you used to scribble at, Eadred! I remember the smell of the pine; so many memories lie here. There were the beds, over in that corner beyond the fire and the little clothes locker was over there.' Eadgifu pointed to the place now occupied by Bica's chair, which dominated a corner of the room. The lurcher had jumped into it and was followed by both boys, who petted and played with it. It foamed at the mouth as it tussled with a branch from the fireside which they had found, showing its great yellow teeth. There were sounds of barking and cries of delight. The chair wobbled.

'Edgar, Eadwig, come here!' Her grandchildren were so like their father and uncle. Eadgifu could be calling to Edmund and Eadred. All blonde, all handsome, all hale. Only Eadred had the cough. In sensibility they were different, she knew. 'Eadwig, don't throw that book. Treat it with respect. That's a bible!'

Bica grabbed the dog and put it into the corridor, where it was greeted by the guard.

The boys came to the table at the sight of food being brought by Hersfig. There was hot fish broth with leeks and turnips, cheese and bread and dried fruits. Vegetables fermented and pickled with honey provided tasty supplementary accompaniments. A vegetable terrine glued together with animal fat completed the array of dishes on offer. Hersfig, in conjunction with the palace kitchen, had done well. Eadred raised a glass to his loyal supporter. Hersfig bowed and kept bringing plates of food.

'Abbot Dunstan, will you say Grace?' Eadgifu threw a warning glance at Edgar, who was about to start eating. Dunstan stood up and raised his hands towards the potted plants in the window.

'For what we are about to receive, may the Lord make us truly grateful.' He lowered his arms. Eadwig sniffed, sitting bold upright, his arms by his sides. Edgar began to eat.

'Where's the meat?' Eadwig liked to tuck in to bloody flesh and expected it at each meal. It was manly to eat animals, especially hunted creatures. 'It's not Friday, is it?' He was becoming aware of the mores of the court.

'Eadwig!' His grandmother hissed. 'You know your uncle does not eat meat unless he has to.'

Edgar looked up from his bowl of soup, spoon in hand. 'Why?'

Eadred came to the rescue of the boys, who he was fond of, especially Edgar. There he was, looking regal, sitting on several cushions to bring him almost up to the height of the adults at the table. Another second son. They had much in common. 'I cannot easily digest flesh, nephew. It makes me bilious. I find fish to be beneficial, and particularly eel, which Hersfig tells me we have today. Try it, you will like it.'

'But I want meat to make me big and strong! I don't want vegetables!' exclaimed Eadwig. He received a sharp tap on the knee from Eadgifu. The boy looked up at her, surprised and frowning.

'Fish is a vegetable, my Lord, it is true.' Dunstan sought to calm the atmosphere, which was in danger of becoming spoilt by the insistence of Edmund's heir. At seven years old, he should be learning to adjust to the requirements of his elders. Less was expected of Edgar; that would come, in time. 'Tomorrow is Friday, when we shall all eat fish and be glad of it, for Our Lord's sake, but it is good to eat vegetables often, when we can, to remind ourselves of our need for gratitude for his saving grace. Meanwhile there is cheese. Have some.' He passed a platter containing a small whole truckle along with a wooden-handled wire with which to cut it.

Eadwig glared at the cheese and waved the cutting implement close to Dunstan's nose. He let out a loud wail. 'I want meat!'

Eadgifu, thinking that a slap would do no good, tried persuasion. 'Look, Eadwig, Edgar is enjoying his eel soup. Here, take up your spoon, eat.'

Eadwig stopped crying and looked at his brother, who was unconcernedly supping and breaking bread into his broth. 'The soup is green! I shall not eat it, not even if it is supposed to make me grateful. It will make me bilious.' He shot a look at Eadred, then folded his arms and sat back, refusing to eat anything. He stared at his platter. A tear rolled down his face.

'What a strong-willed little man, you have there, Madam,' commented Half-king. 'I would not like to meet him in battle, but no doubt he will fare well in his own quarters, when he will have the roasted guinea fowl which I hear is ordered for the feast later tonight.' The Bear took up his own spoon and took a slurp of fish stew. He too would be grateful for the flesh of creatures, well cooked with spices, tonight. In the meantime, he could, unwillingly, adjust to the requirements of this second son's sanctuary. He had seen how Eadred tackled meat in public, when he had to. It was not a pleasant sight. He turned to Eadred, who, as host, had almost been forgotten, in the room's attempt to placate Eadwig. Perhaps the boy had his father's temper and could not help himself. Out of the corner of his eye, he noticed Edgar, quietly munching his soggy bread. There was the more biddable boy, as Eadred had been in his childhood. Thank goodness he would be instructing him, not the other. He looked at Dunstan, who, like Eadwig, had folded his arms, having quickly finished a small amount of food, and was now frowning at his charge. Eadwig continued to display morose determination and would eat nothing.

'Perhaps it may be best, Madam, to begin another line of conversation?' Half-king pushed his platter away and picked up a ginger cake. 'My Lord Eadred, how does the ship-building on the south coast fare?' He knew more than most of the court the exact nature of the war machine employed by the English court; he had signed many documents after hours of discussion in the witan about the price of oak planks, caulking and sails as well as manpower to make and employ the ships, but Eadred had the management of the navy and its economies as his major responsibility. He might learn something new in an update, though he supposed he would not.

Eadred, keen to lighten the mood of the meal, and aware of his mother's gaze as he revealed his competence at mundane manufacturing, gave an account of the increase in the number of ships being built, their place of manufacture and the speed of their building. Manpower was discussed in some detail, but not for long. The boys were soon restless; even Edgar had wriggled off his cushions and was now listening to the dog beyond the door, which was whining and scratching to be allowed in.

'Grandmother, can he be let in?' Edgar tugged at Eadgifu's skirt. The meal broke up, the guests moved to the fireplace, the dog was reprieved and the boys, with the dog, leapt into Bica's chair once more.

Bica, clearing away the half-eaten lunch, made a harrumphing sound of distaste, which was not lost on Hersfig or Eadred, but which they ignored. He must expect to have to adapt to others sometimes, though it might prove unwelcome and difficult. He would soon be back on his throne, giving them orders. A flagon of wine would improve his mood. By nightfall, he would be joking again.

'Your man has a nasty cough, Eadred.' Eadgifu, who had settled into a rocking chair with an intricately embroidered back, allowed herself to comment on Bica's evident dislike of the situation. 'Have you tried medicine on him? I could recommend something which could relieve him...perhaps a good dose of fresh air might improve his chest?' She cast a look at Bica, who had a pile of platters balanced on both hands and was exiting the door to take them to the wash house. 'How old is he, anyway?' She stared at Bica's feet. He was wearing the distinctive moorish leather shoes which she had given Eadred for the previous Christmas festivities.

Bica would have been prepared to answer for his age to the queen-mother, but knew that he was not required to. Her curiosity, and the level of medicinal advice she would proffer Eadred for him, depended on her estimation of his age. He seemed young, to her short-sighted eyes. But how young?

This had been his problem, when, years before, he had been stolen and taken by Cornish slave-traders from his home in Devon, before being washed up and saved by Eadred and Hersfig. He appeared much younger than he really was. His black wayward hair should, according to his years, have turned grey by now. His stature, though grown portly, was like a pre-pubescent eleven-year-old's. Eadwig was not much shorter than him. He only displayed his age when he ate and when he laughed, when his teeth, having benefited from several years of imbibing honeyed figs showed their extensive decay. He continued out of the door, his ears burning and beginning to hate, if he had not before, the grand dame of the court, with her gold earrings and high-heeled shoes. She was no taller than him, no younger than him, but what sway she had in this place! Some thought it witchcraft, and he was inclined to this view. The power of giving birth to two generations of kings had gone to her head. Females had uncanny means of persuasion. What did he have? Only the ear of the second son, but perhaps it would be enough to see him to a comfortable grave.

After the conversation about the navy had been exhausted, Eadgifu remarked on the chair in which she sat, which had been her old nursing chair, and described her memories of others who had used the chairs in which Dunstan, Eadred and Half-king now sat. These antiques had been features of Winchester palace for years, outside the nursery as well as in it. As time went on, their former positions of grandeur in the main halls had been demoted. They had been replaced by modern equivalents, which were, in Half-king's view, more decorative but less comfortable. Dunstan's chair, she could remember being told by her husband Edward, was once in Alfred's father's palace. She pointed out the difference in the style of the craftsman which an earlier century had wrought. She then introduced the topic which she knew would engage the boys and which she wanted them to hear in detail. It had been a plan which they had made in the corridor before entering the room, knowing that the attention span of at least one child would be difficult to maintain.

'Tell us about the battle of Brunanburh, my Lord Half-king.' It was time the boys should know some of the history of their line. 'Come and sit on Uncle Half-king's knee, Edgar.' She indicated that he should launch quickly into his tale, before the boys were completely engrossed by playing with the dog. 'Eadwig, come and sit by Uncle Athelstan. And look, Abbot Dunstan has a ginger cake for you.'

Edgar climbed onto the large knee of the Bear and was enfolded by an arm. Eadwig jumped off Bica's chair but, passing by Dunstan, he snatched the cake held out for him and sat on the floor near Eadred. Bica moved sharply across the room to rescue his seat, taking the dog roughly by its scruff and putting it again outside the door, where it was addressed in surprise by the guard.

'He is not my uncle. The other one was.' Eadwig was aware of his father's brother Athelstan, who had been king before him. The Bear may be a mighty warrior, but bloodline was all.

Eadgifu ignored this. It was a weary battle each day to persuade Eadwig to behave.

The boys knew of the Bear's first-hand experience of the great battle against the Vikings in the north, but had never had the opportunity, so far, of hearing the gory details. Eadgifu and Dunstan had hoped that the great man would be able to make as good a story-teller as a scop; it was important that the boys should come to value this right-hand man to Edmund, and that Edgar, especially, who was soon to enter his household in East Anglia, would appreciate the fatherly qualities as well as the diplomatic accomplishments of his new guardian. The boys would for the first time be separated. It would be for their own good. Edgar should not learn to emulate his wayward older brother's ways. For Eadwig, it was too late to be trained in another household; Dunstan and Aethelwold would have to do what they could. Besides, it was important that the first heir should remain in central Wessex.

Half-king placed his sword on the rug by the fire and invited Eadwig and Edgar to examine it. They both eagerly played with the weapon, running their fingers along both scabbard and blade, while the great Bear regaled them with his tale of how this very same sword had taken the lives of several men of Northumbria, as well as Vikings, at the famous battle. A shortened version, without poetic elaboration, took the group back in time and with vivid descriptions of blood and gore, and satisfied the requirement for violence in their minds. The boys asked for more, but Eadgifu was keen to return to the sewing rooms and for the boys to their lessons with Dunstan and Aethelwold. They were not anxious to go.

'Uncle Eadred,' Eadwig suddenly remembered that boys were not the only children of his grandmother, having noticed a doll on a shelf. 'Did you share this room and the beds with your sisters?'

'Eadwig!' Eadgifu had been trying to put the matter of sex, which he had recently become curious about, out of the young boy's mind. The sisters and their part in the daily life at court were beginning to be a favourite theme of Eadwig's. He was an imaginative and emotional child. He had no sisters of his own.

'That's alright, Mother. Eadwig, there were quite a few of us, boys and girls, here and we were all instructed in polite manners by Uncle Dunstan here, amongst others.' He looked for help from Dunstan.

'He's not my uncle, either. Uncle Eadred, why have you not married?' Eadwig had opened a door which the adults would rather have shut.

Dunstan took up the responsibility of steering the boy, needing to show his authority. 'Many men do not choose to marry, Eadwig. Priests do not. I have not.'

'But some priests do,' Half-king muttered under his breath, but audibly enough to be heard by Eadwig. Dunstan looked alarmed. 'But they need to pray for all our souls. That is their prime concern and why we so value them.' Half-king looked again at Dunstan. Had he done enough to correct the prince?

Eadwig was warming to his theme. 'Yes, some priests do, so why did you not marry the lady who you had to do with in Kent that Father told me about? Your girlfriend?' Eadwig looked from the priest to his uncle for help, but none was forthcoming. 'Ah, but Uncle, you don't have a woman to your bed, either, do you?'

It was time to box an ear. The boy yelled. If only that would suffice to quell the rebellion in this heir's nature. Eadwig kicked the chair in which Dunstan sat, displaying aggression of a level which the guests had not seen before. The dog barked, thinking a game had begun. The last rose petals dropped suddenly onto the table top in a dramatic comment on the disruption of proceedings.

Eadgifu held the screaming child by the arm and dragged him down the corridor. He shouted back at the embarrassed group.

'Father says women control your life. He says a man should not marry! Why? Grandma, let me goooo!' He was taken back to the schoolroom. Dunstan followed. Eadred and Half-king looked at each other and at the heap of petals. The meal had not been a success.

But Eadwig, still on the great Bear's knee, looked up at Half-king's face, his eyes shining.

The Black Sheep

A DAY LATER the sun, after two weeks of incessant rain, poured in through the Winchester schoolroom window. Dunstan, who had been prevented from returning to Glastonbury by the weather, decided that two days might allow floodwaters to recede and mud to dry. He would meantime continue to supervise Eadwig's studies. In particular, the question of the legitimacy and purpose of matrimony and the position of women in the family's business needed to be broached. Eadwig was old enough; he had demonstrated that at the meeting with Eadred. Erroneous ideas had to be quashed, before they could take hold. Clarity was needed. Eadgifu could have instructed him, but she was a woman. Tomorrow, as long as the floods cleared, he would travel westwards. New building work had to be observed, the accounts settled. His aged patron near the abbey needed to see him; she was approaching death and wanted his prayerful presence. There had been a promise of a substantial gift to the abbey in her will, but these things could not be taken for granted. If necessary, he could rewrite it for her.

'Eadwig, come over here to the window. I have something to show you.' Dunstan feigned a pedagogic interest in the birdlife which danced on the grassy walk below.

'But I am busy.' Eadwig was hunched over a large piece of waste parchment on the floor. Red chalk powder surrounded him and covered his hands. Once it had been a map; now it was covered with a large, colourful scrawl.

'There is a bird I wish to show you. You may be able to identify it for me.' Dunstan had often appealed, successfully, to his pupil's assumed superior knowledge.

Eadwig threw his chalk onto the floor, scrambled to his feet with a shrug and sigh and made his way slowly to join Dunstan at the window. 'Well, my lord abbot, which bird? There are several.'

With physical movement towards him achieved, Dunstan could attempt now to hold the attention of this precocious, but awkward, seven-year-old. 'That one.' Dunstan pointed to a crow which was surveying the path for leatherjackets. He attempted to show affection by placing a hand on the boy's shoulder. Eadwig shook it off.

'It's a blackbird.'

'No, look again.'

'Yes, it is, it's a big black bird. Just like you!' Eadwig pointed to Dunstan's nose. 'Beaky!'

'The bird is a crow.' Dunstan dusted the front of his robe. The cheek of the lad was becoming intolerable. 'I have to explain something to you, Eadwig.'

'My lord, to you!'

'My lord Eadwig, yes, you are an aetheling of Wessex indeed.' Dunstan frowned. Eadwig smiled.

'So like his father,' Dunstan murmured, looking out of the window. 'Here is a story of your grandfather's grandfather, which you will like. You have heard of Offa, the former king of Mercia?' Eadwig stopped smiling and looked serious. Dunstan had his attention. Offa was notorious. Family history, and in particular its glories in battle, the bloodier the better, caught his imagination and, for a half-an-hour, or more, perhaps, Eadwig would listen to what Dunstan had to say. He continued. 'You mentioned yesterday your father's sisters and asked why your uncle and I did not have wives. You know already that your uncle Athelstan the king had no wife. It is understandable that you should wonder about this. As one destined to be king one day, yourself, you might consider it right to know the law and practice of the family. You will be expecting one day to be betrothed, no doubt, and would like to be prepared. And there is the question of your brother. Should he remain unmarried, as Eadred has done? Of course, priests in these days are being urged to reject wives, if they have one. Chasity is a strict rule of the Benedictine order. We can no longer have priests operating in our monasteries who have not espoused this rule.'

Eadwig pouted. 'Of course I have heard of Offa. He ate human flesh. What does "espoused" mean?'

'No, he did not. Think, my lord. Espoused, spouse, married. To be loyal to a law.'

'Oh, yes, go on. Espoused. I like that word.'

Dunstan continued. They sat together, looking inward to the room, on the sill-seat, the boy at one end, Dunstan at the other. 'Are you warm enough, my lord?' Dunstan endeavoured to arrange complete comfort for the boy. He produced a cake, kept back from the day before, and offered it to Eadwig. He took it and began nibbling.

'Thanks. I am warm. Go on. What about Offa.'

'Your great, great grandfather Ecgberht, he of the stone of that name at Brixton, you remember we pass by it on our way to Cheddar...'

'Yes, yes.'

'You know that he became king of Wessex, the first in your line, removing the Mercians from their sphere of influence in the south.'

'And they have never got over it!'

The boy had grasped some concepts early, thought Dunstan, but he could do without the constant interruptions. He produced another cake from inside his black outer clothing. Eadwig was curious to know if he had more. 'No. No more. Now listen and I will tell you about Offa's beautiful daughter. Or you can return to the mathematical principles which I note you have been neglecting of late.' The boy sat up, chewing on his second cake.

'Go on. I will be good.'

Dunstan stretched his arms and pulled his cape around

him, choosing his words carefully to suit Eadwig's age and understanding. 'The king of Mercia, who also ruled in Wessex before Ecgberht, was called Beorhtric. He had a wife, the daughter of the mighty king Offa, called Eadburh. She was a great beauty, but a tyrant like her father, her viciousness learned at his knee. As a wife, she tried to rule in her husband's stead. She poisoned courtiers in order to get her way and even killed her own husband by mistake, when trying to remove one of his companions.'

'She sounds as though she was a black sheep?'

'Indeed.'

'What happened to her?'

'After killing King Beorhtric she fled to Charlemagne, along with a large part of the royal treasure. She hoped to remarry a king or prince in Frankia. It is said that she asked Charlemagne's son to marry her. He wanted her for himself, it is said, and took it amiss that she chose the younger man.'

'Younger is better, eh, Dunstan?'

Dunstan ignored the signs of sexual interest in such a young boy. 'Eadburh was sent to a nunnery, where she continued her misdeeds by engaging in debauchery...'

'What's that?'

'I think you can guess. Eadburh ended her days in poverty, regretting her actions and her character, which had led her into such a scrape. The kings of Wessex have never since allowed themselves to be overwhelmed by lust for their wives or concubines. They must be kept firmly in their place. They are consorts rather than queens, mothers of the dynasty. Steeped in the proper religion, they keep to their rooms and quietly support their husbands. That has become the rule for the ladies of this family.'

'But Grandmother is not quiet! She boxed my ear yesterday. Is that not being a tyrant? Should she not be sent to a nunnery?'

Dunstan sighed. 'Since your grandfather Edward's time, your grandmother Eadgifu has been a loyal supporter of both your uncle Athelstan and your father, Edmund, through difficult times. The position of the kings' wife is ceremonial, as with your mother before she died, but essential. The queen-mother was not anointed, but continues to work quietly for the right order of the court. She never gets above herself, at least, not with me.'

'I think Grandmother does with some people.'

'Not so.' Dunstan reviewed his years with Eadgifu. 'She has worked selflessly for peace and in support of the church. In support of what I must do.'

'And perhaps it is now time that she was in support of me, but she seems to prefer Edgar.'

'There are no preferences for the queen-mother. She loves you equally, as do your parents.'

'My father's wife is not my mother. Father is always away somewhere. Edgar and I have to stay here in Winchester for our lessons. Mother is dead. Do you think she was poisoned? Will someone poison my father? Will a woman poison me?'

Eadwig began to fantasise and as Dunstan had feared, to become hysterical. The basic facts had been given; he would have to hope that after a nightmare or two, understanding of the inevitable division of labour in the royal household would lead to a calmer and smoother period in Eadwig's education. For now, he must leave him to the clerks to continue lessons. Dunstan had to prepare to go west.

The Devil's Nose

E ADGIFU, WEARING COMFORTABLE clothes, flat shoes and without her earrings, walked slowly round the boy lying on the floor.
'What are you drawing, Eadwig?'

She had her grandchildren under her tutelage until Aethelwold could return from duties at Abingdon to take over control of the schoolroom. The lessons today were in reading, but Eadwig preferred painting and drawing and this was his earned break from earlier concentration on Alfred's translation of Boethius' Consolation of Philosophy. Edgar was quietly studying the pictures of a missal at a chair near the window, stroking the raised gold leaf.

Eadwig could not reply immediately; he had several inky drawing implements in his mouth. Red lines had spilled out from the parchment on which he was drawing to the floor beyond.

'Eadwig?'

Eadwig shifted his position from prone to kneeling. 'Dunstan's nightmare.'

'You mean Abbot Dunstan. Let me see.'

Eadgifu knelt on the floor next to her grandson. Between his arms and by the side of his head, which was so close to the paper as to raise fears of short-sightedness, she could see the highly coloured vague shape of a human with a large head and black body. There was another shape, mostly red and yellow, which was the source of the floor spillage.

'I see Dunstan. He is the black shape. What is the other?' Dunstan's dreams were notable; she was not aware of a recent one or of any which Eadwig might have discovered. 'When did you hear about a dream?'

Eadwig mumbled, still drawing the details of the red shape. 'He called it a nightmare, not a dream. Yesterday. He said he was going to Glastonbury which is where his forge is and that he hoped not to see the devil there again.' He drew two giant noses on each shape. The proboscis of both was severely exaggerated.

'Why are the noses so big, Eadwig?'

Eadwig jumped up to a standing position, annoyed at the interruption. He shouted. 'Because the devil has a snout like a pig and Dunstan has a snout like a bird and he told me that he caught the devil by his snout with his tongs and sent him running. That is the scene which I am drawing.' He sank back down again to his work. 'Dunstan says that women are tyrants but that you are not one.'

'There has been some misunderstanding. No, I am not one and nor is your mother.'

'Step-mother.'

'Others perhaps may have been...' Eadgifu thought of Edward's second wife, Aelfflaed. 'What do you understand a tyrant to be, Eadwig?'

'A woman.'

Corrections would have to be made. Evidently there had been a conversation between tutor and student which, in Dunstan's haste to get to Glastonbury, had not been completed.

'Not all women are tyrants, Eadwig. You know of the precious head of St Radegund which is in the relic room here? She was a woman. She was not a tyrant, nor were any of the female saints which we pray to.' Eadgifu fingered the small relic box which hung from her belt. It formed a lump under her work-clothes, alongside the treasure-chest keys. 'Edgar, come here, and you too, Eadwig. I wish to tell you about St Radegund.'

Both boys stopped their own activities and sat by their grandmother on stools. She had the tutor's comfortable chair. Saints' stories usually involved some form of torture or extreme violence and were therefore not to be missed. Eadgifu silently asked for inspiration from her dead husband, Edward. The promotion of women and their place in the realm was a thing dear to her heart and since Edward's demise she had tried to use her position to help them, not to equality, but to be regarded as voices worth listening to. Her efforts over several years had, she felt, had an effect on producing stability between the sexes and a measure of settled peace, in England, at least, or so she hoped. She began.

'Radegund. She was not a tyrant.' Edgar looked puzzled. Eadgifu sighed. 'She was a saint, though this was not recognised until after her death, as you may understand. She defied her husband.'

'You mean, like Eadburgh?' Eadwig interjected.

'No, not like Eadburgh.'

'Who?' Edgar had not caught up with the family history. He was too young.

'I will tell you later about Queen Eadburgh, Edgar. Radegund was a maiden who, hundreds of years ago, in Thuringia, married a French king and lived in Poitiers. She was very holy. She prayed, fasted and flagellated herself.'

'What's that?' Both boys spoke together. Eadwig sat, open-mouthed. 'You mean, hurt herself?'

'Yes.'

'What sort of fagllelation, Grandma?'

'Flagellation. She wore iron bands which her skin grew around and lay upon a brazier of hot coals in the shape of a cross.'

'Why?'

'Why did her husband let her do this?' Eadwig enquired.

'She had become a nun. She was, as I said, very holy and he could not abide her. She wished to help the poor and ill.'

'Like Mother,' Edgar piped up.

'So, you see, she was not a tyrant.'

Eadwig looked doubtful. 'But if she was not obeying her husband, wasn't that bad?'

'The story is at an end. Return, now, to your studies. And, Eadwig, tonight we will go to the haligdom. I will show you the reliquary of Radegund. You may ask her yourself whether she was right to obey or disobey her husband.' She said a prayer to Edward, her male guiding light, as the two boys began reading psalms together at the window. Their high voices piped back and forth. The vexed question of male and female accountability at court would have to be sorted, as the children grew. It was unfortunate that they did not have sisters to inform them of the accepted norms of behaviour. She might have to have a word with Aethelwold, whose views were not necessarily her own. To the question 'are women tyrants?' he was one who might be likely to answer 'yes'. Life was complicated.

The Black Pool, Dublin, January 946

I T IS MID-JANUARY, the dark storm-times. The windows of the guest rooms at St Mary's Abbey are steamed up. The small square panes of thick glass lock in cooking smells, the vapour from stews being made in the nearby kitchen, our own damp breath, our bodies, our thoughts. I, Leofa, am cooped up with my young ones, my wife a sick soul, beautiful in her tragic illness. She has a corruption of the lungs, which comes to so many who are still young. She lies behind me on the bed, looking inward to her memories, while I make a circle in the steam on one small pane, endeavouring to look out. Leonada coughs and spits. There will be colour, I know, she knows. Turned away from her, I cross myself and say a prayer, but it will do no good. Nonna has written, a letter which makes me long to be in Wessex.

Below the window is the Pool. The harbour water laps darkly today, lightening to grey only in summer months and sometimes, startlingly, to blue like my wife's eyes when her soul is happy. It was summertime blue when we first arrived here from Wessex several years ago. A flurry of sleet briefly blurs my vision.

I view the scene outside, trying to forget my wife's inevitable, imminent demise. She seems to be sleeping after her coughing fit; the breathing is altered. Sleep is her only relief, now. The small black cat, which Anlaf's cook gave us after discovering the litter in his pantry, snuggles beside her.

In the large dock there are a hundred raven-ships, wave stallions, freshly painted black with caulk against the winter, their sculpted prow heads bobbing gently in the winter wind eddies of the harbour. They are sturdily roped together like rafts, ten deep from the lakeside, affording merchants in charge of the outer boats the facility of carrying their goods across the bridge of wood. The heavy rope knots of moorings attract gulls who sit in hope of an edible dropping. Some slaves are clearing out casks of fish in one end of a flat-bottomed trader, washing out wooden barrels with sea water. Its tall mast and folded red sail sway as they move, throwing rotting fish over the side, sweeping the deck of fetid remnants, fish tails and scales, heads and spines, of a multiplicity of sea creatures. A few desperate crabs crawl along the deck, seeking escape. Other slaves, stronger in appearance, crawl over the flotilla of boats, carrying the previous week's trade, wine, wooden vessels, barrels of fish, spices, dried fruits, cloth. Slaves feed well here. The sturdy work and victuals make some weak captives strong. Those who were once monks even begin to enjoy their less stringent enslavement.

A trade delegation from the Frisian islands has arrived in the last few days, men accompanied by their wives, dressed in colourful finery, plying new wares and amber, exchanging these with slaves and hunting dogs to take back with them for exchange with the southern sea nations. They bring pottery vessels with them, but the woodworkers, who hold a monopoly on domestic items as well as architecture, stage protests when there is the likelihood of encouraging the use of clay. It is something the Vikings and Saxons have in common, this distaste for objects made of earth. The magical craft of woodworking, they say, is our skill, trees are the living material of the gods. For some, I know, stone has been the resource most required; for the Romans, everything was a resource. For us, leather and wood, animals and trees; those are the focus of our culture. We travel lightly in this life. Flexibility is our gift to young men.

On the opposite shore of the harbour, I can see the smaller figures of a different group of burly slaves. They are releasing a batch of twenty or so new arrivals for the market. Freed of their foot bondages, they stagger across the raven ships, looking exhausted, hungry, but probably relieved to be off the ship which held them in its belly. Some look back to note the style of the beast at the prow of their ship. They will never forget it, the fearsome brute which ate their lives, signalled the burning of their homes, the killing of those who tried to rescue them, the sense of shame on the faces of those who did not try.

The female slaves among them, mostly young, are nimbler than the gawky young men. They are lined up on the grassy bank, given some kind of instruction by a Norseman I recognise, and are taken off to the slave store, a two-tier structure with separate bunk rooms for males and females, for sprucing up, feeding and assessment for talent, work ability and potential. A few will enter the service of St Mary's; I know their kitchen has required more help in the last few days; the loud grumblings from the food preparation staff down below in the open sided cooking-yard have been distracting. Visitor numbers, when they swell rapidly as they have at present, are a kitchen manager's headache.

For the unfortunates whose homes have been raided, probably from Kernow and Brittany, by the style of their dress, slavery will be a mixed blessing. I know what exile feels like. I too have little choice in what I do and where I go. It is one way of discovering a talent or learning a trade which may help towards survival. That is the way of the world. Some young men and women would have had a worse life in their homelands, that is sure. They are unleashed from the certainties and limitations of a family's or a lord's requirements. Some, though, will never meet a benevolent new master or mistress. Some will travel far and see the hot lands, if they are deemed to be worthwhile goods, even as far as Constantinople. They may go further. Raids for slaves are becoming more refined; Anlaf's friends know what they are looking for, young trainable beings, not the old or middle-aged, who have little worth. They pass through as figures in the account books which I keep. There are girls in this current batch who may fetch a good price.

Picky, but still ruthless, the Norse who organise the trade, extending to the ports of western Britain, Bristow and the

Liver Pool harbour, are building up gold and warrior forces, constructing more boats, urged on by Anlaf who wants to raid again into English territory in the spring; he has scores to settle.

I continue to watch the new arrivals. The younger women, ignorant of the ways of men, reveal heads of gold or raven black. If their faces and figures suit, their destiny is clear, but some will learn new trades as seamstresses or weavers or cooks. A few may be taken by a royal court to be trained in making fine embroideries. If they serve their new mistresses and masters well, they may even, in time, be freed. I cannot feel sorrow for everyone. My children, my wife, are free, for now, as long as I do the bidding of Anlaf and his men. I am grateful to him for sheltering us, but I know what he wants from me. The time is coming when he will call in his favour.

He is not a bad man, but like all Norse who have taken to warfare and trading as a way of life, he is a hard-nosed negotiator, a merchant by nature, dealing in men's hearts, minds and bodies. He learns from defeat and it makes him hard. A need for revenge, that canker, is growing in him. He is back in Dublin temporarily from his base in York where that traitor to Athelstan, Wulfstan the Archbishop, tolerates him as king in Northumbria. Blacaire, his brother, rules the roost here in his absence, though it is understood that Anlaf is the true king of both Dublin and Northumbria. Blacaire may succeed him, but there are children in York, three sons, all being trained to be astute in war, trade and diplomacy. Wulfstan no doubt sits them on his knee to teach them how to lie, the cunning wolf. Ragnald eyes the throne of York; Anlaf holds him at bay. Even for their own kind, the Norse reserve a snarl.

I can do business with Blacaire; he is tolerant of other races, other ways. Not so his deputy, Ragnald, son of the very same Guthrum who gave way to Alfred all those years ago. He is a brute, like the heads of these ships. He saw the humiliation of his father at the Battle of Edington and swore never to bend to a Christian's will. It is he who keeps the sign of swart black, the raven's wings, and the fierce creatures of Viking sagas and beliefs alive on their sails, their armlets, their belt buckles, their wolf-pelt cloaks. Ragnald is useful; every leader must have his berserkers, ready to do what a king cannot be seen to do.

Leonada coughs again. I am not a nurse by nature. Her suffering affects me, but I must smile, soothe her, for the children's sake. They sit on the floor in this upper room, playing their game of snakes and ladders by the small fire. There is much of the dark winter to come. I must begin to teach them more; Leonada will never undertake that task again.

I look down at my writing. Grudgingly the Norse have recognised the use of the written word for accounting. They are very fond of feeling their gold and, through me, they can hear it amassed. One day soon they will be able to read, too. They want precision in their trade exchanges, want to know to whom they owe (they avoid this if they can) and more particularly who owes them. They prefer to deal in coin, or failing that, melted down gold or gems. Monastic jewelled books have been useful to them in this respect, many raided from the communities in Ireland, who smoulder in resentment outside Dublin's gates and walls. St Mary's is a rare monastery which has not been plundered or destroyed; it has been lately realised by the conquerors of this place that the skills of monastic communities are worth having. Letters can be sent, threats made, communications between Viking colonies, poetry, even, can be written down. But those wealth accounts are the most valued and that is my task today, the accounts for the conference of the past week, with Anlaf and his family in attendance, checking up on his very worldly goods.

Young Aethelred gets up from the fireplace to come to me. He looks at my work and the moving hand, writing, copying.

'Father, when will we do more writing? I wish you would let me try.'

He is a quiet, small person, gratifyingly given to book reading and learning, curious to know more of the world surrounding him but impressionable. If I can ensure his survival, he will do well. But like his mother when I met her, this depends on his obscurity. I call him 'Red' for short, which obscures his origin as a prince of Mercia. He should not be entirely denied his birthright. He knows he has royal blood, but for the present, we are safe enough in Dublin. We stand out as a kin group at feasts. His sister has a golden sheen to her hair, like some of the slaves I have just witnessed. What will become of her, once her mother is gone? Can I protect my children for ever?

There is a knock at the door. Aethelred opens it to the monk who brings us food and ale. He comes into the room, bearing bread, fish soup, cheese and fruit, a flagon of beer and mead for Leonada.

Aethelred speaks to the young man. 'Mother will have fruit, not much else. My sister and I are hungry. Father, too, will eat.'

'Red, that will do. Bring us all that you have, on the table over there,' I indicate a low table in a corner of the room away from my wife. The smell of hot food makes her feel ill.

The young monk, a fresh face to us, is graceful, a rare thing in one so young. He carefully places the tray of food and broth down, spilling nothing. He seems genuinely concerned for our well-being.

'Do you wish for wine?'

The repast is generous, both in food and in drink.

'No, thank you, that is enough.' I wag a finger at Red, who is surveying the dishes, seemingly displeased with the size of portions allotted to us.

The young man turns towards the door, then pauses and turns back. 'King Anlaf has asked me to tell you that he wishes to speak with you tonight. He wants you to bring your son with you to conference after Vespers. He particularly wants to interview the lad.'

I nod, do not answer. This is the beginning of a new career for a young man; he is growing into the confidential spy which I have been in another's court. I have almost forgotten the ambition which I once had. He will receive no help from me; none is necessary. It is my son's career which is now at stake; Anlaf's request fills me with dread. I have bred a Mercian heir. Anlaf knows it and he has returned yet again from York to Dublin to recoup his treasure, slaves and power. And to make use of my son. It is time to summon what wits I have left.

The spring tides of February had enabled more great ships to access the Viking harbour; many slaves had been brought in from southern lands. As the daylight faltered, the last of them, tied together by ropes, green with the sea swell, young and middle-aged, male and female, dark-skinned as well as light, staggered across the path of planks between moored ships to the comparative safety and stability of the wooden jetty. Traders hastened their cargo on into the warehouses further up the slope, away from the shoreline. The straggle of sea-sick humanity passed out of sight, swallowed by a large dragon-capped gate. It swung shut with a clang.

Leofa turned away from the first-floor window of Anlaf's hall. This time the cargo of the slave-ships was different; many this time were brown-skinned. He turned to Anlaf, who was seated at a low table in the centre of the room. A board game was in progress. Anlaf was still choosing his move. Leofa returned to the table and picked up a counter. It was too easy.

'You will be richer still when the Bristow merchants line up for your latest batch. There are some good specimens among them and some handsome girls.'

Anlaf was becoming bored with the third game of that morning. Leofa had ceased allowing him to win.

'It all depends what they are good for. I am picky these days. There's more to be made from skilled craftsmen and cooks than cattle herders. Boys for the eunuch market: now that's where real money can be made. The monasteries of the east can't get enough of good trebles. The brawn market is drying up. I'm insisting that my men are more discerning on the raids than they used to be; I have some hopes for better prices. Better quality, fewer of them. Slaves make unwilling soldiers, especially Christians; in any case we have enough motivated young men of our own, coming monthly from the home country. Sit down again, Leofa. We haven't finished our game.' Anlaf sat back in his chair by the fire and raised his goblet to his gaming companion, waving it towards Leofa's empty glass.

Anlaf continued. 'Don't make yourself miserable thinking about them. Your god or mine will seal their fate, for good or ill. There's nothing we can do about it. They will be slaves forever or they will be saints.' Anlaf caught a sharp look from Leofa. 'Oh, sit down and let me beat you.' He waved a beautiful blue and white glass counter by its four-pronged head. The gaming board was more attractive than many of its players. It had been stolen from an unnamed Scottish monastery. 'Have you thought any more about what we discussed, the last time I was here? Your son, you know? A fine lad. I have been considering his future, how we might help him.'

Leofa sat on the fleece-covered stool. The same game was played often, its simplicity appealing to Anlaf's mind. Leofa played it to please the Viking leader, always conceding defeat or at best a draw. He had forgotten whether he made himself lose for Anlaf's sake or whether the boredom of the game had dulled his wits. Anlaf was not stupid, but he was vain. Archbishop Wulfstan, when he visited Dublin two years before, told him that he regarded him as cunning and bold, rather than intelligent. The single-minded Viking was easy to read and usually successful at achieving his goals. Winning at anything was forever a novelty to him and would be to his dying day. Losing was unacceptable. Leofa said nothing. The game of chance would develop, without his help, like it or not.

Anlaf poured wine into Leofa's goblet, replenished his own, and sat back in his chair.

'Actually, Leofa- and I know how fond you are of this game- I want to talk business with you. Bjork!' Anlaf shouted to the guard outside the hall door. 'Bjork, I need you.'

The door opened and a tall, well-built young man lowered his head to pass under the door frame.

'Come in.' Anlaf indicated a stool on the far side of the gaming table from the fireplace. Bjork put his lance against a wall, heaved his sword belt into a more comfortable position below his belly and sank on the low stool. He tidied a lank lock of hair with his right hand. Anlaf was notoriously impeccable with his own appearance. He was a man to emulate.

'Leofa, I see that you two like each other,' Anlaf gave both men a light touch on the shoulder, 'and you know that I trust both of you. Bjork has told me about his trips to Hywel Dda in Wales, carrying certain missives...ah of course he would tell me, Leofa, I am his lord and he is my cousin, after all.' Leofa made to stand up, but sat again as Anlaf continued to speak. There was a look, that look of cunning which Wulfstan had noted, in Anlaf's eyes. 'You have spent many years here, my friend, and we have played many games. We have given you and your family shelter and watched your son grow into a fine young man. You will understand what I am about to ask you. Need I spell it out?'

Leofa was too self-contained to openly squirm with fear. He had been dreading this, knowing the risk of sending letters overseas. How much did Anlaf ken of his requests to Hywel Dda? Was he aware of his letters to Nonna in the heart of Wessex?

'No, you need not spell it out.' Leofa gritted his teeth.

'Your wife's letter last year to the queen began it. She gave me the idea, which I have in any case, been mulling over during our times together, of a way for you to show your gratitude to your father's kin. There are openings for boys on the continent...

they are valuable goods, as well as young girls. Need I say more?'

Leofa restrained himself from rising. Letters then, had been intercepted and understood, despite the use of code. He pictured his son, a eunuch in the depraved court of Constantinople, his daughter a plaything for foreign magnates. They would pay well for the offspring of a Mercian royal court. So, the time for Anlaf's reward had come.

'What do want of me, Anlaf? I have little choice but to do as you ask. But you must promise safe passage for my family to Hywel.'

'That I can do, Leofa. Bjork will see to that.' Anlaf signalled to Bjork to come closer to the table.

'Come in towards the fire, lad. Here is my scheme to make us all rich and to put your lad of Mercia on the throne of Wessex, Leofa. Wulfstan in York confirms that he is willing to play a part. It only needs courage, a bit of disguise when travelling, and you can be back where you evidently feel you belong, playing and winning your board games with whomever you like. Bjork here will assist with the detailed planning. Your wife will remain in Wales with Bjork while our plan is carried out. If it fails and the king lives, you will rue the consequence. The warm countries of the south will welcome your family, no doubt...now listen. Here is what I want you to do once you cross into Mercia and Wessex...'

Leofa listened. He had to. Could there be some merit, after all, in what Anlaf had suggested? But a puppet king, his son, Aethelred, was what Anlaf would want. Or to be king, himself. This was another game he had to try to lose. He could lose all, or win.

Bromborough, The Wirral, March 946

THE IRISH SEA was its usual green-grey at this time of year; breaking waves foamed cream-coloured. Strong gusts of wind swept the coastline, bending low scabby trees and clumps of spiky grasses struggling to start their spring growth after the ice-hard winter. A single large trading ship with a dragon head was being heaved onto the sand; a dozen men made heavy work of the job of securing it as wave after wave lapped without enthusiasm at its clinkered sides, wetting them but assisting little. One of the men stepped away from his sweating companions and walked along the shore to meet a group who were approaching on horse. They trotted towards the ship. A cloud cleared the sun, shedding light on the near coastline. The sky beyond the flat land and sea sparkled, a glimmer of blue among the grey on the horizon.

'See, I bring the golden light of success to your shores, my friend.' Anlaf shouted to the tallest of the horsemen, now within range of being heard above the suck of the sea. The next cloud covered the sun. Colour reduced in the scene once more.

'Hail, Anlaf, I see you have brought your best boat...' Skallagrimsson dismounted and strode forward. 'But the sun is unreliable here. It's better in Wessex where the spring flowers are blooming.'

'Unreliable, heh, like me, do you mean?' Anlaf and Egil greeted each other. There was a slapping of shoulders, a manhandling of their bodies which restored cultural familiarity. The men placed their arms on each other's shoulders. Tattoos and arm rings clashed; snakes' heads intertwined along the length of their arms.

'Wet, cold and unreliable, as usual. But the hug was warm.'
Egil smiled and looked deep into the shorter man's eyes. Most
men were smaller in stature than him; whole nations had
become used to having to look upwards to his eyes. It made many
otherwise well-built men of Wessex feel humiliated. They grinned
at each other.

'By Odin, ugly as ever. Uglier than a penitent backside from
hell. Care for a fish?' Anlaf drew an object from a bag at his side.
He threw the mackerel at Egil, who caught and examined it.

'My favourite supper. Got any more? I see you are getting
used to the names of some Christian destinations. They say hell is
not so much fun.'

'Plenty, if you will supply a place where I can get this wet
clothing off and get a good night's sleep. I should like some of
the warmth of a Christian hell just at the moment. This sand is
stinging my eyes. We have a lot of talking to do. But what is this,'
Anlaf tugged at Egil's beard, 'the latest fashion, my friend?'

'Why have one beard when you can have two? I like to annoy
my Saxon masters.'

'I would pay you to remove that forked beard. It does not add
to your beauty.'

'How much would you pay? I would take it off for you.'

'I couldn't afford your price!'

The sailors and horsemen blended into a tight circle of fur-
clad warriors. Leading the horses, they left the ship and climbed
the tussocky dunes, disappearing inland towards a group of
wooden fishermen's huts on the side of a sandy creek.

The sun reappeared, but only briefly.

'Speak slowly, Egil; your Icelandic accent is growing away from
me. Your time in the soft South has not helped.'

The group of Norsemen had moved further inland from the fishing huts to a more wind and sand-proof shelter, a thatched extension to what had once been a substantial stone church, now derelict after being burnt several years before. There was warmth and comfort in the one-roomed home, commandeered by a family of women, grandmothers, daughters and young grandchildren. Egil had secured a Viking welcome for the king of Dublin, a house of survivors and relatives of the troubled times nearly ten years before when so many of their kin had been killed. There were few men left of Norse descent on the Wirral who could become husbands or fathers. The women had made a living from collecting and selling artefacts from the Brunanburh battle site. They continued to find and bury bird-scavenged bones, mostly of Norse soldiers and sailors who had gone to Valhalla on that fateful day. Some of their finds were on display, trophies of Saxons killed, on a great beeswax-polished table. Egil and Anlaf sat on cushioned barrels with their feet up on a fur-clad bench. Their eyes met over a skull being used as a candle-lamp.

Egil leaned back against the stone wall of the old church. His huge mass covered the remainder of the stone bench almost completely.

'A Saxon's head, the women say. This was the altar, they tell me.' Egil looked down his great nose at his Viking compatriot. 'It is in my poet's nature to be slow-spoken and precise, Anlaf. As for my Icelandic accent, well, I do not apologise. Perhaps you would like me to come and live with you one day in Winchester to teach your lads how to read and spell like the students they must become when you are king? They could all benefit from a little cultural education. I could give them a taster session in Dublin on the next tide perhaps? They might appreciate my poetry better than Edmund's clowns, though they thumped the table and whistled when I recited "Brunanburh" for them.'

'You did that? Did you spare them any gruesome details? But they paid you magnificently to fight for them. I suppose I should forgive a Viking brother for making hay while he can. I prefer to be more honest in my dealings to make a profit, but I appreciate that your way of life may be making you a very rich man.'

'There is a difference between us, Anlaf. I do not desire to be king. I just want to live long and retire to my Icelandic farm to breed ponies.'

'And breed other things no doubt. As you say, we will be in Winchester soon enough, handling the jewels and silver chests of Edmund and playing at being educated gentlemen with the ladies of the court, if some are still alive to take part in our games. I hear the royal women are dropping from their perches as fast as they are born. I hope that there will be one left for me to couple with. One will be required to bear my sons, after I have wiped the world clean of the old Saxon family. By the way, who do you suggest I take as a bride? Perhaps more than one?'

'There's no choice, Anlaf,' Egil was enjoying this Viking banter. It was something he missed sorely. Thank Odin for his close companion, Bjork. 'Only one woman will do for you. Eadgifu.'

'The old woman! She must be fifty if she is a day. Haven't you someone better suited to being my mate? And anyway, I have heard that she gives birth to cats.'

Egil laughed again. 'She will outlive both of us, my friend. If you catch her soon you may squeeze a legitimate child out of her. You'll have your own dynasty to think of. As for cats, you may be sure she can conjure them, but the palace mousers do not resemble her.'

'Doesn't she have a tail? Isn't she tall, taller than me, as tall as you, Egil? I cannot abide looking up to your ugly face. Looking up, or down, for that matter, to an old woman's face would not raise my cock.'

Egil chuckled. 'Seriously, if you want to rule England you would do well to consider her as a matrimonial partner. The priests would come along with her. They worship her. Actually, it would not be such a bad idea. You could do worse. And her height is not what it seems; she gives herself airs and the ability to look down on others by the stuffed shoes she wears.'

'High heels, hmm. I might have to consider those...but let us discuss our plans, now, the serious matters. You will return tomorrow to Wessex. Is there any suspicion of our movements? What are the arrangements for the seating of guests at the gathering? What do we do with Eadred? Tell me all you know.'

'You needn't consider Eadred. He is a wimp. He cannot even eat meat. You can leave him to me.' Egil made a squeezing motion with his fist. He could act out his gory poems, as well as speak them.

Anlaf poured ale into the other's horn cup. This would be a long night.

Dublin, March 946

To my Lord Hywel Dda of Wales, I, Leofa, formerly of Wessex, greet you. I hear much in praise of you, my lord, perched as I am in this god-forsaken abbey of Dublin. The good that I hear of you sustains me in my dark recess inside this place, once of learning, now of charnel, blood and swearing. The smell of rotting fish and men in the slave camp nearby my cell, I am used to after all these years. You know why I was sent here. The official reason was that I was a thief. My sentence was unjust, my exile a punishment for being faithful to my lord and your friend, Athelstan, king of all England.

I played a part in the birthing of the dream of the empire of Britain, with England and its people, leaders of commerce and Christianity, a beacon of light on the flank of the continent and successor to the enlightened world of Charlemagne and Bede. We all contributed to the effort to unify Britain; that effort killed Athelstan in the end and it caused me to leave, and later to be exiled.

You will know, too, that while at the court of my king, I acted diligently and with fairness in my duties with you and the ambassadors from the countries beyond England, assisting with translation and information gathering. I was held in high esteem. There are always enemies who, having no wish to be held liable for their part in any unsuccessful secret mission, will point the finger of blame, especially towards one who is seen as an outsider. My mongrel Viking blood was once valued. I was useful as an interpreter and as a poet but I became the scapegoat. My Lord, you are aware of my paternity. My Viking background, my father's part in the attempt to defeat Wessex, I cannot deny. I must be punished for the sins of my father.

I am weary of exile, fearful for my family. My wife is ill. Anlaf harbours jealousy. He wishes to cement the north within the Viking crown, to join the Scandinavian countries to his own fiefdom in Ireland. He is bereft of sensitivity, alive only to his own restlessness at being kept at bay by the English forces for so long. He is gathering strength, building his forces and his ships, brainwashing men and their sons (and mine) into becoming bloodthirsty fighters, rejecting the approaches of any who dare to call themselves Christian.

I beg for your help in restoring me to British shores, away from these pagans, for my children's sake as well as my own. You have met Leonada; you were kind enough to give us shelter in Dyfed on our journey here. I fear for her health. There is no healing medicine here like that which can be found commonly in any palace and monastery of England. She worries for our daughter, surrounded as she is by unfettered Viking youth who have little common sense and no discipline in the company of women.

My wife has written to Edmund's wife, but has had no return from her. That letter may have been indiscreet, but, my lord, you will feel for our discomfort here and understand my wish to be of use to yourself, and to the kingdom of Wessex.

Tell me soon if you can help me and be an intermediary for me; I have nothing to lose from leaving this place and much to offer the forces of good: Anlaf's head.

From this blasted black pool of a town,

Yours in desperation,

Your friend, Leofa

Pucklechurch, April 946

Friend Leofa, give my greetings to your master there. Arrangements have been made to meet your ship outside the harbour of Fishguard on the thirteenth day of the next month, weather permitting. Your family will be taken to St David's for shelter with Hywel Dda to whom I send a copy of this letter. You will travel on alone to Mercia under the protection of Bjork. I cannot guarantee the safety of anyone else. You know how to handle yourself, or you did. Arm yourself well. I am here in Pucklechurch to make arrangements for the Augustine feast. The Danish guard will be armed. Security will be tight; the king is growing nervous. I am instructed that weapons will not be allowed by guests to be carried inside the hall. Wear only English clothes and a large hat while in this land, to hide your Viking colouring. Shave your beard.

There is only one chance for your return, my friend. You know what you have to do. You are not popular here. Say your farewells to Ireland and perhaps to this world. May Odin be with you.

Egil Skallagrimsson

Dublin Castle, April 946

To my old friend Nonna from your friend Leofa. Bjork was slow to bring me your letter; a storm was bad on the crossing, he said, and a return to the Welsh mainland was required, without which much of the valuable cargo would have been lost. Your letter was more valuable to me! Things here are on the move.

There was bullion aboard in the form of metal scraps, regarded these days as payment for slaves in the market at Bristow, some of which was gold brought from the eastern kingdom (they have carefully guarded heaps of treasure looted from monasteries many years ago which they are now beginning to release). Anlaf's speciality is the melting down of such stuff, now nearly valueless to anyone as it is so mangled, to make coin for the coffers of war. I have seen some of the artefacts which go into the forge; you would weep, my friend, to see the low glint of gold of the figures of saints on torn reliquary caskets, on ornaments from English abbeys and monasteries, melting into mere liquid metal. But neither you nor I are English; we need not weep for their loss; our charms arise from other sources. I must confess to a certain small satisfaction that our old foes' history and wealth suffers by these desecrations. But perhaps you do not now think of them as your foes? Have you become a full Saxon in your mind and soul?

I continue mouldering in this benighted place, weary now of my people's ridicule at the idea of education in writing form. They insist on behaving, as the English did in our youth, with contempt for anything but the spoken word. Despite this, I suspect some of the younger warriors, or traders as they are becoming, have some interest in what they see me doing everyday as I try to record events. Some watch my quill move across the parchment open-mouthed, but they never dare to ask me what it is I am writing, or how I do it. Like most adults who have had no contact with learning or understanding of other cultures except in terms of trade or violence, they regard my work, at best, with suspicion and at worst as black magic. I have to confess that I miss the Wessex court. It has realised at last that the written word is a necessity.

You ask about my family. I fear for the mind and life of my son. He is now almost as old as we were, Nonna, when we were given first sight of the library at Glastonbury. I have tried to instil the love of learning into him, but I often see him on the wharf-side, watching or trying to assist the merchants as they unload or load their goods. He badly wants to wear an arm-ring like the soldiers amongst them and I have even caught him drawing one, with my best feathered pen and ink, on his arm, to represent where he says he wants one to be. It will be silver and decorated with the dragon figure-heads of the ships, he says. I told him it would be better to have a silver tongue, to use as strength in argument, but he has warriors in his bloodline; he has changed; he is for fighting, not thinking. My daughter looks like her mother and is led by her, thankfully, though I wonder for how much longer. They both keep to our rooms in the abbey. There is plenty of sewing and mending for them to do for the family and sometimes for others. Young men of the merchant class admire some of their embroidery; perhaps Leonada will have more success with her needle in turning them towards culture than I have had with my records. Her health is poor. She prays for warmer weather.

My time with Anlaf has become wearying, as you can imagine. He is all for attacking the mainland of Britain, as I am sure you in that blessed place are all aware; I have tried to dissuade him from it but warships are being built and become more numerous daily. The Black Pool is full of the sounds of clinker woodwork and armament making, the warehouses full of hanging sails and carved figure-headed prows, waiting to be attached to ships when the weather has improved. Trading has ceased; full attention is being given to assault across the Irish Sea. These new ships are huge. You have never seen the like of these, my friend, nor would you wish to. Their cargo on return to Ireland, too, will be fearsome, one day, unless a truce and payment can be agreed between the Saxons and these determined men.

There are things which I can tell you about the intentions of Anlaf in more detail, which would be of use to the court, but I dare not say them here, even in our chosen language. I will say this: I intend to outsmart my warders (they have become my prison keepers after all this time) with my son and to try to buy a passage to Wales, to Hywel Dda's court. He will be sympathetic to my plight. From thence I may be able to travel alone across the Severn to the outward reaches of Wessex or Mercia. I intend to ask for Edmund's mercy. Perhaps Hywel Dda will take care of my son. He will at any rate be safe with the Welsh king, and your relatives in St David's will be aware of him. I rather wish he had the dark hair of the Welsh, not the red of my father's race, but I must hope that the gentle courtesy which Hywel has bestowed on other visitors will be given to him. As Athelstan used to do, Hywel protects the high born who are in danger and gives them room under his roof.

I am expecting the annual feast of St Augustine to take place at Pucklechurch as usual in May. With assistance from Egil Skallagrimsson and Bjork (Egil has sent me word) you may count a hooded head amongst the Welsh guests, if my plan to escape is successful. I am changed, my friend. The Black Pool has taken my youth. I hope you will recognise me. We may meet again, Nonna. I hope so, my friend.

My fond affection to you,
Leofa

Archbishop's Residence, York, April 946

To the King's armourer Egil Skallagrimsson from Wulfstan, Archbishop of York.

Greetings. I have heard from our mutual friend in Dublin that there are movements afoot which interest me. Can I take it that you and Anlaf have come to some agreement to support our northern cause? Our attempt to sway matters ended badly last year. We should not repeat that failure.

The matter needs confirmation so that I will know how to act, should the time come when we have a new dynasty on the throne of Wessex.

I must obey the summons to be at Pucklechurch for the Augustinian celebrations on the 26th May. If necessary, my men will assist, but be in no doubt, if there are unforeseen problems, there will be no rescue for the thief or yourself.

Wulfstan.

To Anlaf, king of The Black Pool, from Wulfstan, Archbishop of York.

Greetings. I could have wished for news sooner, but I understand the Wessex matter has been under discussion without resolution for some time. Leofa can be persuaded, but not by an offering of gold, I think. He must have some just cause to act against Edmund. His honorable intentions need to be undermined, perhaps through a threat to his family.

We must be sure that this plan will work. My men will be at table on the occasion in question and I intend to be present to witness the encounter, but as you may understand, I cannot be involved.

Will Leofa be armed? Has he been persuaded to approach the king as a former friend, pleading for a merciful retuturn to his country or has he developed the mindset of a useful assassin?

Do your job, Anlaf, and twist his arm. This will be our last, best hope to steal the kingdom back.

You must assist his escape to England. Make it look real or Leofa will smell a rat. I hear from Skallagrimsson that arrangements have been made with Hywel in Wales.

I look forward to seeing you on the English throne and crowning you. First York, then Dublin, and finally England is within your grasp. Or do you intend the Mercian brat to rule in your stead? St Augustine's day should be very memorable. Succeed, my friend. Northumbria needs you.

Wulfstan.

Part 3
The Red Tent

Aelfwolde hyre twegen wesendhornas an hors hyre re'a'de geteld.

"And she grants to Aelfwolde her two buffalo-horns and a horse and her red tent."

Will of Wynflaed, c. 955

Cheddar Palace

EADGIFU PACED THE women's room, muttering. She was alone, the court having gone to supper. She could not eat. Male blackbirds in thorn bushes outside quarrelled their way into a crescendo of violent song.

'Be quiet!' Eadgifu needed to think. The distracting noise of nature tried to pull her back from the brink. Geese honked loudly on the mere and the nearby farm pigs squealed as they were fed. But it was no good. Beauty and nature's bounty in this spring of 946 had been forgotten by this queen. Inside her head, the world was in chaos.

It was raining, again. The crops might fail, the mud might bake to rock-like clay. The backdrop to her thoughts was of a dismal future, a starving autumn. If the sun would only appear for more than a single useless day, there could be hope, but no. Eadgifu felt uncommonly morose.

She stopped pacing in the middle of the room, having received one of those revelations which pierce, shining and swift, into the soul at times of need. Radegund had spoken. Who else could it be? The idea came not in words, but as a plan of action. The clouds cleared; the rain ceased. The birds, silent, listened to what she had to say.

'Wynflaed. I must go to Wynflaed, before she sets out for Pucklechurch. It is time to use a woman's skills!'

Nonna's Diary

It was at Cheddar that Eadgifu first heard of the existence of the child. I am glad that it was not my fault. It seems that a court visitor, who had heard it from a Viking source, had mentioned the rumour while visiting the royal sewing room. Gossip travels quickly. Egil Skallagrimsson had let slip, during some drunken meal, that the Viking king Anlaf in Dublin held an interesting prisoner. Eadgifu, whose ears and eyes are sharp, has begun to ask searching questions. Thankfully, as yet, no links seem to have been made to Athelstan, Leofa and Shaftesbury. Dunstan was able to deflect her enquiries, but by his tone, I could tell that he could not do this for ever. The queen-mother has spies of her own. Who has not?

Gwladys told me that Eadgifu had interviewed Skallagrimsson, becoming rough-tongued. The Viking bodyguard, taken aback by her sudden change in humour, apparently made things worse by trying to retract what he had said. The queen-mother shouted at him, in an unusual display of loss of control, whereupon Edmund, who was present at the meal-table while this occurred, shooed her out of the hall, following her into a private chamber, where 'words' were heard for several minutes. Both lost their tempers. Edmund is learning to say 'No' to his mother. The matter was put to rest, then. The next day, the atmosphere at court was changed. The expected boar hunt was cancelled, to the disappointment of many. Egil had disappeared, as he often did. There were icy encounters for a few days, then Eadgifu went to Shaftesbury. The queen-mother was beginning to suspect that a royal bastard was growing up in Dublin. There had been others, too, born to Edmund, though these were female and of little consequence. Eadgifu was angry, but not unduly worried. I do not know the extent of the gossip, or how much Eadgifu has been told. There has been no mention of the secret of Radegund's head.

I fear, though, that the unravelling of private affairs, born of the time of King Athelstan, has begun. A royal crisis, the first of the new reign, is upon us.

Grandmothers:
Eadgifu and Wynflaed at Charlton Horethorne

WYNFLAED GAVE EADGIFU a hug as they greeted each other. The queen-mother kissed her almost as heartily. They said prayers together in the chapel, to calm their thoughts. They sat together in the great hall, where the steward Martin had lit a fire despite the arrival of summery weather. Wynflaed's whole household had eaten together on a table nearby, and the detritus of the meal was being cleared away, but she made Eadgifu comfortable on a cushioned settle while she sat opposite the fireplace in a rocking chair. Supper on a tray was brought for the tired visitor. She had no time to change out of her riding gear; the matter in hand was burgeoning to be out.

They were alone. Only the iron firedogs observed them, their snouts deafly pointing, as if begging for food. Eadgifu leaned over the end of the settle and gave one of them a caress. They had been a gift to Wynflaed by Edward, on her marriage, and designed by Eadgifu, with Dunstan's help. They had been awakened from their summer slumber, polished and glowing in the candle light of sundown and the fire's flames. The sun retreated behind the hills, showering the sky in glorious russet streaks. It disappeared as the women talked. Night had arrived, the time for deep discussion. Eadgifu nibbled at bread, fruit, dried meat and cheese and a plate of cooked leeks. Ale in a pottery mug washed down the food. She sighed and leaned back. The initial pleasantries were almost over.

'A good show, to end the day,' Wynflaed remarked. She had

been patient while Eadgifu refreshed herself. 'Now tell me what it is that brings you here today. I will be discreet.'

'Edmund did not want my presence at the witan; the matters were of little interest to me, he said. He did not wish to bore me. But whether I would be bored or not, that was not the point. He is closing the door on my involvement with court business. I hoped to continue as in former days. However, I have learned other ways of hearing news. Not everything escapes the eyes and ears of wives of the court. No man can ensure that his wife is not a fool, though many consider that they ought to be.' Eadgifu paused to allow Wynflaed to speak, but she said nothing.

Eadgifu went on. 'I have heard through a visitor's wife about a threat to our kin.'

Wynflaed sat up. Her bracelets clattered together as she dropped her arms. 'More?' Wynflaed offered the flagon of ale and poured herself a drink. It would soon be midnight. Eadgifu waved her hand in refusal. 'Go on, my friend. I am listening.'

Wynflaed peered intensely at Eadgifu. Candlelight revealed, as well as concealed. Firelight cast the shadows into which those born to rule must peer, if they had the courage. The dark as well as the light must be considered; Edward and Athelstan had been right about that. There were things which only experience could teach; they were not found in books.

Eadgifu stood and walked slowly around the hall, beyond the firelight and into the gloom beyond. She needed to compose and clarify her thoughts and to remove herself, for a moment, from Wynflaed's perceptive gaze. There were things which she was prepared to think and do which she preferred to keep to herself. Wynflaed's weather-beaten face followed hers. She looked away. Her eye drifted over the trappings of the room. There were many decorative items, inherited gifts from many generations. Fire-light reflected flaming orange from polished metal and glass. Small metal figurines from ruined villas dotted cupboard and table tops. They displayed the vigour of former landscape beliefs in their miniature bodies. There were layers of meaning behind the outstretched arm, the open mouth, the smiling eyes. Were they listening, too, like the fire dogs?

The moon had risen. It shot a beam onto a polished bronze mirror. Stained red-gold, there she stood, her hood thrown back. Her hair was plaited but becoming loose, her green cape was similarly trying to release itself, prevented at the neck from doing so by the wooden toggle and large brooch. There was the high forehead, a mobile mouth, a long neck and medium height female body, covered with linen to ankle and wrist. The riding apparel had trews like a man and a short-skirted tunic to match. A middle-aged, active woman looked back from the mirror. There were deep furrows on the brow. The left cheek twitched, like Edmund's.

Eadgifu turned back to face Wynflaed. She now felt ready to tell her fears. The words as they flowed chased emotion away.

'The family of Edmund's new wife are proving intrusive; God help us if ever she should produce an heir. If she does, may the saints ensure that it is female. She has turned Edmund against me.'

Wynflaed tutted.

'Edward told me that there would be a problem with Mercia. He said that it would be born of Athelstan's line.'

'When did he tell you that?'

'I often ask him for advice.'

'You ask your dead husband for advice? Mine is best left alone to stew in purgatory.'

'Edward is my sole support, apart from Radegund, and of course Dunstan, though even he is beginning to avoid me. He is getting busier with each passing year.' Eadgifu's twitch again trembled across her face. She blinked.

'Wait, be clear, slow down, Eadgifu. Sit down. Begin with Edmund. Tell me about him.' There were layers of complaint which must be worked through, starting with the least painful.

Dread would come last.

Eadgifu sat down again on the settle, in the full light of the fire and candles. She began to get into her stride. 'Edmund often rides his fast mare to Glastonbury to visit Dunstan and to watch the restoration works. He's consulting the abbot on planning for his own mausoleum there. It's a little early in life for that, I tell him, but he seems to think it necessary. He has nightmares of dying. Of course, he still has horrific visions after the gorge experience; that is to be expected. He has become a nervous wreck. Dunstan tells him such things may be dispelled by prayer, that there is no need to go to Glastonbury to see him so frequently, but he does. I wonder if he dislikes his new wife. He is not alone, but she brought useful allies with her in the marriage. Well, he chose her. He would not listen to me.' She paused. 'Edmund's ministers have decided that I interfere too much at witans. They say I talk too much. I learned only at the last minute that the door of the great old hall of Alfred and Aethelwulf was to be closed to me. This, just at a time when I needed to be present at the witan, to assess the mood of Edmund's closest advisors and to discover whether they have heard what I have.'

'And what is that?'

'Something of it was brought originally to me at the last witan. A Mercian minister's consort took me aside while we were sewing. She said then that there was a rumour about a secret child of Athelstan's. I tried to tell Edmund, but he fobbed me off, saying that I was listening to too many unfounded conspiracies. I put the matter to the back of my mind, but the woman has spoken to me again at Cheddar and I am concerned. I cannot speak to Edmund; he will not listen.' Eadgifu checked her flow of words and gulped back a tear. Wynflaed nodded. 'The problem lies with Mercia. It will never rest from its petty jealousies. My home of Kent has learnt to regard itself as a part of Wessex and a small part of England, but Mercia will never forget that it once held the reins of power. I tried to find a way to be present at today's meeting, though it would take a quantity of silver. I had my private purse ready to bribe someone,' Eadgifu sighed deeply, 'but they said the king had ordered that no women were allowed into the hall. They told me to go away! Oh Lord, make me not become like the old queen Aelfflaed before she died, forever rehearsing her loop of woes. It is a trial to be an able queen, to witness disasters made by men.' The tear escaped and fell down Eadgifu's face. She quickly wiped it away.

Wynflaed nodded.

'Yes, I tried. I displayed my packet of silver, but they would not let me in,' she repeated. The Mercian minister's concubine, the one I met before, joined me in the sewing room. She began by talking gossip. I still feel the shock of what she told me. I asked her to speak quietly, as what she was saying was outrageous. She whispered, barely understandable, her Mercian accent was so strong. It was just as well. She said things which should not be overheard by the rest of the women. She stuttered and lisped, so that it was difficult to follow her. She was bright enough to realise, thank Radegund, that what she had to tell me, in response to a gold coin, was to be said in low tones.

'I led her behind a heavy curtain leading from the main embroidery room to the materials store. She told me that her husband was the son of a Danish woman who in turn had contacts abroad. This lisping whisperer expected me to pay her well for information. She held out her hand for more coin. I refused. After a moment, she went on. She told me that Edmund should look abroad to discern his next engagement with enemy foes. This was not new to me or to anyone else. Do the nobles think we are stupid? She continued. They were not the Norse in the east and north, she said, or the Scots far away, nor the Welsh or Cumbrians. I remarked that Brittany and France were safe places of peacefulness, full of concern for their own business. She shook her head. The problem lay in the west, she told me. Could I guess the Name of the Beast? Was I blind? I slapped her face, the impudent woman. She gasped, burst into tears and knelt at my feet. She said the word "Ireland".

'Ireland. I should have guessed. She was repeating what I had heard Skallagrimsson say. It is a breeding-ground for rebellious upstarts born to that race of violent thieves, the Vikings, in particular the nest which reside in Dublin. The snake's head is growing and its body coils around us. Edmund admires their style and wit and heroic tales, but I have so often told him to watch his back. Bravado does not mix with loyalty. Skallagrimsson, though he is not Norse, is not all he seems to be. Iceland is part of their northern world. He mixes with the Norse visitors to court. Dunstan does not trust him. Aethelwold hates him.' Eadgifu paused. She sipped at her ale.

'"Dublin?" I asked. I thought there might be more to learn and lifted her up from the floor. She was weeping and holding her face. I had to take the opportunity to squeeze as much as possible from the frightened mouse. "The Black Pool?" "Yes, Madam," she said.

'I waited for her to continue. I looked at the coin, held in her still open hand, that I had already given her. I considered taking it back She turned away, wiping her eyes, closing her hand around the coin. A red patch had appeared on her face. I brought out my cross relic, the finger of Radegund, that very same which was once owned by Wulfstan, the traitor of York. He is still the Archbishop in that city, despite everything. Edmund is too soft, needs my guidance. Safe far away, like Anlaf in Dublin, the devil Wulfstan cooks his plots. I suspect that he and that serpent Skallagrimsson, and countless others are waiting, biding their time, to bring this house to ruin. It hurts that I am not listened to.' Eadgifu sighed again. She had become aware of the alleys of deceit and despair which flooded her mind and which were now causing fog in her delivery. Frustration and jealousy had reduced her talent for clarity.

Wynflaed had seen this frustration before in her friend.

Born at the end of Alfred's reign, they had both seen many spiders' webs grow and be destroyed. The women knew their history. Poison, daggers and swords come easily to the hands of many who would wish to harness providence; in particular the gouging out of eyes, that means of exclusion for a hopeful prince in an unguarded moment. Athelstan had narrowly avoided being blinded. Words are just as effective; gossip can ruin an aspiring ruler's future, destroy his youth and manhood with a mere eyebrow's rise, take away the power of the throne and cast it to another. The smiles of deliberate propaganda cloak threats. Sons and grandsons could be taught how to act ruthlessly as adults; but the years between childhood and maturity, combined with a rebellious nature, could dispel a mother's influence and aggression could be turned against a tutor. Wynflaed could see that this had happened with Edmund; there had been symptoms of a growing dissatisfaction with his mother since the battle of Brunanburh.

Eadgifu grimaced. 'I was taught as a child never to trust the ones who smile. Skallagrimsson grins. Archbishop Wulfstan bares his teeth. There is little distance between a smile and a snarl. I can discern danger, but Edmund ignores me. Is this the fate of all mothers of grown sons?'

Wynflaed nodded. It was. 'Go on.'

'As I said, I showed the trembling mouse the small coffin-shaped box which holds the finger of Radegund. This one.' Eadgifu pulled out the relic case which was attached by a chain to her belt. Keys jangled. 'She started to cry. I grabbed her wrist. She gasped. The gold coin fell to the floor and rolled beyond the curtain. I paused. There was no sound beyond but a buzz of light conversation by the ladies. There was no break in their talk; they had not heard us. I squeezed her arm and presented the relic close to her red face. "You know what this small relic box may contain," I said. "You are in the presence of Radegund. Tell me everything you have heard. Tell me now. But bear in mind, for the future, that the king cannot abide others' discussion, mistaken or otherwise, of the business of my family. Of my family, do you hear?" I had to be careful not to raise my voice. The mouse had good ears, or a delicate pain threshold. She winced as I twisted her wrist and nodded at my hiss of impatience. She trembled, but said nothing. "On the finger of holy Radegund whose spirit is before you, speak and tell the truth of what you know," I said. I screwed her flesh again. It was soft. I rarely use physical threats but she had raised my anxiety. She started to reveal all she knew, which was a great deal. The Vikings are better informed than many in Wessex.

'You remember, Wynflaed, how many years ago one of Athelstan's court clerks, a man called Leofa, disappeared suddenly from court. There were three men particularly close to the king (Dunstan was one of them,) standing ready to interpret the foreign visitor's words, to assist him in pulling wool over their eyes when necessary, diverting ill-tempered talk, making vital notes. Some of their productions are probably on your walls; they have written or commissioned many books.' Eadgifu looked enquiringly at Wynflaed.

'Yes, I remember Athelstan's trio of spies, though two of them not well. Dunstan is a distant relation of mine. But tell me more about this Leofa.' Wynflaed's mouth settled into a line.

'It seems that he has been living in the Black Pool.'

'Where?'

'Dublin. It's what the Irish call it. In Irish, of course. He was forced into exile by Athelstan. He has relations among the heathen there who use Dublin as their base. Leofa was not exiled alone. He has a family there.'

'Go on.' Wynflaed gripped the chair arm, downplaying the movement by readjusting her stole. Firelight played on one side of her face; the house was silent. An owl began to hoot.

'Apparently, Leofa arrived many years ago in Dublin, demanding to meet the Viking chieftain and also the abbot of St

Mary's Abbey. Whichever would take him in, he said, he would be his servant. He had a family with him and he needed shelter, was willing to act for whoever would pay him most. He had a red-haired woman with him and two small children.' Eadgifu looked to see if this meant anything to her friend. Wynflaed blinked. It was as new to her as to the queen-mother.

'The woman was apparently Athelstan's daughter by Aelfwynn...'

'Aelfwynn! Athelstan has a daughter?' Wynflaed was a student of dynastic history and understood that Eadgifu was talking about the daughter of Aethelflaed, the Lady of the Mercians, who had done such great things to recoup the midlands from the Vikings. She grasped immediately what this could mean. 'So she's alive? Didn't your husband put Aelfwynn somewhere safe? And there were children with them, you say?'

'Yes, he put her where the Mercians couldn't get hold of her to try to make her a focus for insurrection, he told me, but wouldn't say where. There are two children, twins. One a girl, the other a boy.'

Wynflaed whistled. 'A boy, how old now? Where was he born?'

'They began living with the Dublin nest of Vikings just before Athelstan died, so about eleven years old. The twins were born, it seems, at our abbey of Shaftesbury. There may have been some subterfuge agreed by Athelstan with the old abbess, right under our noses. If so, she kept the births very quiet, for love, or money. So, the Mercian heir was born there, and lived there for some years before they were taken to Dublin.'

'And so, there is another aetheling waiting in the wings under the tutelage of the Dubliners, who, whatever their religion, mean us harm. What was the mother's name?'

'Leofa's wife is called Leonada. Dublin is far away, Wynflaed, but possibly, yes, there is trouble brewing, unless the woman has fantasised everything. The details were too plausible. And the

Mercians will never give up the hope of having one of their own on the throne.'

Eadgifu stopped, allowing time for them both to come to terms with the potential threat. Blinding, poisoning, knifing, drowning. All royal heirs were in need of protection. The best form of defence was to attack, they say, or to enlist dark arts. It was their right to consider subtle weapons when the blood kin received threats, as any woman would do.

'Is Leofa himself connected in any way to the Wessex or Mercian royal family?' Wynflaed understood how important bloodlines were. Families and slaves, servants and thegns; you could trust a kin to keep its own order.

'No, he is part Viking, but he has a great deal of knowledge of our family. I understand that Leonada is largely ignorant of her Mercian background. There is more. Leofa, I remember, boasted of being part of the expedition to Chester-le-Street in 934. When he was exiled, he claimed that he was not involved in a plot to obtain a relic from Cuthbert's monks there. I thought nothing of it. Relics are often stolen. I remember Edmund telling me about his experience in the chapel crypt. He said the first visit to view the body of the saint was overwhelming but that the second, on the return journey from the north, was less inspiring, but he did not say why. There might have been something about it which made him feel uneasy. Leofa was banished for a good reason and it may have something to do with this as well as his surreptitious marriage. He was branded a thief, though he had no trial. He may think that his reputation matters, that his son might be able to restore it. When I asked Dunstan about the second visit to Cuthbert's tomb, he was unusually reticent in describing what had upset Edmund. The door to this particular episode has been closed, to me, anyway.'

'And we must try to open it. An exiled thief is unusual; they normally suffer the gallows unless the church is involved. Was Leofa a priest or monk?'

'Neither. A clerk.'

They paused, leaned back and took a sip of from their cups. Was this just another gossip-led conspiracy? Were they seeing more than need be in this double-headed secrecy? The existence of a Mercian prince being brought up beyond any Wessex influence was one thing. The exile of an important, albeit secular, court official for the crime of theft would usually attract the death penalty. That was another. There were still questions which had not been answered. What, exactly, had been stolen, to give rise to this mess?

The women tried to answer their own enquiries. Wynflaed was the first to speak. 'What was the purpose of the second visit to Chester-le-Street? I understand that Athelstan and Edmund had been there on the way up to Scotland and of course would wish to view St Cuthbert.' Wynflaed was thinking about the secular and sacred connections. They were never far apart, in the Christian world in which they lived.

'To give thanks, I suppose, to Cuthbert, for the success of the mission as it was viewed then. Of course, the euphoria didn't last long; the battle at Brunanburh put paid to that. But I see what you are getting at. Dunstan or Leofa or someone engineered a second meeting for a specific purpose.'

'Was there anything else in the crypt with Cuthbert which Athelstan may have wanted to see but dare not reveal his need? He was an avid collector of relics as all his family are.'

Eadgifu drummed the chair arm. 'Athelstan died at Gloucester, having been brought there, it seemed, to be near the foundation of his aunt and uncle of Mercia and within the Priory of St Oswald. He was very anxious to have Oswald's body parts reunited, I remember. He could not rest until they were. There was some sort of presentation to the priory shortly after Christmas in 935. The witan at Cirencester that year would have given him a chance for him to visit nearby Gloucester. I wonder if he had something with him to take there, something particularly precious?'

'I do not attach such importance to relics. They seem to be favoured by the more conservative types of wives and widows. Land holdings are more valuable; this world, not so much the next.'

'Yes, but we have to be able to see what makes a man tick in order to understand the background to this latest problem. 'So, we have an exiled man who has a royal son and who was also something to do with the second as well as the first visit to Chester-le-Street and some subterfuge involving it.'

Wynflaed got up from her chair and went to the nearest bookcase, carrying a candle which she lit from the fire. She peered in the gloom along the shelves.

'What have you thought of, Wynflaed?'

'Father Bede. His History of the English Church and People. I have a copy here, somewhere. I read it first as a girl and often consult it. Ah, here it is.'

She returned to her chair with a large tome. It looked immaculate, though it must have been two centuries old. Wynflaed had originals of many Saxon books.

'Bede may give us an indication of who it was that Athelstan may have been interested in in the north.'

Wynflaed could read the spidery writing of many scribes of past centuries. She had read some of it to Eadgifu before.

'Yes, here it is.' She read a passage. 'After Oswald's death in 641 his bones were taken to Lindsey near the city we call Lincoln, at the Abbey of Bardney.' Wynflaed paused. 'Ah, but not all.' She continued reading. 'His head and hands were hacked off by his killer and fixed on stakes. His brother Oswy rescued them later and placed the head in the church at Lindisfarne.'

'Are they still there?'

'I remember Grandfather saying that the Lindisfarne monks were continually attacked by the Vikings in his lifetime. It is likely that the monks fled and took their most precious items with them.'

There was a gap in their information. The two women continued to consult books. As the fire died down, they both realised, at the same time, who might be able to assist them and who would also be discreet about their enquiries, both on the theme of Leonada and on Oswald.

'Aelfthrith.' They spoke together. 'Aelfthrith the abbess of Shaftesbury.'

'We'll go to Shaftesbury tomorrow.' Wynflaed leapt like a girl from her chair. She took Eadgifu's hand in hers. They both stood. 'To bed, now, and sleep. We will get to the bottom of this, I am sure of it. Some may call it interference, but so be it. The men have made a complicated mess. We will have to produce a little of our own womanly magic. St Radegund will help us. And luck.'

The following morning, as the horses were being saddled, the women continued their conversation of the previous night. 'What happened to the concubine who told you about this business?' Wynflaed stifled a yawn. There hadn't been much sleep for either.

'I dismissed the lisper. I pushed her through the heavy curtain, after admonishing her to silence. She had the sense to pick up the coin from the floor. She won't speak to anyone else, but if she does, she knows what will happen to her.'

'What about Dunstan? Does he know anything?'

'I am sure that he knows more than he has told me about Leofa and the red-haired girl and their issue. I sent a servant for him, but I was too late, she told me, the witan had begun. He was called away straight after to Winchester on some urgent business. Nonna was in Frome. I had to bide my time or come to you.'

They climbed their mounts and wheeled about. The witan and all its slow-witted men be hanged. Grandmothers are agents for the spirit. Their sharp sewing needles stitched the facts of history, their minds guided the young. Who to hate and who to love, that was the most important part of education. They shaped the destiny of a bloodline, defended it from harm.

Eadgifu shouted to Wynflaed as they cantered off. 'Now I understand how Aelfflaed felt when she lost Aelfweard and Edwin, her sons by Edward. I had contempt for her, then.' Eadgifu, queen and mother, grandmother and king-maker, had compassion at her core, still, though not much. She could deal in death. A man and his child must die, or her grandsons, perhaps her son, would lose their lives. There was no choice. Sentimentality and conscience would be put aside.

Nonna had to be interviewed, but first they must interview the abbess of the abbey in the sky.

Nonna's Diary, May 946

I HEARD FROM Gwladys that the queen-mother wanted to talk to me urgently, but I was busy at Frome with court business and could not get away. The following day, I travelled with the courier back to Cheddar, but she had left the palace. Her women said that she had taken a fast horse with the intention of visiting Charlton Horethorne.

I had no idea why she should want me. Dunstan was her usual source of information, but he was in Winchester, three days journey away. Aethelwold was viewing building works at Ely.

There had been an upset in the sewing room at Cheddar, it seemed. I wasn't unduly worried, except that interviews with the queen-mother had become uncomfortable affairs of late. It was not to be long before I discovered that the secrets were out.

To Shaftesbury

THE TWO GRANDMOTHERS set off across country eastwards to Shaftesbury, a half-day ride across the vale of Blackmore. They passed ruined remains of ancient farmsteads and houses. Their stone walls and field enclosures, studded with mature oaks, littered the countryside. Long, overgrown hollows and drives led up to shambling, abandoned villas and workshops, glimpsed through acres of foxgloves and nettles. The tumbled stones and half-fallen roofs mutely held the memories of a once dense population. Some were being restored. What had once been a well-ordered landscape was in the process of becoming so again. The Vikings could not, must not, threaten again.

They rode hard through Wilkin Throop, Abbas Combe, Kington Magna and East Stour, heading for the great hill of Duncliffe and, beyond it, the commanding hilltop town, site of the market burh of Alfred and the great abbey, founded by him for his daughter, the first abbess. In the few years since its founding, the abbey had grown quickly in size. Its church tower rose on the horizon like a solid, immoveable flag of Christianity. Huge nave windows glittered in the spring sunshine.

They arrived, walking and exhausted, at the top of the steep hill to Shaftesbury, at midday. They looked back, as they and their horses panted, across the land they had covered. Shaftesbury commanded views for many miles. In the distant north-west, the impressive hill of Lamyatt Beacon indicated the nearby old Roman frontier road of the Fosse. They leaned against a rail outside The Paladur Inn, a tavern at the junction of the hill path with the town, taking a momentary glimpse of the great beauty and marvel of the springtime. Would they live to see another? A weather-beaten wooden tavern sign, swinging from a single chain, squeaked a welcome to the women.

As they arrived at the abbey gates the bell in the church tower was ringing for sext. The women dismounted. Their horses were led to the abbey stables by the gate-house groom. They put on dark cloaks and veils and joined the sisters in the church. They were greeted afterwards by Abbess Aelfthrith in her parlour. She was a quiet spearhead of culture, a promoter of peace, aided by the wealth at her disposal. The lengthy formalities of greeting normally required were dispensed with. The abbess patiently waited for Eadgifu to begin. Wynflaed she knew well, but the queen-mother was her equal, possibly, even, her superior, and less familiar. Her eyes twinkled in her wrinkled face. The visitors tucked their dusty shoes under their cloaks.

'Mother Abbess, we are making urgent enquiries about a birth which we think happened here some time ago - about ten years ago, we think. May we consult your records?' Eadgifu had rarely been examined more closely. She felt uncomfortable. She could learn from this older woman; how to be strong, how to be silent, how to pray. How to be resigned.

Aelfthrith was a wise, middle-aged woman, energetic, alert and careful. When she walked, it was purposefully. Her robes flapped as she moved, even in the still air of endless corridors. Her slow measured stride when in procession displayed her self-control. Her antennae for picking up family discord or jealousy was remarkable. She took her time, guessing the reason for the visit. Discretion might have to bow to need. A visit from the queen-mother meant urgent business was at hand. Secrets could not be kept forever.

'I'll have the scriptorium sister bring the records of new life.' She rang a small hand-bell on a table by a bowl of holy water. Like the light of candles, priest-blessed water helped to keep dark things at bay. Eadgifu placed a large purse of coin discreetly on the table beside her. There was a clinking sound as the coins settled.

The three settled down to a long discussion.

A nightmare was coming. The great embroidery on Wynflaed's hall wall might have to be resewn.

The old willow by the river, devoid of its crashed lower limbs, its trunk still leaning to its fellow creature of life, the flowing water, listened to the bells of St John's church of Frome, mother of its region, the old shire of Selwood. It swayed and shuddered in the wind, dancing, as the insistent monastic call to prayer rang out in the late spring evening. Men and women, resting after their labours in the town, heard it and paused, their spoons, half-way to their mouths, dripping broth. A Hail Mary touched their lips. On its remaining upper boughs, a territorial owl settled with its talons gripping firmly onto its hunting roost. It waited for full darkness to deliver its deadliness to small, furry, creeping creatures. A reckless water vole hastened across the river from bank to bank, its fur drenched red by the setting sun.

The owl willow raised its limbs in the cool air in response to the singing which, following the bells, emanated from the monastic church. A sudden strong gust lifted the angelic sound to the lower levels of heaven, just as the monks intended. Heaven sighed in reply. As the last Gloria joined with more ringing the owl, a lone hunter since the death of a partner in the previous summer, took flight across the sluggish water, ignoring the vole which had found its nest in the damp reeds, safe from the eyes of feathered creatures. Not so the smaller animals who inhabited a large midden beside the monastery refectory, some of which had seen their last day on earth. Brown rats with pointed noses scurried to safety as the owl flew down, seeking the sanctuary of tiled pipes and labyrinths of water conduits criss-crossing the land. Creatures and monks, nature and man, harmonious in their reverence for the Creator, fearful and greedy in their extremes, were driven by a force to live and to copulate, to create themselves in perpetuity, to seek everlasting life in this world and the next. They found their boltholes and waited for their murderer to pass.

Rats and men; cunning and clever, they lived together, worshipping their gods and fighting for survival. Together they congregated in the edifices of house, home, workplace and monastery, bringing nature and contempt for it within the same bounds.

Night and the wind descended. The moon was full. The Compline bell tolled. The monastery evening meal was ending, after which the midden would be refreshed. Candlelight replaced the sun's glow, closing in upon the faces of a small monastic congregation of tardy souls, quickly and quietly eating a comfortable repast: rye bread, fish paste. It was a Thursday and therefore not a fasting day, and so there was a light chicken broth. Ale accompanied the feast, poured from a set of pottery jars. The old leather jugs had been thrown out, along with much that was decaying and fetid in the religious establishment. All would be swept clean; these were the coming times in the church. Happily, strong ale was still allowed. Thor, ancestor of some but now displaced as chief deity, would be pleased.

On the heights of Shaftesbury, at the abbey, the local population of owls, out in great numbers and calling to their mates, woke the lighter sleepers amongst the nuns. Compline had been said and gone; Nocturnes awaited. The royal visitors had gone to bed. In the room set aside for them, they removed their heavy black veils, revealing long tresses of well controlled hair, both greying blondes. Grandmothers in their forties, they were comfortable in their rounding bodies, familiar with discussion, political, religious and secular. They were skilled in the making of mead, the weaving of wool, the shape and design in silk of a horse's head in embroidery. Their personal antennae, as mothers, worked day and night to solve the problem of the frailties of their children's characters, the antagonism of other jealous parents. Sleep came to them, at last.

Amongst the few still awake, the abbess and three of her immediate inferiors were holding an important meeting in her chambers; there was business which must be dealt with even though the daily habit was to remain silent after the evening meal. Their wimples fluttered and conjoined in the candlelight as they conferred around a wooden table, its woven cloth covering their laps, the bowl of hot ashes beneath warming their perpetually invisible legs. Like the rest of the monastic world, they too would fast in silence on the next day, but this night was for thoughts to be expressed.

The nuns sat back. The flowing wimples separated.

An abbey full of women is a dangerous thing. They spin and weave; their souls, as well as others. Their guests' path was woven of the glorious colour of their kind, the dynasty into which they had been born, that of the House of Wessex. The nuns practised magic at a deeper level. There was serious business to discuss and to decide upon. A Mercian potential heir had been discovered by the outside world. Could the abbey be held accountable for not recognising the importance of the birth to the princess while she was with them? Of allowing a romance to flourish under their roof? Eadwig was now known to have a rival in a child which they had sheltered. The wealth of the abbey could be affected, if the Wessex family chose to punish them. Edmund and his line were under threat. Words are swords but real swords might become necessary. This was no longer a matter of church, but of state. There were few reassurances which the abbess could give. The child left the abbey long ago, along with its mother, father and sister. All the nuns could do now was pray. There would be many daily hours of prayer, the guests could be reassured.

In the morning, the abbess reported to her guests what she had learned. The child had probably gone to Ireland. It was abroad and in pagan hands. The notorious thief, Leofa, was the father.

Shocked to find their fears confirmed, Eadgifu and Wynflaed returned to Charlton. Matters were in their hands. Prayer might help, but more was needed. Could Edmund be persuaded to listen to their womanly fears? The court was on the move. They must make their case at Pucklechurch.

The owls of Frome, of Shaftesbury, of the world, careless of man's machinations, or the songs of monks or dancing trees, continued their eerie noise in the valley beyond Shaftesbury. The night retained its secrets, the willows of Frome listened to the sighs of men, their hopes, waiting for the bells of dawn, for the candle of vespers to be lit, for the light of the world to be born again.

'A cock is lord of his own dungheap.' Dunstan, referring to Eadwig.
William of Malmesbury, The Deeds of the Bishops of England.

Cheddar Palace, early May 946

A CHILD'S VOICE, screaming in rage, made lounging dogs
in the yard bark and scatter. Huntsmen looked up from
grooming the underside of horses. A cockerel on a dung heap
took another opportunity to crow.

'Vile, vile, vile. No, no, I shan't.'

'Eadwig's temper needs curbing. He is worse than his father.
Let me deal with him. I shall soon show him how to control
himself.' Aethelwold grabbed the wayward child's arm and
yanked him from a desk and stool. He dragged him to a corner
of the main lodge room, away from the smoking fire. He planted
him firmly, facing the wall. Eadwig continued to shout. Novel
obscenties emanated from the corner, quieting into mumbling.

'I think it unlikely that we shall be able to train this one,'
Dunstan observed. 'What do you intend to do with him?'

'The dung midden might suffice to alter his behaviour. The
cock may rule the muddy, stinking heap, above this snivelling
monstrosity of a princeling. He needs to realise what can happen
to one who resists his teachers. He is no better than a brat in the
kitchens.'

Dunstan sighed. Aethelwold was given to discipline which
could have life-changing effects. A roll in pig manure and a few
straws in his breeches might do no lasting harm at this stage of
the boy's life. 'See that he comes to no physical harm...'

'If he doesn't stop this yelling and soon, he will get my stick
as well as a smelly backside.' Aethelwold had reached the end of

his tether. Edmund, the boy's father, had never been as bad as this, but then, he had not had much to do with Edmund until his puberty. Athelstan and Dunstan had been soft on Edmund as a child. By the time Aethelwold had taken over his academic training, the anger had been largely concealed, covered up by years of conciliatory kindness.

'The boy has spirit; he may make a good soldier, at least...' Dunstan could see some merit in the lad's prospects. If only Edgar had been first-born. That child had entered the world with a psalter in his hand, already reading it. He and Aethelwold could have done something with him. Kings are not made by God alone. He heard a door open and shut.

There was an almighty yell, followed by a squawk from the cockerel outside. Eadwig had had his salutary lesson. It was never forgotten. Aethelwold had become Eadwig's first enemy. What might be the consequences of discipling a seven-year-old future king with an excellent memory and a tendency towards the frequent rehearsal of grudge?

Malmesbury Abbey, mid May 946

Aethelwold and Dunstan walked slowly along the path outside the abbey church which led to the town walls. Conversations which needed to be secure were best limited between two. They paused and looked over the steep defile to the gardens and small fields beside the river. From the woods beyond, a raven cronked and flew up from its nest. They both watched the noisy bird flap by. Ravens, for the superstitiously inclined, or those who were concerned, could bear omens.

'There are not so many of them about, to pick at the corpses of our warriors.' Dunstan had once tried to predict by observation of bird behaviour in Baltonsborough when he was a boy. Black birds had a certain unassailable magic. Corvids were as intelligent as dogs, it was thought by some. One bird, however, was not a threat, just a bird. The bones of Oswald, reposing at Gloucester, were doing their job. His plan to secure the venerable head of the hero and saint had proven wise and practical. England was secure.

'But wolves are still aplenty. We cannot see behind those trees to what may lie beyond and in the forests are the creatures we fear, lying in wait. They may have had their skins removed and they may be hanging on our walls, but they have remarkable magic in their bones. They will return.' Aethelwold was more disposed to creative pessimism. 'Mark my words, we have not heard the last of our Northumbrian friends.' Aethelwold was not familiar with all the details of the visit to Chester-le-Street, but knew there had been an exchange of some kind with the northern monks. Dunstan had many irons, in many fires, which had to be diplomatically handled. Secrets. He told Aethelwold about his headaches and dreams.

'Have you heard of anything new which could cause you to be doubtful, or are you having trouble with your digestion again, Aethelwold?'

'The sermon was dismal this morning, I think you will agree. Skallagrimsson's bloody rendition of Brunanburh at the last witan was certainly more attractive. But it is not that.'

'Then what?' Dunstan felt a growing unease about his companion's doubt about the safety of Wessex, his continuing and deepening dislike of the number of foreigners at court. The sermon delivered a few minutes before by the secular priest ("did you see his painted wife in the congregation," had muttered Aethelwold) had set off a bad mood. There had been converted Danes at the service, standing as guards at the church entrance and later sitting close to Edmund. Granted, they made no attempt to adopt Saxon dress or hairstyles. They could not be confused with their Saxon masters.Their height made them stand out. Their insistence on completing their outlandish attire with ceremonial axes hanging at their waistbands, ready to be used in some imagined emergency, gave rise to grumbling amongst some of the older nobles. They clung to their culture and their language. Their conversion, Aethelwold feared, was not even sartorial in kind, yet here they were, taking a greater part, as each day passed, in the nation's affairs. 'Edmund dotes on his Viking guard and they are paid remarkably well.' Dunstan was reluctant to take on another fear. He leaned forward on the wall, as though intending to lean away from his troubles.

Aethelwold persisted. 'Haven't you noticed how their numbers have grown in recent weeks? It's as if the family know something that we don't. They are getting nervous. And didn't you see: Skallagrimsson is not amongst them. Where is he? But I can answer that. Somewhere where the pile of silver offered is largest.'

Dunstan said nothing. He hadn't noticed the bodyguard's absence. Perhaps he was at Pucklechurch, in preparation for the witan there. Had he, Dunstan, chief advisor to the king, relaxed too much in recent times? Was Aethelwold right to continually distrust foreigners? But Aethelwold distrusted women, other monks, dogs, everyone. They could all leap out at him; his throat was ever their target. In annoyance at his companion's unchangeable mood, he shrugged and looked away from him to the greening woods. The raven was flying over the fields and came back towards them. It wasn't going anywhere, just surveying its territory, reviewing its defences.

'Cronk!' The sound was unmistakable. War was in the air.

Pucklechurch, near Bristol, 22 May 946

WOMEN DARTED ABOUT the interior of a large red leather tent, the size of a small hall, distributing lightweight items of furniture which were being offloaded by male slaves from the cart outside. Piebald carthorses with muddy, feathered fetlocks and gaily ribboned manes stood patiently in their harness. The slaves and servants wore yellow overshirts, dun-coloured trews and red sleeveless tunics. Red, stripes of red and yellow were the colour and design announcing the estates of Wynflaed, together with the emblem of a golden horse. At a distance, other tents were being erected. Pinks, blues, stripes of black and white, greens and mauve clashed and competed in size, convenience and audacity. The temporary hunting lodges of the visitors shouted out their intent: to be the best, the most outrageous, the most courageous, in every way, at the late-spring meet.

'Man, put that down at once. Sprow, do likewise.' Wulfwaru launched herself at the slave called Man, who was carrying one end of a heavy chest and entering the tent. Man did not have age on his side; he shouldn't have been carrying this weight, but he was keen to please. Freedom awaited a willing slave. He stumbled.

The younger slave carrying the chest, hardly visible because of its size, groaned and started to lower his end, making Man drop the chest. There was a thump, a crashing sound and another yell from one of the women.

Wulfwaru was in charge. She tutted and shook her head. The final positioning of the chest and the disaster it might contain could wait. It held crockery freshly made and brought from Charlton. Man had fallen over against one of the entrance poles. It sagged and creaked.

'Come here, both of you. Never mind the chest for now. The entrance poles need realigning, and quickly.' Wulfwaru stood, arms folded, by one of the inner supporting poles which gave height to a conical section of the tent.

The labour required was like erecting a small house, each time they did this. Every time, something went wrong.

'How many times have we put this tent up, tell me? Sprow? Thirty times in two years and you still can't get it right. Come here.'

So much leather, so many horses and other animals to make this blasted tent and to carry it around the country. So much expense at the tanners to make it red coloured. Sprow, who had accountancy on his young mind, being comptroller of the estate at Charlton, counted the cost of everything. *I have a brain; I am not cut out for heavy lifting. I was bought for my mind. Man should have picked someone else for this task. Just because I am male...* He said nothing. He walked reluctantly towards Wulfwaru. She cuffed him on the ear. There was a hierarchy in everything and punishment was meted out accordingly. Wulfwaru was a slave, like himself, but higher in the order of the household, in superiority as well as years served.

She was dressed in Golden Horse work clothes, with a brown linen tunic over a dark red, calf-length skirt. Strapped high boots denoted her high status in the household. A linen scarf had fallen back to reveal her white hair, neatly tied back into a long plait and falling to her waist. No ribbons today, no earrings. Finery would be donned tomorrow, when the whole court had assembled. Her mistress, Wynflaed, would need her to wait upon her and her guests. The red tent had seen some illustrious visitors in the past and tomorrow there would be more. The abbot of Glastonbury and his associates were due to call in the afternoon and in the evening the king would pay his respects. A second chest of undamaged crockery would be soon carried safely in. The beefier guards would be used instead of Man and Sprow, useless creatures.

'Tighten the props outside, now. Make this pole vertical, or by St Radegund I shall have to do it myself.' Wulfwaru was infuriated by incompetence and particularly the damage to valuable goods. She contained her annoyance with difficulty.

Sprow reacted swiftly to Wulfwaru's commands. For his own good, he obeyed immediately. He ran outside, shouting to the nearby cartmen to help him to tighten the ropes, to secure the peg in the soft rain-drenched ground and to heave the supporting poles into place. There was a strain on the central part of the tent as a consequence of their efforts. Wulfwaru sighed audibly as she observed the work, the time it took. She looked briefly at the position of the sun.

She gave an upright a slap in disgust, and marched into the circular section, where it was intended to dine the noble visitors. She brushed away the colourful silk ribbons which dangled from the cartwheel frame in the roof of the tent, waiting to be decoratively plaited and placed around sacred and mundane articles yet to be brought in. She beckoned to one of the women who was starting to dust a table and chairs. They looked alike, to the casual observer, except for the grey in Wulfflaed's dark hair. She would be white, like her older sister, in time.

'Sister, put down that chair and come over here. There is something I have to tell you.'

Wulfflaed obeyed immediately. The chair rocked over as it hit the ground. Her older sister was head of the slave community of all the estates held by Wynflaed. Her future life depended on the whim of this trusted advisor and housekeeper. She hoped, but could not guarantee, that Wulfwaru, who had been promised her own freedom soon in addition to a substantial reward for her many years of service, would promote her own freedom too. But sisters are not necessarily friends; Wulfflaed had to take the commands of her superior and senior sister, if she wished to achieve freedom which might, or might not, come in a few years' time. More than Wulfwaru, her freedom depended on the generosity of the noblewoman who owned her. Wynflaed had told her older slaves that they could expect a reward through her will, but sometimes slaves were simply given clothes or a coin and then gifted to another member of the family to continue their service. A change was not necessarily a rest.

There were considerations for the owner in the matter of slave freedom. Manumission was not just a magnanimous gesture. For noblewomen such as Wynflaed, entry to heaven would be more easily accessed by generous gestures made in the hours after she had departed this life. But what use was it to be free but penniless? Wulfflaed had reached thirty-five summers, the beginning of old age. Wynflaed was a caring mistress, but what might she expect to receive other than the ability to walk alone, unmolested by landowners and other slaves, beyond the confines of Charlton after a public rite in the abbey church at Shaftesbury? When would it happen? Might she, in the meantime, be able to marry whom she pleased? Please God (and not forgetting Radegund) a marriage might take place soon. Martin of Chinnock was willing. Time was running out. She was still vigorous. Two of her teeth were loose. She could move furniture around, a frequent task, and was an experienced spinner and weaver. She had value and could ask, perhaps, for a time when she might leave the household. It must come soon or it would be too late. Martin was still a bondman at Chinnock. Might she be allowed to live with him there? Could she risk asking for this? She had never liked to ask for anything. Years had gone by, clouded by her indecision. Her woes looped around inside her head. She righted the chair and placed it at random in the middle of the freshly fern-carpeted grass, joining her sister at the entrance to the bedchamber section of the tent, where it was darkest.

'What, what now, Wulfwaru? There is so much to do and I thought that you were anxious to get it done before nightfall?' Wulfflaed allowed herself to push back a little at her sister's commands.

Wulfwaru put a finger to her mouth. 'Sshhush.' She had something of importance to share. There was no other slave nearby who was as intelligent as her sister or who would understand the gravity of what she had noticed. The sisters were as one mind when discussing the travails of others. 'I saw HIM this morning.'

'Him? Him who?' But Wulfflaed knew who her sister meant. A rumour was circulating that a famous thief might return from exile. The camp was alert to the possibility of a sighting of a red-haired man. Unexpected visitors gate-crashed witan meetings regularly and the guards were especially wary to be on the look-out for unpopular thegns, returning exiles and renegades at these times. 'Oh, HIM, you mean.'

The sisters were aware of a certain piquancy which was added to the general excitement of the peripatetic court, but were not unduly worried by the possible arrival of a criminal. Their house guards were capable of preventing more than the theft of a chicken or two. However, in this case, they knew him, or rather, knew of him. Many years before they had both noted the effect of a tall Viking man on the younger nuns of Shaftesbury, when accompanying their mistress. And there were rumours of a secret liaison there. Neither woman could read, or they might have learned more. They recapped what they remembered and discussed what they should do about Wulfwaru's sighting. A reward, or more, might be in store for them both, if they told the right person in the right way.

The image of the man in question rose in Wulfflaed's mind. She recalled a shadowy figure, Athelstan's half-Viking attendant, who spent so long loitering around their abbey, getting to know someone very well. She remembered his name, Leofa, and that he had vanished with a cloud hanging over him. The thief, the robber of peace in the court, the disturber of politics, the traitor.

Servants and slaves were trained to be discreet holders of their masters' secrets, but they could speak amongst themselves.

No harm could come of that. The stimulation or withholding of gossip by servants closest to royalty gave them a status among their own kind which they could never claim in the free world. The sisters shared their memories. Neither was stupid; their knowledge of royal matters and the potential of this sighting to alter their own futures needed urgent discussion. This time, their needs came first, before their mistress and her kind, generous though she was. Sightings of a red-haired intruder were beginning to be reported by others. How could they capitalise on Wulfwaru's luck?

'Are you sure it was him?' Wulfflaed had heard the rumours. Perhaps they were just that.

'Yes, I tell you, it was him. Red hair. I saw red hair, just like they are talking about.'

'Who do we go to? Our mistress?'

'Of course. She is anxious. So's the queen-mother. This is our chance, Wulfflaed.'

A servant or slave in a noble household or in the royal palaces themselves was able to deduce much. If you combed the queen's hair every night or heard her sighing over her embroidery, you could guess at the cause of any distress or happiness, sometimes more than surmise, but because it was always in vogue, gossip remained just that. The reign of Edmund the Deed-doer began; the enemies beyond his realm were forgotten. Their names were used to quell unruly children, nothing more.

'Leofa the thief. That was his name.' Wulfwaru looked around her before mentioning the name aloud. 'I saw him at dawn this morning as I was feeding the riding horses. I swear it was him. He was riding away from the high land into the forest.'

'Are you sure? Was he alone?'

Wulfwaru was not used to having her sister doubt her. She shouted. 'Yes, it was him!' She calmed down. 'I saw no one else nearby. His horse was well furnished. He had weaponry about his person but did not appear to be ready to launch an attack single-handedly. He had more the appearance of a spy. He was wearing a red cape. He flew off into the air. His horse had wings.'

'Wings? What will you do?'

'This must be reported. An alert must be given. The princes will have to have a double guard over them.'

Wulfflaed considered the urgent need of certainty for her future life. Might there be a coming opportunity of turmoil, of chaos which could facilitate her yearning to be elsewhere, to be released from Wynflaed's demands, her sister's orders? In times of war or emergency changes occur. Individuals walk through ruined fields, past burned churches, to new fates. Might a time have arrived, when fear, or the threat of it, would open a door for her and for Martin? Could there be a reward of great value? It would be nothing to others, but to a woman whose time for birthing a child was running out...she turned and ran out of the tent.

Wulfwaru stared at a retreating back. Her sister was gone, had left the tent in its state of unreadiness. But she was right; Wynflaed must be warned, whether or not the sisters would get a reward. There was a red-headed devil on the loose.

Pucklechurch, evening, 22 May 946

THE GRANDMOTHERS SAT at a far corner of the fully furnished tent. They watched the gathering of twilight from comfortable seats. In the morning the red tent of Wynflaed would host the wives and families of arriving nobles in its core. An area at one end was curtained off for ablutions and costume changes for the women. A gated area with playthings for the younger children had been constructed near the entrance. Three stuffed hobbyhorses poked like strange flowers from a decorative urn.

'What can we do?' Wynflaed was having an uncharacteristic moment of panic. 'There aren't many red-haired men about. The Danes in the camp are mostly fair-haired. It must be him. I suppose that we could suggest that Edmund should send out a search party, but it may be too late. It is already growing dark. We should alert the guards. The palace will turn from looking like a pleasure-ground to a fortress, though, if we do that.' The St Augustine celebrations, so important in representing the state of the realm to foreign dignitaries, needed to avoid displaying the panic of a state under siege.

'It is no good, Edmund won't let me near him. In any case, he won't believe us, and especially not a slave.' Eadgifu slapped the table. Why was Edmund so unreasonable, when all she had ever done was to protect him? 'And in any case, Wulfflaed might be imagining things.'

A rumour cannot be suppressed for long. The report of a spy, his face covered in red paint, the colour of hell, had flown around the camp. He had a winged horse. The feast could not be cancelled, there was no question of that, but a reduction in the number of guests might assist the vetting which would be necessary. Skallagrimsson would be in charge of that.

Wynflaed and Eadgifu looked at Wulfwaru, standing nervously in a corner, anxiously wringing her hands. They looked around the interior of the red tent. They considered the number of weapons at hand. The children must be guarded when they were with them. There were several decorative hunting spears, propped up, like the hobby horses, in jars. Hanging by the stuffed head of a boar, in a food preparation area, there were some dangerous-looking kitchen knives. The male slaves were not allowed to carry legitimate weapons. They were bulky, physical men, but only few in number and not young. There was little protection for anyone, except behind the stone walls of the palace. Tents, large and small, had become the commonplace shelter of visiting diplomats and dignitaries; the security of a hall's solid walling with its small army of guards was reserved for the immediate royal family. What good would a tent, even though a sturdy leather one, be against sword and fire? But who would have thought that there might be violence in the land again? The north, that vengeful, pagan place, had become a toothless shadow over their lives. It was a shock to discover it might regain its bite. A red headed monster, a flame of vitriol, had ascended from hell's mouth. What would this day, this May day of St Augustine, bring to them all? Could their fears be realised so quickly? Would the saint protect them? Sensible women though they were, the queen-mother and her fellow grandmother feared the potent unknown.

Who knew if this was all just the product of self-serving imaginative fancy of an anxious female slave? And who had now absconded?

Pucklechurch, 23 May 946

EDMUND COULD NOT hear his mother speak. He was not deaf, it was just that, with the criticism of his new wife and her overbearing attitude to his personal choices, his hairstyle included, Eadgifu had overstepped a mark. He could not abide her voice, her look of wild, possessive involvement. Egil Skallagrimsson had become his advisor-in-chief, after Dunstan. He did not wish to hear from the older women in his family and so he could not.

Dunstan was delayed in Malmesbury. Aethelwold was present, preparing for the ceremonies. Egil was off-duty, probably admonishing or cavorting with the Viking contingent at a nearby hostelry; they were not lovers of tents. The only person nearby who he could trust was Nonna, the safe and boring one. Nonna would tell him what Eadgifu and Wynflaed were anxious about. They were forever troubled about something; usually it was what the children were or were not doing, what Eadred was eating and vomiting up, about herbs and healing and behaviour; about what other women had said or done. Women's concerns. He found Nonna talking to a foreign visitor's servant beside the hall entrance. He beckoned to him to step away.

'Nonna! You don't look quite as busy as everybody else. Tell me what the women are saying. I've no time for their perambulations around the subject of the court's misdeeds or mine. Tell me in a few words whatever is the matter, if you think that I should know. Come with me.'

Edmund and Nonna walked to the stables. Edmund patted his horse and began to brush down Sian. The motion soothed man and beast. Like his dead wife Elgiva, he was fond of all horses.

Their smell calmed him. He could speak to them. This horse shared a special bond with him. Neither could forget their time on the heights of Cheddar. His new wife had brought land, but they had no shared interests. She had banished dogs from their bedchamber. There was little chance of her becoming close to his children; Eadgifu had seen to that. She might, in time, produce more heirs; that was the contract between them and no more.

Nonna felt uncomfortable. 'I feel out of place somewhat, my lord, on such occasions; there being no witan meeting to work for until the day after tomorrow and not being involved with the affairs of the church. The steward has all in hand for the feasting and the procession for tomorrow is being conducted by Aethelwold; I am pleased to say I am allowed to be idle, though my pen and my memory are always available to you and my eyes, thank Christ, are not yet dim.' Nonna, nervous of the large flank of Sian which shifted sideways in response to his appearance at the stable entrance, shrank back into the courtyard. Edmund joined him outside, patting the horse on its rump.

'I'll be back soon, Sian, I have not finished my conversation with you, my friend. Well, go on, Nonna, what is the trouble with the women?'

'My lord, they have been told by one of their slaves that a red-haired man has been sighted in the vicinity of the palace.'

'Another one? That's four this week. Egil has been telling me about such a man who is supposed to come from the west. Mother has told me before to beware of a red monster, but that was in her dreams. Dunstan has devils attacking him in his nightmares every night. Red is the colour of hell. If I were to take notice of everyone who dreams in colour and who insists on omens, I would not get out of bed in the morning.'

'My lord, they say that the man is Leofa. They also think that his intentions are malicious.'

'Leofa? Malicious? He was once a friend. But Leofa would not return to these shores. His exile was permanent, for his safety as well as my own. Why should he come back, unannounced? Have you had any more communication from him?' Edmund leaned against the stable wall and folded his arms. This might be more serious that he had thought.

Nonna had to choose now between loyalty to his king and to his friend. He could not believe that Leofa had the intention to cause problems at court, but could he admit that he had had direct dealings with him in recent times?

His quandary was resolved by a shout from the palace entrance. A scuffle had broken out between a small group of Mercians and a Danish guard. Nonna and Edmund ran to the doorway. Edmund stepped between them, narrowly missing being hit by a fist intended for the guard. The obscenities continued. The Mercians were objecting to a new rule: no wearing of daggers inside the palace. The Dane had been goaded by the Mercian men, calling him an old woman for insisting on their removal of weaponry from about their persons. He had tried to frisk them. It was the new rule for feasts, the guard insisted.

'The guard is right, my friends, it has been decided by the witan that ceremonial daggers are not allowed to be worn inside the hall. It is a matter of security for all of us. We will store your weapons safely for you in the stables here. Implements will be provided for the feast.' Edmund expected the Mercians, who he had personally invited, to give way. Instead, they flourished their daggers and looked furious. Dunstan's idea of using forks and short knives to eat with, which he had seen on the continent, was going to take time to be accepted.

'We cannot accept this rule. It is a dishonour to be bereft of our personal knives.' One man, a giant who had been useful at Brunanburh, spoke out. 'And get your hands off me you Viking scum.' He shouted and spat at another guard who was preventing him from going inside the hall.

'Come here, over to the stables. Are you Aelfweard?' Edmund turned his back on the group and began to walk down the cobbled yard towards Sian, who was watching the men from the stable with interest.

'Yes, Aelfweard is my name.' The tall man put his dagger into its sheath and followed Edmund. The two men argued as Sian whinnied and shook her head. At the palace door, tempers cooled. The discussion progressed.

Edmund pulled a purse from his belt, poured something out of it into the giant's hand, picked something from the floor which had escaped and added it to the outstretched palm of the Mercian.

The deal was concluded. The waiting Danes were grinning, the Mercians frowning. Edmund and Aelfweard marched back, step for step, to the others. Aelfweard revealed small silver coins in his hand. Whoops of glee echoed round the yard.

Aelfweard was smiling. 'Fear not, my friends, we shall wear our jewels and knives tonight, but tomorrow we shall be good lads as we depart. In our meeting and for the next embassy, I have agreed that we will wear our scabbards only. Wessex will have no personal daggers, either.'

The cheers subsided. Forks were an easterners' invention to take away their manhood. Meat was eaten in the warrior's way, using daggers and hands. Edmund waved his arm at the Mercians, who, disgruntled but appeased, backed away. Edmund had given the Mercians what they most loved; a valuable piece of silver for each man who would promise to cast aside his weapon for tonight's feast. More might follow, to soothe a Mercian's esteem. They would get used to it; nobody relishes change.

There would be no weapons at the feast, except his own. By his act of diplomacy and generosity, Edmund had just sealed his fate.

Nonna retreated to the tent allotted for clerks. It was too late to get a message to Leofa, much too late. He might be arriving here, or he might be still in Dublin, or in Wales. Hywel Dda would be arriving soon; perhaps he might have news. What had his friend decided to do? What had others, not as friendly to

Edmund, decided for him? Like everyone at the court, Nonna looked for red hair in the crowds. There were some, but none with the age and assurance of the man who had been Athelstan's chief advisor before Dunstan had taken over that role. After all these years away, who would recognise him? Dunstan was on a mission elsewhere, Aethelwold had barely known him and Athelstan was dead. Only he, Nonna, and Edmund, of the present generation of court clerks, had known him well. Only he and Edmund could recognise the voice, the looks, of the person who had shared their adventures to the shrine of Cuthbert at Chester-le-Street. And years of boredom in Dublin might have taken their toll.

Nonna's Diary

I, NONNA, REMEMBER well the events of that fateful day at Pucklechurch in May 946. How could a nation forget? I wish to share the details, some of which I witnessed and gleaned from others, the day that all our lives changed, when war and the thought of war was once again on everyone's lips, in everyone's hearts. That day I was no longer a young man. I passed, as so many did in despair, into the ranks of the fearful middle-aged. From that moment on, I could hear the bells of approaching death, smell its fetid breath.

I must set the scene. Pucklechurch palace, more of a hunting lodge than a conventional hall, sat on a brow of open land, its great door facing south-east to the warming sun and to the depths of the territory of Western Wessex. Everything as far as the eye could see, land, trees, animals, farmsteads and people was the property or in the gift of Alfred's dynasty or the church. In the distance lay the great Severn river and beyond that, the land of Wales, of the foreigners, though they were less like enemies in those days than formerly. Hywel Dda ruled there then, a trusted friend.

The palace, though not the best-appointed hall, nor best equipped for hunting (though the nearby forest of Kingswood afforded reasonable mixed game) was nevertheless a well-built stone edifice, like its nearby church of St Aldhelm, which gave shelter from winter winds. The combination of hunting establishment and church was appearing in most of the popular areas of Wessex; building in stone was financed by the wealthy who had vastly increased their treasures after the successful battles of recent years. Churches and their priests were showered with gifts; the idea of purgatory was taking hold. I had my doubts about it, but many new monasteries were built or restored, particularly in the east. Their patrons were guaranteed short stays in God's waiting-room. If only some of that wealth could have been spent at Frome, but the older missionary monasteries along the Dumnonian frontier were neglected, except for Dunstan's Glastonbury. The Saxons were in their second phase of conversion; they had left paganism firmly behind; next they needed to become reformed Christians. Aethelwold had the matter in hand.

The hall at Pucklechurch served as a spacious reception for large groups of visiting nobility and their families, with a cleared and hedged enclosure nearby, suitable for a number of tents, big and small, at the time of witans and celebrations. It was used primarily in late May as a suitable venue for the celebration of the two great saints, Aldhelm and Augustine, whose feast days were held on the twenty-fifth and twenty-sixth of the month. Its thatched roof was readily repaired from the reeds of the marshes by the side of the river and its small glass windows helped to illuminate the interior. Glazed windows were a recent addition to the palaces, especially in the renovations and new-builds in stone which were being undertaken under Athelstan and Edmund. The royal treasury was full. The church was spending a flood of fresh income. Former luxuries were becoming almost commonplace. Dunstan's ideas were flying from paper to stone, being turned into edifices of splendour.

Monastic buildings had used glass for years as part of their lighting requirements, as the continent had taught us. Glass was much prized in the homes of thegns, though fire and candlelight were still the main means of illuminating older halls. They seemed to reveal not just that which could be seen externally but also that which was internal, Dunstan said.

Look into a man's eyes by the light of a candle and you will see the truth, as well as any demons dancing on the wall behind.

The sanitary conditions at Pucklechurch, always an important consideration for the growing witan meets, were not as good as at Cheddar and especially not for the increasing number of wives and daughters who accompanied their lords. The chance to meet their sisters who had been married into the house of Mercia and the relatives partnered with Welsh nobles made it a venue of interest, a place to discover new cultures or fashions and to exchange vows of betrothal. It was an airy, uplifting site, somehow encouraging fresh ideas, blowing away the detritus of the old and marked the end of winter. On the edge of former kingdoms, away from the conservative heartlands, it was open to the new, or different.

The Welsh contingent could easily travel there, taking a ferry across the Sabrina, as they called it, the mighty Severn river, from St Brides near the New Port to the old Roman port of Abona. They call this today Sea Mills. From the settlement of King's Weston nearby it was only a few miles from the busy slave port of Bristow. Less than a day's ride after landing brought them to the palace at Pucklechurch, when their presence and their assigned tribute, usually wolf skins, was requested by Edmund. The gatherings were cordial; Hywel Dda, king of the Welsh, friend of Athelstan, continued on good terms with Edmund who was the same age as his sons. The language of the foreigners, together with their colourful woollen garments and metal jewellery was heard at most of the witans, preferable, many thought, to the sound of the Danish tongue. The Welsh brought musicians and dancers with them, introducing us to melodies which filled the rest periods between intense negotiations and law making. Some meetings were memorable for their failures or disappointments. The bread had been sour, the servants less than pleasing. Disgruntlement sometimes changed to murderous intent when confinement caused by arguments about boundaries and ownership led to frustration. Like their dogs in the barns outside, the younger men sometimes howled with temper and boredom. Hywel Dda's flautists had soothed and saved many a meeting from disaster, though not on this fateful day. Everything happened too quickly.

The trouble ought to have been limited to a dispute, as so often happened, between the hot-blooded young men of the Mercian and Wessex contingents. The king's steward, by judicious supply of ale, wine and plentiful food, as well as arranging hunting and hawking expeditions, could moderate any anticipated quarrels. The arrival of a large number of Danes, however, had brought new challenges. Edmund's choice to mark his incipient fatherhood by sporting a Viking style hairstyle, had been unfortunate. Suddenly everything Danish was in vogue. The Mercians remained suspicious of change. They were wary of the influx of any foreigners who attended court. Vikings, in particular, were regarded by the more conservative members of the government as loud-mouthed upstarts. They had poor table manners, incomprehensible accents, had little or no family pedigree and had showy, exotic weaponry and clothing styles. Strangers to modesty, they flaunted their wealth. They did not apologise for their obvious enjoyment of high status in the land, won by dubious means, not years of tradition. Dead animals hung around their necks as additional ornamentation, reeking. Ostentatious Thor necklaces and arm rings declared their opposition to conversion. The Christians among them had taken their new faith to mean that they had the right to wear more jewellery, added to the decorations of their fathers. It was just a different design, very fashionable, to them, to wear a cross. The Mercians viewed their dancing with distaste. It was too vigorous. They laughed too loudly. Their insolent existence was personified in the ever-present person of the Icelander Egil Skallagrimsson.

I could see what they meant. The king's chief guard was a giant, ugly-headed man, wearing the same hairstyle as Edmund, sporting a fixed grin which said it all: *I am this man's protector and he is mine. I empty this man's pisspot, I am so close. Remove me at your peril. Come on, I dare you.* He stood within yards of Edmund at witans with folded arms and legs apart, challenging with his eyes beneath their bushy brows, a long-bladed sword at his side. You could see runes sparkling along its edge. No-one understood what they meant. He washed, they said, only in cold butt water, or in any adjacent river. In the winter he would charge out from the hall to leap, with others of his kind, into iced river water, accompanied by frenzied yelling. He had been a berserker in his youth. His air of suppressed violence made him an excellent personal guard. He was like the geysers that I hear Iceland has. He could blow at any time. He smelt of death, death to others, for a price. His price was high and Edmund paid it.

On that fateful day, he disappeared.

The Red Tent at Pucklechurch, 25 May, 946

E ADGIFU LIFTED HER feet to a low stool. 'One down, one to go.'
'One what? Oh, you mean, feast.' Eadgifu looked tired,
Wynflaed thought.

*We are both getting on. I will have fifty summers soon and she has
forty-six. We have both experienced much in our time, bad as well as
good. God grant that we will be able to see our families and their line
into the next generation. The wars are over, but the jealousies are just
as deadly. Will the wisdom of age count for much when youth holds the
reins of power?*

These thoughts flowed like a nebulous river beneath the
actions of the moment, at some point colliding with those of
others. Wynflaed realised that though she herself was exhausted,
conversation should be restarted. There had been much to think
about. It would be best to begin with untroubling speech.

'The greeting supper went very well, last night, I thought. The
procession to church, taking in the town and making dramatic
use of the sunset from the brow as a focus for prayer and then
continuing eastwards to pray for St Aldhelm, was a fine touch of
Dunstan's.'

'Dunstan's, you think? Only his?' Eadgifu winked over her
goblet. 'And what do you think I was praying for as we looked to
the west?'

'Ah, I thought you might have had something to do with it.
I'm surprised, though, that Aethelwold passed it as acceptable?'
Wynflaed, having made the effort to attend to her friend, began to
wake up. They had both slept, tired and stressed, from the journey
and other matters, during the day. 'I suppose you were thinking of
Dublin.'

'You can send more than prayers across the world, if you wish. I sent an arrow.'

Eadgifu was not ready for bed. The nap had refreshed her. She had more to say.

'Thankfully, Dunstan doesn't discuss everything he plans with Aethelwold. Aethelwold's turn comes tomorrow. There will be less concern with the sunset, more monsters involved, more slaying of devils, you can be sure. He can conjure the devil or multiples of him with a mere wave of his bejewelled aestel. For one who likes drama, he is remarkably difficult about secular dress. He looked askance last week when he saw my daughter wearing a low-cut dress without a veil. He berated her in the abbey cloister because she had bright colour in her skirts. And she was just a visitor. It was a pity that he happened to be visiting Wilton too.'

Eagifu put down her glass, lifted her feet off the stool and leaned forward. 'But never mind him. Send out the slave. I wish to discuss matters with you in private. It is time to put on our veils and to consult the relics.'

'Ah, the magic bones.' Wynflaed rose and signalled to Wulfgyth, a deaf slave girl who attended her. 'Come here, I need some help to robe.' *She is a pretty girl; I drag her around with me. She would do well as a farmer's wife. She will be free after I am gone. She would not hear what transpires between us, but Eadgifu is right to be wary; the girl is intelligent. Actions and lip reading may give more away that we would like. A veil can be useful, as well as obscuring vision, but, God knows, I need help with that putting it on. My fingers fumble. My sewing days will soon be over.* Wynflaed opened a small chest and brought out her light veil. Eadgifu pulled out her summer veil from a tasselled leather bag.

With the veil tidily in place and the head band straightened, Wulfgyth was dismissed. Nuns' robes were put on. Together the two women moved to a darkened inner area of the tent which had been reserved for private worship and relic consultation. A large pole in its centre gave height. A heavy curtain could be drawn across for complete privacy. Wynflaed, straightening her robe, approached a metal box, gilded and decorated, standing on a chest. The box contained divining equipment and relics and acted as a travelling altar. Three candles nearby were already lit. Wulfgyth had anticipated the requirements of her mistress.

Wynflaed knelt, muttered a prayer, then stood and unlocked the box using one of many keys hanging from her girdle. Again she knelt, prayed, rose again, made the sign of the cross and moved behind the chest, lifting the lid slowly with both hands at its sides as though it was a breakable object. The idea of the relic could be fragile, if not the outer casing. In this case the belief and casing were both strong.

Eadgifu leaned over the contents which faced her and lifted a red silk-wrapped item from its interior. It was round and heavy. The beaky nose shape could be seen through the cloth. She cradled the article, then passed it to Wynflaed.

The relic had been touched by both women; both were now charged with the mighty powers of divination. The head was returned to its box. Lips moved in the unison of prayer. The two women knelt in front of each other, holding each other's hands. Behind the veils their eyes were shut.

In prayer, dreams are messages from the gods. In the close presence of a participant of equal status, or of the same sex, they are charged with foretelling.

Or so it was thought. A flying red enemy met the head of a saint and did battle in the air above them. This was the magic of prayer.

Pucklechurch, 26 May, 946

THE WELSH CONTINGENT had arrived, a day late.

'By Aldhelm, Hywel, you have been busy!'

Edmund was untroubled by the talk of a red-headed monster with wings possibly lurking outside his encampment. Nonna had finally revealed what others were saying. It would not look good to spread alarm, and in any case, the rumour, born of hysteria, was based on the word of a slave girl, not a phrophetess. His mother was a nervous wreck, a nightmare zone. Ghosts could be red-headed. People see, or imagine, strange beings. Dunstan was always conjuring devils. But ghosts seen in colour? His own mind was a fertile place of other-worldly action, nightly. Why should others not be similar? He blamed the lurid dooms which had appeared on many internal church walls. Dunstan had certainly lit the imagination of his subjects. The treasury was overflowing as a result, but there were unforeseen consequences. He put his mother and her fears to the back of his mind.

'How many pelts have you brought with you, Hywel? Is the sacrifice of my tribute going to bite you where it hurts?'

The plump Welsh king walked uphill, leading his family and a dozen of his ministers and clerks, to the church, swathed in the finery of an almost entire wolf pelt, its head and front legs hanging at his crotch. He grinned.

'Only as many as I am told to by your good self, Edmund. It is good to see you again.'

Hywel bowed, the publicly required saluation of a subject king, and gave Edmund an informal hug. 'I can promise you, there are few wolves left now on Machen mountain. I have most of them here with me. There are two hundred dead in my wagon, skinned and tanned. And I have two living cubs for your sons.'

'Wolf cubs? The wolf hounds will love them, though whether they will play with them or eat them, we shall see. Come, stand here with me. We are just about to begin our parade.'

The second day's procession, the celebrations of St Augustine and St Bede, banners waving, bells ringing, monks chanting, reliquaries and their occupants rising and falling with the sway of the slow-moving crowd, made its way slowly and with due pomp from the palace to the church. It passed the cluster of thatched homes, pausing at a stepped cross in the dusty highway for an encircling prayer for the outcome of the coming hunt. Most of the court business would be done in the days after the feasts, when sobriety would be more likely. Some was achieved during the regular processions which had become an important part of civic life. They were important rituals of inclusion. If you were not involved, you lost your place in society. Archbishop Wulfstan was again missing, said to be on his way, held up by muddy ruts. York was a far-off place, almost as far away as Dublin. It was understandable. Perhaps he would not be missed.

The weather was kind for the lengthy procession. Everybody took part, from the high to the low. The holy day's spring wind toyed playfully with tapestry and embroidered banners, fluttering them with vigour on this blue-skied day. Like the cloth put out to dry on lines and hedges after washing or fulling, the winging material accentuated the benign beauty of the day. Bright linen garments, worn by both sexes, tossed and flapped, their decorative edging catching the acquisitive eye of rooks whose nearby nests were now full of young birds. Gold, silver and red-embroidered stitching framed the bodies of nobles; red, yellow and blue silk ribbons danced over the bosoms of commoners. Garlands of flowers, loosely tied, drooped over the arms of lower orders, freemen and slaves alike, attracted to the hunting lodge and palace from miles around to view and to petition their masters. Between and throughout, the mist and smell of incense wove its way, rising and falling, encompassing and enchanting the collective nostrils of the crowd, linking them with the smell and taste of heaven. It was a bright day in the late spring of peaceful England.

The main body of the procession, following bishops and abbots, was made up of colourful families of the nobility. In order, behind them, came the peasants, dressed in more sombre clothing. Continental visitors and the Welsh contingent, sporting green trews under their furs and resembling hybrids of animal and vegetable, clumped along in the central part of the long line of humans.The foreign guests had a sparkling and adventurous array of clothing and headdresses; the colours of silk and linen reflected their homes and culture. The Welsh invariably adopted deep greens and deep blues to represent their hills, rivers and seas; the small Scottish group represented tribes and clans with purple checks reminiscent of heather moorland and grey skies; the Bretons tended to favour sea-turquoise and bright orange. All wore gold and silver jewellery in abundance. A dozen or so tall men and women from the Danelaw walked gracefully. Their fathers had been with Guthrum when he had accepted baptism at Aller in Alfred's time. Egil Skallagrimsson accompanied them, a head taller than the rest. His religious persuasion was dubious. He wore no obvious symbols of faith. The matter of his religious leanings was in dispute among Edmund's closest followers, but his bulk and position at court were unassailable, unquestionable. No-one dared to challenge him; but perhaps a time would come.

Within the small group of Danes were some older men, similar in stature and dress and adorned with battle-won arm rings and ceremonial daggers. The Viking guests, against Dunstan's advice, had been allowed to wear their personal adornments for the procession. The argument from the visitors, as with the Mercians, was that they felt naked without their knives, bereft of a major symbol of their culture and beliefs. It was a part of their being, as was their distinctive hairstyling. The men had carefully combed their hair, where they had it still, into tight loops at the back of the head; the women wore short, transparent wimples which were tied back from the head and held in place by headbands of precious metal across the forehead, showing their hair. The younger women wore their tresses, (*their distractions*, thought Aethelwold), loose, others used multiple plaiting to accentuate density and blondeness. (*Vanity*, thought Aethelwold). The golden or red lights in their hair echoed that of their husbands and fathers, whose beards were also plaited or forked and bright blonde or red or grey. Their level of fastidious personal display annoyed many, particularly as it produced sights of beauty which were nourished by their ancestral heathen beliefs. It would take more than a single generation to stamp them out entirely.

At the door and porch of the church, the procession leaders, the Archbishop of Canterbury, Oda, himself a converted Dane, and Aethelwold paused. Dunstan was absent, having been called away the night before to Malmesbury to pray at the death-bed of a monk. They separated from the serpent of walkers, taking only a small thurible-bearer with them, a lad of nine years. The procession stopped. The intimate magic of the almighty is best announced to few and in a language which only the trained ear can understand. They moved forward to the door of the church, requesting the dead saints Augustine and Aldhelm for entry. Oda raised his heavy staff to bang on the decorative metal. The stout door would allow centuries of ritual to dent its magical face; it would withstand devils and their wiles. The blow brought an answer: voices, young voices within the church began to sing. The sound of angels flooded through the closed door, calling to the faithful. The anthem was one which Aethelwold had composed afresh for this occasion.

The crowd outside the church, mesmerised by the spell of slow, controlled walking, swayed slightly. At the end of the anthem, the door opened inwards as if moved by an invisible force and the priests entered the holy space. Their backs disappearing into the nave were a sign to the following nobles to also enter, bowing or bending to curtsey as they applied holy water to their foreheads and chests. The sign of the holy cross was made countless times as each person, from noble to poor, king to slave, shuffled into the church and responded with awe as they entered this place of heaven on earth. It was better to exaggerate the physical act than to exhibit feeble belief. Banners and bulky items were propped by the door outside, but the holy relics, including the newest purchases by Edmund of St Wenceslaus, his right arm and finger, were carried to the altar and placed at its foot. Greenery from the hedges and woods festooned the altar, the nave and the relics. Commoners and the low-born, along with slaves, sat on the grass outside the church, listening to the glories within.

The service continued, with eulogies, prayers and song, ending in the ritual of freeing an elderly slave of the royal household of Pucklechurch who had reached the end of his useful days as a ploughman on the estate.

After the church rituals came the reward for patience by the secular nobles, believers and heretics alike; the returning walk back to the palace was short, noisy and shambling. Released from the requirements of duty for these few minutes, family groups chattered their way into the hall, some via the latrine and midden, some to the women's quarters in a wooden hall nearby. They would join the menfolk later. Meanwhile the kitchens buzzed. Smoke from the spit roasts, the smell of the fat frying, the aroma of bread baking, rose into the air to glorify God and to lift the mood of the congregation. They took their places, men and sons, brothers and nephews, priests (now relieved of their black outer garments and looking much like their noble brothers), men of power and those who would succeed them, on benches, ready to gorge. Short, blunted knives were handed out to those who had been required to leave their ornaments behind by the guards and who insisted that they could not eat without a knife. Two-pronged forks were available, placed significantly by individual wooden cups. The meat would be tender and the round breads, acting as plates, a delight to tear. There would be crumbs for the dogs, later, and not much else.

Edmund, Eadred his brother, Oda and Aethelwold sat at one end of the hall at the high table. Eadgifu, Edmund's wife and the women and children were seated at at a long trestle nearby. A flash followed by a rumble of summer thunder caused the diners to pause as they lifted portions of the first course, fish, to their mouths. Some younger men, seated just below the high table, watched the king enjoying his repast, studying his costume and hairstyle. Eadred was as usual picking through his fish, separating bones, skin and fin. He was slow to eat, examining closely each morsel before eating, leaving large quantities of half masticated flesh in a wooden bowl especially provided for him, dipping his fingers into a warmed bowl of water and wiping them on a bleached linen cloth between each mouthful. It had become something of a joke to parody, in private, the picky eating habits of the king's brother. He was no less fastidious in dress, preferring to wear a huntsman's tunic with leather guards at the shoulders and wrists, enlivened by striped red and green hose, along with a feathered cap which looked out of place in a sea of headdress-free male guests. The guests noted a short, dark manservant, or was he a boy, called Bica waited on him, a personal friend, some said. Apart from their objections to his sartorial style and his repulsive eating habits, there were no objections to Eadred from the nobility; he had openly declared that he would remain unmarried. There would be no challenge when the time came for the child Eadwig to take his place as king after Edmund's demise, which, the Lady Mary be hoped, would be many years into the future.

The conversation was quiet; concentration was upon the meat course and how to tackle it. Eadred was inspecting his dish with concern. Aethelwold was helping himself to vegetable dumplings from a tureen. An explosion of laughter came from a table near the hall entrance, where the Welsh had been placed. Edmund suddenly jumped out of his seat. Eadgifu, scrutinising closely the feasting behaviour of her two sons, the one prone to anger, the other to annoying table manners, stood up and looked around. What could have caused Edmund to make a violent movement? Had he imbibed too much wine? The hall had suddenly silenced. Here he was, her kingly son, now looking as though he was on a battlefield, reaching for a spear in the hands of the nearest guard standing behind him. What had angered him? She looked along the line of surprised guests. Forks were awkwardly raised mid-air. There was one who was not surprised, she noted. He stood. He made no move.

'Leofa!'

A body flashed by the queen-mother. Edmund had snatched the spear and was blindly rushing down from the wooden dais, followed by Egil Skallagrimsson and two armed guards. Edmund ran, scattering guests, towards the group of Welshmen. A mixture of incredulity and shock stunned the guests into frozen watchfulness as Edmund threw himself, yelling, at what he perceived was his deadly enemy, and his son's. Eadwig, supping with the women at their table, burst into tears, quickly followed by Edgar. Women screamed. Eadwig screeched at being manhandled roughly by his nurse, with dramatic gestures of defence. He was bundled under clothing, an ample wimple, and thrust under the table, his cries hightening the terror of the moment. Edgar joined him.

Leofa remained still, watching Edmund moving rapidly towards him. Eyes swivelled to him. Who was this? There had been a laugh. A Welshman who laughed? What was unusual about him? Was he the thief who was supposed to be lurking in the vicinity? But there was no red hair, only grey. Rage settled upon the crowd. There was uproar. Whoever he was, he was an enemy of the king, that much was clear. How...

But the many questions which needed to be answered would have to wait. Eadgifu watched, mouth open, as Edmund rushed at Leofa, getting closer to his physical body, somehow avoiding harming others with the long-headed hunting spear. The men on benches leaned away from his heated rush.

'Leofa, I charge you to remain where you are; you will be removed by my guards.'

Edmund turned, his mother had spoken, not him. Spurred by self loathing, dislike of feminine instructions ringing out in the company of his court, superceeding his own, he launched himself on Leofa, who now brandished, in self-defence, a small dagger which had escaped frisking by the guards. Other knives, also missed, began to appear amongst the guests in response.

Leofa put out his other hand. 'Peace, Edmund, I come in peace...'

'Do not believe him, he comes direct from Anlaf with a message for you- he brings you death!' Egil Skallagrimsson, now beside Edmund, shouted.

Edmund threw down his spear and launched himself at Leofa, pulling back his head by the hair. As an act of defence, Leofa thrust his knife at Edmund behind him. Edmund let go of Leofa's hair and faced him. Two Danish guards, Skallgrimsson's paid men, kept onlookers at bay. Was it an honourable act by the king to fight this man alone? Whose side was anybody on? The grappling pair pushed and pulled. Edmund threw his taller body at the smaller and slighter man. They rolled on the floor. There was groaning and puffing. Aethelwold and Eadgifu watched with horror from behind the high table. Eadgifu was screaming. Hywel Dda tried to separate the two men but failed.

Aethelwold shouted to Eadgifu above the din which ensued. 'I thought it was too easy on Leofa to just banish him. I begged Athelstan to do more to be certain of the dynasty, but he would not have him killed.' There was no time for more. The horror was upon them all.

Edmund's body, lying on Leofa's, suddenly went limp. Leofa's weapon had found its way, deliberately or otherwise, deep into the chest of the king. He retracted it as Edmund was pulled off him and stared at it in disbelief. Edmund, on the hall floor, blood gushing from his wound, was surrounded by guests now recovering from their fright. In their panic to protect him, they had pushed Edmund onto the implement. Skallagrimsson, waving his sword, stood over the king, who doubled up, clutching his stomach, yelling in pain. Wynflaed and Eadgifu rushed to him. Eadgifu shouted to servants to lift the king. He was carried out of the hall to the nearest large tent, away from the crowds. The two guards who had appeared to hold up any rescue retreated through the kitchen. Skallagrimsson followed.

It was like this in the hunt; it was chaotic. This should have been a boar, not a man, not the king. Friends of the king stabbed at the enemy. Leofa disappeared beneath a tussle of angry men. Blood began to spread in a pool across the floor as Edmund was carried away. Skewered, Leofa's soul left his body. The grey-haired man was dead, torn into pieces by forks and knives.

946. *In this year king Edmund was stabbed to death on St Augustine's day.*

Anglo-Saxon Chronicle.

Pucklechurch, 26 May, 946

A T THIS FIRST stage of grief, there was silence. In the red tent of Wynflaed the Wessex family members and their trusted servants knelt, their hands clasped at their hearts or around their chests, nursing the realisation of what they had just witnessed. Two young children, Eadwig and Edgar, were being held, but not shielded from the sight of their dying father, by an older woman. A young woman knelt by a portable shrine nearby.

Edmund lay on two tables, breathing his last. The blood loss had already paled his face. He was losing consciousness. His mouth hung open. A priest-physician to the court and Nonna as his assistant were hovering over the near-corpse, ripping apart fine clothing to reveal the stab wound to staunch blood if they could, but the visible pouring of life from the body was too terrible, too final.

There was a commotion at the entrance to the tent.

'Let me through!' Dunstan had arrived late to the scene, declaring that a devil had danced in his path, preventing him from saving or warning Edmund. He said that he had feared that the king would die. He had had a vision. He was too late to assist in warning or saving his king, but the abbot of Glastonbury was an important and necessary figure at this tragic time in the nation's history. He must be present at the leaving of his lord from the mortal coil, this snake-ring of licentiousness, pride, greed, toil and tears. Still in his muddy travelling robes, returned from an urgent task elsewhere, expecting to take part in a feast to honour St Augustine, he now had to summon his repertoire of prayer to publicly shrive the dying young man, whose head fell to the side. The chest lifted once and then no more.

Dunstan rushed to the body. Latin poured hurriedly from his lips, like the flow of life force leaving Edmund in front of him. The last seconds of life would be accompanied by a personal protection for Edmund from the gates of hell. What had happened to bring about this sorry state of affairs, he would learn later. He pushed the hovering and defeated healers aside. Nonna would inform him of events after he had done his necessary job. It was not too late. He held the corpse's hands in his own, muttering the prayer for extreme unction for the dying. Would the fading man hear? Perhaps, in those moments before the soul and mind shut down completely, there would be recognition of the sound of prayer to accompany him on his last great journey. Regret, his own as well as theirs, would journey with him, too.

Eadred stood by his mother. Within the few moments that he had been in the tent, seeing how Edmund was fading, seeing his eyes closing, they were both considering the effects of the calamity. None were more adept at viewing the future than Eadgifu and Dunstan, who was now closing Edmund's eyes on this world and exhorting him to look upon his maker in the next. The abbot shot a look at the queen-mother.

Dunstan knelt at Edmund's side. A rattle escaped the corpse. It was over. The women of the family wailed and clutched each other in earnest, as their fear was unleashed. This was a genuinely loved ruler. His public fits of anger were forgiven. What they had lost was more present in their minds than his obvious flaws: order, stability, protection. Edmund had been, in his short reign, a fearless leader of men, a lover of women, a faithful husband to two wives, a father to his children, a worthy leader of the united nation of England.

After some moments, Dunstan stood up, crossing himself.

The others present, witnesses of the passing of the annointed king, did likewise. They waited for his next move, which they would also emulate. Dunstan looked at Eadred. Edmund's brother shifted closer to his mother, putting an arm around her. Eadwig, half enclosed by her arms and silk gown, looked up at them both.

'King Eadwig.' Dunstan bowed to the six-year-old. 'You must now take on the mantle of kingship. Your father has joined the heavenly host.' He waited as the child, pushed forward from her skirts by his grandmother, came towards his tutor, his tormentor.

'Does that mean I can command you?' Eadwig's voice was high. 'I don't want you at my court, or that man over there.' The child pointed at Aethelwold. 'He called me "cock of the heap". He shall rue that day.'

'My lord, you shall have your way in many things. But kings must learn, not only about their lands and their subjects, but to contain their own natures. Yours is kingly, Eadwig, but as yet uninformed. We, your devoted tutors, will guide you.' Dunstan met Aethelwold's eyes and then appealed to Eadgifu. 'Madam, we must hastily come to some arrangement for your son. You, of course, must be consulted about his needs and requirements. Edgar, also, must be involved. He must be groomed to prepare in case Eadwig...' Dunstan did not finish his sentence.

'My grandsons will continue to benefit from your advice, lord abbot, and yours, Aethelwold,' Eadgifu nodded at the priest. 'I will, of course, act as regent while my son matures.'

Eadwig wriggled and looked up at Eadgifu. 'What does "mature" mean, grandmother? If it means that I cannot rule now, then I don't like it.' There were further exchanges of looks between the tutors and Eadgifu. This was going to be difficult.

At the Gate of Heaven

THE PAIN, THE pain, ah I cannot breathe. I cannot move. Wolves snap and tear at my limbs. The vortex comes, the vision underlying all my thoughts. The colours...of life, whirling around me endlessly, the sound of wind. The tunnel comes with visions of the past flashing in its sides, now darkness.

Now light, bright light. I have a thinking mind, in this white place. No, it has a rose colour about it. It changes. Angry colours are here, wavering on the edges. I can keep them at bay by my will, I learn, travelling towards the door I now see.

Not several doors in a passage, as in life, but one only, a simple door with light behind seeping past its edges. It is shut. My floating soul flies towards it and is forced to wait. At its sides stand the patient but unspeaking souls of many others, who turn away from me. They do not seek another, but there is one fresh soul who does; he is familiar. The white and gold strands of his hair and the emotion of pain accompany him as I am accompanied. I feel the yearning he has for life, the regrets. He recognises me. It is the voice that I chiefly recognise.

Edmund.

Leofa.

Is this place the purgatory which we have been taught will be our home? We cannot return, we cannot go forward. The light which draws us is barred to us. There must be prayer below on earth to set us free. The bindings which now appear on our bodies, round and round like thorns, draw us close. We become as one.

I see no devils to torment us.

Tell those fearful below, love will unbind our souls, tell them!

I felt the division of my flesh as sharp metal pierced me deep within; they say that you cannot feel the wound, only the screaming pain of it a moment later, but I felt the stab and the slow retrieval of the metal afterwards, which caused the blood to flow from my side.

So much blood, I could see, pooling around me on the tiled floor. It slithered in a rush to the feet of men standing nearby, staining their shoes.

I tried to rise, but I could not. I pushed at the flesh lying under me. I heard a sickening blow as the halberd struck his head.

My eyesight failed; my mind wandered. The pain became all. Someone lifted my head. My vision was lost.

Then the falling. I was on Sian, flying backwards, tossed and rolling downwards, my feet loose from the stirrups, our cries mingling, animal and man, as we cascaded from the heights of the gorge to join the deer and dogs below.

I do not remember the smash of our bones as we hit the gorge floor; I remember the scream of the horse and the bellows of outrage around my head from those who rushed to save me. Before the total darkness, there was Elgiva, standing as if at an altar, her hands clasped in prayer, her eyes, those large blue eyes, lifted to heaven. She cast her eyes to look at me without emotion. No words were said.

Recognition and acceptance were a wave which passed through me; too late I repented of a need to express my anger; anger at myself, anger at my mother.

I was sorry that Leofa, my former friend, had brought this about.

I was sorry.

I am sorry....Eadred.
I am sorry, Eadwig and Edgar.
I am sorry, England.

Nonna's Diary: Aftermath

THE RED TENT acted as a temporary shrine at Pucklechurch for the first hours after the double deaths of the two former allies, Edmund and Leofa. The bodies, slashed and broken, lay there, unwashed, for some hours. Indecision followed stunned grief. In the late spring warmth the corpses began to rot; I remember the smell of them and the clouds of incense as Dunstan, Aethelwold and Oda argued about what to do, trying to perceive what the saints would wish for them, trying to decide whether Edmund should be declared a saint. Was he a martyr? Saint or martyr, no miracles occurred that day at Pucklechurch. It was eventually decided that Leofa's body, in its entirety, would be buried immediately on the north side of St Aldhelm's chuch. It was a lonely spot, shaded and without a view. He received no marker. I stood with him there as they buried him and said goodbye. There would be no reunion. Even I had not recognised my aged friend.

There were long discussions about Edmund's final resting place.

'It has to be Winchester.'Aethelwold was keen for any royal event of importance to be held in the Wessex capital. 'Forget Athelstan's choice of Malmesbury. He was a maverick and biased towards Mercia.' He folded his arms.

I waited to hear how Dunstan would counter his argument, knowing that Edmund had said, in the hearing of the witan, that all his worldly goods, including himself, would be showered on Glastonbury, Dunstan's abbey. That had been declared in the first few days after the Cheddar hunt and Edmund's escape from death. It might be thought that this promise was made without great consideration, at a time of high emotion. Edmund, spared from death, might reasonably expect not to be faced with choice about his legacy for some time to come.

Dunstan stood his ground. 'There are cogent arguments for a change of burial place for the Wessex kings. We have shifted our kingdom to the west; the shire of Somerset is now a central place in England. Edmund was emotionally attached to the abbey, as were the earliest Saxon rulers. It would cement Glastonbury's importance as a cultural and pilgrimage centre. Edmund was well-liked by the West Wessex people; his corpse will bring in revenue.' And the abbot needed funds for his restoration works. That was obvious to all.

Athelstan had been buried in Malmesbury, as he requested, despite claims by Mercian lords for him to be near St Oswald in Gloucester. Archbishop Oda, perceiving that change was in the air, favoured his own establishment, Canterbury, in the old Kentish kingdom. Though encompassed by Wessex, it had never been a traditional resting place for Wessex kings or foreign saints. That changed later, as both he and Dunstan removed saints from their chosen places of rest to take them to Canterbury. Aldhelm and Wilfrid were exhumed from their chosen burial places and given glorious shrines. Pilgrims flocked; Canterbury grew wealthier still. Besides, Oda's Canterbury had enough riches to maintain itself in comfort, almost as much as Glastonbury. Oda, disgruntled, was called away to business, or to the wash-house.

In his absence, Dunstan continued. 'Oda should be ignored. He and his archbishopric are already wealthy. The Kentish folk have for long pulled the purse strings of the whole of Wessex. We need to share out the income of our holdings, whether land, relic or kingly corpse, to other parts of the kingdom.' Dunstan's birthplace was Baltonsborough in Somerset. Naturally, he wished to see more income graviating westwards. He changed his mind later, when he became archbishop himself. He stood up, suddenly flushed, looming over the seated Aethelwold. Aethelwold unfolded his arms and gripped the chair.

'Edmund called to me. My being rescued him from certain death. I have the choice in this matter, no other.'

It was the first occasion that I saw the determination of Dunstan take on a different guise, one of a messianic quality. He seemed to threaten; even his body appeared to grow. In the small side chapel of the church at Pucklechurch in which we clerks and prelates were meeting, there was a glow, an undeniable light, around his person.

Aethelwold recognised the resolution in Dunstan. Perhaps he had seen it before. 'Then how will we organise the burial service, in such a tumbledown place as Glastonbury? How will we accommodate the guests? The kitchens are in need of rebuilding and the hostelry is without most of its roof.'

Dunstan had evidently thought about the possible arrangements. 'The court is now used to travelling with tents. They have their own kitchen staff with them here, in Pucklechurch. The event need not take many days.'

'But the extra cost...' Aethelwold was not yet defeated. 'Winchester is well set-up to accommodate visitors and the New Minster is weatherproof, which the nave at Glastonbury is not, besides, it is so small.' He stood up. If Dunstan got his way, there would be no holding him in future. Aethelwold had dreams, too of a future archbishopric, though first he had to become a bishop. He had Winchester in mind. Both men could see themselves high up on Jacob's ladder to heaven. Their souls' time in purgatory need not be long, a fortnight, perhaps, at most.

'This is not a matter of cost. I have consulted the gospels. An angel has come to me. The land of milk and honey is the land of West Wessex. It is there that the church's fortunes lie. Edmund's grave will cement our power there. This is the will of God.' Dunstan glared at Aethelwold. I thought he was going to push him over, but he merely took a step towards him. After a brief moment, Aethelwold placed his hands together in a submitting, silent prayer. The tussle was over. Dunstan, and Glastonbury, had won. The angel's appearance had underscored his wish. Aethelwold was not as gifted in positive visions. Dunstan's continuous dealings with devils and angels, which he often related, trumped Aethelwold's imagined ogres and monsters.

Oda returned to the chapel to an accomplished decision. There was no denying the charged atmosphere of consent between Dunstan and Aethelwold. Discussion moved on, with everybody seated. Wine and bread was brought into the room, while the prelates calmed down. I melted into the shadows, taking note, listening. There was still the matter of the succession to decide.

There would be no doubts about it. Eadwig was the first choice of the witan. He represented Winchester, the Wessex of old. Edgar could be offered to Mercia as an under-king. Would they accept this compromise? Arguments continued for some time, while Edmund's soul flew up from his stinking body in the temporary bier in the red, now bloody, tent. Leofa's soul would, no doubt, be consigned to hell, if Eadgifu had her way. His body had been torn into many parts. She was satisfied that he would not rise on the day of judgement. It was judgement, of a sort.

But Eadwig was only six. A child had never ruled the Wessex dynasty. Brothers of kings, rather than children, had been chosen to prevent the weakening of the crown by regency rule, often led by a female relative. The state was now too large, too powerful, to be risked in a minor's, or a woman's, hands. Marriage and legitimacy of heirs, and primogenture, were required, but the desirable straight line of descent was not always the best. Vikings might vote their charismatic leaders into positions of power; that might be democratic and it worked for them, but a settled, landed aristocracy needed clearer demarcation. After the birth of two sons to secure a dynasty, the nobles hoped for daughters as most useful in forging family ties.

Then there was Eadred, Edmund's sickly and unpopular brother. Could he be an acceptable leader? His inclinations seemed to be to the church more than to state, but that was probably the result of years of bullying by his mother. Edmund had always been her golden son. It would take a great deal to awaken the soldier in the dun coloured Eadred. Nevertheless, might he not be a better choice than obstinate Eadwig who would be combined with the formidable regency of his grandmother, Eadgifu? Edmund's second wife, the barren Aethelflaed of Damerham, would be dismissed back to her family to be married off again to an obscure noble. She was a weak character, thankfully, who had taken her fate without emotion, perhaps glad to be removed from the feverish court life and temper tantrums characteristic of the Wessex family. She had been of use; the manor of Damerham had been gifted to Dunstan's abbey by Edmund on their marriage and it would remain there. Glastonbury would rise again.

Athelstan Half-king was consulted. It became clear to the main players in the land that Eadred was the only practical choice for Wessex and England and that his chief advisor, Dunstan, would support him on the throne, rather than the boy. The queen-mother would still have a part to play; Eadred was a more compliant character than his brother had been. The second boy of Eadgifu, the one with the troubled stomach and difficult eating habits would have to do. Eadgifu, Dunstan and Half-king would instruct him how to act and take his place when feasts were necessary. The nation would not see his illness, only experience the strengths of his advisors. A four-strong leadership, with the weakest of them being the king, would rule. What could go wrong? The witan must be persuaded to accept the untried eater of soup, to put aside its boy-king. Eadred, with a stammer to hamper his effectiveness, would not be a popular choice, but he was Dunstan's, and that, in the end, was what mattered.

Nonna's Diary: Hindsight.

W HAT MIGHT LEOFA have told them, had he been able to, had not Edmund, in one of his drunken moods, attacked him? Might he have offered a tale of how, at the end of his many years of exile, he had returned to give him information about the Norse proposals to regain Northumbria? Could he have persuaded him that his own son, though Mercian by birth, was never to be a threat to Edmund or his family as far as the kingship was concerned? That he wished to return to the Saxon court, be useful to it if he could, to act as liason with Anlaf, using his investigative skills to restore the balance of power to England?

But he could not tell them, nor change his mind. The violence which had been unleashed on him by his recognition by Edmund, a man charged with and obsessed by intimate family tales throughout his childhood as heir of Wessex, determined his fate. Leofa's own distinctive laugh had revealed his presence earlier than he had intended. The sound of merriment had killed him.The court had underestimated the power of hatred. Years of insistence by a mother or grandmother about threats to her own kin and their potential perpetrators had corroded Edmund's ability to be rational. Their badgering, in my view, produced an emotional outburst in this vulnerable son. No diplomacy, the overiding of unrational thought, could overcome the tendency of violence born of dislike.

Leofa had become more than a traitor, to Edmund. He was a devil, a competitor for the highest position in the kingdom. The king's death in the red tent would be an image woven into hangings in later years; one hangs in the burial crypt in the

Old Minster of Winchester, another in the rebuilt church of St Mary in Glastonbury, where Edmund was eventually buried. Like Athelstan before him, he had chosen to rest away from the Wessex capital. Edmund's violent death was recorded in many ways; it became a memory recorded in the Welsh Annals, as well as our own, Hywel Dda saw to that.

St Augustine's feast: it was, that year, a celebration of meat, both animal and human. I left the priests arguing and went back to join the queen-mother. In the red tent on that dreadful evening, as the prelates argued about what to do with Edmund's body, Eadgifu and Wynflaed sobbed. Slaves and servants wailed. Eadwig and his baby brother, in the arms of their stepmother, wriggled and cried too, adding their shrill voices to the cacophony of grief. Eadred, having abandoned the hall and the food which so upset him, was now, potentially, the new king. He was silent, standing near the bloodied body, his hands wringing in unconscious agony. He looked stunned. Dunstan and Aethelwold accompanied Edmund's body to Malmesbury abbey first and some weeks later, with a suitable train of mourners, to Glastonbury. The abbot would take care of his soul and in return Edmund would return the favour, he told me.

And what of Egil Skallagrimsson? No-one noticed him disappear. We heard later that he was seen riding hard towards Abona, presumably to take ship overseas. Anlaf, who seemed to be the instigator of the assassination, was known to be in Dublin, no doubt considering another plan to take over our lands. Archbishop Wulfstan, who had failed, unsurprisingly, to join the Augustine celebrations, was under suspicion for collusion. In times like these, where life can be cut short by illness or injury, the conspirators would be unlikely to immediately lead another campaign, though others would fill Anlaf's place, were he to die or lose heart. We were to face more threats from the Norse and their allies again and at a time when we were vulnerable. The head of the Viking snake, cut off, would give birth to more cunning foes.

Eadred, or rather, Half-king, briefly imprisoned and interrogated the innocent Danish and some Welsh visitors, but they insisted that they had had no knowledge of Leofa, his motivations or his presence at Pucklechurch.They blamed the Dublin pagan Norse. We looked to Eadred to recover from the shock and grief of his brother's loss. Would he be strong enough to lift the spirits of the nation? Without an able warrior king, ready to crush our enemies, Wessex and England could fail, we could be pushed back into the marshes of Somerset. For weeks, the witan debated whether to act against the devil's nest, the Black Pool of Dublin. While they raged and ruminated on this matter, led by Half-king, the matter of succession continued to be hotly debated by the royal family and Dunstan. Eadwig was old enough to understand his rights of primogenture but too young to realise the meaning of regency, his grandmother's regency, and what that might entail. Eadgifu pushed back.

Egil Skallagrimsson was never seen in Wessex again. He ended his journeys, no doubt via others who would pay him, in Iceland, breeding ponies and counting his silver. To this day, I hear, he sends missives to his friends in Norway, asking for revolution, never satisfied with the ruler who rises above him. He knocks the heads off stolen wooden statues with his wearied sword arm, practising daily for the fight against an enemy which he will never conquer, the battle against death, writing his poems and telling his tales by the fires of his life. His children rue that he is as tall, as ugly, as famous as he is; they would never match him. Such is the sadness of the father, of the child. He never confessed to any part in Edmund's downfall.

So passed a king and another took his place. What could not be foretold, even by Dunstan, was how vicious a foe Wulfstan, Archbishop of York, ardent follower of that illustrious northern saint, Wilfrid, would become and how an ambitious and fearless young man named Erik would come to dominate our nightmares.

We called him Bloodaxe.

Mourning

IN THE FIRST few weeks following Edmund's death and after his interment, with great pomp, at Glastonbury with a service devised by Dunstan, the court and royal family retreated to Winchester, to its heartland in central Wessex. The Old Minster and the New, together with the Nunnaminster nearby, formed the centre of a solid fortification against the ravaging world and the after-effects of regicide. The palace of Winchester, crawling with the ghosts of royal ancestors, was filled with an influx of client kings from Wales and Scotland as well as diplomats from further afield. They brought tokens of loyalty or fellow-feeling at the inevitable alteration in the nation's state and took part in an emergency witan.

Indecision followed grief and anger. The witan dithered about who to have as its king. Arguments raged. Priests should not have it all their own way. Was Britain to be led by a child, a precocious but wayward infant with its mother as regent? The nobles took their time. What alternatives were there? Dunstan and Aethelwold, while acknowledging the right of young Eadwig to succeed, were not yet convinced, nor was the majority of the witan, that the primogentiure rule, recently established, should be invoked. They consulted elderly men, whose memories could reach back to Alfred's day. Sons had not necessarily followed their fathers onto the throne. Brothers had taken the place of kings whose sons had been deemed unsuitable, or too young to hold the mantle of power. The retired ministers agreed unanimously that a woman should be excluded from wielding power.The memory of 'bad' queens had been kept alive by the scops. Women were not to be trusted. The much admired Eadgifu of Kent had not been given the sanctifying approval of an anointing. Should such a woman, energetic and able though she was, be given the freedom to order the realm, hard-won by the warriors of the Wessex family into which she had married, just because she had given birth to a king?

For days the arguments and concerns flowed back and forth through the nunneries, monasteries, churches, palaces and halls of the capital of the nation. Visiting diplomats veered between wishing for a collapse of confidence, a crack in witan indecision, and resolution in favour of strength. After two weeks, the witan members and the royal family itself were in favour of making a decision about the right to rule of a son or a brother. The food stores and ale were running low. Prayers were said, day and night, for the matter to be brought to a close.

The choice was clear; Eadgifu and Eadwig, or Eadred the brother, supported by Ealdorman Athelstan Half-king. There was a third possibility, which Aethelwold and Dunstan were mooting, of the younger son of Edmund, Edgar, to rule, together with Eadgifu. Archbishop Oda consulted the relics held in the haligdom at Winchester, a vast array of potent religious items hoarded by Wessex kings, some bearing direct transmission of touch of the sacred apostles, even of Christ himself. Like a shaman in a trance, Oda, assisted by the monks of the Old Minster, visited the shades which lie beyond this world. In fairness and in strict order, to keep peace in the land, it was given to him that Edgar should rule Mercia and Northumbria and Eadwig, Wessex, but that overall, their uncle, the sickly Eadred, should bear the weight of the crown for the time being, until one of his nephews should be of age or competency to take over.

The family discussed the options. Eadred, at twenty-one, should remain unmarried. He consented. No children of his line, as the second son of a king, would be allowed to claim the throne. There had been no potential spouses for him on the horizon; Eadred, a more introverted character than his brother had been, had shown no interest in marriage, of convenience or otherwise. This was a point in his favour, but could he be a decisive defender of the state? The shadows, which Eadred had so far inhabited, had not yet revealed his ability as a war commander, but it seemed unlikely that he would be active and energetic in battle, or give the all-important appearance of it. Non-meat eaters were usually monks. Monks prayed for peace, did not go into battle. There were no immediate threats to the nation, but the north, sensing the indecision and navel-gazing of the south, was considering its options. The Norse and Danish settlers and fresh immigrants, who still poured into York and the hinterland around it, intended to flex their muscles. There had been whispers of a clamp-down on the numbers of families speaking Danish, of a cull, even, of their number. The Northumbrian Danes were beginning to bare their teeth against such an idea, though for now, they held their hand. Trade was good across the Viking world; war might divert wealth from the merchants; they would watch and wait.

At last a decision was made by a majority vote in the witan. Eadred, in receipt of Oda's official advice from the relics, became undisputed, though temporary, new leader of the united nation of England and Emperor of Britain, the best taxed, the best governed, the brightest and most secure nation, with defined borders and a natural moat around it, of all the European states.

The diplomats and client kings could return to their realms. Pantries could be replenished. The detritus surrounding the tents on Winchester green could be shovelled up. No-one thought that Eadred's reign would be long, but as a caretaker, he would do. He would be the necessary guardian, to keep the peace, to allow the nation to breathe. Eadwig and Edgar could grow into manhood. Eadgifu could be encouraged to do the right thing. Wilton Abbey, perhaps, or Shaftesbury; she could choose her own fate.

There was another requirement in balancing the authority of state and church; there came a change with Edmund's demise, a great alteration in the affairs of one noble family; Half-king rose to prominence. After the disappearance of Egil Skallagrimsson, into the void left by him stepped Athelstan of East Anglia, hailing Eadred as a competent leader. Though less imposing as a right-hand man than Egil, he was a convincing and erudite man, skilled in diplomacy as well as warfare. He carried the power and authority which was his due as an experienced courtier and warrior, having witnessed the capture of Constantine of Scotland in 934 and the battle of Brunanburh in 937. He made up for Eadred's lack of the golden element with which his older brother had dazzled his subjects. A month after his coronation, Eadred adopted Edmund's elder son Eadwig as his heir. Half-king adopted Edgar. The queen-mother lost control of her grandsons.

During the month of June, Edmund's burial cortege made its slow way to Glastonbury and his beloved gorge. A procession of carts, soldiers and priests made its way to the coast from Pucklechurch and followed the shoreline to the opening at Brean Down of the Severn sea to the inland seas of Somerset, traversing by punt, dry causeway and track to the abbey site of Glastonbury, the legendary tor always in their sight. Access to the abbey was by a newly built western gate which Dunstan had designed and had constructed in stone the previous summer. The body rested in the chapel above the gate for one full day as the rites were prepared and then in splendour and in full view of the blood-red tent and its female occupants, owners and slaves, the interment took place beyond the east window of the old wooden church. The children of the dead king fidgeted in the company of the black-robed priests, Eadwig gloomily holding the hand of his uncle Eadred, Edgar being controlled by Dunstan, with some success. He would be the easier to tame, of the two boys. It seemed already too late for Eadwig. The seven-year-old was a swearing, screaming embarrassment.

Nonna's Diary

A YEAR WENT by before I saw the colourful tent again, at Charlton, when I was accompanying Dunstan. It was being utilised for spinning, weaving and craftsmanship in general. Embroideries were under way; the slaves appointed to make short and long hall tapestries were getting to grips with the design for a celebration of the life of Edmund and Saint Elgiva, as she had become known. Eadred had taken up the mantle of kingship in the meantime. He had made an agreement with the officers of the church that he would give way to Eadwig when he came of age or when he was deemed to be capable. Eadgifu did not object. Her bloodline would be part of the kings of England for decades, hundreds of years, if the dreaded millenium could be survived. Eadwig might improve, with time, as Edmund had done. Meanwhile, she remained at court, improving her relationship with Eadred.

Two old women were sitting under the canopy of the tent at Charlton Horethorne, absorbed in their creative work, one sewing a part of a death scene as drawn on parchment by Dunstan, another weaving a linen base for attachment to the long "short" hanging which would be placed opposite the entrance to the grand hall of the manor. I asked them about themselves. They reminded me of my own wife, Gwladys, my dark beauty.

They did not remember their true names. As small children they were rescued, they said, from the hot lands, near the reaches of hell. Yes, they were grateful to be here, well cared for by the household in their occupations as weavers and seamstresses. I do not recall their Saxon names, but they ill-fitted the colourful complexions of these creatures. When they looked into a mirror they did not see the faces of an Elgiva or an Eadgifu, who should be long-jawed, fair haired and blue-eyed; they saw the dark faces and hair and black eyes of another race. How they came to be here, people had forgotten; they had been passed down the generations along with furniture, as old as some of the pieces they were sitting on. They remembered the lady Wynflaed's mother, Brihtwyn and her husband, bringing them as children to this place; they could recall being taken to the pool at the church and being baptised. These were their first memories. The other thoughts, the dangerous ones, they had blocked out. Here they were, sitting in safety, protected by the family, guarded and guided by the holy Mary, doing the work required of them and at which they were highly skilled; weaving linen with Christian hands, sewing scenes of blood, mayhem and murder so that the memory of the achievements of Wessex would never fade, spinning their fates. Madder-dyed wool, used in abundance, spilled from workboxes.

We could not foresee, though some might have guessed, that we had more strife and eventually more embroideries to make, under the new king, Eadred. There is always one enemy who stands out on the calamitous and colourful scene of enmity. More red thread would be required and sooner than we all thought.

There is one more question which I hear you asking: what became of Leofa's son, the young Aethelred? Many years later I heard that he was taken back to Dublin from Wales, along with his sister. They may have been sold abroad as slaves. Hopefully he found a way to exist in some learned court of Europe, but he may have followed his yearnings to become a Viking pirate. Leofa's wife died in Hywel Dda's court in Wales shortly after her husband's demise.

I could not bear to think more of my friend and his fate. At that time my wife, Gwladys, caught a chill and died. I became a monk shortly after I lost them both to the afterlife. I gave in to Dunstan's demands. For many years, his certainty became my refuge. I was tonsured. It no longer mattered what I believed, or that my doubts plagued me still.

Kingston-on-Thames, 16 August, 946

A FIGURE LAY snoring, wrapped like a cocoon in a highly decorated, but sleep-mangled bed covering. It was frayed, as were Eadred's nerves.

Eadred had managed an hour of slumber, not more, on the night before his anointing. Strange beds were never friends to him, and the coverlets in each different palace rubbed or rustled. His skin was sensitive, as was his stomach.

'Good morning, my Lord, I trust you slept well on this auspicious night?' Hersfig knew what the honest answer to his enquiry would be, but he hoped to inject optimism into the daily grind of the reluctant king's life.

Eadred groaned. 'Hersfig, good morning. No, I did not.' He yawned and stretched, throwing the hot bedding with which he had been wrestling to the floor in a final defeat of the enemy.

'And how are my Lord's innards today?' Hersfig had particular concern for his master's liver and lights. The forthcoming ceremony might have to be curtailed, if the answer to this question was not the usual one. Eadred's undisturbed daily routine was already a requirement before the imposition and stress of kingship. Since Edmund's death and his accession, Eadred had been struck down many times by his personal maladies. He would get through the ritual of transubstantiation into a king chosen by God, but he would have preferred that God could be in a hurry. With Dunstan's rewriting of the service for Kingston, there might be a few minutes less to endure, but it would take all of Eadred's stamina and a stronger sense of self-importance to survive the day without embarrassment. Had he not become king, could he have kept the problem to himself and his near family? His mother would also have had a sleepless night.

'Get me the bucket and I will tell you.' Eadred and his personal bucket travelled together around Wessex. In future they would go further, to Mercia, to Northumberland. 'I must have slept, at least, for I remember my dream.'

Hersfig put the bucket into the commode by the bed. He waited. Eadred's dreams were not uncommon and their recitation frequently accompanied the evacuation of his bowels. Eadred mounted his comforter.

'I dreamed of the northern nations. I dreamed of being in Ripon, standing by Half-king, waiting for something.' He sneezed, and then sneezed again. 'Hand me a rag, Hersfig. Where was I?'

'In Ripon, my Lord.' Time was getting on, there was a requirement for Eadred's dress to be made before a family breakfast, then the ceremony. The schedule was tight.

Eadred sneezed a third time, being blessed each time by his man. A sneeze brought one near to the other world or to the saints; the soul must be saved from evil spirits which might invade the body. Eadred could not afford to have more afflictions. His function as a man, let alone a king, depended on warding off any fresh malaise.

'Ah yes, thank you, Hersfig. The dream is fading, alas, but it was vivid.'

Hersfig smiled. There might be only a small delay in the morning's ablutions, after all.

'Ripon, yes. I've never been there, but Edmund told me about it. I remember Archbishop Wulfstan had a great deal to do with the dream. He was being awkward in some way. We were in a place which seemed to be his home, a fortified house of some sort, the Archbishop's palace, I suppose. I've seen pictures of it in books. And behind him there was someone else, someone who started to roar at me. Ah yes! He stepped out in front of Wulfstan and threatened me. A pagan, a Viking. His roaring became like thunder and the screeching of eagles, combined. The dream filled with smoke and flame. The roaring is with me now...' Eadred moved to the wash basin, allowing Hersfig to swab him down.

'Never mind, my Lord, your dreams are only that, they cannot harm you.' Hersfig prepared the shaving equipment and started on Eadred's face.

Eadred, soothed by Hersfig's attentions, his day-old beard half removed, had an optimistic thought. 'Tonight I will be a king, anointed, a divine being. Does not that make me a visionary?'

Hersfig paused his shaving knife, its soapy foam dripping to the planked floor. He could not answer Eadred, he was not qualified in kingship. 'Abbot Dunstan will be able to tell you that, my Lord. I cannot.' He continued shaving Eadred.

A young man, laid low by multiple illnesses, real and imagined, would soon be that dread figure, a ruler of the constructed state of England, the defeater of its foes. He would know soon enough that his dreams were, indeed, sometimes to be relied on as prophecy. He and Dunstan had much in common.

'Would you say that my son is incompetent, my lord?' Eadgifu was in her finery, sitting next to Half-king at the feast following the anointment.

It was diplomatic, and expected, that a straight answer should be given to the queen-mother. She had assumed her former place at court. The rejuvenation had increased the number of bracelets on her arms and the heaviness and splendour of her earrings. There was a difference in her, though. The silks she wore were grey, as befitted her advancing years, half-way to black.

'He is untried, Madam. He has been thrust into a situation for which he has not been trained.'

'Then you agree with me, Athelstan.'

Frome, Summer 985

SWALLOWS SCREAMED, TEARING around in the rafters of the roof of St John's monastery church with its broken stone tiles, holes to let light, God and the rain in. They few restlessly in and out of the open west doors, uncaring of the solemnity and ritual below them. The single-bellow organ piped a faltering note as the choir of men and boys sang the first performance of Aethelwold's introit written especially for services of manumission. Having recently lost the bishop of Winchester, he would hear it from his seat in heaven. Archbishop Dunstan led the way down the nave while Nonna, ever present in support of Dunstan, croaked along with the choir, back home again with ageing monastic friends of this once beautiful place, established and built by St Aldhelm centuries before. Nonna prayed, as he sang, for the court treasurer to cast his eye on this beautiful, decrepit ruin. He was not hopeful: it was unlikely that funds would come. Frome was too far away from Canterbury or Winchester. Missionary monasteries were no longer required.

The Procession of the Golden Chains wound, swaying slowly along the nave, between the sloping pillars, extracting maximum essence from the solemn ritual. Six tall monks led four men, one half-grown boy and a woman by the lightest of neck fetters, string-like in their strength but shining with gilt and symbolic glory. Dunstan, as chief priest, was preceded by a carved and gilded cross carried by a tonsured bearer. The archbishop was here, visiting western Wessex, his land of birth, to free, among others, the serving boy, Algar. The boy's mother, a native of Frome, stood just inside the west door. He had no known father. The birds took their opportunity to bring pace to the proceedings, adding their discordant cries to the sounds of the tower bells and choir. The cacophony could be regarded by an onlooker as comical in such a ruined place, but the archbishop's face, stern and composed, retained the solemnity required for this special day. He walked towards the doom before the chancel which he had painted many years before. There was no need to point a finger towards it to remind those present of what it represented or who gave it life; it still had power to awe, though the paint in some places was peeling.

Outside, mid-summer blazed. The church was a cool place of refuge. A pigeon fluttered in through a hole in the roof and started to coo. The sacring bell chimed and tolled the beat of the marchers. A gust of incense from a heavily decorated, swinging thurible drove a large family group of swallows arching back towards the door. They gave a last screech and swooped outside to return to the flies buzzing over street gutters. The slaves who were still in thrall to the ancient monastery knew their role: they closed the doors, keeping wild nature firmly out. Only the pigeon remained inside. It seemed to realise that something serious was about to occur and watched silently from a beam. Its white stillness lent an air of sanctity to the proceedings, as the incessantly moving swallows could not.

Step by step, the procession moved onwards down the nave, past the lower orders crammed in at the back, past freemen family members of those who were the subjects of the morning service. Behind the clergy and slaves, with much pomp and display, barrows laden with colourful copes, gilt reliquaries of bones, glass vials of blood, hair shirts, combs of saints and virgins, drapes and cushions of magnificent coloured embroidery trundled by. They groaned and creaked under the weight of treasures. The archbishop was joined by as many parts of saints as could be mustered from the land hereabouts; King Aethelred had opened his relic room of Glastonbury for this special event. Last came the silvered box reliquary containing what was thought by the masses to be the head of Radegund herself, that exemplar of sixth century womanhood, a thing as valuable as the single finger bone and portion of hair shirt of St John owned by the monastic community of Frome. For this occasion, Aethelred's queen, Aethelfleda, had loaned her out. Frome was, after all, an important centre for the beginnings of the Catholic life of Christ in these parts. The relics were a temporary reminder of its place in the missionary life of the church in Wessex. Today, and for the last time, Frome received its recognition in the history of the family Wessex. It hoped to also receive, in time, its fair share of the tax revenues to allow restoration, but that was a matter for the church courts and to be argued elsewhere. Revenue was needed for the coming wars. St Aldhelm's foundation, important though it was, would have to wait, and meantime moulder.

There were others witnessing the spectacle besides the living; leaning against pillars and walls, some highlighted in bright, magical colours by sunlight streaming through stained-glass windows, were carved and painted life-size wooden statues of saints. Some held holy books; some had staves of healing or cloth bales, some carried babes, some lay on deathbeds, some appeared to be angels, their wings and hands extended to the living, beckoning them to the life beyond the grave. Each one was dressed to resemble the living. Painted eyes gazed upon sinners with reproof or encouragement. The saints responded to the shafts of sunlight by reflecting bright colours of their own on the stone pillars and paving around them. They wore robes of shining satin, embroidered linen and silver shoes. Feathers and flowers adorned their heads, candles burned at their feet. At midday on this day in late June, wax candles on the altars of the church were lit; there was no expense too great for the feast day of St John the Baptist, the day when the severing of his head by the jezebel Salome was remembered, the day of the leaving of the sun on its long journey to the short days of winter, back to its own brief burial in Winter's dark nights. By the side of the high altar, carved in oak from Selwood forest, stood the image of the head of St John, painted in the colours of gore, red drops of blood dripping from the bearded neck. Heavy brown eyes drooped in death. Green foliage around its neck likened the image to the wooden carving of the green man on the roof truss above. Like the doom, it was impossible to ignore. By its side, the life-sized statue of St Radegund, the virgin queen of Thuringia, gave alms to small, wooden, kneeling lepers, extending her graceful hand, welcoming the believer and the unbeliever, the diseased and whole alike. As the barrowed reliquaries passed by, their skirts of satin dragging along the stones, the watching penitents, whether wealthy Dives or poor Lazarus, crossed themselves and kissed their rosaries. Women curtsied; their heads bowed almost to the floor. The clergy took their places by the altar before the rood, itself ablaze with its own rich colour scheme. The doom arched over its viewers, resplendent in its unmissable message.

Dunstan had done his job well. The paint of the doom, for the most part, was as bright as the day he completed it, fifty years before. Nonna wondered, would he design it differently now? Christ was on his throne, gazing at the participants, flanked by angels with eyes upturned in bliss, pointing with their over-large hands to the sky beyond the battered church roof, beyond the embossed beams with their images of the flowers to be found in heaven. Roses, lilies and irises crept up and throughout the tendrils of stony interlace, challenging the old-fashioned beaks and tails of imagined creatures with their fear-inspiring messages to the religious and others.

The cross-bearer turned towards the congregation. The sacring bell sounded again. Above in the tower, the deep voice of a heavy bell tolled once in response. Incense swirled. The barrowed reliquaries were deposited by the altar. The drama came to its crescendo. The six monks selected as bearers of the relics in procession because of their similar height and age, as well as their strength, led the slaves forward. The men, boy and woman, their hands loosely tied with rosary beads and each clutching a borrowed psalter for the occasion, shuffled three times around the altar on their knees. One, two, three. The group came to a halt in front of the archbishop and the cross.

Dunstan removed the rosaries from the hands of each, coming to the woman last.

'I free your hands of toil and give their strength to each one of you, to do the work of the Lord in freedom. Do you accept this responsibility, to work now for the life beyond this?' The archbishop lifted the golden fetter from each kneeling neck.

Each man, in turn, muttered 'Yes.' The woman mumbled an affirmation. Dunstan reached the boy. He touched him on the neck, lifted the delicate cord.

'Algar, do you accept the responsibility of freedom in the sight of the Lord?'

Algar did, as did the men and the woman, whose raw knuckles and goitre displayed the many years of her life as a washer of monastic gowns, as cook and fish de-scaler. It was to be seen whether her former masters would now care for her, but her family, sitting at the back of the nave, free peasants themselves, would make room for her cot in their thatched home above the marsh. She would now be able to grow her own foodstuffs, pluck her own chickens, spin her own wool and sell it if she wished. Life would be hard but good, her whole family now free of the restraint and command of authority, her purchase paid off.

The symbolic fetters removed, the former slaves now greeted their friends and supporters. The adult freemen were in middle or late middle age, selected as worthy recipients of the Church's magnanimity and generosity. Each were given a silver coin with which to exit their servitude. They could now face the crossroads of their lives, no longer secure in the certainty of a bed and food. Their replacements had already been bought at Bristow's slave market. The boy Algar was different. He had potential. No boy had been purchased to replace him. No-one else could. Dunstan had found a willing pupil for his music-school. Nonna had found his burial-place guarantor and a fellow historian with an open heart and mind.

Algar's destiny was certain. All he owned was his silver coin. He had, though, talent, including a perfectly pitched singing voice. He had been noticed. The church had a career for him, ready-made, if he would agree, and if he survived the physical ordeal which would change, but make him valued by all. Was it sometimes best to remain in the shadows, one's talent unmarked, to remain sane, to remain safe?

The new freemen and woman left the church to walk across the town bridge to North Hill crossroads, free to choose their own destiny from here, free to retire in old age to the comfort of a brewhouse room or to die with a wife or child to comfort them, on a small plot of land and garden. They would return to the soil of the place in which they were born as their forefathers had.

Nonna grew wistful, seeing them go out of the church. He had returned to the ancient monastery which nourished him, and here he would stay. The last few monks still left in the monastery hospital, the old men who had tended King Eadred in his last days, would see him to his grave. He did not expect to travel further, so did not need to pack any baggage for the life ahead, if such existed. It would not be long. He travelled light; he always had. Algar had possession of his diaries and most of his few goods; they were small things, a few books, a brooch from the old times in Dumnonia, some scribbles by writers of long ago. There was comfort in his interest and their safety would be assured in the chained library of Canterbury. Who knows, someone, many years from now, might wish to read his account. What the worth of his words might be, he could not tell, but he had seen much through many years and never sought to impose his own opinions, as others had done, in the affairs of the nation. He saw good and bad, and made note of both. The remorseless passage of time now took him onwards to the grave.

His record was his own. He made no apology for writing truth. Recollections vary, but Nonna felt that his truth was, at least, valid, and an independent record.

"I think ye have heard of St Blasis heart which is at Malvern, and of St Algar's bones, how long they deluded the people."
Hugh Latimer, 1536, in Sermons of Hugh Latimer, ed. G.E. Corrie, Parker Society, 1844

"...at a chapel in the forest of Selwood...be buried the bones of s Algar, of late tymes superstitiously soute of by the folische..."
John Leland's Itinerary of the west country, 1542

Offices of Thomas Cromwell, Chelsea, late afternoon, February 1540

TWO SOMBRELY CLAD academics sat in comfort by a large window, drinking mulled winter wine from glass goblets. One leaned forward to refill his partner's emptying vessel.

'I heartily agree with you, John. There were swivelling eyes behind the screen, manipulated by a very bored monk. You should have seen the faces of the dunces as they were mesmerised by the supposedly living sainted remains. All they were missing was a spoken homily straight out of the mouth of a penitent in purgatory.'

'Or out of hell, you mean, where the holy one probably was in all likelihood and I hope he will remain. I take it you are referring to the Rood of Boxley?'

Hugh Latimer laughed. John Leland was a bird of his feather, though he thought that sending the saints to hell was going a bit too far. The reformers had all had, in recent years, great success in moving things forward, but some were excessively manic. Madness was the next stop on the route to Protestantism and some had already arrived. One could be unpleasantly over-religious. It was too late to rein in the extremists. They had burning brands in their hands, ready to torch any heretic Papist, perhaps rightly so.

The men were sharing a break from paperwork at dusk in the heavily oak panelled reception room of Thomas Cromwell, awaiting his arrival. They were contented men. Job satisfaction under Cromwell's leadership, that arch spymaster, was supreme. Cromwell could handle the king, even in his bad tempered and frankly murderous moods. How to avoid the bad leg humours had become a knack which most courtiers had had to learn in recent years. How to flatter and cajole were new essentials of the courtly handbook. They were honed and practised in whispers in many dark palace rooms and over the benches and tables of groaning feasts on the many saints' days still kept by Henry. Truth and reality had flown far away.

Old men were appalled by the thought of a seventeen-year-old new queen, Katherine, a flirt and whore, who seemed to be destined for the throne and bed of the ageing monarch. What did the Bible have to say about such naked lust? Young men shrugged and said it was one less maiden for them, but if the king was of a mind and able, then why not? A diseased limb needed soothing and tempers might improve in the short term.

Thomas could juggle them all.

We hate Katherine because she has the same name as the old catholic Queen Katherine, who we loved, the old men thought, but did not say. Younger men, amazed by the king's success at attracting Katherine, revered him as an example of God-given libido. The bedding of a pretty girl by a sick old man raised eyebrows but also ambitions by the elderly, anxious to recapture their youths. Middle-aged land-owners preened and sought out their wives' young maids, pushed years aside, inked greying beards and fought for the possession of vigour once again. Court ambassadors laughed at their attempts to dress in louder colours, to dance with fanatic gusto while failing to hide a weakening musculature. Calves were padded and encumbered with hose to suggest athleticism. Exaggerated codpieces became a fashion necessity, with knobs on.

John Leland drained and moved his glass towards the empty decanter. An elderly servant appeared out of the gloomy woodwork, dressed in a brown and fawn doublet. Cromwell's servants dressed in twilight livery, the better to be unnoticed. The usefulness of camouflage was beginning to be understood. He refilled the glass decanter from a large green jug and offered more to Latimer. Latimer waved him away. A nearby chapel clock struck the hour.

'Five o'clock. He should be here soon. Tell me, Hugh, what is the latest from Bristow?'

'As you know, we have converted the whole town into a healthy hotbed of reform. There's no going back for the townsfolk. They know they have been duped by papists for centuries and have been carrying out systematic removal of the idolatrous parts of their churches for several years. Of course, there are objectors, and sometimes compromises have to be made where architectural items are impossible to remove or would affect the stability of the building, but on the whole, the edifices of most religious buildings in Bristow have been losing the battle to Saint Whitewash, inside and out.'

'Thank God for the sanctity of blessed snow and its whiteness, covering all that revolting colour and ghastly imagery. Thank God for the purity of limewash and the practicality of a paintbrush. They feared that devils would be unleashed when the images were gone, but what fools folk were to think so. We shall soon have converted many of the rural churches and chapels, too. The monastic houses had to come down entirely, but you know how the country people cling on to their old ways. They are the last to welcome change. The only problem is to get enough wash to the right people and to pay them for the work.'

'It may take years, this cleansing task which has been given us by God, John, but we shall win in the end. Did I tell you about the roasting of the papist John Forest?'

Latimer began a description of the burning of an enemy, one who would have had him burned, if he could. He took his time. The image of the slowly cooking man, the sound, smell and taste in the air of papist pig as he screamed his way to hell was strong in his mind and he knew the power of description when displayed on the screen of the imagination. Speech, used well, could make or destroy a mind. Leland leaned back and closed his eyes to enjoy the image conjured by the wit and wordplay of the powerful Latimer.

'Did you stay for the end?'

'Ultimately the smoke of the faggots obscured a good deal. I saw his head fall forward not long after the last screech. I suppose that was the departing of the soul.'

'Assuming that he had one. Talking of heads, did you see what they brought in from the west country today? Two skull reliquaries. Said to be a Radegund and an Oswald. Fine workmanship. The heads turned to powder as soon as they were opened.' Leyland pointed to two metal busts on a shelf in an unlit corner of the room.

Latimer glanced into the dark. 'Hmm.'

Refilling both goblets, Leland began a discussion of the separation of the soul from the body. When did it occur? Could it be seen? Could it be measured?

They had not gone far into this subject when outer doors could be heard opening and shutting. Much later than expected, the great man himself, the Earl of Essex, Cromwell, entered the room with the fog of a late winter's day in London around him, his breath condensing in the warm room. He stripped off his gloves to greet the men supping his wine.

'What, no candles lit, my friends? Come over to the fire.' Cromwell threw a hefty log onto lightless embers. New flames sprung to life. 'What dark discussions have you entered into in my parlour and how much of my best wine have you consumed?' Cromwell held out another goblet for the servant who stepped forward, filled it and retreated back into the shadows.

Cromwell, with the usual furrowed frown on his face, a perpetual expression born of years of careful manoeuvring amongst men of all types, slapped both of his supporters and enquired after their health. He was exhausted. The king was being difficult again. There had been another disagreement between them today. But when were there any calm days at court? With greater age, Henry was becoming more like a madman each day, waking up sore legged, continuing sore headed. The child within was crying, Cromwell knew, and disliked having to pander to it. He threw back his head and drank deeply.

'Pass the decanter, Latimer, before it's all gone.' Cromwell waved a hand at the servant, who deposited the full green jug on a nearby table and crept silently out of the room. The three men were alone.

'Was the king in good health, Thomas?' Latimer obliged, getting up from his fireside stool to pour for the older man.

The king's health was on all their minds. Would he continue to support the reform movement, or throw a fit and all its followers to the dogs, the dungeon or the gallows? One had to tread carefully in the court hours of daylight. The hours of night were the business of men of the bedchamber, men who were well acquainted with the royal body. What horrors took place in darkness were beginning to be understood by more than just the cup bearers and privy pages. You could smell the fetid necrosis that was Henry. A heady perfume, used to disguise himself, crept along the narrow corridors leading from the royal chambers. The two smells mixed together were unforgettable. The last years of a dying king were dangerous, particularly when endgames had not yet been completely played out. What positive life there was in the old king, flailing to maintain the illusion of hearty youthful exuberance in his best moments, could turn in a moment to depraved cursing and summary execution. It was revenge for the realisation of the rapid coming of death. Laughter about the king's choice for the next queen, ludicrous to all who knew it, was enjoyed only when far away in the safety of stonewalled ancestral mansions in shires many miles from court and its whispers. Henry would take men with him, if he could, to that nether world beyond life, especially those who laughed at him, not with him.

'No.'

Cromwell tore off his black cape and sank into a cross-legged chair with a groan. His dark clothes highlighted his ruddy, angry face. A white lace collar was the only fanciful and unnecessary decoration of his outfit. That came off, too, in his desire to denude himself of courtly compromise. He threw it on the floor. He turned from the fading light of the window to the freshly firelit interior. The heavy jowls and furrows of a man of character and action threw shadows across his face. He was a formidable sight to the younger men who watched him turn from courtier to relaxed but frustrated lawyer. He turned to Leland.

'So, John, have you been down to the west country yet?'

'I am planning to go soon. I hear from your friends in Bristow that the region needs great attention. The common folk are determined to cling to their superstitious ways.'

'Your presence and your written record will make a considerable difference in our plans to rid the idolatries of the past. I have seen myself the rootedness and determination of yokels in those parts. I urge you to make your journey within the year to observe their follies. I hear pilgrimages constantly criss-cross the counties of Somerset, Devon and Cornwall. It is reported by my men that in every town and village there are churches and chapels festooned with colourful ribbons, bones and relics of all types. The images of saints in gaudy red and blue cover the inside walls and the outer doorways. Bells and songs are forever in the air for christenings and burials. Honest labour is forgotten in favour of marriage feasts and saints' day festivities. You know what it is like in Norfolk. In the south-west it seems that this folly is even more deep-rooted. It is a wonder that the harvest is ever brought in.'

Cromwell drank slowly, his legs outstretched, leather boots pointed towards the flames of the fire. Yokels, and a mad king. The fire of the Book would scorch them all. Let it be so. There was no going back.

Leland nudged Latimer. 'Those boots will soon start to smell like a burning papist, eh Hugh?' He laughed.

Cromwell grunted into his glass. *The end of a reign. The continuation of a scheme to rid the country of papist superstition, of the idea of payment for time spent in purgatory. Monasteries demoted or destroyed. Pilgrimages prevented. A life's work. From dissolution to reformation in a few short years. A life's work, which would end in death, perhaps sooner than he wished. More wine. Try to forget, for a few hours, the difficulties he had to encounter. That leg, the stinking leg.*

He threw a wet log onto the fire. It hissed and spat, as he knew it would. For now, he had survived the king. But oh God, to bow to a teenage strumpet, it was more than he could bear. Queen Katherine the child whore. Henry an old man, deluded. The prince a small child. Princesses divided in their beliefs. The management of the realm, to bring it from darkness to light; it was too much for one man.

But he had begun. Others would follow. There was no going back.

Cromwell lit a triple candlestick from a taper at the fire. The fresh light penetrated the shadows, casting his compatriots' faces into co-conspirators'. He was reminded of wolves and dogs, clever, cunning and fearsome. There were devil shadows on the wall behind them, dancing. He sighed.

They were men like himself, who make and mould a king. But a woman, that Katherine...might kill him.

No, there was no going back.

Reference

"*946. In this year king Edmund passed away on St Augustine's day (26 May). It was widely known how he met his end, that Leofa stabbed him at Pucklechurch.*"

Anglo-Saxon Chronicle

"*A certain robber named Leofa, whom he had banished for his crimes, returning after six years' absence totally unexpected, was sitting.... among the royal guests at Puckle-church. This....was perceived by the king alone....he leapt from the table, caught the robber by the hair, and dragged him to the floor, but he secretly drawing a dagger from its sheath plunged it with all his force into the breast of the king....The robber was shortly torn limb from limb by the attendants who rushed in....*"

William of Malmesbury, Chronicle of the Kings of England, (12th century)

Discussion

The Old King

A THELSTAN (OR AETHELSTAN), king of Wessex, overking of England (sometimes called Englaland in the sources), Emperor of Britain, having ruled for fourteen years and ten weeks (someone recording events for the Anglo-Saxon Chronicle was counting the days, for some reason), died in his bed on 27 October 939, aged about 47, probably of mental and physical exhaustion.

Athelstan had held onto the power handed down to him from his grandfather Alfred and his father, Edward. He had extended their dynastic remit to bring the entire islands of Britain (barring Ireland) under his sway. This was a notable achievement, from the English point of view.

Athelstan died in the knowledge that his reign had been fruitful, if turbulent, and that he had done all that could be reasonably asked of him. With the prayed-for support of saints and their relics, in particular Aldhelm, Oswald and Cuthbert, Britain at his death was free of disturbance from the north. Scotland had failed in its attempt to wrest Northumbria and Cumbria from his oversight and the troublesome Norse leaders had retreated to Dublin to lick their wounds after the decisive battle of Brunanburh, probably at Bromborough in the Wirral, in 937. There was peace, order and stability in England. The Welsh kings were Athelstan's allies for the most part and the laws of the land dealt harshly with thieves, theft being one of Athelstan's chief concerns. The king had been tough, on his enemies and on himself. No wonder Athelstan could take no more.

The sources suggest that he had an altruistic nature. Raised in Mercia, a proud kingdom in the Midlands, Athelstan took on the mantle of kingship as the eldest son of Edward against fierce opposition in Wessex. They had wanted a younger son, born to his second wife Aelfflaed and raised in Wessex, to become king. Athelstan promised not to marry and to therefore not deliver heirs of his body who might challenge his half-brothers Edmund and Eadred, more younger sons of Edward by his third wife, Eadgifu. He went out of his way to assist exiled princes from other lands, who were connected to the Wessex dynasty, to regain their thrones. For a king of the troubled pre-conquest period, he is generally regarded by the sources and by modern scholars as a good egg. But there was a problem with his legacy, which it is difficult to fathom.

Athelstan was virtually written out of the Anglo-Saxon Chronicle, with only the barest details being recorded and there is that tell-tale comment, 'King Athelstan had ruled fourteen years and ten weeks.' Perhaps it simply means that the scribe was deeply involved with court life, knew the king intimately and so was able to give precise dates, though the year of death varies according to the type of Chronicle; sometimes it is 939, 940 or 941. Athelstan's immediate successors, however, who were favourite scions of Wessex, were given death dates to the merest vague half-year. Even Edmund, whose shocking death by stabbing after only a few years' rule, at the age of 23 was recorded by a scribe using the half yearly laconical style. The 'holy bishop Dunstan', a benefactor of the church and significant player in the politics of the time, died in 988, after a long life, without a comment from the Anglo-Saxon Chronicle on his lengthy sojourn in the world. He merely 'departed this life and attained the heavenly.'

Edmund's succession in 939 was smooth. He was already married to a potential saint, Aelfgifu, later known as Elgiva of Shaftesbury, and had produced one son by the age of 18, Eadwig, with another, Edgar, soon to follow. The education of princes, aethelings, was in the hands of king-makers or destroyers, the active reformers of the church, Dunstan, Aethelwold and Oswald, who, like Thomas Cromwell and other reformers of the 16th century, were determined to have control of the psyche of the royal family brand, in this case of the Ecgbert/Alfredian dynasty, secular creators of the new nation of England. Their remit was to maintain and enhance the status of the papacy and to ensure investment in the edifice of Roman Christianity. The Wessex-born kings held the land and temporal power, but the church held the mind of the nation in its grip, with an increasingly complex reliance on the ideas of purgatory, pilgrimage and relics, payment for indulgences and a growing network of monasteries and churches to minister to the religious requirements of the nation. It encouraged, with stick as well as carrot, the populace to toe the pope's as well as the state's taxation and legal line. Dunstan and Aethelwod were the main instigators of the tenth century Benedictine reform of the monasteries. Aethelwold rebuilt many institutions which had been destroyed in the earlier Viking wars, including Ely and Peterborough.

Two events during Edmund's reign, directly involving the king, altered the course of history. The first was his recall of Dunstan after banishing him in 943. Edmund was nearly killed during a cliff hunt at Cheddar Gorge and felt that he had been saved by divine intervention. The second, his dramatic death, ensured the acceleration of the Benedictine reform movement, by bringing a more compliant Eadred to the throne. Both events helped to cement Catholicism's power over the culture and wealth of England in the approach to the end of the western world's first millennium. Massive religious reorganisation took place in England. This trend, upholding the Papacy's rules and restrictions, came to an end, after protests in different centuries against it, in the sixteenth century under Thomas Cromwell and Henry VIII.

Government of the empire of Britain grew increasing more complex as the tenth century wore on and stability brought wealth in trade. The gift of land to loyal supporters, whether secular or belonging to the church, could make the difference between the success of a reign or failure. Surviving charters of land transfer, signed at witans, show the support for the kings by their nobles and bishops and vice versa.

The combination of strong government by king and church enabled the nation to be well fed, peaceful and generally untroubled, by external forces as well as internal, for half a century after the initial Viking wars of the late ninth century. The Wessex dynasty was able to train its new recruits to kingship from birth to take on the tasks which their forebears had handed down to them. Increasing use, by the mid tenth century, of the written word provided proof of ownership, which was formerly established by oath-taking and corrected by blood feud. Society was structured to control every class of inhabitant, from the king down through the ealdormen and thanes, to peasants and slaves. The latter, consisting of convicted criminals as well as subject peoples (mostly taken from the conquered countries of Wales, Scotland and Ireland) were an important part of the agricultural and industrial workforce. Slaves would not merge with peasants as potential freemen until the 11th century, disappearing as a separate class in records in the 12th century.

Priests, monks and bishops had their own hierarchy. Movement up the social ladder by achievement and patronage was not impossible, though it appears that many of the successful church characters of the 10th century were, by birth, already well connected, including Dunstan. The Vikings were an extreme example of the great leap by potential from peasant pirate to king. Force of personality, whether Saxon or Viking, could overcome fixed social stratigraphy. It inevitably enabled the great characters of the time to shine out in the records. They seized the day. Some were women. Eadgifu, mother of Edmund and Eadred, was one.

Emma of Normandy was another.

In the recoverable history of kings, bishops and nations, even as far back in time as the tenth century, we can sometimes perceive, reading between the lines, lives of ordinary people, servants and slaves. Archaeology can assist, as at Shaftesbury and Glastonbury Abbeys and Cheddar palace. A view of a landscape in all its synthesised, palimpsest glory can part the curtains to an English past. In this story, as in Flesh and Bones of Frome Selwood and Wessex, I have tried to do this.

This World and the Next

The medieval mind, formed by the religious doctrine of Catholicism, acted as an editor and censor of a person's inner world. The powerful culture of the later Anglo-Saxons in terms of language, laws, religion, art and poetry appears to have imbued its entire subject community, enjoyed or tolerated by all in Britain. Like the Roman empire before them, their rule of law, both secular and religious, brought stability. Religious rituals and requirements exerted control with increasingly forceful images intended to colour the imagination, providing entertainment and stimulus. For the individual, this could degenerate into fear. Hell was becoming a dreadful stick, used to produce submission; alms and indulgences, to lessen its perils, became the carrot.

By the mid-late tenth century the idea of having to wait, in limbo, before entering heaven, was gaining ascendancy. Purgatory was quickly linked to payment. This was a costly process, in time as well as money, which could be reduced by prayer by the living and by indulgences which could be purchased. The use of colourful imagery in sculpture, glass, wall painting, embroideries and books as well as, perhaps, on the external stone edifices of churches, shows a willingness to use a multiplicity of art forms to dazzle and amaze in a kaleidoscope of theatre.

Education was not only for monks; Wynflaed's will of the

mid-tenth century includes a gift of books, which were evidently common-place among the wealthy. Education for noble women was not a rarity as the century progressed, indicating access to alternative thought processes. Secular priests (married men) and surviving heathen beliefs were derided, distorted into tokens of evil. Dunstan's "Lives" and other hagiographies are full of the battle against perceived devils. The original nature-based Celtic Christianity of Britain retreated in the centuries following the Synod of Whitby in 664, but its shadow still persisted. Processions, rituals, relics and indulgences began to proliferate. Saints days grew in number. Fast days preceded feast days; bounds were protected from the devil whose presence was now seen to be everywhere. Shouting him out, church clipping and ringing bells to ward off evil spirits became the peasants' means of warding off his presence. By the time of the 16th century reformation, purgatory, which was banned at that time, was the chief concern of most people born into the religious system of the British nation. How long was a soul likely to have to be in heaven's waiting room? Medieval churches are full of expensive memorials to those who had been persuaded that a shorter time could be bought. The early church thrived on the promotion of its imagery, as the billion-pound social media giants of the late 20th and early 21st centuries have grown. People need something to believe in or if not, something to relieve our awareness of the brevity of life.

The Lower Orders

S LAVERY, AN INDISPENSABLE managerial device of the Roman and post-Roman world, was practised in the tenth century in England as a legitimate business. It was an important part of Viking trade, though the church (notably the early 11th century Archbishop Wulfstan, not the 10th century Wulfstan of the novel) was beginning to object to it. Slaves were generally captives from places regarded as heathen. For a time, raids into Cornwall probably supplied the Wessex court with its ploughmen and workers, but the slave markets of Bristol (Bristow) would have brought in humans from many non-Christian places more far flung. The church hung onto its slaves longer than any secular institution. In Somerset, Devon, parts of Wiltshire and Dorset, the remaining population identifying itself as British, rather than English, would probably have been vulnerable to slave-taking, even in the 10th century. The Bishop of Crediton, Algar, was said to be a refugee from Viking slave trading in Ireland, having been taken by them from Devon. The possibility of enslavement became less of a threat to Britons as the tenth century wore on and natural assimilation of the British occurred. Over the next two hundred years the status of slaves and their protection under law improved, becoming merged with general peasantry soon after the Norman conquest.

By 1066 a recognisable and well-ordered state had developed after several centuries of post-Roman factional strife. Democracy and equality were not options; but they might have been thought of, especially in an age when the written word was spreading ideas and education was being promulgated, at least for the wealthy. In 955, Wynflaed could talk of leaving her "books and such small things", in her will, as if they were common items of daily use. She gifted them to a relative, also a woman. Female autonomy was possible, especially in the case of the widowed vowess, as she was. Thought is free and some, with access to Roman and Greek philosophy, must have developed advanced ideas for their times.

How true can history be? It is subject to interpretation, to styles and expectations of the age. We see the world as we are. We shall never know the full truth of the lives of those people long ago who were subject not only to their climate and landscape but to the cultural mores and strictures of the times in which they lived. The early medieval mind was very different from our own secularised mindset. There are strongly-held beliefs in all ages which proscribe how we perceive the world around us. This story is one person's best guess at looking through a dark (distorted) glass to try to fathom the motivations of the major protagonists of the tenth century. They were part of the great drama of events in the years preceding the Norman conquest of Britain, a period which suffers from neglect, being overshadowed by the more dramatic events of the eleventh century.

As Edmund inherited the responsibilities of the Wessex dynasty and wore its crown, would he be a king to be loved, or feared? There was one character who would oversee the progress and pitfalls of almost the entire Wessex dynasty: the long-lived Dunstan. He would ensure the legacy of Wessex, or condemn it. In Canterbury at the end of his life, having witnessed and set in train many of the events of the tenth century, he would be the editor of the histories of the kings he had personally known, the truth-maker. He saw, through his own broken images of records made before the second Viking onslaught, back to the golden age of Bede, Aldhelm and Wilfrid, forward to the approaching apocalypse, the coming of the anti-christ, the one thousandth year after Christ's birth. He had a determined message to the world: be Christian or be dead, in hell. His point of view was uncompromising.

Edmund was saved from falling at Cheddar Gorge, but the nation went over a metaphorical cliff instead...

Glossary

Aetheling or atheling: prince.

Aestel: a pointer for reading. The Alfred and Warminster jewels were probably decorative heads for these.

Behindtown: The original name of Christchurch Street, Frome.

Beowulf poem: Scholars consider that the famous poem was written during the reign of Athelstan.

Bimport: Street name (port means town or market) in Malmesbury and Shaftesbury. Both were part of Alfred's Burghal Hideage defensive system of towns, established in the late 9th century against Viking attack.

Black Pool: Dublin. Dubhlinn is Irish for Dubh (dark, or black) and linn (pool, or lake). Blackpool, Lancashire, England, lies on the opposite shore of the Irish sea.

Blood-eagle: a particularly gruesome form of execution used by Vikings, involving the chest cavity and lungs. King Aella of Northumbria (9th century) is said to have suffered it.

Bristow: Bristol.

Brunanburh: battle, 937, between the forces of England and Vikings and Cumbrians, said to have taken place on the Wirral, Cheshire. Athelstan and Edmund defeated their foes in a great slaughter which was remembered in a poem recorded by the Anglo-Saxon Chronicle for that year.

Burh: defended town.

Cley: Cley Hill, east of Frome and west of Warminster. 'y glea', 'The Place' in Old Welsh.

Cwtch: Welsh for hug.

Dublin: means black pool in Irish (see Black Pool, above).

Dumnonia: Former British Kingdom in the south-west peninsula, roughly today's Cornwall, Devon and Somerset. Conquered by Saxons at the end of the seventh century, apart from Cornwall.

Ealdorman: Saxon equivalent of an earl.

Hagiography: a saint's biography.

Haligdom: relic room or store.

Introit: anthem sung at the beginning of a mass.

Mancuse: a gold coin, worth approximately one month's wages for a skilled worker, estimated at about £2,500 in today's values. Wynflaed's old filigree brooch, which she left to her granddaughter Eadgifu, was worth six mancuses.

Manumission: ritualistic setting free of a slave.

Midden: rubbish heap.

Missal: small prayer-book.

Nunnaminster, Winchester: a convent in the same area as the Old Minster and New Minster.

Reliquary: container, often highly decorative, for a saint's relic.

Sabrina: River Severn between Wales and England.

Scop: Anglo-Saxon poet.

Scriptorium: a writing room for scribes in a monastery.

Secular priests: Married priests who were the norm until Dunstan and Aethelwold's Benedictine reformation.

Skald: Viking poet.

Swart: black.

Thegn: noble.

Thurible: incense container.

Thurifer: one who carries the thurible, an incense burner.

Tonsure: the hairstyle of a European monk. Bare head with surrounding fringe of hair.

Vowess: usually a widow practising a religious way of life but not in holy orders.

West tower balcony on a church: a west tower existed at Deerhurst, Gloucestershire, which retains much of its mid-Saxon architecture. There is no certain explanation for its use.

Others may have existed on towers which have long gone or
been rebuilt.

Wild Hunt: in Welsh folklore The Wild Hunt rides at the end of
October across stormy skies, gathering souls of the recently
dead to travel to the otherworld. Its leader is Gywn ap Nudd.

Witan: Saxon parliament which met in many different places in
England. Legal charters were signed at the witans.

Benedictine Offices

Matins/Vigils/Nocturnes	12 midnight
Lauds	Dawn or 3am
Prime	6am
Terce	9am
Sext	12 noon
None	3pm
Vespers	6pm
Compline	9pm

Saints

St Aldhelm: Much revered by both kings and churchmen of the
Wessex dynasty. Educated and became abbot at Malmesbury,
first Saxon bishop west of Selwood, of Sherborne and founder
of missionary monasteries in the late 7th Century at Frome
and Bradford-on-Avon. He was admired by Dunstan and
Aethelwold for his learned and elaborate prose. He died at
Doulting, Somerset in 709. He was buried at Malmesbury.
His relics were removed by Dunstan and taken to Canterbury
in 980.

St Algar: There is no certainty about who he was and why he was sainted, but notes made by H.M.Porter in the mid-1960s and seen by the author suggest that he may have been a bishop of Crediton in Devon, also known as Aethelgar. He was elected bishop in 934, dying in 952/3. Some exchange of land between the diocese of Crediton and the abbey of Cirencester may have occurred at the time of the setting up in the 12th century of the small religious house at Langley at West Woodlands, Frome, (now part of the farmhouse called St Algar's). There is also a legend, also recorded by Porter, that he was captured by Vikings as a young man and taken as a slave to Ireland, where he acted as executioner for the king of Connaught before returning to Britain. In this story of Edmund he is given the persona of a boy in the service of Dunstan and the fictional Nonna. Whoever he was and whatever brought him the status of saint, some or all of his bones must have been revered by local people at St Algar's chapel (see below), as recorded with disdain by John Leyland in the 16th century.

St Cuthbert: It could be said that whoever had control of the remains of this 7th century Northumbrian saint (monk, bishop and hermit, associated with the monasteries of Melrose and Lindisfarne) had sway over northern Britain and possibly the south as well. His body was taken for safety from Viking attack from Lindisfarne to Chester-le-Street in Northumbria and eventually to Durham Cathedral. He was accompanied in his coffin by the head of Oswald, king and saint. Four other heads of Oswald have been claimed by continental countries. An important spiritual guide for King Alfred and others of his dynasty.

St Elgiva: Also known as Aelfgifu of Shaftesbury, first wife of Edmund I. Died 944, buried at Shaftesbury Abbey. Feast day 18 May. Mother of Kings Eadwig and Edgar. William of Malmesbury (12th c.) claimed that Aelfgifu would secretly redeem those who were publicly condemned to severe punishment, gave expensive clothes to the poor and had prophetic powers as well as powers of healing. She suffered from an undiagnosed illness during the last few years of her short life.

St Oswald: 7th century king of Northumbria, regarded by the later Saxon kings as one of the great Christian Anglo-Saxon heroes. He was killed by the pagan king Penda of Mercia at the battle of Maserfield. His body was dismembered and sacrificed to the god Woden in a pagan ritual. His remains were moved several times; his skull is said to be in the coffin of St Cuthbert in Durham Cathedral but the torso and some limbs were taken to Gloucester (St Oswald's Priory) by Aethelflaed of Mercia, Athelstan's aunt. A right arm was said to have been washed and kissed by Hugh the Chronicler, a monk of Peterborough, in the 12th century. With Cuthbert, Oswald was possibly the most important saint in the spiritual life of the Wessex kings.

St Radegund: A 6th century Thuringian queen who suffered persecution at the hands of her husband. She founded the monastery of Sainte-Croix in Poitiers, where she cared for the infirm. She was admired by the 7th century saint, St Aldhelm, who as Bishop of Sherborne brought Roman Christianity to the south-west peninsula, establishing the church of St John at Frome, along with others. He, in turn, was much admired by the Wessex dynasty. Radegund's head is imagined in this story as the replacement for the storyline theft of Oswald's head. Theft and replica production of revered saints' parts was rife.

St Swithun: 9th century bishop of Winchester and subsequently patron saint of Winchester Cathedral. He was renowned, as all the other Anglo-Saxon saints were, for performing miracles. According to tradition, if it rains on Swithun's day, it will continue to do so for forty days.

St Wenceslaus: Duke of Bohemia, assassinated 935. Considered by the English to be a fine example of piety and princely vigour. Dunstan might have thought of him as a role model for the Anglo-Saxon kings of his time.

St Wilfrid: Operating as a missionary in Northumbria and the midlands in the 7th century, Wilfrid gained notoriety as a hard man, prone to a liking for pomp. He was the main protagonist for Roman Catholicism at the Synod of Whitby in 664 against the Celtic Christian grouping, led by Abbess Hilda. He died at Oundle, Northamptonshire, one of his monastic foundations, but buried in Ripon. Archbishop Oda removed his remains to Canterbury in the 10th century. The 10th century Archbishop Wulfstan of York died and was buried in Oundle.

The Battle of Brunanburh 937

KING ATHELSTAN AND his brother Edmund fought a decisive battle against the combined forces of the Dublin Norse, Strathclyde Britons and Scots. The enemies of Wessex were determined, after the defeat of Constantine of Scotland in 934, to overcome Athelstan and to make England into a Viking state. Five northern kings and eight jarls, along with Constantine of Scotland's son, were killed in the battle.

The site of the battle is uncertain but considered to be at Bromborough in the Wirral. Charters of the 13th century refer to this town as formerly called Brunanburh. In October 2019 Wirral Archaeology reported finding metal associated with warfare of the right date.

A poem commemorating the battle appears in the Anglo-Saxon Chronicle for 937:

In this year king Athelstan, lord of warriors,
Ring-giver of men, with his brother prince Edmund,

Won undying glory with the edges of swords,
In warfare around Brunanburh.
With their hammered blades, the sons of Edward
Clove the shield-wall and hacked the linden bucklers,
As was instinctive in them, from their ancestry,
To defend their land, their treasures and their homes,
In frequent battle against each enemy.
The foemen were laid low: the Scots
And the host from the ships fell doomed. The field
Grew dark with the blood of men after the sun,
That glorious luminary, God's brightest candle,
Rose high in the morning above the horizon,
Until the noble being of the Lord Eternal
Sank to its rest. There lay many a warrior
Of the men of the North, torn by spears,
Shot o'er his shield; likewise many a Scot
Sated with battle, lay lifeless.
All through the day the West Saxons in troops
Pressed on in pursuit of the hostile peoples,
Fiercely, with swords sharpened on grindstone,
They cut down the fugitives as they fled.
Nor did the Mercians refuse hard fighting
To any of Anlaf's warriors, who invaded
Our land across the tossing waters,
In the ship's bosom, to meet their doom
In the fight. Five young kings,
Stretched lifeless by the swords,
Lay on the field, likewise seven
Of Anlaf's jarls, and a countless host
Of seamen and Scots. There the prince
Of Norsemen, compelled by necessity,
Was forced to flee to the prow of his ship
With a handful of men. In haste the ship
Was launched, and the king fled hence,

Over the waters grey, to save his life.
There, likewise, the aged Constantine,
The grey-haired warrior, set off in flight,
North to his native land. No cause
Had he to exult in that clash of swords,
Bereaved of his kinsmen, robbed of his friends
On the field of battle, by violence deprived
Of them in the struggle. On the place of slaughter
He left his young son, mangled by wounds,
Received in the fight. No need to exult
In that clash of blades had the grey-haired warrior,
That practiced scoundrel, and no more had Anlaf
Need to gloat, amid the remnants of their host,
That they excelled in martial deeds
Where standards clashed, and spear met spear
And man fought man, upon a field
Where swords were crossed, when they in battle
Fought Edward's sons upon the fateful field.
The sorry Norsemen who escaped the spears
Set out upon the sea of Ding, making for Dublin
O'er deep waters, in ships with nailed sides,
Ashamed and shameless back to Ireland.
Likewise the English king and the prince,
Brothers triumphant in war, together
Returned to their home, the land of Wessex.
To enjoy the carnage, they left behind
The horn-beaked raven with dusky plumage,
And the hungry hawk of battle, the dun-coated
Eagle, who with the white-tipped tail shared
The feast with the wolf, grey beast of the forest.
Never before in this island, as the books
Of ancient historians tell us, was an army
Put to greater slaughter by the sword
Since the time when Angles and Saxons landed,

Invading Britain across the wide seas
From the east, when warriors eager for fame,
Proud forgers of war, the Welsh overcame,
And won for themselves a kingdom.

The Byzantine Connection

I T IS NOT unreasonable to speculate that there was a connection between the mid-10th century Saxon court and the far-flung corners of the post-Roman empire in Constantinople (Istanbul). Alfred is said to have sent emissaries to India. It is also not unlikely that the English court would broker trade agreements between foreign states or individuals. Commodities such as preserved foodstuffs, medicines, spices, silk, relics and hunting dogs would have been of interest to traders of western Europe. Trade deals and their associated information on, for instance, weaponry development would have been as important then as today. Slaves were also an important commodity.

In The Early Lives of Dunstan, written shortly after his death in 986, there is mention of Dunstan, having been banished by Edmund 'in a towering rage', requesting 'important persons' (who were guests of the king at the Cheddar witan in 941) to take him home with them. They were 'on an embassy from the eastern kingdom'. Scholars have deduced that this kingdom was not East Anglia or Kent, which were under the control of Wessex by the mid-940s, but that the commentary referred to Byzantium. It is known that a Greek bishop named Nikephoros, whose see was probably Heraklia near Constantinople, was present at the court of King Edgar. I have made him appear at Edmund's court in Cheddar in 941 as a younger man.

For details, see Winterbottom and Lapidge, (edit. and transl.) *The Early Lives of Dunstan*, Clarendon Press, Oxford 2012, p 47.

Leofa's Exile

THE ANGLO-SAXON CHRONICLE for 946 tells that Edmund died on St Augustine's day (26 May) and that 'it was widely known how he met his end, that Liofa stabbed him at Pucklechurch'. William of Malmesbury, in his Chronicle of the Kings of England (12th century), says 'A certain robber named Leofa, whom he had banished for his crimes, returning after six years' absence totally unexpected, was sitting...among the royal guests at Pucklechurch...near a nobleman whom the king had condescended to make his guest.'

Theft was a serious crime in the mid-10th century. Athelstan's law code demanded the death penalty for what we would now regard as petty crime. The law's ability to hang a miscreant of 12 years of age was raised during his reign to 15 years. Other crimes were subject to ordeal by fire or water. This was a time of strong belief in the efficacy of holiness. It was thought to be in God's gift to judge a person guilty or innocent. Miracles of healing were attributed to the relics of many saints. Why was Leofa not hung or given the chance to prove his innocence by undergoing an ordeal? That he was exiled suggests that he was a person of some importance, perhaps a royal family member, someone close to the throne or perhaps a priest or monk, like Dunstan, who was exiled himself twice. Perhaps Leofa knew too much. Edmund, or perhaps Athelstan before him, was not willing to kill him for some reason, though when he was discovered at Pucklechurch, fear or hatred drove Edmund to attack him. In the heat of the moment Leofa stabbed Edmund in self-defence and was immediately killed by the other guests or guards.

That the name of the criminal is mentioned in the Chronicle and remembered by William of Malmesbury suggests that Leofa figured in court circles and the story is based on this premise.

Five Boroughs Poem
(From the Anglo-Saxon Chronicle 942, Laud E)
In this year king Edmund, lord of the English,
Guardian of kinsmen, loved doer of deeds, conquered Mercia
As far as Dore and Whitwell Gap the boundary form
And Humber river, that broad ocean-stream;
The Boroughs Five he won, Leicester and Lincoln,
Nottingham, Derby and Stamford too.
Long had the Danes under the Norsemen
Been subjected by force to heathen bondage,
Until finally liberated by the valour of Edward's son,
King Edmund, protector of warriors.

Wynflaed's Will

P ROBABLY MADE ABOUT 955-960. An 11thc. copy is in the British Library, Cotton Charters viii.38, Sawyer charter 1539. She may have lived to 960 or later as a Wynflaed occurs as a beneficiary of land in Hampshire in Sawyer charter 754.

Wynflaed is considered by historians to be the mother of Edmund's first queen Aelfgifu/Elgiva of Shaftesbury. She owned land at a variety of manors including Charlton Horethorne, a few miles to the west of Shaftesbury in Dorset. She is thought to have been a vowess, a widow who lived in accordance with Benedictine customs and rules but on her own property, some of which had been inherited from her own mother, Brihtwyn. She would have attended services on occasion at the abbey in Shaftesbury where she may have been educated as her daughter was. For the purposes of this story, she has been based at Charlton Horethorne.

Her will is an excellent source for understanding how a

wealthy late Saxon noblewoman dressed, what her interests were, what she regarded her most valuable items to be, how a home owned and lived in by her or other well-connected females might look, how valuably she regarded books (she owned many "books and such small things"). This indicates that reading and book owning was commonplace at the time and that some women were well educated.

Familial relationships as evidenced by this will are complicated and understanding of them is subjective, but it appears that Wynflaed had two grown up children, Eadmaer and Aethelflaed (son and daughter) at the time of the making of her will.

I have divided up the will into convenient lists for ease of reference.

Land holdings:

Estates at: Charlton (Horethorne), Ebbesborne, Chinnock, Coleshill, Inglesham, Faccombe, Adderbury, Shrivenham, Childrey.

Animals:

General stock including 6 oxen, a horse, 4 cows and their calves, untamed horses and tame horses.

Family:

Mother: Brihtwyn.

Husband (?)Ealhhelm.

Daughter or step daughter: Aethelflaed ("the White"?). Another daughter, Aelfgifu/Elgiva, who married Edmund, is not mentioned in the will, probably because the will was made after Elgiva's death in 944.

Son: Eadmaer

Grandchildren: Eadmaer(?)'s daughter Eadgifu and his son, Eadwold

Named Slaves or workers, unfree:

Men and stock at Ebbesborne, Charlton, 31 others either

freed at her death or given away including Wulfwaru, Wulfflaed, Eadgifu (woman weaver), Aethelgifu (seamstress), Gerburg, Miscin, Aelfsige, Ceolstan's wife, Pifus, Eadwyn, Eadhelm, Man, Johanna, Sprow, Gersand, Snel, Aethelgyth, Bica's wife, Aeffa, Beda, Gurhann's wife, Wulfwaru's sister, Wulfgyth, Ceolstan, Burhwyn, Martin, Hisfig, Aelsige the cook, Aelfwaru, Herestan, Ecghelm, Cynestan, Wynsige, Eadwyn. (Plus others, mostly related to the above).

Items gifted in the will:

Offering cloths, a cross, nun's vestments, black tunics (which may be secular in use), holy veils.

Coins and gold:

A mancuse of gold to every nun at Shaftesbury Abbey (a mancuse is either a gold coin or 4,25g of gold or a unit of account of 30 silver pence, worth £2500 in today's currency), I mancuse each to servants or slaves, I pound (of gold?) to Wilton Abbey, one mancuse to another person, perhaps at Wilton.

Furniture:

4 chests, 2 large chests, a clothes chest and 2 old chests. Useful utensils inside something else, possibly another chest.

Soft furnishings:

Set of bed-clothing, bed-curtain, linen covering for bed and bed-clothing that goes with it, a long-hall tapestry, a short hall-tapestry, 3 seat coverings and other tapestries, large and small. A long hall tapestry reminds one of the Bayeux tapestry.

Personal items:

2 silver cups, 2 buffalo horns, an engraved bracelet, a brooch, an old filigree brooch (plus gold coins), a cup with a lid, a gold adorned wooden cup and 2 wooden cups ornamented with dots. Red gold is mentioned (gold and copper alloy).

Clothing:

Double badger-skin gown, gown of linen, best dun tunic, cloaks, black tunics (already mentioned in religious items) headbands, caps and more gowns.

Miscellaneous:
A red tent, a little spinning box, books and other 'small things'.

Places Mentioned in the Text, with Sources

Cheddar Palace: *The Saxon and Medieval Palaces at Cheddar, Somerset, an interim report of excavations in 1960-62, Philip Rahtz, Proceedings of the Natural History and Archaeological Society of Somerset, 1964.* The excavations revealed a series of palaces dated from the 9th century (Alfred) or earlier to the fourteenth century. It was a popular place with the Wessex dynasty and survived into the Norman period. The witan met at Cheddar in 940, 956 and 968, (Kings Edmund, Eadwig and Edgar). Henry I visited in 1121 and 1130. Henry II visited in 1158. King John spent £40 on the 'king's houses of Cheddar' in 1209-11 but soon after that the palace was given to the dean and chapter of Wells.

Gibbet Hill, Frome: On the west side of Frome, part of Critch Hill, the road to Nunney. OS475763

Glastonbury Abbey: Founded, probably on the site of an earlier Celtic Christian monastery, by the conqueror of Dumnonia, Saxon King Ine in the 7th century.

Longaleta: Longleat. The name occurs on an early medieval seal of the priory of St Radegund over which Longleat House was built in the late sixteenth century.

Shaftesbury Abbey: Founded by King Alfred, probably in 888.

St Algar's chapel: The farm of the same name lies on the road from Frome to Maiden Bradley near the county boundary with Wiltshire. There were brothers or canons living at a house dedicated to St Mary here at Langley, said to be in Selwood Forest. It disappeared very quickly, leaving a manor of Langley with a chapel dedicated to St Algar, held by the abbey of Cirencester. The relationship between the small religious house at Langley (West Woodlands) and the Priory of St Radegund at Longleat is unclear. There is a partially excavated Romano-British villa complex in the fields nearby. Finds, in addition to coins and pottery, included lead and silver working, glass working and a mausoleum or shrine. The medieval chapel site may indicate a memory of Iron Age and Romano-British religious activity. The finds indicated that the villa and industrial site were occupied from the early/mid-1st century through to the late 4th century AD. There are indications of a roadside settlement to the north and north-east of the villa. Iron Age and medieval pottery was also found. *Victoria County History, Bath and Camerton Archaeological Society, Historic England, Scheduled Monument no. 1006153, Lambdin, C and Holley R, St Algar's Project Group, 2011-2012.*

St Mary and St Lazarus Priory, Maiden Bradley: A 12th century hospital foundation for the treatment of lepers.

St Radegund's Priory: the crypt of the 13th century Augustinian Priory lies under the main house at Longleat (Longaleta)and is the cellar café today. Its origin is obscure but thought to be related to the 12th century chapel and monastic community at Langley, where St Algar's farm now stands, only two miles away. It was in existence by 1235 and suppressed in 1529. Did it possess a relic of St Radegund, perhaps a significant one? *Victoria County History.*

Further Reading

Alexander, Michael, (trans), 1991, *The Earliest English Poems*, Penguin.

Chandler, John, 1993, *John Leland's Itinerary, Travels in Tudor England*, Alan Sutton.

Chandler, John, 2003, *A Higher Reality, the History of Shaftesbury's Royal Nunnery*, Hobnob Press.

Duffy, Eamon, 1992, *The Stripping of the Altars, Traditional Religion in England 1400-1580*, Yale University Press.

Ewing, Thor, 2008, *Gods and Worshippers in the Viking and Germanic World*, The History Press.

Ewing, Thor, 2006, *Viking Clothing*, The History Press.

Foot, Sarah, 2000, *Veiled Women II, Female Religious Communities in England, 871-1066*, Ashgate.

Foot, Sarah, 2011, *Athelstan, the First king of England*, Yale U P.

Gittos, Helen, 2013, *Liturgy, Architecture, and Sacred Places in Anglo-Saxon England*, Oxford University Press.

Higham, N J and Ryan, J, 2015, *The Anglo-Saxon World*, Yale University Press.

Higham, N J, 1997, *The Death of Anglo-Saxon England*, Sutton Publishing.

Higham, N J (ed), 2007, *Britons in Anglo-Saxon England*, The Boydell Press.

Hill, David, 1981, *An Atlas of Anglo-Saxon England*, Blackwell, Oxford.

Holland, Tom, 2016, *Athelstan, The Making of England*, Allen Lane.

Holland, Tom, 2008, *Millennium*, Abacus.

Lapidge, Michael, 1988, 'Aethelwold as Scholar and Teacher', in *Bishop Aethelwold, His Career and Influence* (ed. Barbara Yorke), Boydell Press, 89-117.

Owen, Gale R, 1979, 'Wynflaed's Wardrobe', in *Anglo-Saxon England 8* (ed. Peter Clemoes), Cambridge University Press, 195-223.

Owen-Crocker, Gale R, 2004, *Dress in Anglo-Saxon England*, Boydell.

Porter, H M, 1971, *The Celtic Church in Somerset*, Morgan Books.

Pelteret, David, A E, 1995, *Slavery in Mediaeval England*, Boydell

Press.

Ramirez, Janina, 2015, *The Private Lives of the Saints*, W H Allen.

Rawcliffe, Carole, 2006 *Leprosy in Medieval England*, Boydell Press.

Ridyard, Susan J, 1988, *The Royal Saints of Anglo-Saxon England*, Cambridge University Press.

Scudder, Bernard, (trans), 2004, *Egil's Saga*, Penguin.

Stafford, Pauline, 1981, *The King's Wife in Wessex 800-1066*, Past and Present vol.1, Oxford University Press.

Stafford, Pauline, 1983, *Queens, Concubines and Dowagers, The King's Wife in the Early Middle Ages*, Batsford Academic and Educational Ltd.

Stafford, Pauline, 1989, *Unification and Conquest*, Edward Arnold.

Victoria County History, Somerset and Wiltshire.

William of Malmesbury, *Chronicle of the Kings of England*, (trans. J A Giles, 1847).

William of Malmesbury, *The Deeds of the Bishops*, (trans. David Preest), Boydell Press, 2002.

Will of Wynflaed, circa AD 950 (11th century copy, British Library Cotton Charters viii.38, Charter S1539 (http://www.esawyer. org.uk/charter/1539.html) at the Electronic Sawyer.

Winterbottom, Michael and Lapidge, Michael (eds. and trans.), 2002, *The Early Lives of St Dunstan*, Oxford University Press.

Wood, Michael, 1999, *In Search of England*, Penguin.

Wood, Michael, 1981, *In Search of the Dark Ages*, BBC Books.

Yorke, Barbara, 1988, 'Aethelwold and the Politics of the Tenth Century', in *Bishop Aethelwold His Career and Influence*, (ed. Barbara Yorke), Boydell Press.

Yorke, Barbara (ed.), 1988, *Bishop Aethelwold, His Career and Influence*, Boydell Press.

Yorke, Barbara, 2003, *Nunneries and the Anglo-Saxon Royal Houses*, Continuum.

Yorke, Barbara, 1995, *Wessex in the Early Middle Ages* Leicester University Press.

Illustrations

*These are the author's simplified versions of items of the Anglo-Saxon
and early medieval periods.*

 Maughold Viking ship tombstone image, Isle
of Man.

 Based on bust of King Athelstan on a coin in the
British Museum.

 The Alfred Jewel.

 One of two Anglo-Saxon cross-shaft
sculptures, St John's church, Frome.

 One of two Anglo-Saxon cross-shaft
sculptures, St John's church, Frome.

 Based on Bradford-on-Avon Saxon church angel.

 Based on an early Anglo-Saxon necklace pendant, British Museum.

 A woman called Aelgiva and unknown priest, Bayeux Tapestry.

 Bishop, based on the Lanalet Pontifical, Rouen, Bibliotheque Municipale, A.27 (368), fo.2.

 Horses in battle, Bayeux Tapestry.

 Church, based on the Lanalet Pontifical, Rouen, Bibliotheque Municipale, A.27 (368), fo.2.

Woman and child, Bayeux Tapestry.

Warriors, based on the Lanalet Pontifical (see above.)

Animal sculpture from Deerhurst church, Gloucestershire.

Reliquary chest (?) from coin of Edward the Elder, ref. Blunt, C.E., Coinage 15 in Tenth-Century England from Edward the Elder to Edgar's reform, Oxford, The British Academy.

Celtic style raven.

Celtic style boar

Warrior, Bayeux Tapestry.

'Nonna's brooch'. A Romano-British horse and rider brooch. See Flesh and Bones of Frome Somerset and Wessex for explanation!

Acknowledgements

THE FOLLOWING GAVE me helpful advice, assisted with proof reading, allowed me to view their homes or gave essential constructive criticism. They helped me to make this book less like a lecture and more like a story.

Tim, my husband, Gill Harry of Frome Writers' Collective, Silver Crow readers, Christine Deed, Mr A M Mackintosh of St Algar's Farm, West Woodlands, Frome, the Stevens family of Priory Farm, Maiden Bradley, residents of Pucklechurch, the Friends of Shaftesbury Abbey, the Hunting Raven bookshop in Frome for its fantastic support for local writers, and the Kings of Wessex Academy in Cheddar, for allowing me to stand on the site of the excavated Saxon palace, imbibing its spirit.

Not forgetting John Chandler of Hobnob Press for taking me on and putting up with my digital incompetence.

Also by Annette Burkitt
Kings of Wessex Series:
Flesh and Bones of Frome Selwood and Wessex (Athelstan)

Articles:
With Tim Burkitt, 'Badon as Bath' in Popular Archaeology, April 1985.
With Tim Burkitt, 'The Frontier Zone and the Siege of Mount Badon: a
Review of the Evidence for their Location.' Proceedings of the Somerset
Archaeological and Natural History Society, vol. 134, 1990.

Of Flesh and Bones of Frome Selwood and Wessex:
'I very much enjoyed the fascinating way in which you encompass this
little known, yet incredibly important period in our local history, into
an imaginative framework, enabling the reader to appreciate the wider
experience of life at this time.'   *Martin Dimery, Frome Festival Director.*

(Your book) 'is clearly a labour of love, and very erudite. It is indeed most
unusual for a historical novel in the depth of its scholarly apparatus, and
written with an exceptionally vivid, and as far as my slightly inexpert eye can
tell, accurate, reconstruction of the historical background. Its relish for the
West Country landscapes is also evident, and pleases me deeply as a local.'
                            Professor Ronald Hutton, Bristol University.

'The period in England between the fall of the Roman Empire and the
Norman Conquest is often dismissed as "The Dark Ages". England may not
have produced an equivalent to the Book of Kells (Ireland) or a mosque at
Cordoba (Al-Andalus, Spain), but civilised life went on. The Celtic British
learned to live with the Anglo-Saxons, just as they had learned to live with
the Romans. King Alfred repulsed the Danes and an increasingly assertive
kingdom of Wessex welded together diverse people into a state almost
recognisable as England.
    This is a remarkable and beautiful book. Wessex is a magical landscape,
and Burkitt has concentrated on the area she knows best, around the
Somerset town of Frome, where history is written into the landscape.
    The author knows all about history and archaeology, but has chosen to
bring her chosen period and place - Wessex in the tenth century CE - to life
in a most original and effective way. To the bones of history - the little we
know for sure - Burkitt has added flesh, a fictional story that brings vividly to
mind the lived reality of those times. Hence the title - Flesh and Bones.
    The story centres on the Christmas gathering of the Wessex witan or
parliament convened by Alfred's grandson, Athelstan at Frome in 934 CE.
There is drama, humour, superstition, belief, love, intrigue, as in any decent
novel, but always that firm backbone of the historical events underpinning
the story.
    A book for anyone who loves a good yarn, and who loves our English
West Country, with its surviving fragments of older Celtic British origins.'
                John Payne, retired Bath University lecturer and writer.